HAVEN OF VIPERS

HAVEN OF VIPERS

A MASON COLLINS CRIME THRILLER 2

JOHN A. CONNELL

NAILHEAD PUBLISHING

GET A FREE MASON COLLINS NOVELLA

The relationship between writer and reader is a special one for me. If you are interested in going beyond what you read here and wish to receive occasional newsletters from me with details on new releases, special offers, and other news relating to the Mason Collins series, you can sign up to my mailing list, and I'll send you a free Mason Collins introductory novella.

See the back of the book for an offer for a free Mason Collins novella that is not available anywhere else!

COPYRIGHT

To my father and uncles who answered their country's call in World War Two.

Garmisch-Partenkirchen, Germany
American Zone of Occupation
March 7, 1946

F or this particular undercover operation, CID criminal investigator Mason Collins had invented the persona of Kurt Wenger, a down-and-out German citizen who moved with languid steps and the lackluster gaze brought on by hunger and a grim future. He wore a threadbare overcoat previously owned by a Wehrmacht soldier, who no longer required such earthly trappings, topped by a fedora most likely orphaned by similar fortunes of war. Other than a three-day beard, Mason had no need of a wig or any other visually altering appliances. Transforming into another personality was all about posture and attitude, expression and mannerisms.

The man he tailed, Sergeant Carl Olsen, walked thirty feet ahead. Mason kept tabs on him by peering through the crowd and catching glimpses of his round head of black hair covered by his khaki service cap. At six feet six and 250 pounds, Olsen lumbered into the oncoming crowds like a snowplow, Mason following in his wake—hardly a challenge for Mason's covert skills, but concealment from Olsen was not his objective. Mason's main concern was with the men who watched Olsen's progress from the shadows and strategic positions, men far more dangerous and clever than the sergeant.

Mason's partner, Specialist Gil Abrams, had a better view of Olsen from across the street. Abrams had come from the military police ranks to act as a CID investigator under Mason's tutelage. His sharp insight and dogged determination had caught Mason's eye, but he still had a lot to learn about the subtleties of surveillance, especially someone like Olsen, who approached murder and mayhem as impassively as tying his shoe. Nervous excitement drove Abrams to eye Olsen with too much regularity, occasionally bumping into a pedestrian or narrowly avoiding a passing wagon or army jeep. He wore a gray wool suit and long black coat that hung from his lanky frame. At twenty-two, his body had grown into manhood, but had left his face behind some-where in cherubic territory; so, despite his adult attire, he reminded Mason of an overgrown kid from a Charles Dickens novel.

Olsen had led them into the poorer and, as a consequence, more sordid part of town, a place that any number of small-time crooks called home and where the black market thrived, where the uninitiated passerby could be bushwhacked for a few Reichs-marks and left lying in the gutter. Makeshift booths of canvas and wood, tents, and lean-tos were crammed along the sidewalks, forcing the throngs of people to spill out onto the streets. Wagons, carts, and bicycles were now the only modes of transportation available to most Germans, and they competed with the pedes-trians for space in this part of town, most overloaded with wood salvaged from the surrounding forests or a family's meager possessions. Street vendors hawked their wares in a dozen languages: pilfered coal, adulterated flour, or cigarettes made from butts discarded by American soldiers. Men and women walked by and opened their overcoats displaying watches, cameras, and jewelry, while the occasional woman would open her fur coat advertising a more carnal commodity.

Die Stunde Null, or Zero Hour, was what the Germans called the time in the immediate aftermath of World War Two. In every practical sense, Germany was to start over from nothing. It had been bombed and shelled back to the Middle Ages. Whole cities and towns were wiped out, with over six million dead. Disease and malnutrition were killing the very young and very old in numbers unseen for centuries. No food, no crops, no coal, no medicine. Industry and agriculture had come to a standstill. With the German Reichsmark rendered almost worthless, bartering became the only real agency of commerce. The black market flourished, and the American cigarette reigned as the king of currency. It was an auspicious time to be a gangster—or an opportunistic soldier like Sergeant Olsen.

Arrested for manslaughter and grand larceny, Olsen had agreed to be Mason's ticket into one of the most successful crime rings in Garmisch: a confederation of Germans, ex-Polish army officers, and low-ranking U.S. soldiers, a group that operated so boldly they even had their own logo and letterhead. With its easy access to Austria, Switzerland, and Italy, Garmisch was Germany's ideal port of entry and exit for every illicit trade, making this picturesque city a vital center for the black market. And while much of the criminal activity was run by a loose confederation of smaller gangs, Hermann Giessen's organization had been different: well organized, powerful, and operating with seeming immunity—a dangerous combination.

Mason had been investigating the ring for two months, but as audacious as they might be, he only had scant information:

rumors, allegations, and the identities of the leaders, those names always mentioned in connection to major crimes, but not a shred of solid evidence that could send them to prison. The only way he could discover more and get the evidence he needed was to infiltrate the gang. He'd spent a month developing Kurt Wenger, using most of this time as the down-and-out gangster, trolling back streets, frequenting notorious bars, and, on occasion, committing petty crimes. That also meant he had to keep out of the limelight as a military policeman. He dressed in civvies for all but formal army occasions—which by regulation he was allowed to do. He avoided the officers' mess, and instead frequented German restaurants and bars, and being a loner by nature, he was rarely in the company of other soldiers. After he'd spread and cultivated his reputation as a gangster for hire, fortune had shined on Mason by dropping Olsen in his lap. And through Olsen, Mason had finally wrangled an introduction.

In the last couple of weeks, two rival leaders had been savagely murdered, rupturing the fragile truce between the gangs. No one admitted to knowing the source, though rumors circulated of a brutal new leadership trying to take over. The ensuing revenge killings and spontaneous shoot-outs had left the city's underworld on high alert. A call had gone out for more hired guns, working to Mason's advantage, but now a bullet or a blade could come from almost any direction. Precaution dictated that Mason and Olsen remain apart. Similar precautions had obliged the gang leaders to go to ground. Today's meeting would be the first since the turf war had broken out, and only the leaders knew when and where. Olsen, being a midlevel player, had to walk the streets in this part of town until intercepted by his contact, who would then lead the way.

Abrams caught Mason's eye and signaled that Olsen had turned left at the intersection. Mason followed suit a few moments later. He figured they must be getting close, as Olsen behaved with increasing nervousness, stopping frequently and looking both ways, only to continue then repeat the process. Mason hoped the sergeant would hold to his side of the bargain and not get spooked and make a dash for it—or perhaps Olsen was nervous because he'd set them up for an ambush.

Olsen stopped abruptly when a man in a brown homburg hat crossed in front of him and kept on going. Olsen took his time lighting a cigarette. Whether that was a signal of acknowledgment or a way to give his contact a lead, Mason didn't know, but after tossing the match to the ground, Olsen turned left and disappeared.

Abrams hurried to the far corner then looked back at Mason with wide-eyed excitement. He was nearly run over by a wagon when he rushed across the street to meet Mason at the corner. "He just went into the Steinadler beer hall."

"Did you forget everything I taught you?" Mason asked. "Keep cool." He nodded toward the other side of the street. "You stay out here."

"I'm supposed to back you up."

"I changed my mind. I know this bar. They'd grind you up and sell you as sausage on the black market. If I don't come out in an hour, call in the cavalry."

"What am I going to do out here for an hour?"

"Wing it."

Mason watched a frustrated Abrams take up a position on the other side of the street, then entered the bar.

Before the war, the Steinadler had been a cheerful watering hole and, like much of Garmisch, it sported interior walls decorated with frescoes and a long bar of oak carved with intricate details. Now neglect—not to mention its somber clientele—had left it joyless. Due to electrical shortages, gas lanterns and candles had been placed sparsely around the room, providing only a murky light. The clientele probably preferred this, as it was now a favored meeting place for smugglers, thieves, and lower-echelon thugs.

As Mason moved through the room, he noticed two muscled bodyguards standing near the front door, and three more stationed by the rear entrance behind the bar. Mason carried a German pistol, a Sauer 38H with eight rounds in the magazine, but it wouldn't be enough to shoot his way out of there. The only way he was going to leave alive was if they let him. The barman looked at him warily until Mason produced a wad of U.S. dollars. He ordered a beer then scanned the room.

Olsen stood at the other end of the bar talking to the owner, Kasim Aslan, a Turk who'd been accused of everything but convicted of nothing. The patrons were mostly German, but there was also a mix of Polish and Russian ex-POWs, Italians, and a handful of American GIs. All here for the purpose of illicit commerce. They talked in hushed tones, some playing cards, some standing at the bar, while others sat at tables placed at discreet distances for deals to be made without the attention of curious neighbors.

Back in a quiet corner, a blond man with an overly developed forehead played chess with a partner whose back was to Mason. The man's name was Anton Plöbsch, the third man on the ring's totem pole. A former Wehrmacht major, with vague roots in aristocracy, he was suspected of rape, murder, extortion, and bribery, but now held a "respectable" role as the commander of the gang's muscle. Purportedly a twisted genius, brilliant but cruel, a highborn henchman.

Plöbsch had glanced at Mason several times. Olsen must have given him a silent signal that Mason—a.k.a. Kurt Wenger—was the man seeking entry into the gang. Plöbsch said something to his dark-haired chess opponent. The dark-haired man rose from the table and moved to the bar, leaving the game half finished. Mason took this as an invitation to join Plöbsch. He crossed the room, feeling the stares of the other patrons as he did so. He stopped at the table. With deep-set eyes that appeared to be devoid of all color, Plöbsch looked up to Mason and waited, indifferent.

"He could have had you in six moves," Mason said in fluent German.

"Ah, then you play chess, Herr Wenger." He indicated the chair with his open hand. "Then sit, and see if you are correct."

Mason hung his overcoat over the chair back, sat, and immediately moved his king's bishop. Neither spoke as they played. Mason felt vulnerable with his back to the room, but he knew that was the intention. Not being sure where etiquette lay when challenging a ruthless and powerful thug, Mason purposefully made two bad moves that lost him his queen.

"Checkmate," Plöbsch said and smiled. "You let me win, Herr Wenger. I appreciate the gesture, but it could also be a sign of disrespect. A mark against you. We shall play again, but this time you will put forth your best effort."

Mason reached into his suit jacket pocket and placed two hundred dollars on the table. "Shall we raise the stakes?"

"You don't look like a man with the means to possess that kind of money. Where did you get it?"

"Playing Ami soldiers."

Plöbsch chuckled. "Americans are bad chess players. You should have more earnings than that if you consider yourself a worthy opponent."

"American chess players are conservative bettors."

"And you hope that I will be more liberal?"

"One has living expenses."

Plöbsch looked at Mason a moment, then moved his pawn. After a few more moves in silence, Plöbsch said, "I hear a Bavarian accent. I've seen you around, and heard of your reputation, but I know little about you. Where are you from?"

"A little town," Mason said. "Wonneberg."

"And during the war?"

"Is that important?"

"I like to know the man sitting across from me."

"Artillery regiment with the 58th Infantry Division... until I got into a little trouble."

"What kind of trouble?"

"We were on the eastern front, and while the commanding staff lived in luxury, we were starving. So, I managed to lighten the staff's burden for about a month before I was caught."

"They shot men for less."

"I guess I got lucky."

Plöbsch eyed Mason skeptically. The barman came over with two more beers. Mason reached for his money, but Plöbsch said, "It's on me. I always buy a drink for the loser."

They continued to play. Plöbsch was very good, but Mason had lost the first game to assess the man's weaknesses. Plöbsch used the same types of aggressive moves and shrewd tactics as in the first, but Mason had already figured him out.

"What did you do after the war?" Plöbsch asked.

"I was with Rudolph Voss. Out of Munich. Did you know him?"

"Yes..." Plöbsch said as he eyed Mason. "It is unfortunate that you ran with an organization that no longer exists. How is one to verify that you are who you claim to be?"

"Yes, Herr Voss is dead, and the organization busted up, but I assure you I am telling the truth. I worked with Captain Wertz cutting penicillin and baby formula, selling snow and H, until he got busted and ratted on us."

In fact, Mason had known Voss and Wertz during his time as a CID investigator in Munich, and he was the one who had busted Wertz through an informant. Mason had built an entire file around his fictitious character, including having a German detective friend in Munich "leak" Wenger's arrest record and police file to the Garmisch authorities. Giving the records to the corrupt elements in the Garmisch police ensured that Plöbsch knew all about Wenger by the time Mason made contact.

"Why did you come down to Garmisch?" Plöbsch asked.

"I heard of a few networks operating out of here. And your group is said to be the most powerful. But you know all this. I'm sure you already checked me out before I came."

Plöbsch simply smiled and moved his queen's knight.

Mason debated whether he should take Plöbsch at his word and play using his best effort. Would winning seal the deal, leading the man to take the introduction to the next level? On the other hand, humiliating a man like Plöbsch could very well get his throat cut. There was only one way to find out… He held back his best moves, sacrificing key pieces, until finally luring his opponent into making a fatal move. "Checkmate."

"You play very well," Plöbsch said with a forced smile, though he looked like he might prefer slashing Mason's throat.

"As do you, Herr Plöbsch."

"You know my name, then."

"I would not do very well in this line of work if I did not find out who I was dealing with."

"I can respect a man who, knowing me and my reputation, has the courage to beat me at chess."

Mason bowed his head.

"Yes, we checked you out," Plöbsch said. "One cannot be too careful these days. Sergeant Olsen says you are interested in joining in our enterprise."

"I am, indeed."

Plöbsch stared at him for a long minute, his nostrils flaring as if sniffing the air for deception. Finally he said, "It's not up to me."

"Though I imagine your approval goes a long way."

Plöbsch grunted. He then nodded to someone behind Mason. Whether this was a sign to fetch his boss, or to be stabbed in the back, Mason wasn't sure. He maintained a neutral expression, while readying himself for an attack. But instead of the rush of an assailant, a door opened behind his left shoulder. He kept his eyes on Plöbsch as footsteps approached—three or four men, judging by the sound of it.

Two men came around to face Mason. They were the number one and two men in the organization, Hermann Giessen and Erich Bachmann. Giessen appeared to be in his fifties, with a rough-hewn face and slicked-back hair that revealed a long scar running from his forehead and into his receding hairline. Bachmann was a small man, more high-school science teacher than mobster, with soft green eyes, a humble chin, and long earlobes.

Plöbsch rose from his chair, and Giessen took his place. Mason felt the looming presence of two or three men behind him.

Giessen studied Mason with intense blue eyes. "How am I to know that you are who you claim to be?" Giessen asked.

"I could tell you anything, but it would still not prove I am telling the truth. I offer a deal. Let's say, a way to buy my way in. Show you that I mean business. Good business for you."

"Go on."

Mason reached into his coat breast pocket with two fingers so as not to alarm them, and removed a cherry-sized, grayish white nugget. "Platinum," he said, and laid it on the table.

Giessen picked it up and examined it closely.

Mason continued, "I assume you have someone here who can verify that it is ninety-nine percent pure. I have four cases full of these."

"And where did you acquire such a treasure?" Giessen asked.

A peculiar odor reached Mason's nose. It floated just under those of spilled beer, body odor, and cigarettes: the distinct odor of burning tobacco he hadn't experienced since… He struggled to repress the memories that scent elicited. After much effort, he said, "A stash left behind by the retreating SS..."

The scent seemed to crawl into his nose and into his brain, triggering an intense instinctive reaction. His gut tensed as if expecting a blow from a truncheon. Mason remembered it all clearly now: He was suddenly back in the winter of 1944 at a temporary Gestapo headquarters in Monschau. He had been captured during the Battle of the Bulge, and because he was an intelligence agent, spoke fluent German, and had been caught behind enemy lines, they had accused him of being a spy. For two interminable weeks an interrogator had been his chief tormentor, alternately beating him and submitting various parts of his body to electrical shock. The interrogator had chained-smoked a particular brand of Turkish cigarette. And it was that sweet, pungent odor of Turkish tobacco, which Mason smelled now, that had always announced the interrogator before he entered Mason's cell and the torture would begin. Mason had never smelled that odor since.

"Is there something the matter, Herr Wenger?" Giessen asked.

Mason tried to control himself, but his mind raced. *It can't be. The man can't be here. It isn't possible.*

SS Sturmbannführer Volker. Mason could remember his precise features, the way he moved. They were burned into his memory. Some primitive part of his brain told him that the SS man had passed near his table and lingered. He fought against the flood of raw panic and rage.

Then he lost control.

2

M ason propelled himself up from the table, but strong hands grabbed his shoulders and shoved him back into the chair. He then heard the click of a revolver's hammer drawn back a second before he felt the cold steel of the barrel against his temple.

"Hands on the table," a man's voice said just behind him in Italian-accented English.

Mason put his hands on the table and took the opportunity to glance at his watch. Fifty minutes had passed. Ten minutes before Abrams would bring in help. Ten minutes too late. He'd be gone by then.

As beefy hands searched him and removed the pistol from his overcoat, Giessen said, "You've been made, whatever your real name is."

"Mr. Collins," the Italian man said. "A detective of the American CID."

Giessen blanched when he heard that.

"You kill an American military investigator," Mason said, "and this town will be turned upside down."

"Herr Giessen wouldn't dare kill an American cop," the

Italian said, "but I have no such problems. Garmisch is not my place of business. I will have vanished before anyone suspects you are gone. They will never find your body. There will be some inconveniences for the local organizations—no offense, Herr Giessen—but little of my concern."

Mason could tell that the man who was speaking also held the gun. By the angle and timbre of his voice, he estimated the man stood around five feet, eight inches tall and stood close to the back of his chair. The dim light from the bar had been eclipsed by at least two other much bigger men. The man's bodyguards, Mason guessed. The distinct aroma of Turkish tobacco had faded, taken over again by the reek of cigars and rancid beer. It was possible that someone else in the bar smoked that same unusual brand of tobacco, but he felt in his gut that Volker had lingered behind him for a few moments before moving away.

The man pressed the gun into Mason's temple. "You will move toward the bar, please."

The front door exploded open. Whistles blew. German police yelled out, *"Polizei! Hände hoch!"*

The momentary distraction gave Mason an opportunity. In a lightning move, he shot to his feet, whirled around and grabbed the man's gun arm, forcing it upward. He slammed his other hand into the man's elbow and heard the crack of bone. The man screamed. Mason still had control of the man's hand. He forced the Italian to aim at one of his charging bodyguards and yanked on the man's trigger finger. The gun fired, hitting the bodyguard in the thigh. The bodyguard collapsed to the floor.

The Italian man struck at Mason, but with little force. Mason elbowed the Italian in the jaw, then swept his fist back, striking the man in the neck directly over the jugular. The Italian dropped to his knees. At the same moment, the second bodyguard struck Mason across the temple with his pistol. Mason's vision went white. His legs turned to rubber, but he managed to grab and hold onto the bodyguard's pistol arm.

The bodyguard kneed Mason in the groin. Mason collapsed. His abdomen felt like a mass of molten rock. He braced for the impact of a bullet, but it never came. Dozens of uniformed legs entered his field of view. Shouts and grunts prompted Mason to look up, and, to his relief, he saw five German police had finally subdued the giant bodyguard.

Two police yanked Mason to his feet. The pain flared in his groin along with a wave of vertigo. He didn't resist. They had saved his life, and he was glad to see them. Though not too long ago, the sight of thirty-plus armed Germans in uniform would have elicited a very different reaction.

Mason held up his hands. "American. CID." The two cops stopped and allowed Mason to carefully remove his hat. He pulled out his CID badge hidden in the lining and showed it to them. "I'm an American. CID. See?"

The two policemen released him and joined the rest hustling the bar patrons outside. Mason bent over and tried deep breathing to assuage the pain in his abdomen. He used a table to brace himself and scanned the arrested bar patrons for Volker, but the man wasn't among them.

Abrams rushed over to him with two MPs. "Are you okay?" Abrams asked.

Mason nodded as he caught his breath. "One of those gorillas kicked me in the balls."

"At least that made you forget about the hole in your head."

Mason touched his temple and brought away blood. He grabbed a towel off the bar and put it to the wound. "You came in early," he said to Abrams.

"I knew there was going to be trouble when a goon came out onto the street and locked the front door. I went for the German police since they were closer."

14

"There are at least five U.S. soldiers..."

"Yeah, there are a handful of MPs out front collecting them. They came running when they saw the squad of German police charging down the street. We'll sort out the non-Germans from the Germans."

Mason and Abrams headed for the door. "There are three Italian mobsters in the group. Make sure our guys get them too. Especially the one with the broken arm. That asshole had a gun to my head."

"I did good, then?"

Mason nodded. "Yeah, you did good."

They exited the bar. Crowds of people looked on as the German police and five American MPs sorted out the arrestees. Mason scanned the German bar patrons but didn't see Volker. Then he noticed with alarm that Giessen, Bachmann, and Plöbsch were not there, either. And Olsen was not among the arrested Americans. "Damn it." Mason grabbed the leading MP sergeant, turned back to the bar, and said to Abrams, "Some of them escaped out the back."

They ran through the bar and out the rear exit. A cluster of surrounding buildings formed an inner courtyard of mud and snow, where garbage and rusted junk had been piled haphazardly. Laundry hung from a web of lines suspended from the buildings and swayed in the biting wind. Mason silently pointed out the footprints in the snow. Groups of prints went down the three narrow passages that accessed the surrounding streets. He signaled for the MP and Abrams to take the left and right alleyways, while Mason took the one running straight from the back door. He drew his gun and moved forward with long strides. Halfway down the alley, he came across a jumble of footprints. It appeared that a large group had stopped at the double doors of a dilapidated, corrugated-tin garage on his right. The prints showed that the larger group went inside but then a smaller group remerged and headed for the street behind the bar. The flimsy doors banged with gusts of wind that felt suddenly very cold.

Mason raised his gun and, as silently as he could, pulled open one of the doors. He swung inside, gun up, and tried to peer into the darkness. Weak sunlight poured into the holes and gaps in the tin walls. The smell of urine and putrid mud assaulted his nostrils. It seemed empty except for some rags and broken crates piled in the corner of the dirt floor. But when his eyes grew accustomed to the dark, he saw two bodies lying facedown among the rags. They had both been shot in the back of the head and dragged into the corner. Mason squatted and turned them enough to see their faces. They were two of Giessen's bodyguards who'd been standing by the rear entrance.

When he stood and turned, he saw three other bodies on the opposite side of the shed. They lay in a row, arms and legs akimbo. Mason approached them and used his cigarette lighter to view their faces. He cursed under his breath. He whistled for Abrams and the MP, then squatted and checked each of them for a pulse. When he heard footsteps coming up the alley, he called out, "In here."

Abrams and the MP sergeant entered the garage and came up to Mason. "All three of the gang leaders," Mason said. "Giessen, Bachmann, and Plöbsch. A single bullet in each of their foreheads. Then two in the chest. Shot at close range. Killed, execution style." He picked up a spent shell casing. "Nine-millimeter," he said and put the casing in his breast pocket. "Giessen had three bodyguards covering the back entrance. Two of them are over there, in the corner."

"That leaves one and Olsen," Abrams said. "Do you think they did this?"

Mason shook his head. "I can't see two guys getting the jump on five armed professionals. There had to be more. More than likely we're going to find Olsen's body in the woods somewhere.

And there's one other guy...." Mason paused, then said more to himself, "I swear he was there, either with Giessen or the Italians."

"Who?" Abrams asked.

Ignoring the question, Mason stood and turned to the sergeant. "Have our guys go over this crime scene, and start canvassing the area. Make sure that gets done first, then notify the German police that they've got five dead bodies back here."

When the MP left, Abrams said, "Who was this other guy you're talking about?"

Mason just shook his head and charged for the doors. With Abrams in tow, Mason blew through the bar and out onto the street. To his left the five MPs guarded the few U.S. soldiers, a handful of Poles and Russians, and the Italians. The two battered Italian bodyguards tried their best to support their boss. The boss grimaced with pain, but managed to lock murderous eyes with Mason.

Mason said to the MPs, "Are you getting some help?"

"Yes, sir," a corporal MP said. "A truck and an ambulance should be here any minute."

Mason pointed to the Italian boss. "Make sure that one doesn't get too comfortable, and isolate him from the rest."

Mason then marched over to the German arrestees. The German police had them lined up by the wall and were in the process of searching them. He headed for the first one in line, grabbed him by the shoulders and shoved him against the wall. "Who set up Giessen and the rest? Who killed them? Where did they take Sergeant Olsen?"

The German stared at Mason and muttered ignorance.

"Major Ernst Volker. Is he one of them?"

"I don't know an Ernst Volker."

Mason went down the line, asking the same questions. "Ernst Volker? Is he the leader? Did he take the American sergeant?"

A German police sergeant followed Mason down the line, protesting Mason's disregard for protocol, the protocol being that German police had authority over German citizens. Mason ignored the sergeant and continued the questioning. He received only defiant stares and claims of innocence.

Abrams said in a calm voice, "Sir, why don't we search the bar? The Germans have jurisdiction over these men."

Mason whirled around. "Not if Olsen is murdered." He then turned to face the entire group and said loud enough for everyone to hear, "Anyone willing to step forward and identify the men responsible for killing Herr Giessen, Bachmann, or Plöbsch, for taking Sergeant Olsen, will be released. Anyone who can confirm Ernst Volker was present and tell us where we can find him will be released."

No one stepped forward. Mason took a few deep breaths to calm himself and watched as the German police began loading their charges into an open-bed truck. Suddenly one of the German arrestees started yelling. Part of it was in German, but the rest was in a dialect that Mason didn't recognize. The thin-faced man yelled out to Mason from the bed of the truck while the police jostled him. The German policemen stopped and looked to Mason for guidance.

Abrams stepped forward and talked to the man in the same language. Then Mason realized they were speaking Yiddish. "What's he saying?"

"That he's not German," Abrams said. "He's a Polish Jew and shouldn't be with those men."

"Get him off the truck and put him with the others," Mason said.

Abrams told the Germans to let him pass. The man jumped down and talked rapidly with Abrams. Mason could tell he was protesting his arrest—that much was clear in any language. Abrams had to cajole him to join the group of Americans and other foreign nationals held by the MPs, then returned to Mason.

"Claims he's innocent, right?" Mason asked.

"He says he just happened to go in for a beer."

"A Jew walks into a bar..." an MP said and chuckled to himself. "Get it? Sounds like the beginning of a joke?"

Mason glared at the MP. "Just get them all to the Sheridan barracks, would you?"

Mason and Abrams reentered the now-deserted Steinadler. Mason went behind the bar, while Abrams searched the tables and the floor.

"You didn't answer me before," Abrams said.

"About what?"

"Who is this other guy you were talking about? This Ernst Volker?"

"I didn't see him, so I don't really know if he was here or not."

"I don't get it."

"I don't have a better answer for you, so forget it."

"Maybe he, the third bodyguard, and Olsen set up this whole thing."

Mason shook his head as he rifled through the cash register. "Olsen doesn't have the clout or the brains to pull off a coup like this. A group of around five guys met them in the alley, by the looks of it. There wasn't much of a struggle, so my guess is they all knew each other or were taken by surprise."

Questions already circulated in Mason's mind: How would the group know that the three leaders would be coming their way? Was it a prearranged ambush? But how would the assailants know where the meeting was taking place? Was it a coincidence that it happened just as Mason had tried to infiltrate the gang? Were they killed because Mason almost succeeded?

Abrams was apparently thinking on similar lines, as he asked,

"How did they identify you? The way you were disguised, even I'd have trouble recognizing you. Maybe Olsen double-crossed you."

Mason thought of the odor of Turkish cigarettes. "My gut tells me it was Volker. He's someone I knew during the war. Someone who nearly killed me when I was a POW."

"But you don't know for sure?"

"My back was to the room."

"Who's been pounding into my head that I should never get into a situation where my back is to the room?"

Mason ignored Abrams and turned his attention back to the filth behind the bar. "I doubt we're going to find much that will help us. Every kind of scumbag used this place to make deals."

"We'll get footprint castings in the snow," Abrams said. "But other than that and those shell casings, we don't have much to go on."

"We'll see what the canvassing turns up."

"Chief Warrant Officer Collins?" a voice inquired from the front door.

Mason looked up to see two men in matching black overcoats and equally black suits standing inside the door. He knew them as U.S. agents with the Counter Intelligence Corps, or CIC, but neither was American. Their names were Werner and Hans, but Mason called them Frick and Frack after the famous comedy ice-skating team, though there was nothing jolly about their stony expressions. They were both former German army intelligence officers, who now worked for the Americans.

Hans said, "Special Agent Winstone would like to have a word with you."

"If you two haven't noticed, we're busy investigating a crime scene at the moment. Tell him I'll see him later."

"I'm afraid he insists."

"Well, you tell him he can shove it where the sun don't shine."

The two agents took a moment to try to process this. Finally, Werner said, "He said you just screwed an old friend. He is outside. It will only take a few minutes."

Mason stopped, wondering how he could have possibly screwed Winstone. Shaking his head, he followed the pair out of the bar and down the street.

It had become too common, in Mason's opinion, for the CIC to recruit Germans for the expanding task of investigating the growing presence of Russian spy networks, hunting down Nazi war criminals, and searching for the missing Nazi gold. Mason understood why: They were better than their American counterparts at using the locals to sniff out hiding places, potential Nazi fanatics, and Germans now working for the Russians. Still, Mason didn't like the idea of the American army employing German ex-intelligence and ex-Gestapo goons, glossing over their Nazi pasts for the sake of solving cases. Times were already changing, the Russians being the new threat, but Mason still had a hard time moving on after all he'd seen in the war.

Frick and Frack finally stopped at a long, black Mercedes 320 Stromlinien-Limousine parked at the curb.

"Does everything have to be black with you guys?" Mason said.

Werner's expression remained frozen as he opened the car's back door. Mason got in. Agent John Winstone waited for him in the backseat. He was in his late thirties, with a round face emphasizing his deep, receding hairline. He was in great shape, though, and had the kind of tan a skier gets from spending hours on the slopes. He wore a tailored blue suit and a gold Swiss watch.

Mason barely settled in before saying, "I don't like being summoned. Even by a friend."

"Who *does* do your tailoring?" Winstone asked sarcastically. "You'll have to give me his name."

"What do you want? I've got a crime scene to search."

"You screwed up my investigation, buddy. I want to know what you were doing in there in the first place."

"Your investigation?"

"I've been watching Giessen and his cronies for months."

"Since when does the CIC investigate black marketers? Aren't you guys busy enough with war criminals and spies?"

"Those gang leaders, or some of the men under their control, were running a ratline helping Nazi war criminals escape out of Germany."

"A ratline? I've been investigation them for two months and haven't heard about them running a ratline. And maybe if the CIC would share information we might have avoided this situation. We've known each other for three years. Since when did we become rivals?"

Mason had gotten to know Agent Winstone when they worked together at the army's G-2 intelligence branch during the war. Winstone had supervised a team of analysts, while Mason had been a field operative for the human intelligence section, gathering local agents, conducting interviews of German POWs, and estimating frontline enemy assets. They'd become friends during that time, but Mason had lost track of Winstone when he'd been captured during the Battle of the Bulge.

Then they bumped into each other shortly after Mason had been reassigned to Garmisch. Winstone had changed from those earlier days; once an intelligent, unassuming guy, he had become a little too self-important and aloof for Mason's tastes. They'd made plans to get together a few times, but it had never worked out, and Mason had cited his need to remain low-key for his undercover work.

"Ever thought to check with us?" Winstone said.

"I don't recall the CID having to check in with you boys when it comes to black market activity and murder."

Winstone studied Mason for a moment. "It's strange that you

meet with Giessen at the very time and place that he and his cronies are assassinated."

"And here you are, moments after it all happened, in your custom-tailored suit, with your fancy car and two German goons. Should I be looking at you for this?"

Winstone paused and smiled. "Looks like we were working at cross purposes."

"Looks like it, but it doesn't matter anymore. The three leaders are dead, and the ones we didn't pick up will go underground."

"They'll rise to the surface again," Winstone said and looked at Mason's head wound. "What happened in there?"

"I was trying to infiltrate. I had it all set up, but someone blew my cover. You wouldn't happen to know anything about an ex-Gestapo major named Ernst Volker, would you?"

"No, but if he's ex-Gestapo then he's probably using an alias."

"Tall, thin, gray haired, with a chiseled chin and pointed nose?"

Mason thought he saw a spark of recognition in Winstone's eyes, then his focus shifted inward as if in deep thought.

"He isn't working for the CIC, is he?" Mason asked. "Another ex-Nazi now spying for our team who just blew my cover?"

"Mason, I don't know this Volker character. All our German agents have been cleared after a thorough vetting process, and many of them have been very effective. I'm not saying forget what we fought for, but there's another war on the horizon."

"I can't forget everything that easily." Just saying that elicited a flash of images to course through his consciousness. "Is that why you joined the CIC? The other horizon?"

"There hasn't been as much of a need for my specialty in German military intelligence since the end of the war. Plus, I thought I could do more good in the CIC fighting against the threat of Russian aggression."

"In Garmisch? Nothing I've turned up has anything to do with Russian spies. I could see Berlin or Frankfurt, even Munich, but not Garmisch."

"You might be surprised. Another team picked up a group of Russians trying to sneak across the border. The Reds are turning out German agents and double agents in the thousands while we're still struggling to establish a democracy. You're an excellent investigator. Why don't you come work with us? With the Russians grabbing up eastern Europe and sending battalions of spies at us, we could use you."

"Mike Forester already tried to recruit me. I'm a cop. It's who I am."

"Well, if Mike couldn't convince you…" Winstone's expression turned dark, and he glanced out the window as if making sure no one was watching. "I agree the rivalry between the CID and CIC should stop. And in that spirit, why don't we share information? I have some items that might interest you, and vice versa."

"Nothing I've turned up has anything to do with ratlines or Russian spies."

"Any other names come up in your investigations besides Ernst Volker?"

"Other than the three merry henchmen, Giessen, Bachmann, and Plöbsch?" Mason shook his head. "None who are above midlevel thug. But, right now, I'm trying to figure out how a Gestapo major, who tortured American soldiers, is still running around loose. I have the impression that there are a bunch of Germans out there who should be locked up for war crimes."

Winstone paused to consider something. "In my digging around, I did hear stories of new leadership coming into town. Somehow the organization running the ratline is connected to the new leadership. Whoever they are, they're slowly taking over, and the other gangs are running scared. I have a few informants on the inside. Like you, we weren't able to penetrate the group, but we did get inside a couple of operations, and what I learned shocked me."

"Like what?"

"I'm not prepared to throw anything out there without substantial proof."

"You give me what you have, and I'll work it from my end. I'll get the proof."

"I'm not prepared to do that, either."

"What happened to the spirit of cooperation? If it's a criminal matter, then you need to hand your information over."

Winstone suddenly had difficulty looking at Mason and turned his attention to the window again. "I'll tell you when the time is right. Only I and General Pritchard know the contents of the files I've collected."

"What's the deputy military governor of Bavaria have to do with a CIC investigation?"

"When I started seeing a connection between the ratlines and the gang activity, I was told by command to coordinate anything related to crime activity directly through General Pritchard. He's taken a personal interest in cleaning up the mess down here."

Mason merely nodded, letting Winstone talk. He knew General Pritchard, but decided not to mention that to Winstone. He studied the man's face and the way he held himself. For his part, Winstone remained as detached and unmoving as a statue.

Winstone continued, "Until I can verify the information, it stays in my hands. There are other issues involved besides local criminal activity. I've just uncovered some things that could shake the army to its core. Undermine everything we're trying to do here in Germany." He held up his hands before Mason could probe deeper. "Look, I can't say any more. I *can* promise that by the end of the week, I'll have what I need, and I'll pass it on to you. That is, if you're really ready to handle a live grenade."

"That's my specialty."

Winstone tried to produce a confident smile, but it failed.

"I'd better get back to it," Mason said and made a move to leave.

"Why don't we catch up?" Winstone said, turning cheery all of a sudden. "How about dinner tonight? You can meet my girl. We're going to the Blue Parrot around eight."

Another thing that had changed in Winstone: Once a devoted husband and father when Mason knew him during the war, and now he had a German mistress.

"Thanks. Maybe another time. My girl's coming in by train this evening. I haven't seen her in over two months."

"Bring her along. We'll make it a foursome."

Mason smiled and nodded. "If things go as planned, I'll be busy tonight."

3

W hen Mason and Abrams arrived at the Rathaus, the sun sat low behind the snow-laden mountains. Church bells announced the five o'clock hour, the sound immediate and sonorous in the dense, frigid air. The Rathaus, or city hall, sat on a large open square in the middle of town, appropriately called Rathausplatz. It had served as the seat of Garmisch-Partenkirchen's local government, but it now housed the local U.S. military government offices, and served as the military police and CID detachment headquarters. The four-story rectangular main building sported an entrance of stone arches supporting ocher walls with painted geometric designs, and capped by a pitched roof, with a cupola.

Mason and Abrams headed for the three-story annex building that sat perpendicular to the city hall proper. The first and second floors served as the principal MP station, with Garmisch's small contingent of CID investigators tucked away in a corner of the third floor. On the front steps, Abrams peeled off to talk to an MP buddy of his, and Mason continued into the building.

"Do you love your country, son?"

Mason hesitated, not because of the question, but because the

Garmisch area's provost marshal, Major Robert "Bronco Bob" Gamin, had asked it. The major stood just inside the entrance, handing out playing cards with the pledge of allegiance printed on the back.

"Uh, yes, sir, I do," Mason finally said.

Bronco Bob Gamin handed Mason a card. "Keep that in your breast pocket, close to your heart. Commies can't stand to do that. That way we'll know." He gave Mason a wink, then finally gave Mason a thorough look. "What are you doing out of uniform? You look like a damn kraut."

"I'm CID, sir. I was working undercover—"

Mason stopped, as Major Gamin had already turned to the next man coming in the door.

As he started to walk away, Gamin called after him, "You're the new CID investigator. Correct?"

"Well, yes, sir. Going on two months now. We've met on several—"

Gamin had turned away again to question Abrams, who looked more flummoxed than Mason. Once Abrams could break away, he joined Mason. They met their CID supervising officer, Patrick Densmore, by the base of the stairs. A former St. Louis police detective, Densmore stood tall and lean. Proud of his Oklahoma roots, he exaggerated his long drawl and spun endless yarns like a cowboy fresh off a cattle drive. At every opportunity he stood with his thumbs in his belt and habitually squinted as if he'd spent too much time gazing into the vast horizons of the sun-baked plains.

Mason and Densmore had the same rank, chief warrant officer 4, but Densmore had been with the detachment since August 1945, making him the most senior criminal investigator. There were only four CID investigators based in Garmisch, with investigators sent down from Munich if they became overloaded with cases. Between the fifty MPs and the four investigators, the entire police detachment felt like a town-sized force taking on a city-sized crime wave.

"What's with the major?" Mason asked Densmore.

"You haven't been around during one of his crazy spells?" When Mason shook his head, Densmore said, "He's a fine officer, a good administrator, but he goes off the deep end from time to time. Some say it started when his plane crashed during Operation Market Garden and he banged his head pretty bad. Some say he had a stroke. Whatever the reason, he gets on these jags about Commie conspiracies."

Mason glanced back down the stairs at Gamin, who looked like one of those blood-and-guts marines with the steely blue eyes, buzz haircut, and prickly mustache. Mason shook his head again.

Densmore continued as they climbed the stairs, "Because he was a war hero, the army—in its infinite wisdom—put him here just to give him something to do. He'll come out of it in a couple of days and be meaner than a hornet. Has he asked you to look into a conspiracy to steal American flags?"

"Nope."

"He will."

They reached the third-floor landing, which serviced two hallways leading to a series of offices. They took the hallway to the right, and Densmore stopped them halfway down. Playing nice was over; his expression had turned grim. He turned to Abrams. "Why don't you start writing up the report? Mr. Collins and I are going to have a few words."

Abrams headed for his office, and Mason followed Densmore down the hall in silence. Densmore tried to emulate the tough-but-sage commander, but those qualities never seemed to gel for the man. This walk of silence was meant to instill a little humility and contrition, like a student being walked to the principal's office, but humility and contrition were not among Mason's strong suits.

They entered a large office with a window overlooking the north end of town and the mountains in the background. It contained a large oak desk, with file cabinets lining one wall. Oversized maps dominated another wall: one of postwar Germany divided into its four zones of occupation—American, British, French, and Russian, one of the American zone, which included Bavaria; and finally a city map of Garmisch-Partenkirchen.

Squeezed between picturesque mountains of the Bavarian Alps, Garmisch-Partenkirchen had been untouched by bombs and surrendered without firing a shot. Her streets were still graced by buildings painted with religious or pastoral scenes and trimmed in carved wood like icing on a wedding cake—neighborhoods of gingerbread houses on Hansel-and-Gretel lanes, as if the town had been lifted out of a fairy tale. But this wasn't a fairy-tale town in some far-away land. It lay within the American occupation zone in defeated Nazi Germany. The vestiges of the 1936 Winter Olympics still stood as monuments to Hitler's dream of a thousand-year empire, but gone were the sea of Nazi banners, the signs saying: "Jews Not Welcome,", the elite Gebirgsjäger soldiers, the shouts of "*Heil Hitler*," and the swastika flag-waving fanatics. Göring had come there to be treated for a bullet wound after Hitler's failed putsch and was given honorary citizen status by the city's leaders. Hitler had wanted to buy farmland there for his mountain retreat, but the farmer wouldn't sell, and Adolf ended up building his Eagle's Nest at Berchtesgaden. A veritable who's who of Nazis had called Garmisch their home away from home. Under the ice and snow, under the pale blue sky of a low winter sun, the town hid its Nazi past well.

The Garmisch-Partenkirchen assignment had been designed to be Mason's punishment, a backwater post where he was to reflect on his reckless behavior and gross insubordination during a turbulent murder case in Munich. That had suited Mason just fine. He'd spent most of his postwar time in the blackened ruins of Frankfurt and Munich, so a posting at a renowned army playground struck him more like reward than punishment. Then he arrived...

Compared to the urban wasteland of those two cities, Garmisch was a clashing, jarring, incongruous place.

As the Third Reich collapsed, the city had become the stem of a funnel of fleeing wealthy Germans and Nazi government heavyweights, SS and Wehrmacht divisions, all bringing with them vast quantities of the Nazis' stolen art masterpieces, the Reichsbank's gold and currency reserves, diamonds, precious stones, and uranium from the failed atomic bomb experiments, all now hidden away or available for purchase on the black market. With millions of dollars to be made, murder, extortion, bribery, and corruption were the norm. Tens of thousands of displaced persons and concentration camp survivors, ex-POWs, arriving by circumstance or purpose, swelled the city to six times the wartime population. Adding to this volatile brew, tens of thousands of bored U.S. Army soldiers ripe for corruption, tempted by wickedness and greed. Criminal gangs thrived, and everyone seemed to look the other way.

So much for a backwater posting....

Densmore leaned against his desk and crossed his arms. Mason ignored Densmore's attempt at cutting an authoritative figure and feigned interest in the wall maps.

"I ought to charge you with insubordination," Densmore said.

"And that would prove what, exactly?"

"That you can't ignore my authority and try this infiltration bullshit without clearing it with me. Why do I only hear the details of this scheme when the thing goes south? Plus, you put yourself and Abrams in danger. If I had known about this stunt of yours, I'd have made sure, first, that you wouldn't have done it, and, second, that if I had approved it, I'd have seen that you'd have proper backup."

"I got the impression that you felt better not knowing. No one seems to give a damn about the gangs operating openly in this town. Everywhere I turn, I see Polish DPs and German ex-soldiers who've just come out of prisoner-of-war camps driving around in sports cars and wearing gold watches. American GIs and military government employees living like royalty. And no one gets busted."

"So you're the sheriff riding into Tombstone to clean up the town?"

"Maybe."

"Good luck with that. I guess the Germans shooting at you in the war wasn't enough."

Mason said nothing.

"As long as I'm your supervising officer, you will limit yourself to the cases at hand. I heard from the CID boys in Munich about you disobeying numerous direct orders in pursuit of that killer. They also said that you thought of yourself as some kind of modern-day Lone Ranger and charged into dangerous situations that almost got several of your fellow investigators killed. You go off the reservation here and I'll have your hide."

Mason decided not to tell Densmore that he'd heard those kinds of threats before from another commanding officer, that he considered direct orders optional if the situation warranted it. He always intended to toe the line, and after the firestorm he'd created in Munich, he had made a promise to stay out of trouble, but sometimes he just couldn't help it.

Densmore must have read his mind. "You told me when you first got here that you wanted to keep a low profile. Stay out of the spotlight after all the shit you got into in Munich. Just fly under the radar until your time is up with the army and you go back to the States."

"That's the thing about me: Just trying to put one foot in front of the other, I manage to step in the biggest pile of manure."

Densmore appeared to be finished with his reprimand, as he let out a sigh and sat at his desk to rifle through a stack of papers.

Mason asked him, "You've been in Garmisch how long?"

"Seven months. Why?"

"It's a small city. You've gotten to know how things work around here. How many MPs or MG officials are taking bribes or just looking the other way to make a few bucks?"

"MG" stood for "military government."

"Hell, everyone in this town is trying to make a few extra bucks."

"That include you?"

Densmore jerked his head up to glare at Mason. "God damn, buddy, who the hell do you think you are? I make a few bucks with the cigarettes, try to make life a little cushier. But I don't do anything that would compromise me as a CID investigator."

"I don't care what you do with your cigarettes. I mainly asked to see how much you know about the crime networks around here."

"If I knew something relevant I'd tell you. So back off."

They fell silent a moment, then Densmore asked, "What did you find in your search of the crime scene?"

"Not much in the bar. The Turk who runs the place knew how to keep it clean. We lifted fingerprints and shoe impressions from the mud in the alley, but I don't expect much concrete evidence to come of it. The canvass turned up nothing. We did pick up the shell casings near the bodies. Looks like two nine-millimeters. I figure they had some kind of sound suppressors since no one heard gunshots. We'll get the shell casings analyzed, and see if we can get the type."

"No line on where Olsen went?"

"None of the residents saw anything. Or at least they claimed not to. I'm betting his body will turn up in the forest once the snow melts—whenever *that* is around here. I'll have Abrams put out a missing-persons bulletins for all the MP patrols to be on the lookout for him."

Densmore took a moment to light a cigarette, then pointed it at Mason. "Next time you walk into a lion's den, you bring enough backup. Besides me, you're the only other investigator with any real experience. Now, get out of those rags and shave, then we'll go at your prisoners."

4

M ason, Abrams, and Densmore pulled into the parking lot of the newly renamed Sheridan barracks. Built on the north side of town for the Third Reich's elite mountain troops, it now housed POW officers of the defeated German army. The Garmisch detachment of the 508th Military Police Battalion had been slowly taking over the facility as the POWs were released or sent to other prisons. The CID offices would eventually be moved into these white, rectangular structures, and though the place was surrounded by incredible scenery, it still smacked of the same dreariness as any army base anywhere in the world. Mason preferred to avoid it all together.

In one of the buildings the ground floor and basement were being transformed into the official 508th jail cells, but in the case of overflow—which seemed to be a permanent condition— makeshift holding cells had been constructed to accommodate the recent American and DP arrestees.

After showing their IDs and signing in, Densmore said, "While you go at the Italians, I'll start with the Americans. Abrams can take the Yid."

"It's Jew, sir," Abrams said.

"Whatever," Densmore said. "We'll get together after that and go at the Russians and Poles."

They split up, but Densmore called after Mason, "No roughing up the wop, even if he did stick a gun to your head."

Mason ignored Densmore as he walked down the hall. MPs stood guard at the cells—really offices with reinforced doors. He entered a room with a narrow bed and a table with two chairs. A thick wire mesh covered the single window, which overlooked the snow-covered parade grounds. Mason's would-be assassin sat on the bed with his back against the concrete wall. He was maybe thirty, and he could have been a good-looking guy except for his prominent overbite and eyes that sat too close together. A sling cradled his broken arm. Mason expected to be greeted by the usual litany of accusations of police brutality and protests of innocence. Instead, the man smiled and struggled to his feet. He tried to act cool and poised as if he owned the room, but there was an edginess behind the movements, like he was wound way too tight.

"How about some coffee before we start?" the man asked; his Italian accent gone and replaced by one typical of the Bronx. He moved to a hot plate that held a pot of coffee. "It takes an Italian to know how to make good coffee."

Mason shrugged an agreement, then said, "What happened to the Italian accent?" He sat at the table while the Italian poured two cups

"When dealing with Germans, an Italian accent is better for business," the man said and winced in pain as he sat.

"I see they fixed your arm," Mason said.

"Nothing for the pain. That your idea?"

Mason ignored the question and referred to the one-page record and the man's identity papers. "Luigi Genovese. From Naples. Neither of those things is true, is it? My guess is, you use that name as a tribute to the Genovese crime family—the crime syndicate you work for. You were born in Italy—probably Sicily

—but grew up in the Bronx, and then sent to the Old World to drum up business for your bosses back home."

Luigi's smile faded for a moment, but he quickly regained his composure. "No hard feelings about the gun to your head? There was nothing personal about it."

"Strictly business," Mason said.

"That's right."

"Your broken arm? That was personal."

Luigi simply shrugged.

"What are you doing in Garmisch?"

"I am on a tour of this lovely countryside."

"Then why the visit with Herr Giessen?" Mason asked.

"He was the man I talked to about Garmisch's top attractions."

"What about a Herr Volker? Did you get tourist tips from him, too?"

"I don't know anything about a Herr Volker."

"He's the one who made me. He'd have been standing right next to you with one of his stinking cigarettes."

"I don't recall a man like that. But somebody in Herr Giessen's gang would have had you dead to rights eventually. A brave but stupid thing for you to try, Investigator Collins." He leaned forward, always with the smile. "You are one of those cops who likes to take risks. Be the hero. Those cops' names end up on memorial plaques on station house walls."

Mason produced a big, theatrical yawn. "You'd be surprised how many times I've heard that same crap from scumbags like you. Then after they realize their bosses have forgotten them. and they're facing years in the joint, just how many of them squeal for clemency or turn state's witness."

Luigi sipped at his coffee to mask whatever was going on in his mind.

Mason said, "I read that the U.S. deported Lucky Luciano and he landed in Naples a week ago. Does that have anything to do with you?"

"Trust me, you don't want a piece of that. On the other hand, we could use some men like yourself, helping grease the wheels."

"For tourism."

"That's right. I know what an American soldier earns. And if you leave the army and go back to the States, you'll be scrapping for a lousy job along with the millions of other former GIs. I could see that you're set, financially speaking. There's enough business to go around. A million bored GIs and sixty-million-plus desperate Germans? That's a market with opportunity. And now that Mussolini and his Fascists are out in Italy, the families are thriving again."

"Does that sales pitch usually work when you turn cops?"

"They usually come to me. I use that pitch when a cop is stupid enough to think he is going to be the big hero and finds out that nobody gives a damn."

Mason downed the rest of the coffee. "You're right. This is good coffee. Your thirty-year-old ass and your coffee ought to get you a fine husband in prison."

Luigi looked like he wanted to kill him at that moment, and Mason hoped he'd try.

"Which brings me to me offering you a deal," Mason said. "Information for a lighter sentence. And if the information's good, I may even drop the assault charges. All you'd have is a charge for illegal entry into the American occupation zone."

"That deal won't be necessary."

"Murdering three Germans is a very serious offense."

"What are you talking about, three murders?"

"Herr Giessen, Bachmann, and Plöbsch. And that doesn't include the two bodyguards."

"I am sorry for their deaths, but I had nothing to do with that."

"You're one of my prime suspects. You'd have a lot to gain by their deaths. I think you were sent here to take over the territory."

"You broke my arm, remember?" He lifted his slung arm to make a point, then winced with pain. "How could I have fucking done it?"

"Conspiracy to commit murder gets you the same thing."

A bead of sweat broke out on Luigi's face. "How about some painkillers?"

"No."

"I didn't have them killed," Luigi said in a raised voice, the pain in his arm trying his patience. "It's not good business to eliminate your customers. And I have better things to do than take over a middling territory like Garmisch."

"Like you said: Germany's a big market. And Garmisch is the perfect entry point from Italy. You and your bosses would have a lot to gain by controlling Garmisch."

"I am telling you, I had nothing to do with their murders."

"Then who did?"

"I don't know! Why don't you look in your own backyard? You might find that you're all alone chasing down the crime rings in this town."

"Thanks for the coffee," Mason said and stood. "I'm going to let you stew awhile. Let you think about what life's going to be like in prison."

"Am I going to get any painkillers anytime soon?"

"Maybe in a while. Enjoy the accommodations. You won't see better for a very long time."

Mason left the room feeling unsettled. Luigi's suggestion that Mason look in his own backyard carried more than a hint of truth to it. Winstone's words, then Luigi's, mirrored something Mason had suspected. With millions to be made and the cavalier attitude toward the rampant crime, U.S. personnel could be—almost undoubtedly were—involved at higher levels. Considering his disastrous actions during his time in the Chicago Police Department and his desire to fly under the army's radar, this was turning out to be exactly the kind of powder keg he wanted to avoid.

Next Mason interviewed the two Italian bodyguards. He had ordered the same thing for them—no painkillers for their wounds. It made no difference. They refused to talk, despite his threats and their obvious discomfort.

Mason met up with Densmore for the final interview of the five American GIs. More stonewalling and obfuscation, claims of innocence and ignorance. Two had been caught with small quantities of morphine, and the other three had charges of desertion, meaning all of them would be on their way to the stockade in Bad Tölz or Munich. Mason hoped that one of them might crack, but all of them seemed ready to opt for jail time rather than give up information or coconspirators.

When Mason and Densmore entered the Jewish man's cell, they found Abrams and the arrestee sitting at the table, with the prisoner talking rapidly and without pause as if they were long-lost friends.

Abrams rose from his chair. "Mr. Collins and Mr. Densmore, this is Yaakov Lubetkin."

Yaakov jumped to his feet and rushed over to shake each man's hand as if jacking a handle on a well pump. "Pleased to meet you, sirs," he said in heavily accented German.

"Do you speak any English?" Mason asked.

Yaakov shook his head and declared proudly, "I am Polish." His broad smile displayed an equally broad set of teeth. He was in his late twenties and stood at the height of Mason's shoulders. He had a boyish face with dark brown eyes, and acted overjoyed just to be alive and in the company of Germany's conquerors.

"Have a seat, Herr Lubetkin," Mason said in German, "while my colleagues and I confer."

Anxious to comply, Yaakov raced over to the chair and sat. Mason, Abrams, and Densmore huddled near the door.

"You get anything out of him yet?" Mason asked Abrams.

"I could barely get a word in edgewise. I got his whole family history, and his experiences at the concentration camps."

"What was he doing at the bar?" Densmore asked.

"He admitted to black marketeering. Mostly currency exchanges. The Germans give him foreign money to exchange for Reichsmarks, and he gets a percentage. He says it's a sweet deal, because it's against the law for Germans to have foreign currency, but the Jews can."

Mason walked over to Yaakov. Yaakov sat up straight as Mason approached, though his smile faded when he saw Mason's expression.

Mason asked in German, "Where do you get the foreign currency to exchange?"

"From many people. Mostly rich Germans. I get twenty percent, and they are happy for that. Both win."

"You know it's illegal to exchange money for Germans."

"Why? No one is hurt by this. I provide a service."

Mason decided against arguing the finer points of the law, and though he would have done it anyway, U.S. policy called for cutting a great deal of slack with surviving Jews when it came to interpreting the law. "Who were you exchanging money for at the Steinadler?"

Yaakov hesitated.

Mason growled a warning, "Herr Lubetkin..."

"Yaakov, please. I was exchanging money for a Herr Giessen. He won't get into trouble because of me, will he?"

"Not likely. He was murdered during the raid."

Yaakov's jaw dropped.

"Do you know where Herr Giessen got the foreign currency?" Mason asked.

Yaakov shook his head. "He was trying to exchange Swiss francs. I usually deal in U.S. dollars or British pounds."

"Do you know a Herr Volker? He'd be about forty-five, tall, gray hair, smokes a particular brand of Turkish cigarette with a gold tip."

Yaakov shook his head again.

"How often do you go to that bar?"

"Maybe once every two weeks."

"And you've had no other black-market dealings with Giessen's gang?"

"No, certainly not."

"Do you know any of the gang members? Could you point any of them out?"

Suddenly, Yaakov looked like he wanted to be anywhere else but in that room. He sank into his chair. "I don't think that would be such a good idea. My clients must remain anonymous or they lose trust in me. Not good for business. And I need the money."

"Yeah, doesn't everybody?"

"I have a new wife. She is pregnant. There is my brother, his wife and children. My brother works but earns very little. I support them. They depend on me."

"There's a Jewish DP camp not far from here. Feldafing. Why don't you and your group go there? They'll feed and protect you, give you shelter."

"And why should I want to go to this camp? There is no money to be made there. We need the money to go to Palestine." Yaakov leaned forward, lowering his voice. "Please, don't make me identify anyone. I have nothing else I can tell you."

Yaakov obviously knew far more than he was saying, but Mason decided not to push him. And since there was the hands-off policy concerning Jewish concentration camp survivors, he wouldn't charge him or hold him any longer. He joined Abrams and Densmore by the door.

"You're not going to book him, are you?" Abrams said. "He survived two years at Birkenau and Sachsenhausen, then a year at Mauthausen. He told me horrible stories. He lost most of his family—"

"Calm down," Mason said. "I'm not going to book him. But before he goes, give him a lecture about the perils of dealing on the black market." He turned to Densmore. "Let's find out how much stonewalling we're going to get from the Russians and Poles."

Someone knocked on the door. An MP poked his head in. "Mr. Collins, Colonel Udahl would like a word with you, sir. He's in the second-floor conference room."

"Colonel Udahl is here? Not in his office?" Densmore asked.

"Yes, sir," the MP said. "His driver told me that the colonel was in Munich for a meeting when he heard about the incident at the Steinadler. He got hopping mad and insisted on coming back down here."

When the MP left, Densmore said, "Garmisch's very own military governor wants to see you personally. You have stirred up a hornets' nest with that stunt you pulled."

5

M ason knocked on the conference room door and entered. The room contained a simple long table, folding chairs and a chalkboard where someone had written out MP manpower allotments and daily patrol assignments. Colonel Franklin Udahl stood staring out the window. Outside, black clouds had blown in, dropping freezing rain and sleet that clacked against the window and made the room lighting brighter than outdoors.

As the U.S. Army had overrun and occupied German territory, it had assigned military governors to administer each region, district, and city in the occupation zone. As representatives of the conquering army, they lorded over the vanquished population with absolute authority. Colonel Udahl was the district governor of Garmisch-Partenkirchen, and his realm measured four-hundred square miles, encompassing twenty municipalities, farmland, and the highest mountains in Germany, making him one of the most powerful lords in the Garmisch fiefdom.

With him was Captain Miller, a bald-headed man with a pinched cranium and round jowls. He was the head of the military government's public safety office, which oversaw the local German police and fire departments. A lawyer and politician by trade, Miller tried to make up for lack of law enforcement experience with bluster and aggression. Before Mason could say anything, Captain Miller came at him, waving his arms like a priest performing an exorcism.

"We're all wondering, Mr. Collins: Where did you learn police work?" Miller said. "Because we're in awe of how well you pulled off that infiltration gambit. Going in there without any backup, no consultation with the other investigative branches—"

"Every time I've consulted you guys, I've been bound up in red tape or something has leaked. I learned that to get anything done around here, I keep it to myself."

"The stink of your reputation wafted down here long before you arrived. We don't need a hotheaded investigator bulling his way into town. We know about your conduct in Munich. Blind ambition put you and your fellow investigators at risk. You disobeyed orders and went rogue."

"With respect, sir, this isn't about what I did in Munich, or not consulting the other branches. You're embarrassed because I was close to busting up a criminal gang that your department can't, or won't, bust up yourselves. The rampant local crime goes on without fear of punishment. Only the petty criminals have their charges stick, while the big boys are set free. What's going on in your department, Captain?"

"You are way out of line, mister, and I'm going to do everything in my power—"

"Captain Miller, that's enough," Colonel Udahl said without turning around.

"But, sir, this man shows no regard for army regulations or protocol. And his willful disdain for military authority is destructive. He's been blackballed from every stateside police department for past actions, and now he wants a free ride on the army's backside."

"Thank you, Marty. I will take care of it. Leave us for a minute, will you?"

Captain Miller stepped out and closed the door. Colonel Udahl finally turned to face the room. He was of medium height and muscular, with gray hair and mustache, and had what some would call a battle-tested face, with creases and crags, a crooked nose where it had been severely broken, and a deep scar that ran across the base of his throat. But it was his eyes that told you he'd seen hard fighting: They had a sharp gloss like alabaster and could pierce and probe, making some men shy away from his gaze.

And the colonel's icy gaze was directed at Mason. After a long moment, he said, "I appreciate you taking the heat for all this. I heard about everything that happened at the Steinadler. I'm sorry it went south, but that was still some fine police work, considering the restraints I put on you."

"Thank you, sir. I might have been able to pull it off if given more time for surveillance, phone taps, and a couple of experienced investigators to assist me."

"I wish I could have given them to you, but we had to move on them quickly. At least we put a dent in their operations. But I want you to continue your investigation into these gangs. We encountered a hitch, but I'm confident that, even if we can't shut down their activities completely, we'll make it very difficult to operate in this town. What's your next step?"

"The Italian-American prisoner knows more than he's saying. I plan to go at him again. We still have the Russians and Poles. Then there are the Germans who their police rounded up in the raid. If we can learn who was behind the killings, we'll learn who's trying to take over the territory."

"All right. I won't be able to offer much in the way of resources. I'm not even supposed to be involved in CID matters, but Major Gamin is not himself these days. I can't rely on him, and you're our best investigator. The crime gangs are getting away with murder out there. It's like Chicago in the '30s, for chrissake."

"Unfortunately, sir, the only reason the gangs are getting away with murder is because there are American servicemen helping them out."

"No doubt about it. And that's where you come in."

"What I mean to say is, the Americans helping are not just low-ranking GIs. To cover this kind of thing up means officers of rank, even command level."

Udahl nodded and took thoughtful steps in Mason's direction. "That's why I want you to keep this between you and me for the moment. We want to nip this problem in the bud before the stories get the general staff riled up and the press and Washington start hurling accusations of corruption and incompetence. Of course, General Pritchard is following this with a sharp eye."

If Udahl had the equivalent power of a big-city mayor, Lieutenant-General Pritchard, being the deputy military governor of Bavaria, was the governor of Texas.

"He's been impressed with your police work here and in Munich," Udahl said. "You proved yourself capable, and you know how to keep your mouth shut. His offer still holds. You get results for us here, and he'll see that you get that position as a sergeant detective in the Boston PD. That's not a load of bull. He intends to follow through on his promise."

Mason couldn't help smiling. It was what he had been praying for since the end of the war. As Captain Miller had said, after breaking the blue code of silence in the Chicago PD and being drummed out due to false charges, Mason had been blackballed from every big-city police force. Now he was offered a chance to become a stateside detective once again.

"There is one point I need to make clear," Udahl said. "If it looks like you're pushing against the army hierarchy, I want to be able to show them irrefutable evidence as to why. You know the army—command is one hundred percent behind the CID until they're the ones being investigated. Tread carefully, or you'll be the one tromped on. You run everything by me. Everything. I want careful police work. I'm on your side, Mr. Collins, and I want to give you every opportunity. We have to stamp out this crime wave no matter who it hurts." He patted Mason's shoulder. "No rest for the wicked, huh?"

"No, sir. And I'll do my best."

"Good. Now get it done."

MASON THREW the dart at the cork target. It struck the bull's-eye, which happened to be Hitler's nose and mustache. He'd asked the police sketch artist draw up a likeness of Hitler, then Mason had fashioned a dartboard to accommodate copies of the drawing. He'd gone through quite a few sketches in recent days. He retrieved the dart, stepped back to the opposite wall, and threw it again. The dart landed just shy of the previous mark. He retrieved the dart again, but this time he played with it in his fingers while he thought.

Mason's office had a simple desk, one file cabinet and two folding chairs. He'd put in a request for a better chair, as the one he had aggravated an old wound in his butt. A large corkboard dominated one wall, and besides furnishing a space for his Hitler target, it held photos and sheets Mason had pinned up with names and question marks delineating the known or suspected gang leaders of six criminal organizations that operated in the area. A separate section held photos of the three now-dead leaders, Giessen, Bachmann and Plöbsch. Beside those were mugshots of most of the arrestees from the Steinadler.

After the meeting with Udahl, Mason had gathered Densmore and Abrams and interviewed the Russian and Polish arrestees.

They were as tight-lipped as the Americans, except when it came to sharing their sad life stories. Most of the Russian and Polish arrestees had been POWs under the Nazis at a notorious prison camp in Ludwigsburg. Starved and beaten for years, many of these men had survived the appalling conditions by forming gangs that exploited others. Mason had heard of this kind of thing at Mauthausen, where the imprisoned crooks ran the barracks. The immoral had managed to survive. Mason came away from the interviews with the impression that any one of them would cut a person's throat without raising his own heartbeat; these were men who had stayed on after liberation to take advantage of the chaos and plunder the countryside.

He and Abrams had also been present during the German police interviews of the German arrestees, but none of them revealed any new information, and no one had admitted to seeing the ex-Gestapo major, Volker, or knowing if Sergeant Olsen had been murdered or escaped. Since they couldn't be charged with anything linked to the raid, Mason had reluctantly agreed to their release.

They had also conducted a search of Giessen's posh mansion, which neighbored that of the famous composer Richard Strauss. The mansion's notorious resident had been common knowledge and searched several times over the last nine months, first in the summer by the CIC to search for Nazis, then the past December by the CID in connection with stolen army property, but nothing had ever turned up. As a matter of course, Mason and Abrams searched it again, with the same results, save for the discovery of one ironic tidbit: Despite Giessen being a devout Catholic with five kids, he had still allowed Bachmann and Plöbsch to live together in one wing of the house like spinster aunts.

Giessen's gang had been suspected of shakedowns, bribery, extortion, and murder for hire, but their main endeavor was trading in stolen petrol, coal, narcotics, food, and medicines in big quantities. Moving such large shipments of illicit goods across borders took travel permits, papers to cross borders controlled by the British and French, and more than a few cooperative MPs and other officials. Mason had inherited the case from a CID investigator who'd been transferred back to the States, leaving Mason with a slim file on the gang. What had caught Mason's eye was the involvement of lower-ranked U.S. soldiers and lower-echelon military government officials, and that the army and military government law enforcement agencies, while expressing concern, seemed uninterested or unwilling to do anything about it. With millions to be made, many who came to Garmisch with high ideals succumbed to its temptations. Rumors even circulated that his predecessor had been transferred for the same reason.

Mason launched the dart again, but this time it stuck in Giessen's forehead. He retrieved the dart and shook his head as he studied Giessen's photograph.

Who had killed Giessen and the rest? Did the killers know of the bust ahead of time, and then lie in wait for their victims? But how could that be if Mason's identity was only blown just before the German police raided the bar? The three German gang leaders appeared surprised at Mason's true identity, so how was it that the very person who could ID him happened to be at the bar at just the right time? It stank of a setup.

Mason threw the dart so hard that it penetrated the board and sank deep into the plaster wall behind it. He walked up to the board and had to yank on the barrel. Plaster dust and bits of the paper target followed the point.

"How many targets you go through in a week?" Abrams asked as he entered the room.

"Depends on how much thinking I have to do."

Abrams stepped around the desk to keep his distance from the target. "It's almost seven. I'm going to get something to eat and drink a gallon of beer. That is, unless there's something you need for me to do."

"No. Enjoy some downtime."

"How about joining me? You look like you could use a drink or four."

"I'm meeting someone at the train station in a half hour."

"That's right. Your girl's coming into town. So that's why you're so tense."

Mason said nothing as he threw the dart, striking a photograph of Plöbsch in his broad forehead. The point sank deep and snapped off where it connected to the barrel.

Abrams shook his head and started to leave.

"Listen," Mason said, "you did all right today."

Abrams nodded as he put on his hat. "Thanks. And good luck with your girl. Or maybe I should wish her luck."

When Abrams left, Mason sat at his desk. He rubbed the weariness from his face, lit a cigarette, and then fished a letter out of his top drawer. He looked at it a moment before unfolding it. The sheet of stationery had deep wrinkles where Mason had crumpled it up and thrown it in the trash, only to retrieve it later and flatten it out again as best he could.

The letter was from Laura. Laura McKinnon. They had met in Munich. Laura was smart, passionate, courageous and beautiful. A volatile relationship, as it turned out, cop and reporter, both ambitious bordering on obsessed, like two fiery celestial bodies attracted by forces of nature, spinning around and away from each other.

A hunt for a vicious killer in Munich had brought them together, but the same case had eventually created the barrier between them. Catching the killer had left Mason satisfied but drained, and Laura shattered. They'd spent a month together after that, until Laura departed to pursue a story about the black market trade routes in and out of Germany, and Mason had opted for an assignment in Garmisch-Partenkirchen. In fact, Mason had pushed for this posting to be closer to Laura. But by the time he'd arrived, she had left for parts unknown.

Finally, without warning, she'd written him. Sighing, he folded the letter with care, inserted it into the envelope, and placed it back in the drawer. Inside that same drawer lay a box of darts. He shut the drawer quickly before temptation drove him to grab a handful of darts to launch at whoever was likely to show up at the station with Laura.

6

M ason waited just inside the front entrance of Garmisch's train station. He paced the area, unaware of the people having to navigate around him. He opened and closed his cigarette lighter and muttered commands to keep cool. Except for wearing a crisply pressed uniform, he might have been mistaken for one of the crazies that haunt every train station.

The interior was like most train stations found in every small city: long and narrow, with the ticket counter at one end, rows of wooden booths in the center. And like all of Garmisch-Partenkirchen, the walls were decorated with carved wood beams and frescoes of some saint and the surrounding countryside.

Through the double doors overlooking the station platform, Mason spotted Laura's train pulling into the station. A few minutes later passengers poured inside. Besides soldiers and busi-nessmen, a large group of German refugees had arrived; after being forced out of Czechoslovakia, many now sought shelter in Germany's cities or with relatives.

Laura stepped up to the door. Mason's heartbeat quickened. Then he saw a tall man with pointed but handsome features hold open the door for Laura. The two stopped just inside the doors and exchanged a few words with comfortable smiles, though Laura's eyes clearly betrayed her nervousness.

Mason remained near the front entrance and watched them. Laura and her companion appeared relaxed standing together. Not the nervous flirting typical of new couples. They obviously had been a couple for a while. That made Mason's sense of loss more acute, and he had to look away for a moment.

Laura scanned the station as she spoke. She wore a knit ski cap and heavy white coat, which enhanced her blue eyes and black hair. She looked beautiful as always—elegant really, with classic New England blue blood features of pronounced cheek-bones and a thin, upturned nose. As the crowd of arriving passen-gers thinned, she spotted him. She turned to the man, putting her hands delicately on his chest, and said something. They both looked in Mason's direction. She smiled at Mason, but with sad eyes, as if observing a crippled soldier. That was what Mason felt, at least.

Laura approached him alone, with assertive steps, like a tomboy who had blossomed into a stunning woman but had never grown out of her rough-and-tumble days. She kissed him on the cheek. "Hello, Mason."

"Hello," was all he could muster in return.

They looked at each other for a moment. Mason found it hard to speak, and it looked as though Laura experienced the same difficulty.

Finally Mason said, "I'm glad to see you're still in one piece. And beautiful as always."

She smiled, her eyes moist. "I see you got my letter."

Mason nodded. "You've met someone," he said softly, though it took strength to say it.

"He's a reporter. Richard Cranston. An Englishman—" She took a deep breath and forced a smile. "Cops and reporters."

"We tried."

"He has the same wanderlust and independence of mind that you and I have. But Richard and I travel in the same hemisphere. We have the same goals. He's always there for me—"

"Good for him. Does Ricky know who I am?"

"Richard," Laura said, raising one eyebrow. "And, yes, he does."

"He looks like a nice enough guy."

"Yes, he is. Would you like to—"

"No."

"Look, I know this is hard for you, but it's hard for me, too. Like I said in the letter, I care enough about you to want to tell you everything to your face."

"And it was a brave thing to do."

Laura looked in his eyes for a moment. "You surprise me sometimes. One minute I feel I know exactly what you're thinking, then you hit me with something I didn't expect."

"You used to like that about me."

"I still do."

Mason needed to change the subject. "I assume you didn't come all the way to Garmisch just to see me."

"The *Washington Post* has agreed to publish my story investigating the black market routes in a four-part series, so I decided to write it up in Garmisch. The legwork is finally done, and I'm exhausted after close to three months on the road. I even disguised myself as an Italian DP and went on a few black market runs into Italy. I saw how they manage to get across the tough British check points between Austria and Italy."

"I still have to wonder why you picked Garmisch, of all places."

Laura only smiled in response.

"Ricky's okay with you risking your life that way?" Mason asked.

"Being in the same town as you, or associating with dangerous black marketers?"

Mason was unsure how to take that, and Laura offered nothing to help him out.

She finally said, "*Richard* and I met in Italy at the end of my last run there."

"So, no."

Laura gave him a don't-go-there look. "What about you? Risking your life on a daily basis?"

"Not in the last"—he looked at his watch —"few hours. There are some pretty ugly black market activities going on around here."

"Maybe we'll compare notes sometime."

"Maybe. Though I don't think I'll be coming around for a social call."

"You could if you wanted."

"I don't think I could stand being near you with Ricky in the shadows."

Laura nodded and looked away to break Mason's gaze. "I hope you'll forgive me... and wish me well."

"I forgive you. Maybe not myself for screwing things up."

"I'm sure you'll find someone else who's far more patient and loving than I was with you."

Mason said nothing.

Laura took a small step forward. "Try to be happy for me. And, on occasion, for yourself."

She started to go, but Mason said, "Maybe we *can* have that tea sometime."

She smiled. "Yes... See you around."

Mason tried to say good-bye as she walked away, but it got stuck in his throat. He left before Laura returned to Richard, before having to watch them walk away arm in arm. The encounter had sapped all his strength, so even pushing open the exit doors took effort, and the walk back felt very long and very cold.

MASON MADE it to the Rathaus parking lot before turning away from the headquarters' entrance at the last minute and walking to his assigned car. And instead of driving to his billet, he crossed the railroad tracks on St.-Martin-Strasse, then turned right and headed for a cluster of streets where restaurants, bars, and night-clubs had sprung up to accommodate the huge influx of soldiers on leave.

It was eight P.M., and Garmisch had begun changing into its second skin. The extreme contrasts of life in this town had struck Mason on the first day of his arrival, and this evening was no exception. During the day the streets filled up with German civil-ians and ex-soldiers and the less-fortunate displaced persons, all seeking ways to survive. They shuffled through the snow in threadbare clothes, with gaunt faces, bartering possessions for food or taking long treks up into the mountains to gather wood for their fires. At night, the town's other half emerged: army GIs and military government officials in their dress uniforms escorting young German ladies. And it was the first time Mason had seen wealthy Germans flaunting their furs, jewels, and tuxedos. The rules were different in Garmisch, at least for Germans of suffi-cient wealth, whether old money or new and nefarious: no curfews, private luxury vehicles, zero restrictions on gathering at restaurants and bars. Just one big demented family.

A sign on a single-story building advertised the Blue Parrot with alternating neon lights that created the illusion of a parrot raising its wing and downing a mug of beer. Unfortunately the middle gesture looked like it was giving a Nazi salute—an unintentional send-up of Hitler by the Americans who had converted the former German beer hall into a bar/eatery for U.S. army and military government personnel.

Mason shook his head at the irony. He crossed the street and entered the establishment. The bar's namesake came from the film *Casablanca*, but the interior looked more like Geppetto's workshop from *Pinocchio*, with the additions of American flags, Coca-Cola and iconic beer signs, and framed photographs of FDR, Truman, and Eisenhower.

Mason nabbed the last spot at the bar and ordered a beer. While he waited for the barman to bring his order, he scanned the crowd. Every stripe and bar of every rank was represented. He recognized some of the locally stationed army and MG personnel, but the majority consisted, as always, of American servicemen and women from all over the American occupation zone.

Mason usually shunned crowded places. Noisy restaurants and cocktail parties bored him. He liked being alone, but seeing Laura at the station had left him feeling empty, and he needed to fill the void. He looked at the other women and wondered if he'd ever meet someone who could knock him over like Laura did. Lust would push him into the arms of another woman, but once that fire was extinguished he'd move on.

His beer arrived, and as he sipped the liquid, his attention turned to the male patrons. Which of the men he saw having a good time took bribes to look the other way, or greased the wheels, or even participated in large-scale black marketeering? Was it the captain in the transportation regiment sitting at a table with two young women? He had access to trucks and trains to transport or divert goods. Was it the major in the MG financial offices in Munich dancing with a girl half his age? That department not only dealt with payroll and funds for government rebuilding projects, but also oversaw the collection of retrieved caches of Nazi-stolen artwork and gold that on too many occasions ended up missing. Then there was the captain of the prison that held suspected Nazi officials and industrialists. It was rumored that for the right price, papers would suddenly appear exonerating wealthy prisoners of all wrongdoing. And when the captain ran out of legitimate prisoners who could pay, he had other moneyed victims arrested on bogus charges, forcing the families to pay for their freedom. Rumor had it, of course...

There were many good men and women in the service who believed in what they were doing, performed their duty and did it well, despite the Gordian knot of bureaucracy and the rivalries between the army and military government. But the opportunities for profiting from a broken country were often too hard to resist. And no other town in occupied Germany offered as much temptation as Garmisch.

Mason spotted Agent Winstone entering the establishment with a beautiful blond on his arm. He nodded to a few people he knew, but didn't stop to talk. Though he and the woman both made the effort to smile, neither came off as genuine. If Winstone wanted to make a show of his trophy date, he was making a bad sell of it.

Winstone spotted Mason and waved. As they came up to the bar, they sported more genuine smiles, like two winners relieved at crossing the finish line.

"Hey, you came," Winstone said. "Where's your girl?"

"It turns out she's not my girl anymore."

Winstone grimaced his sympathy. "Sorry to hear that, pal. Still, I'm glad you came." He slid sideways to present his companion. "Allow me to introduce Hilda Schmidt." He said to Hilda, "Mason is a top-notch detective with the military police."

Hilda bowed slightly and shook his hand. "How do you do?"

she said in accented English. She looked to be twenty-three or twenty-four, and while not having movie-star looks, she could have been cast as the enchanting girl next door, with her full figure, round face, prominent cheekbones and broad forehead that framed sage green eyes.

"Hilda is a world-class ice skater and dancer," Winstone said. "She performs at the Casa Carioca. You must have seen her there."

"I've never been."

"You've got to go sometime. Great place."

An awkward moment passed between them. Mason had met Winstone's wife in London when she and her daughters had come to live with her husband. She had stayed only a month before deciding she couldn't tolerate the "foreignness" of England and she returned to the States.

Winstone squeezed Hilda's arm as a way of telling Mason that their coupling was more than a financial transaction. "I hope you still want to have dinner with us."

"That's why I'm here," Mason said as cheerily as he could.

Winstone gave Hilda a sideways glance. Hilda displayed a polite smile. "I'll be right back."

"We'll find a table," Winstone said to Hilda, and she headed for the restrooms.

"I don't see one available," Mason said.

"No worries. I know the proprietors."

And sure enough, after Winstone arched his eyebrows and snapped his fingers at the manager, two waiters brought out a small table and chairs and made room in a corner. When he and Mason sat, Winstone ordered a bottle of champagne. "And forget the menus, Franz. We'll take three prime rib dinners with the works." He turned to Mason when the waiter left. "This is all on me."

"Maybe I should screw up more of your investigations."

Winstone laughed as if he didn't have a care in the world. They stood when Hilda came to the table. She gave Winstone a knowing smile as she settled in her seat.

"Seriously," Mason said. "I appreciate the drinks and dinner. What's the occasion?"

"A renewed friendship. And word is, you don't get out much. But that's all going to change, as of now."

The champagne came, and they toasted to good health and good friends. And by the time the prime rib dinners arrived, the bottle was empty. Winstone ordered another. All the while they made chitchat, or shared war stories about this bizarre foreign agent or that asshole commander. Mason learned that Hilda had been skating and dancing most of her life. She was even in Garmisch-Partenkirchen for the 1936 Winter Olympics as a young teenager and used in a Nazi propaganda exhibition showing off future athletes of the Third Reich. She traveled in ice shows all over Germany and Nazi-occupied territories during the war, and had ended up skating for her life and her family. Her mother was discovered to be half Jewish, and her father sent to a work camp for violating the racial purity laws. Hilda had used her charm and talents to help her parents avoid harsher punishment in return for performing in front of Nazi dignitaries. "Like a circus animal," she said bitterly.

Mason had heard many Germans exaggerate—to use a polite term—about their innocence or hatred of Hitler, but his cop training told him that Hilda's feelings were genuine.

The alcohol had wakened Mason's libido, and he found himself enjoying Hilda's attention, her touching his arm when she wanted to make a point, her perfume, her utter charm. But amid the carnal attraction, his detective's instincts also made him wonder why Winstone was wining and dining him. What was the real reason for Winstone's generosity, his theatrical joie de vivre? What was his angle?

But by the time the third bottle had arrived, Mason had abandoned all doubts and cares. And the pain of seeing Laura at the train station had faded to a dull throb.

Suddenly he was aware of another woman coming up to their table and saying hello to Hilda. The men stood to greet her. Hilda introduced Mason and said her name was Adelle Holtz. Winstone and the women exchanged remarks about how coincidental it was that they were all there at the same time, and Adelle was saying that she was there to meet a soldier, who'd apparently stood her up.

Mason hardly listened. He was too busy considering the reasons for this seeming coincidence. First the free-flowing champagne and massive steaks, and now a beautiful woman jilted by a thoughtless soldier. It could be a genuine attempt by an old friend to assuage his pain caused by Laura's rejection, though he felt there was another agenda behind it. But at that moment it didn't matter; he willingly let his guard down and allowed himself to be beguiled. He'd always had a thing for Paulette Goddard, ever since seeing the actress in *The Ghost Breakers*. Adelle could have been her twin, down to her long thin nose, full lips and almond-shaped eyes. She even sported the same roguish grin when she saw Mason staring at her.

"Does your friend speak, or is he the silent, he-man, silent type?"

"Sorry, it's just that you just remind me of someone," Mason said.

They all sat, and Winstone poured another round.

"I hope I remind you of someone in a good way," Adelle said to Mason.

"Not an ex, if that's what you were wondering."

"Do you have an ex?"

"Several."

"Anyone current?"

"I've sworn off relationships."

"Oh…" Adelle said, as she studied him a moment. "Your girl-friend just left you."

"And what makes you say that?" Mason said, then looked at Winstone. Winstone held up his hands in denial.

"It's written all over your face," Adelle said.

"What you're seeing is only the effects of too much champagne."

"Oh, not nearly enough of that," Winstone said and filled Mason's glass. He said to Adelle, "Mason's been living the life of a monk since he's been here—relatively speaking, of course. And I think it's high time we changed that, don't you?"

"I hope he hasn't adopted all the virtues of a monk," Adelle said.

"I'm a detective. I think I've broken most of the commandments by now."

"Oh, a policeman. Then I should be careful of what I say."

"Say what you like. I'm off duty."

"I thought policemen were never off duty."

"We policemen do find time to relax," Mason said. He raised his glass and clinked it with Adelle's.

"Mason was the one who was responsible for busting up that bar, the Steinadler, this afternoon," Winstone said.

Adelle put her hand to her mouth. "Where all those people were killed?"

"The very same," Winstone said.

Mason shot Winstone a look of irritation.

"Sorry, old man," Winstone said. "I didn't mean to spill the beans."

"You were injured?" Adelle asked Mason, looking at Mason's bandaged temple.

"Mostly my pride."

"Anything come of your interviews?" Winstone asked.

"They were all tight-lipped. But it all made me think about your theories."

"You two aren't going to talk about work, are you?" Hilda said. "With two young and charming ladies to entertain?"

Winstone flashed a serious look as if he wanted to tell Mason something, but the moment passed a heartbeat later, and he became Mr. Jovial once again. "Of course, darling." He looked at his watch and said, "It's almost eleven. Why don't we move the festivities to my place?"

Hilda and Adelle agreed, but Mason hesitated. This meant Mason and Adelle would be forced together in an intimate setting. He liked to pick the time and place to be with a woman, not be coerced into it no matter how innocent the gesture. Usually this was when he would bow out. But the last thing he wanted to do was go back to his place, where he'd think too much about Laura, and have another sleepless night. Right then he needed the touch of a woman.

Mason acquiesced, and they left the restaurant, Mason taking Adelle in his car and following Winstone's Maybach. Adelle talked about skating at the Casa Carioca with Hilda. Mason listened as he wondered how a CIC agent could have acquired a Maybach Special Roadster, even with the enormous buying power of the almighty American dollar on the black market. It would have still taken an awful lot of dollars or cigarettes or whatever he traded to wrench that beauty from the clutches of its hapless owner.

Winstone drove east, through town, and up a winding hill that rose above Garmisch. They entered an elegant neighborhood where mansions disguised as Alpine chalets lined both sides of the streets, each on a sprawling lot and surrounded by walls. On the final turn, they cleared the trees, which revealed the city below. Mason assumed Winstone used this street to get to whatever humble billet the CIC had found for him. Something certainly more humble than the neighborhood they were passing through. But Winstone pulled up to an iron gate in a six-foot wall that surrounded a palatial estate. He opened the gate, and they proceeded up a long driveway to a side portico.

When they all piled out, Mason said, "This is your place?"

"Courtesy of the CIC. I told them I needed something private to conduct my investigations, and they gave me this. The owners fled to Switzerland or some such place. Now, if you'd stayed in intelligence, you might have had one of these babies."

A short, bald, barrel-chested man greeted them as they entered the side door. He wore a white suit and black bow tie. He bowed as they passed, and Mason noticed that he'd barely refrained from clicking his heels.

"Oh, come on, John," Mason said. "You actually have a butler?"

"This is my chef and butler extraordinaire," Winstone said, and while he introduced Otto Kremmel, Otto's facial muscles never moved, but his eyes said plenty: He would bear the indignities of serving people far below the status of his former employers, and Americans to boot.

"I prepared an evening meal, sir," Otto said. "Which I could reheat, if you like."

"That won't be necessary," Winstone said.

Otto's eyes were quite adept at showing his displeasure. "Do you require anything else this evening before I retire?"

"No, thanks. In fact, why don't you take the rest of the night off? Go home and see your wife."

"It's rather late, sir. I appreciate the offer, but—"

"Nonsense, Otto. I insist."

Otto bowed mechanically and nearly clicked his heels again.

Mason hesitated, tempted to learn more about Otto and his background, but instead, he followed the group through a large foyer.

Winstone leaned in to them to avoid Otto overhearing. "I don't want him lurking around while we have fun."

Winstone took Adelle and Mason on a tour of the villa, as Winstone called it. Even through the haze of alcohol, and with the distraction of Adelle on his arm, Mason wondered if the CIC had really arranged this life of luxury for Winstone, and if not, what exactly Winstone was mixed up in to acquire all this: the Maybach Roadster, with a Mercedes touring car in the garage, Persian rugs, porcelain china, crystal, silver. Mason didn't know a Titian from a Picasso, but the paintings on the walls looked expensive. If the previous owners had fled, surely they would have taken anything valuable they could carry.

Adelle squeezed his arm against her breast and said under her breath, "I can see you thinking like a cop. For a night, forget. For a night, be enchanted." She gave him a peck on the cheek.

Mason smiled and resolved that he would try.

Winstone took them through ten rooms: a massive living room with a carved marble fireplace, a dining "hall," a sun room, a library, an expansive kitchen, then the five bedrooms and three bathrooms upstairs. All the rooms were king-sized, all with antique furniture, intricate architectural details, and wooden or marble floors.

They returned back to the living room. Winstone retrieved four bottles of vintage French wine from the cellar. They spun 78s on the gramophone. They danced and flirted. They smoked cigars and ate caviar.

At least two bottles of wine later, Mason had sunk deep into the plush sofa cushions, his legs and arms splayed out, his body warmed from the fire that crackled in the enormous fireplace. His head lay back on the rear cushion, and he puffed on a cigar as he studied the intricately carved ceiling and listened to a bouncy French tune on the phonograph. Adelle and Hilda had just left to go upstairs to the bathroom, leaving the men in silent reverie.

"I could get used to this," Mason said.

"You could stay, you know," Winstone said.

Mason lifted his head. "What do you mean? Live here?"

"Why not? It's a big house, and it's just Hilda and me."

Mason found the proposal extremely appealing, that little voice prodding him along, saying it was about time he indulged in luxury and pleasure. And it surprised him that the notion would actually cross his mind. It unsettled him how easy it would be for him to fall for the temptation and embrace this lifestyle. He shook his head. "Nah, I might get to like it too much."

"You don't think you deserve a little luxury?"

Mason sat up and leaned on his knees. He studied Winstone as the man blew smoke rings at the ceiling. He'd seen his friend revert back to the old Winstone over the course of the evening, the frank, amiable, and humble guy he once was. But Mason was concerned that this kingly lifestyle had already seduced his old friend.

Mason said, "Look, I'm all for a man getting what he deserves—"

"But you keep thinking that all this isn't courtesy of the CIC," Winstone said. He sat up and flicked his cigar ashes in a crystal ashtray. "The owners left in a hurry and were forced to abandon a lot of what you see. Some of the art and the cars were confiscated from Nazis by the CIC and consigned to me. They're all registered and destined to be sent to Frankfurt's central repository when I'm done with my investigation."

"The wads of cash, vintage wines, the caviar?" Mason asked. "What does that have to do with investigating ratlines?"

Winstone shrugged. "If they see you as corrupt, you're less of a threat. Considered more predictable, weak and malleable. I even deal with some of them on a business level."

"And how do I fit into your plans? I can't help wondering why the VIP treatment?"

Winstone looked like he'd been stung by the comment. "You're an old friend. I haven't seen you in a long time, and I wanted to show you a good time."

"Don't get me wrong, I'm enjoying myself, but I think it's also because someone or something has got you spooked."

Winstone puffed on his cigar as if using the pause to come up with a response. "What I'm starting to uncover would make anyone nervous. The idea of you staying here as a"—Winstone searched for the right word—"deterrent? That didn't occur to me until just now. I saw you enjoying yourself and thought you could work your job, stay here, and give me a little peace of mind."

"Deterrent against what?"

"About a month ago, I hired some security, but they were unreliable, and I had the sense they were working for someone else. I decided I need someone I can trust. It's not a big deal. I'm not asking you to stand guard all night. And cops take side jobs, right? Think of it as that: make a little extra cash and enjoy the perks, while helping out an old friend."

"Is Adelle part of the compensation package?"

"I'm offended you think so little of me. Or her. She's a nice girl. I admit we wanted to fix you two up, and you *did* hit it off, just like Hilda thought you would. That's it."

They heard Hilda and Adelle coming down the stairs. Winstone leaned in and said, "Think it over. Stay the night. Otto comes in at seven every morning and cooks up a mean breakfast. I promise we'll talk it all over in the morning. Meanwhile, it wouldn't hurt you to live a little, would it?" Winstone whispered the last sentence before the women entered the room.

Adelle smiled warmly at Mason and returned to his side. Her touch, her smell, her warmth worked better than any of Winstone's words. Maybe he would take Winstone's advice. Just for the night.

They danced some more and drank more wine. Mason and

Adelle's flirtations turned to intimate caresses, and Mason became aware only of Adelle, her breasts against his chest, her hips pushing into his as they danced. At some point late in the evening, Winstone and Hilda slipped away. Mason and Adelle danced another three songs. Then, already half naked, they went upstairs and made love in one of the bedrooms on a thick mattress under a lace canopy.

Lost in the luxury of Adelle's embrace, Mason allowed himself to forget Laura for an evening, to be enchanted....

At around three A.M., Mason woke up with Adelle sleeping at his side. His prodigious consumption of alcohol was now compelling him to go to the bathroom. When he staggered out into the hallway, he heard Winstone and Hilda inside their bedroom speaking with raised voices. The thick door muffled most of what they were saying, but he detected either anger or fear in Hilda's voice. She yelled, with Winstone trying to calm her with a more measured tone. He could make out Hilda shouting his and Adelle's names. And that someone should go, and go now.

Mason continued quickly to the bathroom, relieved himself, then crept back to the bedroom and gently prodded Adelle awake.

"We should go," Mason said.

Adelle yawned and stretched. "We can't. Hilda will be upset if we leave before morning."

"I've got to be at headquarters in about four hours."

Adelle took his hand. "Please. Let's stay."

"Stay if you like, but I've got to go."

Adelle held her breath when she heard Winstone and Hilda's distant argument. She rose quickly. "Not if you're leaving."

Mason and Adelle dressed and left quietly. They barely spoke as Mason drove them back into town. She directed him to her apartment, and he promised to see her as soon as he had a chance. Then he managed to find his way to his billet, a place on Frühlingstrasse by the Loisach River, a cottage compared to Winstone's villa.

The time for forgetting came to a close. Mason remembered as he slept. He remembered the torture, the misery at the prison camps, the death march, and a little girl, Hana, dead in a snowy field.

7

M ason entered police headquarters an hour late, and a little worse for wear. Two hours of sleep and a gallon of champagne. Not so long ago, he could have done that and be ready to tackle the day. Last night seemed like a dream now, Adelle a divine apparition sent to help him forget Laura for a brief time, and the darker things in his mind. He would definitely see Adelle again.

Copious amounts of water and coffee, that was what he needed at that particular moment. But when he saw an MP, Private Stratford, heading for him as if competing for the land speed record, he knew he should have stopped by the officers' mess before showing his face at headquarters.

"What is it, Private?"

"Sir, there's been a double homicide. I'm to take you there. Mr. Densmore will meet you."

"Densmore?"

Mason found that odd, as Densmore was the supervising officer and usually coordinated investigations from headquarters.

"Yes, sir. He wanted to be in this one, for some reason."

What, at first, had simply been a bone-chilling trip in an open jeep across town turned to unease when the Private Stratford took a now-familiar path. Unease turned to dread when the jeep rose above town on the same winding road.

"This can't be," Mason said.

"What's that, sir?"

"Nothing," Mason said as they passed the same row of mansions.

The private stopped at the gate to Winstone's villa. Two other MP jeeps were parked at the curb, and an MP stood guard at the open gate.

"When you get back to headquarters, tell Mr. Abrams to get his ass up here."

"He's already inside."

Mason nodded then got out of the jeep. The MP guard waved him through the iron gate. Mason stopped halfway up the front walkway and lit a cigarette. He needed time to steel his nerves. A double homicide. Winstone and Hilda.

He cursed at the tragedy of it and hurled the cigarette down onto the snowy walkway. Abrams intercepted him as he took quick strides toward the villa he'd left only a few hours ago.

Mason asked, "What have we got?"

"The victims are a man and woman. A CIC agent, John Winstone…."

Mason cursed again under his breath.

"What's wrong?" Abrams asked.

"He's a friend of mine. I'm guessing the other victim is Hilda Schmidt."

"Damn. How do you…? I'm not going to ask."

"I was here last night."

"Damn," was all Abrams could get out.

They entered the front door of the villa and stepped into the vast foyer. Three MPs stood outside the living room door.

Abrams continued, "Winstone left a suicide note—"

"Suicide note?"

"You'll have to see for yourself, sir, but it's pretty simple: 'I can't come back from this dark place. I've committed too many sins to go on.' Looks like a murder-suicide to me. No signs of a forced entry, no tracks leading up to the house, no sign of a struggle."

They entered the villa's living room. Densmore was already there, crouched near Winstone's and Hilda's bodies, with the tips of his shoes touching a pool of blood spread across a Persian rug.

As Mason took in the scene, he struggled to maintain his composure.

Winstone sat cross-legged, cradling Hilda's head with a lifeless arm. He had a bullet hole just above his right eyebrow with a chunk the size of a baseball missing behind and below his left ear. Hilda had been tortured: cuts, burns, and bruises everywhere her shredded nightgown exposed skin. She had at least ten stabs wounds to the chest and stomach that Mason could see. But worst of all, her nose, lips, and ears had been cut off, and her eyes gouged out, giving her the appearance of a grinning skull wearing a fleshy mask.

After four years as a homicide detective in Chicago, two years of war as a soldier, and time in several POW camps, Mason should have been used to seeing the barbarity of man, but that had never been the case. And now he looked upon the bodies of his friend and a woman he'd grown fond of over the course of a few hours.

Obviously Densmore didn't feel the same way: "Ain't this romantic?"

Mason ignored the morbid crack and moved to the left side of Hilda's body. He crouched to get a better look at Winstone's wound. Being so close made his body feel cold. He summoned all his experience as a detective and imagined he was examining any other corpse, and not that of a friend.

Winstone's head hung forward with his chin buried in his plaid bathrobe. His right eye was half open and full of blood. His left eye and mouth were clenched tightly closed in a frozen last moment of waiting for the impact of the bullet.

"A murder-suicide if I ever saw one," Densmore said.

Mason needed a smoke at that moment, but the pack stayed in his pocket. It struck him as disrespectful to light up even if the two were long past caring. He sighed instead.

Densmore began to report impassively, "A CIC agent, John Winstone—"

"Yeah, I know this guy. A friend of mine."

"Pretty fancy digs for a CIC agent. What do you know about him?"

"He was investigating some ex-Nazis who he suspected were running a ratline."

"What do you know about the dame?"

"Hilda Schmidt. Winstone's girlfriend. The two of them came across as really close. She worked at the Casa Carioca as a skater."

"A real looker. Or she was."

Mason closed the woman's open robe to cover her nakedness. Densmore's childish humor was getting on Mason's nerves. He clamped his jaw to suppress it. He bent low to examine a carving knife that lay on the floor a few feet from Hilda's hand. The blade and handle were caked in dried blood.

"Pretty clear fingerprints on the handle," Densmore said. "I'm gonna bet that they're Winstone's."

On the surface, it appeared Densmore was right. Mason pointed out the lack of blood in Winstone's lap. "Looks like she was dead by the time he sat down and propped up her head. Why would he go through the effort to cut her up then cradle her in his arms and shoot himself? Doesn't make sense."

"Now, don't go complicating things."

Mason indicated the champagne bottle lying on its side by the fireplace and the two broken champagne glasses. "They decide to celebrate her butchering?"

"Look, it's simple enough for me. He finds out she's fucking some other guy, loses his head, and cuts her up. As soon as his head clears, he starts bawling: 'What have I done? Oh, God, what have I done?'"

Mason looked up to Abrams, who had turned pale while staring at the two corpses. "Were you the first to arrive on the scene?"

"Yes, sir," Abrams said, then pointed toward the living room door. "Me and Specialist Tandy."

"Did either of you find the woman's body parts?"

Abrams shook his head. "Everything was as you see it. And it looks like nothing was taken. His wallet with a wad of cash and his gold engraved pocket watch are still on the bedroom dresser."

"And you've searched the grounds?"

Abrams nodded. "Wilson and Tandy are still out there."

Mason looked closer at Winstone's head wound. "Odd way to shoot himself. Above the right eyebrow."

"He could've been nervous and slipped. Or bawling so hard his aim was bad. Could be any number of reasons why he shot himself there."

"So, you're certain this is a suicide?"

"There's nothing to indicate it was anything else. Nothing. And if we throw around the speculation that a CIC agent was murdered, it's going to create a real shit storm."

Mason looked up at Densmore, surprised by his remark. "I don't like tossing out other possibilities because it might complicate the job."

"You're the one who said you wanted to keep a low profile."

"This one's different. I was here last night, and neither of them showed—"

"Wait, wait, wait…" Densmore said, holding up his hands. "You were here last night?"

"I met Winstone and Hilda for dinner, and he invited me back here." Mason decided to leave Adelle out of it for the moment. "We drank and talked. They looked happy together. They were having a lovers' quarrel when I left, but most of the time it was nothing but smiles and kisses."

"What time did you leave?"

"About three in the morning."

"By the looks of it, I'd say they died very early this morning. Maybe even as early as three."

"Oh, come on, Pat. You should know better than that."

"No, I shouldn't. Can anyone corroborate you leaving before they died?"

Mason hesitated. "I was with a girl. We left together, and there was no one in the living room. Like I said, Winstone and Hilda were having a little argument, but I think it was about me and the girl still being here. Look, don't start in with the questions if you really think this is a murder-suicide."

"Is that what you think?"

Mason pondered a moment. "He did hire a security team about a month ago because he was spooked about investigating a ratline. He asked me to stay with him for the same reason."

"Was the team here last night?"

He didn't trust them, and let them go over a month ago."

"He was so spooked he fired them and asked you to do a sleepover."

Mason had to admit, Densmore had a point.

Densmore said, "I'll ask you again. Based on what we have, what do you think?"

Mason had his suspicions, but he sighed and said, "Everything seems to point in that direction." He felt ashamed for saying it, but Winstone and Hilda *were* having a heated argument. Still, that didn't explain such a brutal slaying.

Densmore stared at him for a moment. Mason dodged the look by going back to considering the scene. A framed eight-by-ten photograph sitting on the mantel caught his eye. He strode over and plucked it off to have a closer look. It was a publicity photo from the Casa Carioca, of seven dancing girls in sparkling outfits in front of a twenty-piece orchestra. A circle was drawn around Hilda's face with the word *mich!*—or me!—then an autograph at the bottom where Mason made out *Hilda*.

Looking upon the smiling young woman with eyes full of hope and youthful energy made her disfigurement more tragic, and he started to feel that familiar slow burn of rage. He put the photograph back in its place. "If Winstone cut her up, what did he do with the body parts? Why get rid of those and leave the body where it was?"

"There you go again."

"And why the nose, lips, ears and eyes? If he wanted to deface her out of jealousy, the usual thing is to slash up the face, not this."

"I don't know what went on in his head, and neither do you."

Mason decided not to push his suspicions too far. "I know he has a chef who also serves as the butler for the place. A villa like this, he must have had other servants."

"Besides the cook, two servants," Densmore said.

"Anyone talk to them yet?"

"I got here five minutes before you did."

"The chef's the one who found them," Abrams said. "Says he came in this morning around seven and found them like that. Apparently the two servants, an elderly husband and wife, have been out of town since yesterday morning. They're expected to come back by train tomorrow."

"Where's the cook?" Densmore said.

"We've got him in the library."

"Why didn't you tell me when I first got here?" Densmore asked.

"You didn't ask."

Mason suppressed a smile. Most of the other investigators and MPs didn't care for Densmore. He acted imperious to the lower ranks and spoke ad nauseam about his experiences as a cop in St. Louis.

Densmore fixed his glare on Abrams. "Anything else you decided not to tell me because I didn't ask?"

Abrams looked to Mason for help.

"Anyone call the crime scene techs and ME?" Mason asked Abrams.

"The techs were busy at another scene, but they should be here anytime now. The ME is up in Frankfurt for a medical summit, so the hospital is sending a doc over, but that could take hours."

"Then get the German ME over here," Mason said.

With a "yes, sir," Abrams moved out, looking relieved at being rescued from Densmore's wrathful glare.

"Damned rookies," Densmore said. "We've got major crimes going on in this city, and the detachment's run like a small-town sheriff's office. Back when I was in St. Louis, we'd've had a whole team swarming over this place—"

"Let's go talk to the chef," Mason said.

Densmore looked annoyed at the interruption, but he got the message. "By all means. Let's go to talk to the kraut."

They crossed the broad dining room with its mahogany-paneled walls and ceiling adorned with intricate molding. At the far end, they came to a door guarded by an MP. The MP stood aside to let them enter.

"The guy's fit to be tied, sir," the MP said. "A real Nazi asshole."

"Thanks for the professional assessment, Private," Mason said.

The two investigators entered a room with floor-to-ceiling bookshelves. Along the back wall stood tall windows overlooking spacious gardens buried in snow. From a seat in one corner, Winstone's butler and chef, Otto Kremmel, eyed Mason with a look of recognition. He shot up from the plush leather chair. "Why am I being kept prisoner?" he barked in German.

Mason introduced Densmore.

"I simply reported this incident to the authorities," Otto went on, "and now I am confined as if guilty."

"Do you speak English?" Densmore asked.

Otto shot a disdainful glance at Densmore. "I speak English, Italian, Polish and Russian."

"English will do, Herr Kremmel," Mason said.

"You're pretty well educated for a cook, Herr Kremmel," Densmore said.

"I am not a cook. I am a chef and have headed kitchens for some of the finest families in Germany."

"What's a Nazi chef doing cooking for an American army captain?" Densmore said.

"I am not a Nazi!"

Mason and Densmore both tensed when Otto went for something in his suit coat breast pocket. Otto opened his wallet and pulled out a fistful of papers. "My denazification certificate and identity papers."

"Put those away, Herr Kremmel," Mason said. "We don't need to see them. We understand you let yourself into the house around seven this morning?"

"Seven-oh-two precisely. I always knock twice at one-minute intervals. If there is no response, I am authorized to enter and begin my day."

"And last night, you left at what time?"

"You saw me leave, sir. At eleven P.M."

"Did Agent Winstone appear agitated, nervous, or angry in any way?" Densmore asked.

Otto looked at Mason with a puzzled look then back to Densmore. "He acted quite cheerful." He looked at Mason again. "Sir, you can vouch for what I am saying."

"I'm asking the questions," Densmore said. "Did Agent Winstone speak of anyone who may have wanted to harm him or Miss Schmidt? Any heated arguments with other visitors or over the telephone?"

"Not that I'm aware of."

Mason said, "But Agent Winstone did hire a security team about a month ago, didn't he?"

"Yes, but that lasted only a week. He decided that was a waste of money and had them leave."

"Would you say Miss Schmidt and Winstone got along okay?"

Otto looked carefully at both Mason and Densmore as if calculating his answer. "If you mean, did they quarrel or have violent disagreements, none that I witnessed."

"You also work as a butler here, don't you?" Mason said. "Hours beyond what's required to prepare the meals?"

"Yes. On Saturday evenings I am allowed to go home to spend Sunday with my wife."

"Winstone dismissed you, and gave the servants the day off. Is it unusual to let the whole staff off on the same evening?"

"Perhaps, but I am not in the habit of questioning my employer's wishes."

A bead of perspiration broke out on Otto's forehead. His eyes lost focus as he thought. Mason watched him closely. There was something Otto was hiding, but before he could press Otto about it, Densmore blurted out, "Otto, you know any reason why Agent Winstone would kill Fräulein Schmidt, then himself?"

Otto's eyes widened. "No. Certainly not."

Densmore looked around the room, taking in the expensive furniture and what appeared to be rare and valuable books. "Do you know if all this fancy stuff was left by the previous owners? Or did Agent Winstone acquire them?"

"Agent Winstone brought me into his employ a month after taking up residence here."

"Does that mean you don't know?"

"That is precisely what I mean. I do know that the previous German owners were an elderly couple and had let the house fall into disrepair. I know nothing about the furnishings, but I was present when Agent Winstone made extensive renovations. He was very fond of this house and put a great deal of money into repairing the many holes and cracks. This room, for instance was of his favorites. It was in terrible shape. The floor, French doors, and sections of the exterior have been completely repaired or replaced."

Densmore blew into his hands. "You'd think he would have put fixing the furnace at the top of his list."

"Agent Winstone had the coal furnace refurbished, but he didn't like using it," Otto said. "He preferred to use the fireplaces for heat."

Densmore's expression turned sly. "It must have been tough for you; after being a cook for the wealthiest families in Germany you come to work for an American soldier."

Otto dabbed his lips with his handkerchief. "Please, gentlemen, may I go now? This... incident has left me distraught."

Mason pulled out a pencil and his notepad and handed them to Otto. "Write down your address in case we have any more questions."

Otto wrote down his address with a slight shake to his hand. When he finished, he bowed his head and moved for the door.

"Oh, one more thing, Herr Kremmel," Mason said. "It's just

for the files. My boss wants detail, you understand.... Where was your last position as chef of a household?"

Otto hesitated.

"We could look it up, but it would save us some time."

Otto almost came to attention again, but his mouth went crooked. "My last employer was the Krupp family."

Densmore's jaw dropped. "The Nazi industrialist Krupp? And you got yourself denazified?"

"Preparing a family's meals does not require sharing their political beliefs."

Mason stepped forward, his eyes bearing in on Otto. "Who certified your denazification card?"

Otto's eyes flitted nervously between the two investigators. "Why, Mr. Winstone."

"Why would he have personally done that? Was it because he wanted a good chef, or was there some other reason?"

"I have done nothing wrong. And now I am being persecuted simply because I performed my civic duty and reported Mr. Winstone's death."

"We can call for a review of your certification, Herr Kremmel."

"Please, sir. Why would you want to do such a thing? I swear to you that I know nothing else."

The man was close to tears, and Mason knew he would get nothing else out of him without pressing him hard—if there were anything left to get. Despite suspecting the man knew more than he was saying, Mason dismissed him. And as he did so, he had the distinct feeling that everyone—from Otto to Densmore to Mason's higher-ups—would have a vested interest in making this case go away.

8

When Mason and Densmore returned to the living room, they found that the crime scene techs had arrived—in reality, one tech, a photographer, and two MPs who'd received cursory training in dusting for fingerprints and crime scene procedures. One took measurements then added them to his sketch of the corpses and the room. The other two were dusting for fingerprints. Flashes from the camera illuminated the corpses in a ghostly light.

Abrams led a bony, gray-haired man up to Mason and Densmore. "This is Dr. Saltzman."

The doctor tipped his hat. "How do you do? I was reluctant to examine the victims until I was sure you were finished with them."

"Sure, yeah, thanks for that," Mason said. "Go ahead, doc."

When the doctor walked away, Abrams said, "Looks more like an undertaker than a doctor."

"In this case," Mason said, "it's about the same thing."

Mason watched the doctor examine Hilda's corpse for a moment, then told Abrams to take two MPs along and canvass the neighborhood, while he and Densmore searched the villa.

The other rooms on the ground floor yielded little. The basement consisted of numerous separate spaces, but the wine cellar appeared to be the only one frequented in the last few years. They finally made their way up to the second floor and the five bedrooms. The sheets on the bed where Mason and Adelle had made love were still rumpled, and Mason felt obliged to tell Densmore that they'd spent two hours in there. They ended their search in Winstone's bedroom. The room was furnished in elegant Biedermeier furniture, including the four-poster bed, with Persian rugs on the floor.

"All this for one guy," Densmore said. "Maybe I should get a job in the CIC."

Densmore had a point: A five-bedroom mansion was a lot for one intelligence officer, though the finest villas and châteaus had been confiscated for army brass and higher-ranking military government officials, many of whom lived like kings.

Mason scanned the surface of a triple dresser. Winstone's gold pocket watch and his wallet containing five hundred dollars were there, just as Abrams had said. Hilda had placed a number of her personal things on top as well. He looked through the drawers—Winstone's affairs on one side and Hilda's on the other—but found nothing significant. Winstone did have a collection of photos of his wife and two daughters hidden under his socks—a testament of his recent feelings toward his stateside family. Notifying Winstone's family of his death would normally fall to his immediate CIC superiors, but since Mason knew Winstone's wife personally, he resolved to call her with the bad news.

Densmore banged around in the armoire, and Mason moved on to an ornate eighteenth-century desk, which sat under a broad window looking down onto Garmisch. All the desk drawers had been pulled out at odd angles. Papers were strewn on the desk's surface and on the floor.

"Someone went through Winstone's desk," Mason said.

"Everything else we've searched has been all neat and tidy. He even trifolded his underwear."

"Maybe he had sloppy work habits. And look at this."

Densmore pulled two suitcases out from behind the clothes in the armoire. He threw them on the bed and opened them. "A his and hers. All you'd need for a romantic weekend somewhere."

"Or to hightail it out of town. He sends the butler home and gives his servants a holiday. His money is ready to go—"

Densmore cut him off. "He invites you and a girl back for fun and frolicking. They're still in their jammies and drinking champagne. How does that fit into skipping town?"

"I don't know what to make of any of this. But I still have a hard time seeing murder-suicide."

"Look, I had a homicide case once where the guy prepared a full-blown candle-lit dinner for his wife, then halfway through, he strangled her. There ain't no rhyme or reason to people."

Mason let Densmore go on about his cases as a St. Louis detective, while he used a handkerchief to go through the contents of the desk drawers: letters from Winstone's wife, a few memorandums from the CIC office in Frankfurt, a few local newspapers from Schenectady, New York, Winstone's hometown, but nothing he could use. Among the papers in the top drawer, he did find a smaller version of the photograph of Hilda and her fellow skaters at the Casa Carioca. He put the photo in his pocket and closed the drawer.

Two hours later, Mason walked out onto the front porch of Winstone's villa. He lit a cigarette, cupping the match with his hand to guard against the biting wind.

Densmore joined him and lit his own cigarette. "A suicide note, no sign of a forced entry. We still have to get fingerprints from the servants and the girl you were with, but I doubt we'll get any matches other than the victims', the help's, and you and your girl. The techs confirmed Winstone's fingerprints on the knife and gun. You say they were having an argument when you left. And we didn't find anything suspicious in the search."

"We still have the autopsy. And I want to check Winstone's office at the CIC and see what he was up to down here." Mason told Densmore about his conversation in Winstone's car the day before, near the Steinadler bar. "After he chewed me out for blowing his investigation, he told me that he suspected that a new leadership was in town and taking over all the crime rings. That the other crime bosses were running scared."

"Did he say who?"

"He wouldn't say until he was sure and had enough evidence to prove it."

"That's why you were so interested in his desk?"

"His desk was the only spot in the house that showed signs of being disturbed. Find out why someone was rifling through his desk, and you might find out why he was murdered. Maybe they tortured Hilda in front of him to make him talk."

"All this from a messy desk and a vague statement from Winstone?"

Mason shrugged. "My grandma always said that I have an overactive imagination."

"And now you want to go through his office at CIC."

"I know what you're going to say: The CIC isn't about to let us rifle through one of its agents' desks."

"That's right. Even with an order from Gamin, I doubt you'll get anywhere."

"Then I'll take it to General Pritchard."

"Good luck with that."

Technically, CID agents could question the highest-ranking officers in a criminal investigation, but it rarely worked out that way. "I still want to go over there and try. At least talk to some people."

"Then I'm going along to make sure you don't step on your

own two feet. You're like the guy who tries to run into a burning house to save his cat while everyone else scrambles to save his ass from his own stupidity."

GARMISCH'S COUNTER INTELLIGENCE CORPS detachment head-quarters occupied a large villa south of town, with the ubiquitous white stucco walls painted with floral patterns, a high-pitched roof of red tile, and an arched doorway, all fit for a fairy tale. At the end of the war it had served as a safe haven for several top Vichy and Mussolini government officials in exile. That was until the CIC decided that this lovely villa would better suit an army intelligence detachment headquarters.

Abrams pulled the olive-drab sedan into the villa's parking lot and whistled. "Why can't we get a villa like this one to work out of? You think they'd have an opening for an ambitious young man such as myself?"

"They have the word 'intelligence' in their title," Mason said. "That's what's going to trip you up."

"A pity you didn't go into vaudeville."

Mason, Abrams, and Densmore got out of the car and crossed the small parking lot. A few army vehicles dotted the lot, but Mercedes, Bugattis, and even a rare Horch 855 dominated the spaces.

"First Winstone's mansion, then this villa and the cars out here," Abrams said. "These guys are living the good life."

Densmore said to Mason, "Think about it: You and I make about two hundred twenty bucks a month. About the same, maybe a little more, back in the States. I don't blame anyone for trying to make some dough on the side. If we were smart, we'd be doing the same."

Mason said nothing. He'd gotten a taste of the good life the previous night, and he'd liked it. A lot. That was what scared him. He'd seen too many cops fall in that black hole and never crawl out again.

They entered the cavernous ground floor, which felt more like the lobby of a luxury hotel. They showed their badges to the uniformed clerk at the front desk and explained what they wanted. The clerk went down the hall to an office door, knocked, entered, and returned a few moments later.

"Major Tavers has agreed to see you. Second door on the left."

The three investigators did as instructed and entered a small but elegant office cluttered with papers, maps, and overflowing file cabinets. Major Tavers looked to be no more than forty, but gravity was already dragging his face earthward, giving him the look of an emaciated bloodhound. His full lips, the only facial feature to have resisted collapse, had formed into a permanent grimace.

"What's this all about?" Major Tavers said lethargically as if he was already bored with the conversation. "One of my agents step on your toes?"

Densmore signaled Mason to take the lead, so Mason said, "Sir, Agent Winstone was found dead this morning in his villa."

"And? Did he die in his sleep?"

Mason wanted to ask him what part of "intelligence" brought him to that conclusion with three CID investigators standing in his office, but instead, he said, "No, sir, he has a bullet wound in his skull—"

"No signs of a struggle," Densmore said. "No forced entry, and there was a suicide note."

Mason glared at Densmore for a moment before turning back to the major.

"The man committed suicide?" Tavers asked.

"We're not certain of that," Mason said. "His girlfriend, Hilda

Schmidt, was with him. She was mutilated and stabbed multiple times. We're looking into every possibility."

"Well, which is it, gentlemen? Murder or suicide?"

Densmore spoke up. "My colleague suspects foul play, but the evidence thus far indicates that Agent Winstone murdered his mistress and then killed himself."

"Jesus," Tavers said.

"Sir," Mason said, "I knew Agent Winstone, and spent time with him and Hilda Schmidt last night. I saw nothing to indicate that hours after I left he intended to murder his girlfriend or shoot himself."

"You two coming to different conclusions doesn't give me much confidence."

"We're here to see if you, or any of your agents, might have any information that could shed light on the situation. I think we owe that to his widow."

"What damn difference does it make?" Tavers said. "He's dead. You're talking about two different cans of worms. Either way it stinks." He sat back with a sigh. "At least this isn't my headache. But you guys better decide quick if there's a chance that a murderer took out one of our own."

"That's why we're here," Mason said. He waited, but the major said nothing. "Did you know Agent Winstone well?"

"He wasn't under my command. He came here on a special assignment and coordinated his efforts with General Pritchard."

"Did he share any aspects of his investigation? Perhaps something that might point to a reason why someone or some group would want him dead?"

"Just the overall parameters. Nothing specific...." He stopped and looked at Mason. "Now I remember. You were the one that barged in on his investigation."

"Same people. Different reasons."

Tavers grunted.

"Sir," Densmore began, "did Agent Winstone say or do anything that would make you consider that he had contemplated taking his own life?"

Tavers thought a moment. Mason thought he took a little too much time glancing over the things on his desk, like he was trying to weigh the headaches involved with murder as opposed to suicide. Finally he said, "He did act sullen at times. Frustrated with the lack of progress with his case."

Mason found that interesting, since Winstone had expressed the opposite to him.

"Any signs of anxiety?" Densmore asked. "Mood swings? Depression?"

"I don't like to talk about a man's personal life. And I'm no expert in psychology."

"We understand that, sir, but any observations could help us determine the cause of death."

"He did have tremendous mood swings. Most of the other agents avoided him. He only had the two Germans with him most of the time, like two guard dogs. I have no idea why his behavior was so inconsistent. I understand the trauma of war can lead men to take their own lives. If that's the case here, then my deepest sympathies to his widow."

A somber silence passed between Tavers and Densmore, as if in a silent prayer for the poor troubled veteran who had committed suicide. Mason wasn't buying any of it. And Densmore was doing his best to lead Tavers through a minefield of lies.

Mason broke the silence. "Agent Winstone mentioned having informants on the inside of several of the smaller gangs. I'd like to talk to them."

"Even if I knew who they were, that's out of the question. You should know that better than anyone."

"We'd also like permission to search his office," Mason said.

"Also out of the question."

"If this is homicide, then there's a high probability that it has something to do with his investigation into Nazi ratlines. He even mentioned to me that he had information that might blow the lid off the criminal gang activity. Too sensational for him to reveal to me. Now, if we could access his files—"

"Access to intelligence files?" Tavers asked. "Are you out of your mind?"

"Sir, his files could lead to the murderers. We have the authority—"

"Show me. Show me specific orders that would grant that permission from someone higher up the chain of command than Bronco Bob Gamin. Someone who has enough authority to make me give a damn. In the meantime, stop wasting my time. Now, get out of here. The three of you."

Back out on the steps leading down to the villa's parking lot, Densmore stopped to light a cigarette. "I told you how this would go down."

"What the hell were you doing in there? You torpedoed me with that line of questioning."

"I'm trying to save your ass. If you push this into murder, you're going to be the first suspect. You were there last night, buddy. You've got your fingerprints all over the place. The only visible tracks, other than the two victims', are yours. It's beyond me why you want to put yourself in the hot seat, unless you're a goddamned fool."

"Why would I bring up possible homicide if I was the one who did it?"

"I've known a lot of murderers who wanted to get caught. Is that the case? You try to shove this down my throat, and I'll turn this on you."

"I knew those people. For all his faults, Winstone was a good guy, and not the suicidal type. And the girl had her whole life ahead of her. Someone carved up that lovely face of hers and snuffed the life out of both of them. They probably tortured her and made him watch. No one should get away with that. And sure as hell not because it might complicate the job. And this in less than twenty-four hours after those three gang bosses were killed, execution style—"

"Mason, come one. It's bad enough you want to throw murder at an obvious open-and-shut case, but then bring up a criminal conspiracy? I'm not going to be dragged into the quicksand with you."

"Why are you so dead set on suicide? What's your angle? Are you afraid, or is it really that you're connected?"

"You can stop right there!" Densmore said. "I'm done saving your ass, and don't ever say I didn't warn you. You piss off the wrong people, and you'll have more than a ruined career to worry about." He threw the cigarette down and stomped on it like he wished it were Mason's skull. "Let's go."

"I have other places to check," Mason said.

"Suit yourself. Keep Abrams, if you like. He'll be Robin to your Batman. It'll make a nice obituary."

Densmore blew past a stunned Abrams, grabbing the keys out of his hand.

Abrams turned back to Mason after watching Densmore drive away. "Well, that's that," he said. "What's next, Batman?"

9

M ason and Abrams waited at the front door for someone to respond to their knocking. Abrams blew into his hands to warm them. Mason's feet stung from the old frostbite wounds he'd received on a death march from a POW camp near the Czech border. They stood on the front porch of a shoebox-sized, two-story house, on a street with other shoebox houses. Hilda Schmidt had shared the two-bedroom with two families, an elderly couple, and two other women skaters.

Finally a woman in her late seventies opened the door just enough to peek through the gap. Mason showed his badge and introduced them in German. She sucked in her breath, stumbled back two steps, then disappeared, leaving the front door open.

Mason and Abrams looked at each other and waited a few moments, but no one appeared at the door. Abrams said, "I guess that means it's okay to come in."

They entered the small foyer and turned right into the living room. The old woman huddled behind one of two round coal-burning stoves sitting in the middle of the room. Several beds lined one wall and were separated by hanging sheets. Two tables and several chairs sat near the stoves, and laundry hung in crisscross patterns throughout the room. An old man sat hunched next to a stove, while a woman and two young children sat by the other. The children had that listless look from constant hunger that Mason had seen many times.

Again, the two inspectors held up their badges and explained they weren't there to arrest anyone, and only wanted to look in Hilda Schmidt's room.

For a long moment, no one moved. Everyone looked to the old woman, who finally mustered up the courage to step out from behind the stove. With brusque gestures, she urged them to follow her. She led them through the living room and down a short hallway to a bedroom shared by Hilda and the two other skaters.

Mason said to her in German, "Ma'am, if you wouldn't mind staying here to witness our search, so there are no accusations of theft by Hilda's roommates."

"Why do you want to look through her things? Has she done something wrong?"

We're not at liberty to say, ma'am."

The woman studied Abrams face, then said, "She's dead, isn't she? And an American soldier killed her."

"We didn't say that," Mason said.

"Why else would American inspectors be here, if it didn't involve an American soldier?" She covered her mouth and began to tear up.

She started to leave, but Mason stopped her. "We need you to stay, ma'am."

The woman nodded, then looked away with tears in her eyes.

The search would be quick, as three twin beds took up most of the floor space. As in the living room, the beds were separated by hanging sheets, and laundry hung from lines strung across the room. Instead of a chest of drawers, open suitcases held the women's clothes, neatly folded. A few dresses and coats hung in the single armoire. The girls had done their best to decorate, with photos of movie stars and dancers cut from magazines, and portraits of family or publicity shots from the Casa Carioca.

Mason had the woman point out which were Hilda's things, and he and Abrams set about their task. They searched through Hilda's clothes and leafed through her novels, a German-English dictionary, and a Bible. Abrams looked behind all the photographs and posters pinned to the walls. Mason took the nightstand and noticed Hilda had the same photo of the skaters as the one on Winstone's fireplace mantel.

Mason asked the woman, "Does she have any family?"

"The only one I know about is her father. And he died in a work camp. She never discussed about anyone else."

Mason held up the framed photograph on Hilda's nightstand. "Are the other two women who live here in this photograph?"

"No, that was taken before the other two girls arrived."

She named the two girls, and Abrams wrote them down. Mason checked the interior of the picture frame, then turned his attention to Hilda's suitcase. He lifted out a small stack of mostly summer clothes and looked through them. The suitcase's side pockets were next, but they contained only a few items of makeup, creams, and toiletries. She obviously kept most of her things at Winstone's villa.

When Mason ran his fingers along the suitcase's inner lining, he pricked his finger on a straight pin. He examined it further and noticed that a small section in the corner of the case had been pinned in place, with the pin hidden under the fabric of a side pocket. He removed the pin and folded back the square of fabric. Between the shell and the lining lay $150 in folded bills and a small piece of paper. He unfolded the paper and saw Hilda had written a single letter then a series of numbers: A47235.

He put the paper in his breast pocket and replaced the money and repinned the lining. Abrams closed the armoire doors, prompting Mason to ask, "Anything?"

"Not much. I guess she'd moved most of her stuff over to Winstone's"

Mason asked the woman, "Did Fräulein Schmidt spend much time here?"

"She always had some kind of man friend she stayed with. She rarely slept here, that I know of. Just come and go on occasion, bring something in and take something out again. Like she wanted people to think she lived here for propriety's sake."

"Did she say anything about going away recently?"

The woman's eyes lit up as if Mason's question reminded her of something. "She came in a little over a week ago, bragging she had a way to get out of Germany. She was so excited that she was bouncing around like a little girl. I told her it's illegal for Germans to leave the country, and that whatever she had cooked up would get her into trouble. She wouldn't listen. And now look what happened. She was a dreamer, that girl."

Abrams asked, "Did she say anything else about that?"

The woman started to tear up again and shook her head.

Mason thanked the woman, and they left. The only clue they walked away with was the piece of paper with the mysterious letter and numbers. Perhaps a code. Perhaps something as simple as a license plate number. Whatever it was, Mason had uncovered a little more about the life and death of Hilda Schmidt—more than he cared to know, because now he felt her death more deeply than before. She deserved justice, and Mason was determined to give it to her.

DENSMORE HAD STILL NOT COME BACK to headquarters when Mason and Abrams returned. That was fine with Mason. And though he wondered where Densmore had gotten to all this time, he was in no mood to try to go through him to get to Major Gamin.

Gamin had taken over the former deputy mayor's office in the main Rathaus building. Mason knocked on his door and wondered if Gamin had regained his senses or was still orbiting Mars. The colonel responded with a "yeah," which was more grunt than actual verbal utterance.

Mason entered a large but modest office. Gamin was a stickler for neatness. Everything in its place, the desk clutter free. A few books lined one shelf, but there were no file cabinets or any other signs of a commander in charge of a detachment of MPs and CID investigators, especially for a crime-ridden town like Garmisch. The only defining feature in the room was the collection of paintings of horses: horses on the plains, horses in rodeos, horses supporting cowboys or Indians. Gamin obviously fancied himself as a rootin' tootin' cowboy—hence the nickname "Bronco Bob."

Gamin sat at his desk with his head buried in an open file. He didn't bother to look up. He devoted his attention solely to turning over a page and placing it carefully facedown and making sure the edges lined up perfectly with the previously read pages.

Mason waited at attention.

Gamin glanced up at Mason then went back to his file. "Looks like you slept in your uniform. I'll not have my men looking like bums just because the war's over."

"Yes, sir. I'll keep that in mind."

"Come back when you've fixed the problem."

"I'm afraid I have a bigger issue that needs addressing at the moment, sir. I need a travel pass to go to Munich this afternoon and see General Pritchard in the matter of an investigation."

"What investigation is that?"

"The possible murder of a CIC agent, John Winstone."

"I heard Winstone killed himself."

"That hasn't been concluded, and I want to explore all possibilities. Agent Winstone and General Pritchard were working on an investigation, and I believe that investigation may have led to Agent Winstone's death."

Gamin finally looked up from his desk. "You think General Pritchard has something to do with it?"

"No, sir," Mason said patiently. "Since he and Agent Winstone were the only two people privy to a certain set of files pertinent to their investigation, I'd like to see if the general can tell me what Agent Winstone discovered while down here."

"You want to see General Pritchard dressed like that? Permission denied."

Mason was about to press further, but stopped when he noticed Gamin was studying some area of space behind Mason as he rolled a pencil around in his fingers. "You play golf, son?"

"I beg your pardon, sir?"

"Golf. Do you play golf?"

"I haven't got the patience for it. I keep hitting the ball and running for first base." Mason thought a little humor might lighten things up, but Gamin furrowed his brow.

"Communists don't like golf," Gamin said.

"They don't like baseball, either, and that's my sport."

Gamin nodded. "You've got a point there."

Mason hesitated. Time to risk another strategy.

"Sir, it's about the theft of the American flags. It could be a bigger Communist conspiracy than we thought. Agent Winstone was investigating a nest of Communist agitators, and he may have been murdered because of it."

"You think I'm a damned fool?"

"No, sir. I thought you were concerned about the theft of American flags, as I am—"

"The CIC doesn't give a damn about American flags. They've got a bunch of krauts working as agents. What kind of half-cocked theory have you cooked up?"

"I thought that, since General Pritchard is personally involved with Agent Winstone's case, he would take the thefts very seriously."

"The flags are just the tip of the iceberg, Collins. Typewriters, chalk and erasers, cases of paper, two cases of army manuals—which I'll attribute to the reason for your dereliction of duty in the proper comportment of a soldier in the U.S. Army."

"All the more reason to make sure General Pritchard is up-to-date and on board."

Gamin thought for a moment. "All right. Tell my assistant what you need, and I'll sign it." He stuck his index finger at Mason and furrowed one brow. "And don't think I don't know what goes on around here. I've got my eye on you."

Mason said, "Yes, sir," and saluted.

Gamin grunted and went back to reading his file. Mason told the assistant what he needed and, with some additional prodding and gentle reminding, persuaded Gamin to sign the travel orders.

Before he caught the train to Munich, he checked out a jeep from the motor pool and drove over to Adelle's apartment. On the drive over and while he knocked on Adelle's door, he had the feeling he was being watched. And his disquiet only grew when Adelle failed to answer the door. In that moment a thought finally surfaced to the forefront of his mind. If he hadn't heard Winstone and Hilda arguing and insisted on leaving last night, then there would have been two more bodies making a trip to the morgue today: his and Adelle's. That eliminated Adelle as a suspect, but made her a potential victim. For all he knew, she lay dead just behind this door. For all he knew, he was next.

10

The journey from relatively pristine Garmisch to the blackened ruins of Munich was jarring for Mason. He found the main train station even more crowded with German refugees from the Sudetenland than when he had been stationed there. And the streets were filled with more misery; the long winter and the extreme shortages of food had taken their toll on the population. Though the rubble had been cleared from the streets, and construction was taking place on numerous corners, the city still faced a long road back from its shattered remains. The only bright note was that the trolley lines were running once again, though where they took people without jobs or money was a mystery to Mason.

The taxi took him southeast of town to the sprawling complex now called the McGraw Kaserne. Built by the Nazis, it had been designed as a mixed-use facility, housing everything from vehicle maintenance to patent offices and the offices regulating uniform patches for the armed forces and uniformed bureaucracy. Now, however, the immense main building housed the American military government of Bavaria.

Mason exited the taxi on the tree-lined cobblestone street that passed along the front of the complex. The buildings' swastikas had been blasted off, of course, but the place still epitomized the Nazi fondness for structures that intimidated through colossal monotony. Instead of black and brown Nazi uniforms, the place now buzzed with army khaki and suited civilians. While the American fighting forces were slowly shrinking, the bureaucracy required to govern the occupied country had mushroomed, easily filling the three hundred offices.

Throughout the American zone of occupation there were more military governors than you could shake a stick at: governors of townships and districts, like Colonel Udahl in Garmisch; then higher in the pecking order the major cities, and the states—or *Länder*; and ultimately the highest of the high, Generals McNarney and Clay, governor and deputy governor, respectively, of the entire American zone. General Pritchard being the deputy military governor of Bavaria, the largest *Land* in Germany, meant his place on the food chain was quite high indeed. To have this man on his side was exactly the kind of support Mason needed.

Pritchard's office was on the fifth floor. Mason had to pass through several checkpoints and reception desks before reaching the general's secretary. When he entered, the master sergeant requested neither his ID nor Gamin's written orders and immediately ushered Mason into the general's office like a visiting VIP.

While General Pritchard talked on the phone, Mason took the moment to look around. Unlike Gamin's sterile surroundings, Pritchard's office had overstuffed file cabinets and a desk cluttered with papers. There were the ubiquitous framed portraits of President Truman and General Eisenhower, but, oddly, there were no pictures of family or friends or other reminders of home.

Pritchard hung up the phone and rose from his chair. Mason saluted and they shook hands. The man was Mason's height, six feet, with a full head of silver hair that broke in waves. His bushy, turbulent eyebrows arched and wagged above jovial eyes, and with his full cheekbones, rounded nose, and pointed chin, he reminded Mason more of a circus ringmaster than the typical dour army general. But despite his theatrical exterior, he exuded strength and trust, and he looked straight in Mason's eyes as they exchanged salutes. Mason found he'd liked him right away.

"I appreciate you coming all the way up here to talk to me about Agent Winstone," Pritchard said as they shook hands.

"I'm grateful for the opportunity, sir."

"Have a seat, Mr. Collins. No need for formality with me."

Before Mason could even settle in his chair, Pritchard said, "So, you don't believe it was suicide."

"Contrary to available evidence, no, sir, I don't."

"I've known John for some time now. I can't, for the life of me, imagine any reason why he would do such a thing. And killing that girl before taking his own life? I don't see it."

"That opinion makes you a member of a very small club, sir."

Pritchard smiled, his waggling eyebrows emphasizing the sentiment. "I've never been swayed by popular opinion. And I can see you feel the same way." He turned serious on a dime. "But I didn't say Winstone murdering his girlfriend then committing suicide was impossible. Just beyond my understanding. Some aspects of the incident have reached my desk, including Winstone leaving a suicide note." He leaned on his elbows and locked on Mason's eyes. "I want you to convince me that Agent Winstone didn't dishonor his name and the army."

The gravity in the general's tone reminded Mason not to let Pritchard's kindly appearance lull him into thinking that the general was any less serious or formidable, and he took a second to regroup his thoughts. Obviously Densmore had already filed his version of the preliminary report and sent it to Munich.

Mason said, "Sir, I believe Agent Winstone was murdered for

something he had or knew or intended to do. Something related to his investigation, and, according to him, he shared the findings of that investigation with you. I—"

"That's all well and good, Mr. Collins, but what about concrete evidence?"

"Sir, I've been a homicide detective for a while now, and I've learned to listen to my gut, even when there's a lack of evidence. The odd angle of the bullet wound in his forehead. The fact that they were dressed in only their bathrobes and drinking champagne in front of the fire. We're still comparing fingerprints lifted at the scene with anyone associated with Winstone's villa. And we're still waiting on the autopsy report. Also, Agent Winstone had hired a security team about a month ago for fear that his investigation might put him in danger."

"Yes, that was in one of his reports. But he let them go a week later. So far you haven't presented anything that convinces me."

Mason took a deep breath and said, "Plus, I was with him the night of the murder."

"You?"

Mason nodded. "And Agent Winstone showed no signs of a man about to murder the woman he loved and take his own life."

The general's expression turned stony as he eyed Mason A long moment passed in silence, then the general sighed and sat back in his chair. "Let's say he was murdered. Why do you think that happened?"

Mason said a silent thank-you for Pritchard being a "bottom-line" kind of man. "Agent Winstone spoke to me in confidence about his work—the day of the murder, in fact. And that evening he expressed some concern for his safety." Mason went on to explain why he believed Winstone had been killed, that while investigating the ratline he'd uncovered a possible conspiracy to take over all the criminal activity in Garmisch. He told Pritchard that Winstone had claimed he'd collected information in a set of secret files, information explosive enough to shake the US military to its core. "He told me only he and you had copies of the files. The CIC detachment commander has refused to grant me access to Agent Winstone's office and papers, so I was hoping you could help."

"By granting you that access?"

"Yes, sir."

Pritchard pressed the intercom button. "Sergeant, could you have all of Agent Winstone's reports brought in to me?" After the sergeant acknowledged, he sat back in his chair and thought a moment. "Would it be possible for you to send me your report on the investigation once you have the autopsy results?"

"Yes, sir... though I doubt it will tell you much more than what I've already laid out."

"Perhaps a second pair of eyes, by someone who shares your theory."

Mason nodded. "I'll send it along."

"Any idea as to who would want him dead?"

"That's what I'm hoping his files will tell me. How long have you worked with Agent Winstone?"

"Three months. He was sent to me by his CIC section chief with the proposal for the investigation in Garmisch."

"In that time, did you become aware of anyone Agent Winstone might have angered, or—"

General Pritchard chuckled. "Angered? You realize he was investigating ratlines involving a very desperate group of individuals. High-ranking Nazis with very powerful friends? Then suspecting that those individuals were somehow connected to criminal elements? I'd say those two activities could produce some enemies. I don't mean to make light of his death; it's simply that that kind of investigative work carries a great deal of risk. Frankly, it comes down to finding the murderer or murderers in a whole crowd of people who wanted him dead."

"If there is a ratline organization Agent Winstone was on to, I doubt murdering him would serve their purpose. They're a covert operation, reluctant to call attention to themselves, especially by killing American intelligence officers. And if Winstone had uncovered something thoroughly damning, they would have made him simply disappear."

The master sergeant entered with a handful of file folders with FOR GENERAL PRITCHARD'S EYES ONLY stamped in red ink across each cover. The sergeant laid them on General Pritchard's desk and left.

While Pritchard looked through the folders, Mason asked, "Did Agent Winstone relay to you he was getting close to discovering the people involved in a powerful gang that is taking over the black market operations in Garmisch?"

Without moving his head, Pritchard raised his thick eyebrows to peer at Mason. "He indicated that he was on to something of the sort, but was unable to produce anything concrete. His updates were usually a weekly affair, so, who knows what he discovered after I'd received his latest report?"

The general shuffled through the files, then opened one with a time stamp of February 23, 1946—almost two weeks back. Pritchard punched the intercom button. "Sergeant, are you sure you gave me everything from Agent Winstone?"

"Yes, sir. From the file cabinets and the safe."

Pritchard shuffled again through the folders as if searching for something. "It appears I haven't received anything later than the twenty-third of last month."

"Agent Winstone mentioned he had a few informants inside a couple of operations. Do you know who they were?"

"Unfortunately, no," Pritchard said and held up a file folder for Mason to see. "He did have a short file on you, by the way." He looked up from the file and studied Mason as if weighing Mason's potential involvement in criminal conspiracy. Apparently satisfied, his eyes turned jovial again and he said, "Nothing damning. He kept tabs on most of the U.S. personnel of German heritage."

"His two assistants are more German than I am. I was born here, but my mother emigrated to the US when I was four."

"Yes, that's in there," Pritchard said and leaned forward. "Is there anything I should know about between you and Winstone?"

"Sir, I was probably the last person to see him alive besides his murderer, and my fingerprints are likely all over the house. I know this makes me suspect, but John and I were friends, and if there were something damning enough to make me want to kill him, it would probably be in that file." It was a long shot, but Mason asked anyway. "Is it possible for me to glance through those files, or even take them with me?"

"I'm afraid not." General Pritchard restacked the file folders —a signal they were done.

"General, I need to know which individuals and groups Agent Winstone was investigating. I'm certain that whoever he was close to exposing are the ones responsible for his death."

"This was a CIC investigation. They have ultimate say-so when divulging aspects of their cases."

"But, sir, you must be aware of the rivalries between the CIC and CID."

"And you have to realize that until you can supply concrete evidence of murder, the CIC is not going to hand over Winstone's files. If you can convince me—and, more important, the CIC— that Agent Winstone was murdered, then I'm sure we can open these files to you. However, I will talk to Major Tavers at the CIC detachment down there and make sure you have access to Winstone's office."

"I appreciate that, sir."

Pritchard stood, prompting Mason to do the same. "I'm afraid that's all the time I can spare," Pritchard said. "But please keep me informed of your progress. If you need anything, let me know, and I'll see what I can do." He became the concerned father counseling his son. "And be careful down there. If you start turning over the same rocks as Winstone, you may end up disturbing the same nest of snakes."

11

M ason exited the train at the Garmisch station after nine P.M. He walked over to Adelle's apartment again and looked around the neighboring houses, the street, the shadows before knocking on her door. Still no answer. She and Mason were the only two direct connections to Winstone. If they had gotten to her, it was now his turn. After several minutes, he returned to headquarters, and there he found Abrams in a second-floor office that he shared with another two other junior investigators, Specialists Wilson and Tandy. The cramped quarters barely accommodated the three small desks. Abrams was sitting at the one jammed against the wall, banging away at the sole typewriter.

"Cozy," Mason said.

"You'd think with all the army's resources, they could come up with a second typewriter for the three of us. I had to come in late just to type up the report."

"It's due to a Communist conspiracy, according to Gamin."

"Huh?"

"Never mind. Have you eaten yet?"

"I'm about to take a bite out of this desk."

"Come with me, then. We'll have a working dinner and do a little digging around at the same time."

IN YET ANOTHER sign that madness had descended upon Garmisch, the Casa Carioca, a nightclub and entertainment venue built for American service members, lay just south of the train station. U.S. Army engineers had built the club in the months following the war. It boasted a retracting roof that transformed the club into an open-air, under-the-stars extravaganza, plus the large dance floor retracted to reveal a skating rink where top skaters performed big choreographed shows. An engineering wonder that seemed conceivable only in a Busby Berkeley Hollywood movie, it had been cobbled together from materials found, pilfered, and confiscated from all over Germany. When the engineers ran out of one type of material, they simply altered the design to accommodate whatever material was available. But no one could answer the question of how this lavish nightclub had been paid for. The amount of money the army had committed to its construction would have been barely enough to build one of the bathrooms. The story was that almost all the money had been acquired under the table, and no one cared to investigate.

"You ever been here before?" Abrams asked Mason as they headed for the entrance.

"First time," Mason said and shook his head as he took in the bizarre design of the building. "Looks like they cut out a Manhattan store front and plastered it onto a part barn, part roadside motel."

"Just wait until you see the interior."

Indeed, the building's facade offered only a taste of what awaited inside. At first glance, it appeared to be like any big-city nightclub—tables on several tiers formed a horseshoe around the dance floor/skating rink, but then Mason saw the two-story-high back wall. "Okay, now we've got half Spanish hacienda, half medieval castle."

Throngs of patrons swayed on the dance floor to the sounds of the twenty-piece orchestra perched on a balcony in the center of the rear wall. A duet sang a rendition of "Petootie Pie," a song Mason and Laura had enjoyed together despite the ridiculous title. The memory gave him a pang of nostalgia as they joined the queue of arriving patrons.

Though the place had been conceived as a club serving U.S. military and government personnel, it was said that for the "right price" anyone could get in. The maitre d' smiled from his podium, then looked beyond Mason and Abrams as if expecting to see two young fräuleins as their dates or—as happened on a rare occasion —wives or American sweethearts.

"Do you have a reservation, sir?" the maitre d' asked in English with a Polish accent. "We can arrange something if you don't." He finished with an it-will-cost-you grin.

"No, we'll grab something at the bar."

"I'm afraid that is reserved for guests awaiting tables." Again the grin and the not-so-subtle arch of his eyebrows.

Mason showed the maitre d' his CID badge. "This is a U.S. military club, isn't it?"

The maitre d's smile faded. "Yes, sir."

"And I see quite a few nonmilitary customers who are not seated with U.S. personnel. Friends of yours, or did they give you bribes?"

The maitre d' motioned for one of the hosts. "Please seat these gentlemen at the bar, and tell the bartender they can order anything they please." His smile returned as he looked to the next couple in anticipation of financial opportunity.

Mason and Abrams wedged their way to the bar and found two

available stools. Suddenly they were VIPs, as the bartender dropped what he was doing and asked for their orders. The bartender had greased-back black hair and was short but muscular with a boxer's nose. Another Polish ex-POW employed by whoever ran the joint. Mason ordered two beers and two plates of bratwurst and sauerkraut.

"I'll take a cheeseburger instead," Abrams said.

"You got something against bratwurst?" Mason asked.

"Jews don't eat pork."

"All right, make it two cheeseburgers," Mason said to the bartender. "Sauerkraut and bratwurst keep me up at night, anyway."

The bartender shot Abrams a wary look before writing the order down and giving it to a waiter. He introduced himself as Bolus and poured them each a glass of cognac.

"On the house, sir," Bolus said.

Free drinks and already on a first-name basis with the bartender. Mason was beginning to see why no one asked questions.

"You haven't been around too many Jews, have you?" Abrams asked Mason.

Mason knew that Abrams had been born to Lithuanian Jews who had emigrated to Ireland. At the age of twelve, the family had moved on to Queens, so Abrams had a curious accent, half Irish brogue and half working-class New Yorker.

"I've met some in the military," Mason said, "but I never checked out what they were eating."

"You have a problem with me being Jewish?"

"Do you have a problem me being German American?"

"No."

"There you are. I don't care one way or the other. You do a good job and we'll get along fine."

They clinked glasses and drank. Mason turned in his stool and surveyed the crowd. Abrams did the same.

"Looks like most of the army brass from the rank of major on up are here," Abrams said.

Mason nodded. "I recognize some from Munich and Third Army headquarters. There are a few out there fox-trotting that I know from supreme headquarters in Frankfurt."

The amount of money that changes hands in this place, Mason thought. *Who's profiting from all this excess?*

Mason wondered if Hilda's murder had anything to do with her associations, direct or indirect, with the club. Could the murderer or murderers be here, running around in black suits and waiting on tables?

The band finished another song, and the audience clapped. The bandleader took the microphone. "Ladies and gentlemen, if you would please take your seats. The show 'Around the World on Skates' is about to begin."

While the couples on the dance floor returned to their seats, a waiter brought Mason's and Abrams' food. The man captured Mason's momentary attention as, unlike most of the waitstaff, who resembled guys in the Wanted posters pinned up on post office walls, this man had the comportment of a fencing champion, as if he approached posture and ambulation with precision and poise. He exuded authority and status, which made Mason think he was no ordinary waiter.

"Compliments of the house, sir," the waiter said in precise and crisp German-accented English.

Abrams simply dug into the hamburger and said thanks around a mouthful of meat. But the curious diction made Mason turn to look at the waiter, noticing his board-straight stance. He figured ex-military, but weren't most age-eligible German males ex-military?

"This, too?" Mason asked the waiter with mock surprise. "I have *got* to meet the manager and thank him personally."

"The manager is not present this evening," the waiter said.

"Well, then, the assistant manager."

"Perhaps after the show. He will be quite busy until then. You gentlemen enjoy your food. And the show is excellent."

The lights dimmed as if on cue. Spotlights threw beams on the now-empty dance floor and swept across it while the drummer beat out a fast roll on the snare drum. Suddenly the dance floor split down the middle and the halves retracted, revealing the skating rink beneath. The drumroll ended with a final pop and cymbal crash when the process was complete. Spotlights swung to the broad arched opening beneath the orchestra's balcony. Male skaters in gold lamé outfits pushed out cartoonish representations of the Eiffel Tower, the Leaning Tower of Pisa, an Indian teepee, and an Egyptian pyramid. When the skaters disappeared back into the arch, the band started up a rendition of Offenbach's "Infernal Galop." Then female skaters came out in typical French cancan outfits of long skirts, petticoats, and stockings.

Mason watched the girls defy the laws of physics by skating in circles while kicking up their petticoats like they were performing at the Moulin Rouge. He scanned their faces to see if Adelle was among them, but he didn't see her.

"They are very lovely ladies, don't you agree?" someone said off to Mason's right.

Mason was suddenly aware that the "waiter" who'd brought their food still stood next to them. The man didn't need to say it; Mason knew: He was the assistant manager. "Haven't you got other things to do?"

"They will be fine without me for a few minutes," the man said.

"I thought you were going to be too busy until after the show,"

Mason said, then turned on his stool and took a bite of his hamburger.

"I wanted to personally make sure that you and your colleague have everything you need."

"And maybe you wanted to check out the two CID investigators who threatened to spoil the party."

The assistant manager smiled confidently. "I assumed that, if there were concerns about how this club is managed, I would have heard them from one of the many high-ranking officers or military government officials who often frequent this establishment. We do try to comply with Third Army wishes."

"I haven't got a problem with it. I just don't like the maitre d' giving us the shakedown."

"We'll see that doesn't happen again."

The band finished the cancan number and the audience applauded. The girls skated backstage, then the band broke out in a westernized version of Middle Eastern music. Male and female skaters came out in Ancient Egyptian costumes. Mason looked for Adelle or any of the other skaters in Hilda's photograph, but all the female skaters wore veils.

Mason assumed the lull in conversation meant the assistant manager would move along and attend to other duties, but the man remained. His decision to do so piqued Mason's curiosity. He leaned back and studied the assistant manager while the man watched the show. Whether the man was born of royalty or not, Mason didn't know, but with his drawn cheeks, protruding chin, his long, delicate nose, and soft eyes, he exuded highborn status. His default expression consisted of a slight frown, which seemed to stem not from disdain, but rather from disappointment in his fellow man.

While continuing to watch the performance, the assistant manager said, "You've been in Garmisch two months, haven't you, Mr. Collins?"

"That's right. And since you know my name, how about giving me yours?"

"Frieder Kessel." He held out his hand. "A pleasure to meet you."

Mason looked at Kessel's hand. It was a long hand with a round scar dead center in the palm.

"A scar from a bullet wound," Kessel said. "The hand works, but I have little feeling in it. It won't hurt if you shake it."

Mason shook his hand. "I could point out my bullet scar but then I'd have to show you my ass."

"Another time perhaps," Kessel said. "If there is nothing else you need, I will return to my duties." He turned to go.

"Actually," Mason said, stopping Kessel, "we do have a few questions. It's in connection with one of the girls who works here," Mason said. "A Hilda Schmidt."

"Oh? Has something happened to her? She failed to come in this evening."

A foursome crowded around Mason's and Abrams's bar stools and proceeded to shout at each other over the loud music.

"Maybe there's somewhere quieter we can talk," Mason said.

"I'm afraid I'm awfully busy."

"I'm afraid I must insist. It will only take a few minutes."

Kessel stared at Mason for a moment. "If you will follow me to my office."

Mason took a last bite of his cheeseburger, then signaled for Abrams to come along. They followed Kessel around the horseshoe of tables to a back corner stairway on the "medieval castle" side of the back wall.

"He's probably got a torture chamber up there," Abrams said as they climbed the stairs.

They came to a landing, which fed into a short hallway serving several offices. The biggest German man Mason had ever seen sat on a stool at the top of the stairs. Mason stopped and turned to him. He pointed to the man's nose, which had as many curves as an alpine switchback. "I recognize you."

The man returned a blank expression, punctuating his indifference by crossing his massive arms. "No, you don't."

"Hans Weissenegger. Heavyweight boxer."

"I don't know what you're talking about."

"I saw you fight in an exhibition match in '35, in Chicago. You gave what's-his-name... Sal..." Mason snapped his fingers as if trying to remember. "Sal..."

"Torrino."

"That's it. Torrino. You gave him a real pounding."

Hans gritted his teeth and puffed out his already expansive chest.

"Did Uncle Adolf make you wear a uniform, or did you get to box during the war?"

"Uniform."

"Pity. You could have gone to the championships, like Max Schmeling."

"I proudly served the Fatherland, putting the hurt on punks like you—"

"Hans," Kessel said firmly.

Hans looked like he wanted to break Mason's jaw, but he took his place on the stool again.

Mason and Abrams followed Kessel to the first office on the left, which was guarded by a guy who should have gone by the moniker "Bennie the Blockhouse." The guard stepped aside and let the three men enter a bare-bones office. Mason felt rather than saw the guard slip in behind them, noting that the guard moved stealthily for such a big man.

Kessel moved to the small window overlooking the club and paused there for a moment with his back to them. Mason and Abrams stopped in the middle of the room, and the guard sidled up behind them.

First the VIP treatment, and now a little dose of intimidation.

Kessel closed the window curtain and sat on the edge of his desk. He appeared completely at ease in having two U.S. Army CID detectives in his office. Usually, no matter how hard-nosed the German interviewee, the person always showed some anxiety at being in the presence of a CID investigator, who represented the absolute power of the conquering army. Kessel had either nothing to hide or else powerful allies.

"What would you like to ask me, detectives?" Kessel asked.

"What do you know about Hilda Schmidt?"

"That she is an excellent skater. Why are you asking about Fräulein Schmidt? Is she in some kind of trouble?"

"You never talked to her personally, or know anything about her private life?"

"Before we go any further, I would like to know why you are interested in her."

"She was murdered last night, Herr Kessel."

Mason watched for Kessel's reaction, but he offered nothing but a slight pucker of his lips—something a potential killer might imagine as the proper expression of sympathy.

"Do I need to repeat the question?" Mason asked.

"Other than greetings or compliments on her performances, I only spoke to her in a professional capacity. I prefer not to know anything of a private nature about my employees. Hilda came in for auditions one day, and the choreographer was impressed with her talents. He hired her on the spot."

"So, she just shows up, dances, skates, you hand her some cash, and she goes home."

"Something like that."

"She must have shown you papers that allow her to work at a U.S. Army club."

"My responsibility is the smooth operation of this establishment. If you have questions about any of the employees you will have to take that up with the manager."

"And who's that?"

"Actually, there are several. Two from the Army Corps of Engineers, one from the special services branch of the military government, and one from the civil administration branch."

"Okay, the principal one, then."

"That would be Major Schaeffer of the special services branch."

"Is he here tonight?"

"I'm afraid not. He, along with the other managers, comes in from time to time; however, I have been entrusted with the daily operations."

"Daily operations? Like hiring and firing?"

"The bandleader is responsible for the musicians and the director-choreographer for the dancers and skaters."

"And the waitstaff?"

"I have some authority in that regard, but the final decisions are up to Major Schaeffer."

"I want to talk to all of them, but we can start with the choreographer."

"By all means, Mr. Collins."

Kessel's smugness was getting on Mason's nerves. "You have a very good command of English, Herr Kessel."

"I studied law at the University of Oxford before answering my family's call to come back to fight against Bolshevism. I, among many Germans, was puzzled why you Americans and the British didn't join with us to stop the Russian Bolshevik menace. It is something I believe you will regret—"

"What did you do during the war, Herr Kessel?"

"That is hardly relevant to your investigation."

"I like to know who I'm dealing with. Barely ten months ago we were trying to kill each other. Now here we are, together in a cozy office, talking about the murder of one of your employees, with one of your gorillas standing at our backs." Mason heard a slight rustle from the troll standing behind him. "Were you a commandant at a concentration camp? Did you dress up in an American uniform and kill U.S. soldiers behind our lines?"

"Now you're getting personal. If I had performed anything deemed a war crime by your army, do you think I would be working here?"

"You tell me. I'm beginning to think that in this town the wolves were left guarding the henhouse."

"I wouldn't know about that. Now, if you gentlemen will please excuse me, I must return to my duties...."

"I see a lot of money changing hands. Who collects the money? This club's supposed to be run by the army."

"You would have to direct those questions to my supervisors."

"I've got to hand it to you, you're pretty slick."

"I'll take that as a compliment."

"Take it any way you want."

Mason and Abrams started to leave, but Mason turned to the muscle-bound bodyguard instead. "Next time you stand behind us like that I'll break your legs."

The bodyguard moved a fraction of an inch toward Mason, but Kessel barked, "Boris!"

Boris gave Mason a carnivorous smile and backed away.

When they reached the door, Kessel said, "Mr. Collins, some friendly advice: I'd step carefully before stirring up more trouble than you can handle. In this city, your friends could be your enemies, and your enemies your friends. You might be alone out there."

A s Mason and Abrams descended the stairs, Mason could pick out the club's waiters and bus boys moving among the patrons. Every one of them stole glances at him and Abrams as if some coded message had been transmitted exclusively to their ears: Their VIP status had been downgraded to enemy combatant.

The spectators broke into applause with the last strain of a tarantella. The skaters left the rink and the curtains closed. The retractable floor transformed from skating rink back to a dance floor. As patrons came out to dance, Mason and Abrams wove through them and slipped behind the curtains.

The backstage security guard didn't blink an eye when the two investigators passed through the bustle of stagehands moving props and lights. They found a door leading to the dressing area, where a small common room serviced hallways in both directions. The bandleader was talking to a man Mason assumed was the director-choreographer—tall and lithe, an aging ex-dancer by all appearances with angular, outsized facial features and theatrical gestures. Mason and Abrams showed their CID badges to the two men. "Do you know why we're here?"

The choreographer nodded and looked at them with glassy

eyes. "Yes. One of Herr Kessel's human Rottweilers just told us. She was such a sweet girl, and a real talent."

"What's your name?" Mason asked.

"Arnie Sobel. I'm the director and choreographer."

Mason pulled out the photograph of Hilda with the other skaters. "We'd like to start with the girls in this photograph."

Sobel examined the photograph. "This was taken four months ago. Four of these girls are no longer here."

"Then we'll talk to the two who are."

"Can't this wait? They're due to perform in another set."

"No, it can't."

Sobel hissed his impatience. "Come with me." He led them down the left hallway reserved for the female performers and past several large dressing rooms packed with women in various states of dress.

Mason noticed Abrams ogling the girls with an open mouth. "Steady there, soldier." Then to Sobel, "We need a couple of quiet rooms. Then bring them out one at a time."

Sobel stopped at an open door and stood aside for the two investigators to enter the small office. Framed photographs of skaters and dancers, and snapshots of Sobel with army brass and celebrities hung on every wall.

"This is my office," Sobel said.

"Yeah, I figured that," Mason said.

"I just ask that you not be too hard on them and scare them with tales of murder. It's hard enough keeping good performers. Half of them are on the lookout for rich husbands or lovers."

"Is that what happened to the other four girls?"

"Two of them, yes." He turned to his wall where he had the same photograph as Hilda's and pointed to a brunette with a crooked smile. "That one liked her dope too much. I took her back once, but never again. The fourth one's husband was a German soldier, and as soon as he was released from a POW camp, he came back here and dragged her away."

"As long as the girls are being cooperative, I'll be gentle."

Before Sobel left the room, Mason said, "The second room is for my partner. He's going to talk to you."

"Me?"

"If Mr. Abrams finds you uncooperative, he has orders *not* to be so gentle."

Once more, Sobel expelled a hiss of irritation and exited the room.

Abrams said, "You get the girls, I get the choreographer?"

"One of the perks of rank, my boy."

Abrams imitated Sobel's hiss and left.

Mason took a tour of the room while waiting for the first girl. Sobel had dance and design books, sketchbooks and photo albums. Nothing out of the ordinary. The pictures on the walls included Sobel posing with a galaxy of one-, two-, and three-star generals, from Third Army and up to USFET, the supreme head-quarters of all U.S. forces in Europe. There were military govern-ment officials and USO celebrities, including Bob Hope and Judy Garland.

The door opened and Sobel led a young woman into the room. He introduced her as Margareta and left them alone. Margareta's frayed terry-cloth robe contrasted with her black nylon stockings and flashy stage makeup. Mason invited her to sit in Sobel's chair. Instead, she nearly slithered over to Mason and sat on the desk, inches from where Mason stood. She crossed her legs and leaned back on her hands in what Mason figured was a much-practiced pinup girl pose.

"You wanted to see me?" she said in her Greta Garbo best, though it lacked the same allure in German. "Could I have a cigarette?"

Mason offered her one and lit it for her. She was all smiles as she took a puff and exhaled as if auditioning in a Hollywood screen test.

"Did Herr Kessel tell you why I'm here?" Mason asked in German.

"He told me to cooperate," she said with half-lidded eyes and parted lips, a parody of the seductress. "Give you anything you want."

"That's kind of Herr Kessel. Is every girl here as cooperative as you?"

"It depends."

"How about Hilda Schmidt?"

Margareta's sultry gaze faltered for just a moment. "She could cooperate, but you'd have to make a bigger noise than being a cop."

"Really? Her latest boyfriend is an intelligence agent, John Winstone."

"It's not the rank, it's the muscle behind it."

"Mr. Winstone's a powerful guy, is he?"

"Maybe not to you."

"Meaning, he could make life easy or hard for Germans?"

Margareta shrugged. "One hears things. Denazification papers, work permits, better ration cards."

Now we're getting somewhere, Mason thought, though he got no pleasure from it. He knew she could be lying, either out of vindictiveness or under instructions to do so. "What else does one hear?"

"Nothing I've had anything to do with. I like to stay out of trouble. I come to work, do my job... maybe make a little on the side. I sleep at night. No problem."

"What can you tell me about Hilda?"

"Whatever you've got on her, it won't stick. She'll get out of it."

"Probably not this time. Hilda was murdered last night."

Margareta maintained her smile, but it went crooked on the ends.

"Agent Winstone's dead, too. It could be that he killed her then committed suicide, or, what I'm inclined to believe, that someone or some group murdered both of them. Can you think of anyone who might have wanted them dead, and why?"

Margareta just shook her head. The cigarette hovered near her mouth, but she seemed too breathless to take a drag.

"Did she mention having any trouble, or an argument, with Agent Winstone?"

"He was like a puppy dog around Hilda."

"Do you know of anyone who threatened her or would want to do her harm?"

"Nothing I heard of. Could be one of her jilted lovers. She had quite a few of those."

"Was Hilda involved in anything illegal?"

"Like what?"

"Con games, gambling, prostitution?"

"Nothing like that she ever told me about."

"What about the black market?"

"Everyone uses the black market."

"I take it she wasn't a friend of yours."

"She only had men friends."

"Can you name any of them?"

"No," she said flatly.

"Are you sure?"

Margareta played with the collar of her robe. "Are you sure I can't help you another way?" She pulled back her robe enough to show she wore little underneath.

"Thanks, but no thanks. What about Germans or DP friends?"

Margareta closed her robe. "Is this going to take all night? I've got another show in an hour."

"This will take as long as it takes to get some information."

Mason leaned against the wall and lit a cigarette as if he were ready to wait all night.

Finally Margareta stubbed out her cigarette and let out a heavy sigh. "Eddie Kantos. A Greek. He owns a nightclub, the Havana. I've seen him with Hilda a few times." She poked her finger at Mason. "But don't you go saying I told you."

"A tough fellow, is he?"

"I wouldn't know anything about that." She slipped off the desk. "Are we done yet? I don't have anything more to tell you, and I've still got to change for the next performance."

Mason handed her one of his cards. "If you think of anything else, give me a call. You might not have liked Hilda, but no one deserves what happened to her."

Margareta took the card. She looked at him for a moment, and her eyes told him what he needed to know: She was frightened. She left without another word.

Next Sobel brought in a perky blonde with curly hair, who clumsily tried the same seductress routine, but she turned out to be Margareta's exact opposite: dull witted and fragile. When Mason informed her of Hilda's death, the girl burst into tears and continued that way until Mason finally gave up, letting her flee the room.

Sobel entered shortly thereafter with Abrams, and Abrams looked close to tears after what must have been a soul-destroying interview. "Please tell me you're finished," Sobel said. "I've got a final show to run, and you've traumatized one of my principal skaters."

"Adelle Holtz is one of your performers, correct?"

"If you want to talk to her, you'll have to come back another time. She never showed up tonight, and not a word—"

Sobel stopped in midsentence when Mason rushed out the door.

13

A delle occupied the basement apartment of a three-story pink stucco building just off Ludwigstrasse. Abrams pulled up the sedan and parked it on the opposite side of the street. Since it was after midnight, the street was quiet.

"You said you've been here twice already," Abrams said. "Maybe she's skipped town." He started to get out of the car, but Mason grabbed his arm to stop him.

"Wait a minute."

With a puzzled look, Abrams obeyed. Mason scanned the street.

"What are you looking for?" Abrams asked.

"I'll know it when I see it. From now on, you and me, we're going to watch our backs. Check the corners and the shadows before you move."

"Now you're just trying to scare me. If you want me to stop being your partner, just say so."

Down the street a block and facing them, a car engine started. The headlights came on and the tires squealed. Temporarily blinded by the bright lights, Mason could only make out two silhouettes of men wearing fedoras as the car sped past. Mason jumped out. The car had no license plate, but Mason identified the make, a German-made 1938 Horch, unfortunately a fairly common vehicle. He then rushed across the street with Abrams in tow. He bounded down the six steps and pounded on Adelle's door. A dog barked, setting off a chain reaction of other dogs. A few lights came on in other houses.

Mason pounded again. "Adelle, it's me, Mason. Open up." He felt the door. "It's pretty solid. Help me kick it in. You hit under the latch, and I'll hit high."

After two hard kicks, the wood around the latch gave way, and the door flew open. Inside, the apartment was pitch-black.

"I told you she wasn't home," Abrams said.

Mason put his finger to his mouth and flicked on his flashlight. He then pulled out his Colt .45 and clicked off the safety. Abrams did the same. They moved slowly down the corridor that led to doorways on both sides. The living room came first. Mason signaled for Abrams to move forward and check the bathroom. He scanned the living room with his flashlight and his gun. He swept the beam across the entire floor, while hoping he didn't discover Adelle butchered the same way as Hilda.

Mason rolled out of the living room and met Abrams just as he exited the bathroom. Abrams shook his head. They moved down the final ten feet of corridor, side by side, flashlights and guns up. Abrams split off to the left to check the kitchen, and Mason stopped at the bedroom's open door. As before, Mason scanned the left side of the bedroom with his flashlight and gun. The bedcovers had been pulled down; coffee cups and a tray with scraps of food lay on the bed stand. The odor of cigarettes lay thick in the still air. He rolled around to view the opposite side, and just as he began his sweep, he heard the click of a gun's hammer being pulled back.

Mason ducked low and swung the flashlight around to the sound. He braced himself for the explosion of gunfire. His finger squeezed lightly on the trigger, but the flashlight found her first. Adelle stood trembling in a corner. She held the gun out straight, though she aimed at nothing. Her eyes were wide and tears slid down her cheeks.

Mason illuminated his own face with the flashlight and spoke in a soft voice. "Adelle, it's Mason. We're here to help you."

Adelle let out a soft sigh, but continued to point the Walther P38 with the hammer locked back and ready to fire. Mason slowly straightened and stretched out his arms so both the flashlight and gun were aimed to the side. He took a step forward.

"Put the gun down, Adelle."

Abrams popped in the room behind Mason, and Adelle took aim at him.

"This is my partner. Another policeman." He turned slightly to Abrams. "Put your gun away." He took another step forward.

"How do I know you're not here to kill me?" Adelle asked in a haunting voice.

"Well, for one thing, I wouldn't have pounded on the door and announced who I was to the neighborhood." He smiled. "I hope you give me more credit than that." He laid his gun and flashlight on a high-backed chair.

Adelle's whole body shuddered, then her arms dropped. Mason stepped over and gently removed the Walther from her hand. He returned the hammer to its resting place. Adelle collapsed into his arms and took deep gulps of air.

Behind Mason, Abrams let go of the breath he'd been holding and said, "Jesus Christ."

"I'm sorry," Adelle said. "I thought you were… were… Oh, God, poor Hilda."

Abrams turned on a floor lamp, while Mason led her to the foot of the bed and helped her sit. "Why do you think men were coming to kill you?"

She looked at him as if confused by the question. "Because of what happened to Mr. Winstone and Hilda."

"Adelle, we're still not sure it was anything more than Agent Winstone murdering Hilda and committing suicide."

"You don't... You can't believe that."

"I don't, but there's no evidence to say otherwise."

"It's because of what Winstone and Hilda found out."

"What did they find out?" Mason asked.

"I don't know. They wouldn't tell me. But whatever it was, Hilda was frightened. Agent Winstone thought she was overreacting, but Hilda claimed they were being followed by some Americans. She told me that's why they wanted you to come home with them. If the men saw a policeman was with them, it would discourage them from doing anything."

"And that's why they asked you to come along? To persuade me to stay the night?"

Adelle nodded and lowered her eyes. "That was Hilda's idea. She called me from the restaurant and asked me to come. I told her no, but Hilda sounded so frightened and desperate. I did it for her. I would have done anything to keep her safe. Hilda was my sister."

"Your sister?"

Adelle nodded. "I'm sorry I deceived you. That was another one of Hilda's ideas, not to tell you we were sister, because you would have figured out the deception right away. I was going to just keep dancing and talking with you until morning, but I guess I got too drunk, and I liked you."

Mason laid his anger and embarrassment aside until later. He looked at Abrams, who still stood near the door. "You don't have to hear any of this. The more you know, the more it could get you in a jam."

"I'm staying, if that's all right with you."

Mason turned back to Adelle. "Did Hilda tell you who the men were, or what they looked like?"

Adelle shook her head.

"You still haven't told me why men would want to kill you."

"They might know what Hilda told me."

Mason knew that, more than likely, Hilda had told them everything under their knives.

"And what did Hilda tell you?"

"Before they fell in love, Hilda was an informant for Agent Winstone...." She paused to fight back tears. Mason remained quiet to let her gather her thoughts. "She was supposed to report on the activities and movements of Herr Giessen, Bachmann, and Plöbsch. What they said, everything. Later, maybe two weeks ago, Agent Winstone had her trying to get information on a man named Lester Abbott."

"Abbott? That doesn't sound German."

Adelle shook her head. "I only overheard her mention his name once or twice. Agent Winstone believed that Abbott had some kind of business relationship with Herr Giessen and was somehow associated with your American intelligence corps."

A gang-related agent in the CIC? Mason looked at Abrams, then turned back to Adelle. "She said nothing else about this man Abbott?"

"No. Then Giessen and Bachmann were killed, and Hilda murdered. I'm sure the murders are connected somehow."

"And she said nothing about what Agent Winstone had discovered?"

"Only that some very scary people are trying to take over all the black market operations."

"Who? Germans? Americans?"

"I think both," Adelle said. She suddenly turned pale and held on to Mason for support. "Please. That is all I know. I'm so afraid they'll come for me now."

"You can stay with me tonight. But it's probably best if you make some arrangements to leave town."

"And go where? I have no family left, and I barely have any money."

"We'll figure it out." He turned to Abrams. "Bring the car around close to the door. Someone could still be watching this place."

~

ABRAMS PULLED the sedan onto Frühlingstrasse, a ridiculously picturesque street running alongside the near-frozen Loisach River. It had much smaller houses than in Winstone's neighborhood, but they were nevertheless lovely, and, of course, gingerbread.

Abrams slowed the car to a stop a block and a half from Mason's house.

"Why are you stopping?" Mason asked.

"You said to be careful from now on."

Mason nodded. "All right. I'd rather you be overly cautious."

"Do you really expect trouble?"

"Whenever there's a lot to gain or lose, there's always trouble."

"Maybe we should get some help."

"Do you know who to go to? I feel like everyone in this town has something to gain or something to lose."

"Including you."

Mason nodded. "Including me." He looked back at Adelle, who lay splayed across the backseat, sleeping. He pointed toward his house. "Go ahead. I don't see anything suspicious."

Abrams parked the car, and Adelle woke up with a start when the car doors opened. Abrams waited until Mason had escorted Adelle safely onto the porch before driving off.

The house had once belonged to a German major in the Gebirgsjäger, the elite mountain troops, stationed in Garmisch. It was a half-timbered two-bedroom home of white stucco, with a pitched roof, arched windows, and a wide front porch. Spindly weeds had taken over the window flower boxes. The house had been abandoned after the major's death and showed signs of neglect, but it still felt palatial compared to the places Mason had hung his hat in the last number of years.

Mason unlocked the door after one last visual sweep of the neighborhood. Inside, Mason helped Adelle remove her overcoat as she looked around the living room. "Everything in its place. I bet you don't even let the dust settle."

"I'm only here to sleep."

Mason had left the furnishings as he found them. The major had been a widower in his final years, and the furniture and decorations exuded a man with conventional tastes: If it had no function, it had no place. The exception was the man's extensive and eclectic collection of 78 records, from French ballads to Croatian folk music. The only things Mason had removed were the once-ubiquitous portrait of Hitler and family photos. Though Mason had not bothered to replace them with any of his own.

"The dedicated officer," Adelle said as she sauntered around the furniture. Her vulnerability had vanished. The lithe, sensual movements had returned. She walked up to Mason and stopped, her face inches from his. He could smell her lipstick and old tears and, below that, a wisp of body odor, which, on her at least, he found erotic.

"You like collecting little birds with broken wings," Adelle said.

"You don't look so broken to me."

"Yes, I am. And your partner: another one you've taken under your wing."

"He can take care of himself."

"Just don't let him fall out of the nest too soon," she said and leaned in to kiss him.

Mason pulled his head back and locked his eyes on her. "Is this another calculated maneuver of yours?"

"What would I gain? You're not the type to keep me around as your house pet to feed scraps of food and throw coins at for tricks. You rescued me and brought me to your home, my knight in shining armor. I haven't met a man who's done that for me in years. I want to kiss you. You can enjoy it... or not."

Mason did kiss her. Deeply. There was little emotion behind it. It was all pure passion, and she knew where to push, where to touch, where to kiss. Their connection lay in knowing just what each of them needed and desired, what intensified each sensation in turn. Normally Mason preferred at least a shared affection behind the lust, but Adelle had a bewitching ability to enflame his desires, and for a second time he gave into it with utter abandon.

THEY MADE love again in the morning, though it failed to reach the same heights of abandonment as the night before. They spoke little over coffee, which Mason appreciated, since his brain was the last organ to wake up in the morning. Adelle ate ravenously, so talking took a backseat to the toast and jam, the cereal, several pieces of fruit, and a quart of milk.

She noticed him watching her eat. "Don't worry. I'm not going to eat you out of house and home. I've hardly had anything for the last day and a half."

"I'll bring more food home tonight. I want you to stay out of sight, at least for a few days."

"You don't have to ask me twice." She took a break from gorging to look at him. "Why are you doing this?"

"You don't think you deserve saving?"

She shrugged, then dug into her cereal again.

"What did you do during the war?" Mason asked.

"Like everybody else: tried to survive."

"Did you skate? Dance? Rob banks?"

Adelle stopped chewing a mouthful of food and looked at him, as if she were going to spit in his direction. "You screw me, then you want to make sure I wasn't a Nazi? Is that it? Do you want to see my denazification papers?"

"A sensitive subject, I see."

"I'm sick of every American asking me the same questions with that smug look of superiority."

"Then skip it. I don't want to know."

"Because you're sure I was a sieg-heiling Nazi fanatic."

Mason found himself on the defensive, which made his temper flare. "Hilda told me your mom was part Jewish, and your family was persecuted because of it. I found Hilda's story compelling, and I simply wondered if you had a similar experience. You don't want to talk about it, that's fine. We'll keep it strictly business: food and shelter for information."

Adelle dropped her spoon in the cereal and sat back in her chair with her arms crossed. "That was a heartless thing to say."

"You're right. I apologize."

Adelle looked at him for a moment, then said, "Hilda was the really talented one. She was eight when she started exhibition skating. I'm five years older than Hilda, and I started about the same time as her. I was good, but too interested in boys to be serious. Then I got pregnant at seventeen."

"You have a child?"

Adelle shook her head. "I lost her in childbirth." She swallowed hard and looked away. "Anyway, the boy who got me pregnant married me. His father was a powerful local Nazi. He loved his son, so he covered up that my mother was part Jewish. My husband..." She made a crooked smile. "He joined the Waffen-SS two years later. I was the upstanding *Hausfrau* to my little Nazi *Soldat*. It kept me out of trouble... for a while." She stopped, and looked as if the remembering was painful. "Then I was impetuous enough to petition for the release of my father. That was just before my husband was killed in '43 in Russia, and my father-in-law died of a heart attack a month later. There went my only protection, and I was arrested. They put me in a camp and I was attached to a work detail, cleaning up after bombing raids and digging defensive trenches against the Russian army. I was a wreck after the war. It was Hilda who convinced me to start skating and dancing again. There you have my sad war story." She pointed her chin at Mason. "I noticed your scars: the one on your left rib cage, your back, and the one on that lovely ass of yours. My little pincushion. Also the scars on your feet. Burns?"

"Frostbite from when your comrades forced me and a thousand other POWs on a death march."

"A big, strong he-man like you... I bet you came out of it just fine. The boy grows up in the American dream to become a war hero. That's what most of the Ami soldiers want you to believe, telling me how wonderful life is in America, so that I'll rend my clothes, pull my hair and curse God for not making me an American."

Mason smiled and leaned on his elbows. "I was born in Augsburg, but when my father died in World War One, my mother, along with my grandparents, emigrated to the U.S. We went to the state of Ohio, where my grandfather had a brother with a farm. My mom married an American, a mean drunk named Robert Collins. Because of the anti-German sentiment, they changed my and my sister's name from Strächer to Collins, my first name from Meinrad to Mason—"

Adelle chuckled. "They did you a favor, there."

"My stepfather left home when I was eight. My sister died of polio, and my mother from booze. My grandmother raised me. I was a cop, then a detective with the Chicago police. Then because I was a detective and fluent in German, army counterintelligence recruited me. I was captured, and became a POW for four months. And now, here I am, fraternizing with a gorgeous ex-Nazi."

"You've come full circle. Back to the Fatherland."

"It's not my fatherland. Not after what Hitler and Germany did. I'm still trying to understand how an entire population supported, even cheered, a man like that."

"We're all innocent, and all guilty. Didn't you know that? All supporters, and detractors. All willing participants, and helpless bystanders. That's the only way it *can* work."

"You're pretty smart for a skater."

"I didn't know there was a maximum IQ requirement for skaters. On the other hand, in my experiences, there is one for cops. Present company excluded, of course."

Mason finished his coffee. "Speaking of being a cop: I still have a few questions."

"For my room and board?"

"To find your sister's killers."

When Adelle didn't respond, Mason asked, "Why did you and Hilda live apart? And why keep the fact that you were sisters a secret?"

"We lived apart because that's how I wanted it. It didn't take long after coming to Garmisch for me to resent her, and I grew angry. She had all the talent. She got all the men. I acted just like when we were kids. Plus, I didn't like some of the things she was getting into. We fought like cats, then I refused to talk to her. Hilda came to me about three weeks ago. She was afraid, and she didn't have anyone else to trust. She told me everything, and through it all, we became close again. And we didn't keep that we were sisters a secret, exactly. Hilda thought I would be safer if we simply kept quiet about our relationship."

Any idea why Winstone recruited Hilda as an informant?

What kind of contact could Hilda have had with Giessen and the rest? How did she know them?"

"This is a small city. Anyone who dealt on the black market—and that's just about everyone—knew of these men."

"But for Hilda to get that close, she must have had some direct connection."

Adelle took interest in her spoon for a moment, turning it over and over in her empty cereal bowl. "Hilda was Herr Giessen's lover."

Mason lit a cigarette to mask his surprise. "Even while she was with Winstone?"

"No. Giessen and she were only together for a few months last summer. Hilda volunteered to strike up a renewed friendship with Giessen for Winstone's investigation."

"She met Winstone when?"

"Sometime in December. She was with Eddie Kantos at the time."

"Kantos? One of the other skaters insinuated he was a pretty tough guy."

Adelle nodded. "I guess he was rough on her. That lasted about five months, until Winstone recruited her to inform on Kantos. She fell in love with Winstone during that time. Poor girl never had much luck with men."

"Do you think Kantos killed them out of revenge?"

"Could be."

"Anyone else you can think of who might have wanted to kill them?"

"Whoever they got too close to in the investigation, I imagine. Whoever is trying to take over the black markets."

"The million-dollar question," Mason said and rose from the table. "Are you going to be here when I get back?"

"I haven't made any plans to do otherwise."

"Then stay out of sight and don't answer the door for anyone but me or my partner." He disappeared into the living room and came back a moment later with Adelle's Walther P38. He laid it on the table in front of her. "Just do me one favor and don't open fire unless you're sure it's not me coming through the door."

Adelle stared at it for a moment then looked up at Mason with alarm in her eyes. "Do you think they know I'm here?"

"No. But you're not the only one they could be coming for. Me, for example. You and me, it seems we're in this mess together, whether we like it or not."

14

M ason ignored Abrams's increasingly insistent questions about where'd he'd been, and why he looked like Jack the Ripper just before plunging his blade into his next victim. He followed Mason across the detachment headquarters and up the stairs, having to take two steps to each of Mason's long strides. On the third floor, Mason zeroed in on Densmore, who once again was bending the ears of three MPs about some case while he was a detective for the St. Louis police department.

Densmore took one look at Mason and dismissed his less-than-enthralled audience before Mason could get there. Abrams wisely fell back so as not to be in the line of fire.

Densmore feigned a smile. "Investigator Collins. You look chipper this fine morning."

"I've just come from the morgue," Mason said. "You'll never guess what I discovered: Winstone's body was shipped out. The ME never had a chance to perform an autopsy."

"Calm down, Mas—"

"Was that your idea? Get rid of the only evidence that could determine whether it was suicide or murder?"

"Just hold on a minute."

"You're deliberately sabotaging this investigation. Why?"

"I'm still your superior, so you *will* calm down," Densmore said. He jerked his finger in the direction of his office. "In my office. Now."

Mason held his glare a moment longer before complying.

Densmore entered and closed the door. "That was not my idea."

"That's a load of crap. You're the supervising investigator. Gamin's out of the picture, so that leaves you."

"The orders came from someone higher than my pay grade. Supposedly the wife refused permission for an autopsy to be performed here. She wanted the local ME in Schenectady to do it."

"A homicide investigation supersedes that."

"This isn't a homicide investigation. For all intents and purposes, it was a suicide."

"So you rolled over on the request."

"This is the army, Mason. When the Third Army provost marshal issues an order, you snap to and do it."

"The only way the provost marshal could have gotten involved is through you."

"I had nothing to do with informing the PM. I don't know where the orders originated or who told the wife it was suicide to begin with. I assumed you'd contacted Mrs. Winstone, since you knew her and were friends with Winstone."

Mason stopped. He'd intended to contact her so she could hear the news from someone she knew and not an impersonal telegram or a phone call from an army clerk. He'd let it slip his mind and got wrapped up in the investigation. It wasn't the first time he'd let his fixation on a case blot out the rest of the world.

"I didn't call her," Mason said.

"Well, someone did. Maybe if you'd called her, you could have convinced her to let the autopsy take place."

140

Densmore had a point, but once Mason had something in his teeth it was hard to let it go. "Someone with authority is trying to cover his tracks."

"We could debate who all day, but there's still Sergeant Olsen, abducted and possibly murdered, and whoever is muscling in on the black market."

"They're all related, and Winstone's the key. Which brings me to the Italian who put a gun to my head. Genovese. He was released last night, when I wasn't here to object. What's going on here?"

"He's an American citizen. You denied him treatment for the broken arm that *you* gave him. You didn't get anything out of interrogating him. Either he or someone on his behalf, alerted some heavy-hitting lawyers in New York, and they put pressure on the Judge Advocate's office. Plus, the Italians had a warrant out on him for racketeering and suspicion of murder. It was a political hot potato for JAG and the brass, so they were more than happy to hand him over to the Italians. I got my ass chewed out by the Third Army provost marshal about that, too. Next time you want to hold a witness and deny him medical attention, make sure he's not connected up the ass. Now get out of here, and don't you ever come storming at me again or you won't know what hit you."

Abrams followed Mason into his office and closed the door.

"Okay, I want to know how to do that," Abrams said.

"Do what?"

"Stick it to your commanding officer and not get busted down to private."

Mason couldn't help cracking a smile. "I wouldn't advise trying until you're too valuable to get rid of."

"I think you're close to spending all your currency in that regard. I'd like you to hang around long enough for me to learn something from you."

Mason walked over to the chalkboard. While he filled Abrams in on what Adelle told him, he wrote down Hilda's name and drew lines to Winstone, Giessen, and Eddie Kantos. Then he added Abbott and CIC with a question mark off to one side. Next to that he added the Casa Carioca with Kessel's and the general manager Schaeffer's names. "We need to find out whatever we can on Kessel, Schaeffer. and Kantos."

"What about Abbott? We should check with the CIC to see if he works there or if they've got anything on the name."

Away from the other names, Mason added Adelle's and Densmore's names with question marks.

"Densmore?" Abrams said. "You think he belongs on the list, or are you trying to piss him off?"

"Could be a little bit of both."

Abrams handed Mason a file. "This just came in from the special services branch. It's all they have on Major Schaeffer."

Mason glanced through the two-page document. Schaeffer, aged thirty-nine, had joined the army in 1926. It cited his two medals, a Silver Star and Legion of Merit, but not what he had done to earn them. He stood six feet, three inches and weighed 190 pounds. His official photo showed a lean, muscular man with a dark complexion, slicked-back black hair, and dark piercing eyes topped by thick eyebrows.

Mason double-checked the thin dossier. "This doesn't go into any detail further back than a year and a half ago, when he joined the Third Army as adjunct administrator to the general staff—which means nothing. Is this all they could give you?"

"That's all they had. The rest is classified."

"CIC?"

"They didn't, or wouldn't, say. And the three other managers Kessel said run the Casa Carioca? The two from Army Corps of Engineers have been in Berlin since the beginning of the year.

And the one from civil administration was mustered out of the army a month ago and is now stateside."

"You mean Kessel didn't tell us the truth?" Mason asked sarcastically.

"I can try to request Schaeffer's classified file."

"Do it, but I don't expect we'll get anywhere." Mason dropped the file on the desk.

There was a knock on the door. A private opened the door and held out an envelope. "Sir, this came down from OMGB."

OMGB was the Office of Military Government, Bavaria.

Mason thanked the private and opened the envelope. After reading the letter, he said to Abrams, "Come on. We're going to the CIC to see if we can piss them off, too."

THE RECEPTION CLERK at the CIC villa headquarters examined General Pritchard's written orders as if great secrets might be revealed to anyone willing to stare at the piece of paper long enough. The grandfather clock and crackling fire were the only sounds in the place. Mason tapped his foot with impatience. He looked at Abrams, who just shrugged. Finally the clerk went to Major Tavers's office door and knocked. He opened the door a crack and spoke at length.

Mason had enough. He tapped Abrams on the arm for him to follow, and he marched down the hall, blowing past the clerk, snatching the letter out of the clerk's hand, and stopping at Tavers's desk. "Written orders from General Pritchard, granting me permission to search Agent Winstone's office and safe."

Tavers stared at Mason for a moment, then took the letter and examined it with the same interminable scrutiny as his time-killing accomplice. Mason noticed Tavers had a partially completed crossword puzzle laid out in front of him. Tavers looked at Mason and, with a slight flush in his cheeks, laid Pritchard's letter on top of the puzzle. He turned to a large safe behind his chair and made sure his body blocked Mason's view as he turned the dial. Once he'd opened the safe, he pulled out a key and a sealed envelope. "Follow me."

As they exited the office, Tavers said, "I suppose you've finally concluded that Agent Winstone was murdered and didn't commit suicide."

"That's my conclusion." And for emphasis, he added, "General Pritchard's as well."

Tavers issued a noncommittal grunt as he unlocked Winstone's office door.

"Anyone been in here since Winstone's death?" Mason asked.

"We locked it up as soon as we heard."

"Which was when?"

"When you two clowns showed up the first time."

"So at least eight hours from the time he was killed?"

"If you say so," Tavers said and escorted them into the office.

Winstone's office had probably been the villa's morning room before the CIC took it over, as the set of windows faced east and overlooked the southern end of the city that doglegged along the Loisach River. The original chairs, settee, and coffee table had been pushed to the windows to make room for the desk and two filing cabinets, one short and one tall. On the floor, along one wall, was a series of cases, and above that, a chalkboard with lists and charts. Mason felt a brief moment of melancholy for his dead friend.

"Everything in this room stays in this room," Tavers said.

"If I find evidence—"

"Your orders grant you permission for a search, not to remove official CIC documents."

Mason turned to Abrams. "Write down the names and draw

out the charts on the chalkboard." He said to Tavers, "If you'd open the safe for me, please."

Tavers led Mason over to a wall safe behind the desk. He broke the wax seal on the envelope and removed a piece of paper listing all the safe combinations in the building. Once again, he used his body to block Mason's view as he turned the dial. He opened the safe door and stepped aside. Inside, a shelf divided the safe into two compartments. The upper part contained a Browning nine-millimeter pistol, along with a file folder containing a handful of photographs. The lower compartment contained a stack of file folders. Each folder had a handwritten label indicating dossiers on individuals. He laid the files on the desk and sifted through them.

"Got everything," Abrams declared from his spot at the chalkboard.

Without looking up, Mason said, "Start with the cases on the floor, then the small file cabinet."

Mason returned his attention to the files and went through them again. The files only contained information on German gang members, and he already knew almost all the people and their particulars. Frustrated, he leaned on the desk. "They're not here."

"What were you hoping to find?" Tavers asked.

Mason ignored the question. "Are you the only one with the combination to this safe?"

"Yeah, but I didn't go in there and take anything, if that's what you're implying."

"Anyone else have the combination to *your* safe?"

"Nope."

Mason strode over to the tall file cabinet and rifled through the hanging files in each drawer.

Abrams said, "One case contains a camera and lenses. The other ones have equipment for wiretaps, listening devices, and a few boxes of unopened tape stock."

"None of the tapes look like they've been used?"

"None that I can tell."

"Even if they were, removing them is not part of your search parameters," Tavers said.

Mason slammed the final cabinet drawer closed. "It looks like someone has cleaned out everything of relevance."

"If you'll just tell me what you're looking for—"

"Major, if you're the only one who has the combination to both your safe and Winstone's, then logically, you know what I'm looking for."

"No, I don't. And I resent the implication."

Mason let him squirm as he studied the major's expression and posture.

Tavers spit out lamely, "Maybe someone cracked the combination."

"Are you telling me that your hotshot CIC agents would let someone wander into their headquarters, break into Winstone's office, and crack his safe? All without being detected?"

Tavers appeared flustered and at a loss for words. From what Mason could determine from Tavers's reaction, the detachment commander truly had no answer.

Mason said, "Then it had to be another one of your agents. What about Winstone's two German assistants?"

"All I know is, they came out of the CIC in Frankfurt. They were not under my command."

"But they could have access to this office and the combination of the safe."

"I haven't seen them in the last couple of days. And to save you the trouble of asking, I don't know where they are or where they're billeted. Why don't you ask your buddy General Pritchard?"

"What about a Lester Abbott? Is he one of your agents?"

"I've never heard of him. And if he was with this detachment, I'd know about him."

"Would it be possible for you to check with CIC central command and see if he is?"

Tavers went to the door and called for his clerk. They talked a moment, then Tavers returned.

"Sir," Abrams said, "could you look at this, please?"

Mason joined Abrams at the chalkboard, and this time Mason blocked Tavers's view. With a subtle nod Abrams indicated a list of names written in chalk at the bottom of a chart. Yaakov Lubetkin was written at the top with two small arrows pointing to Giessen and Bachmann, then one to Kantos.

"You think Yaakov was an informant for Winstone?" Abrams whispered.

In the middle of the intersecting branches, Winstone had written Eddie Kantos's name. The man seemed to be connected in one way or another to just about everyone on the board. Mason followed one branch that led from Kantos to Frieder Kessel, the assistant manager of the Casa Carioca. Winstone had written *SS?* beside Kessel's name, and next to that, he had written *Herr Z* with a question mark and *Gestapo Major, Intelligence,* also with a question mark.

The hairs on the back of Mason's neck stood up. He could not have said why, but suddenly he felt certain that Herr Z was Volker, the Turkish-cigarette-smoking Gestapo interrogator who had tortured him. The one who Mason would swear had also been at the Steinadler and who'd blown Mason's cover.

"You got all this down, right?" Mason asked.

Abrams nodded and then pointed to two more entries. "Then you've got 'Herr X' and 'Herr Y' set off from the rest. No names, but Winstone connects them with everyone on this board, including our dead German gang bosses. Who do you think Winstone was referring to there?"

"Whoever they are—"

"What are you two doing, skulking over there?" Tavers said. "Are you about finished?"

"Anxious to get back to your crossword puzzle?"

"I don't have to stand for this," Tavers said and stormed out.

The clerk appeared a moment later, and Mason asked, "Did you find anything on Abbott?"

"Sir, that could take days," the clerk said. "If he's in special operations, they may not admit he's one of theirs."

With the clerk now assigned to watch them, Mason and Abrams set to work: Abrams dusting for fingerprints, and Mason studying the documents from the safe. The files yielded little new information. The safe's combination dial had obviously been wiped clean, as there was just one set of prints, and those could have only been Tavers's. If Winstone had kept an agenda book or diary, it was gone. And no copies existed of the reports Winstone had sent to Pritchard.

An hour later, they returned to their car and drove away from CIC headquarters.

"Whoever cleaned out Winstone's records knew what they were looking for," Mason said.

"If they wanted to cover their tracks, why did they leave all that stuff up on the chalkboard?"

Mason shrugged. "Actually, they might have added stuff just to throw us off."

Abrams looked deflated. "That idea makes my head hurt."

"Did you check up on the address that Yaakov gave us from that first interview?"

"Yep. Unless he lives under the Olympic skating rink parking lot, he gave us a bogus address."

Mason pulled out his cigarette lighter and flicked it open and closed as he thought. Finally he said, "All the lines on the chalkboard converged on Eddie Kantos. We'll start with him."

E ddie Kantos covered his tracks well. He had a clean police record, both American and German. In the public records he was listed as an upstanding citizen and sole proprietor of the Club Havana, which interestingly was his only known address. Mason and Abrams stopped by the Club Havana, a bar-night-club-restaurant that catered to Americans and locals with enough money for the overpriced drinks. The lunch crowd filled the tables, most of whom preferred a liquid diet. The Latin music and a few ferns were the only indications that the place had anything to do with its namesake. Mason talked to the barman, who said Eddie never came in before ten P.M. After a considerable amount of coercion, the barman gave up Eddie's home address.

They found the house, an alpine-style affair of medium size and surrounded by a high row of shrubs, situated in an upscale part of town. That was the thing about Garmisch: Even the dangerous gangsters lived in charming gingerbread houses on Hansel-and-Gretel lanes. Another reminder that, in this town, nothing was as it appeared.

Mason and Abrams entered the property via a gate in a white-picket fence painted with pink roses. Mason held the cowbell hung from the latch to keep it from clanging their presence. They had expected at least one guard to be watching from a discreet distance, but none appeared. Perhaps the guards were inside, as it had turned bitterly cold, with the sun hidden behind a thick cover of clouds. Their boots crunched in the hard-crusted snow, and Mason noticed a whole series of footprints climbing and descending the steps that led up to a high porch.

"Even lace curtains on the front door windows," Abrams said. "This guy's thought of everything. Probably has doilies on the sofa arms."

Mason knocked, and they waited.

"You think the bartender gave us a bogus address?" Abrams asked.

Mason knocked harder.

"Could be he's not home," Abrams said.

"Do you plan to have a running commentary the rest of the afternoon?"

"Jeez. Just thinking out loud. I figured you'd be in a better mood after getting laid."

Mason pointed to the corner of the house. "Check out the back. See if you can get a look inside from one of the rear windows. Stay alert. Someone could be in there with an itchy trigger finger."

They stepped off the porch and proceeded around the house in different directions. Mason tried to see in the front picture window, but the curtains were drawn closed. Then he noticed a brick red splatter stain on the lower edge of the curtain.

"Abrams," Mason said in a loud whisper.

Abrams stopped. Mason removed his pistol and headed back to the front door. With a look of alarm, Abrams did the same. At the front door, they took opposite sides, using the door frame as cover. Mason used the barrel of his pistol to break a lower pane of glass. He waited a moment, then reached inside and unlocked the door. He ducked back behind the door frame and opened the door. Mason signaled for Abrams go in on the right side, and he'd take the left. Abrams nodded, and, with guns at the ready, they slipped inside.

The living room had a high-sloped ceiling. A freestanding fireplace separated the living room from the dining room. A high-backed sofa and chairs were clustered in the middle. Mason and Abrams slid along opposite walls, checking the open balconies that spanned the two long sides of the room. As Mason cleared the sofa, he saw why the place had been so quiet.

A man's body lay on its back, with one bullet hole in the fore-head. He had a look of surprise on his gray face. It was Hans Engel—Frack, of Frick and Frack, one of the two German CIC agents working for Winstone. The splattered bloodstain on the curtain had come from the exit wound in the back of Engel's head. Two more bullets had punctured his chest. No time to wonder what Frack was doing here; they had to clear the rest of the house.

Mason and Abrams alternated rooms, covering each other, as they searched the house. They didn't have to go far before finding a second body in the kitchen. Werner Schluser, a.k.a. Frick, had the same look of surprise on his face. A half-eaten sandwich still lay on the breakfast table. The bullet had entered the back of his head. And like Frack, two more bullet wounds in the chest. And like Giessen, Bachmann, and Plöbsch, both had been killed execution style.

No sign of a struggle; Frick contentedly eating his sandwich, then dead. His suit coat lay open, exposing a nine-millimeter still in its shoulder holster.

"What were these two doing here?" Abrams said.

Mason shook his head and pointed to the upper floor. They climbed the stairs and moved silently from room to room. Finally Abrams whistled softly for Mason's attention.

A man lay naked, facedown, on the bathroom floor. He was tall and muscle-bound, with a series of scars across one shoulder, hip, and back. Like the others, he had been shot in the head with two in the chest.

They still had two bedrooms to go. On the other side of the sink, a door fed into what Mason presumed was the master bedroom. Mason signaled for Abrams to approach the bedroom from the hallway. He waited for Abrams to get into position, then he stepped over the corpse and peeked into the room. The master bedroom took up a third of the second floor. A massive canopy bed sat in the middle. Mason checked the corners and entered. Abrams did the same thing from the hallway door. A second later, Abrams hissed and pointed to the far corner on the other side of the bed.

When Mason went around the bed, he saw a woman in a white nightgown curled up in a ball, lifeless on the floor. She looked to be in her early thirties, with long, dark hair. She'd been shot in the head and chest, like the others, but there was a bullet wound in the back of her shoulder. Mason figured she'd heard the pop of a silencer and Kantos fall. When she tried to run from the killers, she'd been hit in the shoulder. She'd curled up on the floor, as if to shield herself. She had a look of terror frozen on her face.

Mason forced himself to breathe; they still had one more bedroom. Abrams must have been feeling the same thing, as his face was tense with dread at what they might find in the final room.

Their worst fears were realized. Lying in bed as if asleep, a boy of eight or nine still had his bedcovers pulled up to his chin. He, too, had been shot in the head but, apparently, even the killers had their limits, as there were no other marks on the boy's body.

Mason stared at the boy's face. The boy's eyes were closed and sunken. His skin pale in contrast to the blood that had spread across the pillow. A flash of memory came to Mason: during the war, another child shot through the head, her blood staining the snow. He slammed his fist against the wall.

After taking another ten minutes clearing the rest of the house, the two investigators returned to the body in the bathroom. Mason turned the corpse onto its back. The exiting bullet had taken out most of the man's forehead and bridge of his nose, and his eyes were filled with blood, but Mason could still make out the face.

"This has to be Kantos," Mason said. "I saw him with Giessen once or twice." He searched the floor in the immediate area of the shooting. "The killers were pros. They picked up the shell casings. We probably won't find a print anywhere."

"There's still the footprints outside. We can see if there are any matches with the prints from the Steinadler. The thing I don't get is, why were Hans and Werner pulling bodyguard duty with one of the men Winstone was investigating?"

Mason shook his head. "Whatever the reason, they must have known the killers. That's the only way they could have gotten inside and surprised two trained agents." He squatted and examined the body. From the condition of the corpse, Mason estimated Kantos was shot six to eight hours before, putting it at early in the morning. "Any visitors before six would have seemed strange, so sometime after that."

"Someone's eliminating the competition," Abrams said.

"Or potential witnesses. It's time to find Yaakov before anyone else does."

"Shouldn't we call this in first?"

"If we do that, we'll be tied up with this for the entire afternoon. We've got to find Yaakov. Now."

"We can't just walk away from these people."

Mason looked up at Abrams. He thought about the woman and the boy lying dead and beginning to decay. He couldn't have cared less about Kantos's remains, but Abrams was right: He wouldn't let the woman and boy lie there any longer. "All right, call it in."

Thirty minutes passed before a contingent of MPs, crime scene techs, and the assistant ME arrived. By that time, Mason and Abrams had searched around the bodies and the house for traces of footprints, hair, or fibers. The search turned up nothing of real value. Mason had hoped to find something that could help tie Kantos in with the other suspects listed on Winstone's chalkboard, or identify the killers and their bosses. They did find a sack of cash: U.S. dollars, British pounds, Swiss francs, and Italian lire. In all, close to ten thousand dollars' worth: a fortune by some standards, but probably pocket change for Kantos. Wherever he kept the majority of his earnings, it wasn't in the house. And, as with Winstone's office, Mason suspected that whatever records or incriminating material had been in the house, the killers had destroyed or taken with them.

The only break came in finding the slug that had passed cleanly through the wife's shoulder and embedded itself in the wall. The relatively intact bullet, a nine-millimeter, would have the distinct striations, the markings, left by the weapon. He could compare those with the compressed bullets from the other gunshot wounds and see if it was the same weapon and determine its make. But in all, they came away with very little useful evidence.

Mason and Abrams were finishing up, and giving instructions to the crime scene techs, when, to Mason's surprise and displeasure, Densmore entered and marched up to them. "Every place you go, another set of corpses turn up. And this time, you're going to have to learn about cooperation. German victims, German police."

"The principal target was Eddie Kantos. A British citizen."

Densmore hissed a curse. "Now, I suppose, we're going to have to involve the Brits on this one."

"The woman and boy were Austrian."

"Boy?" Densmore said with dismay.

"Kantos's wife and her son. I found the marriage certificate along with their passports. The son was from a previous marriage."

Densmore let out a tired sigh, then eyed Mason. "Why were you here, anyway?"

"To question Kantos. I got access to Winstone's office and saw he'd drawn out a chart with a whole web of unsavory characters, living and dead, with Kantos at the center of it all."

"You're still circling around Winstone being murdered? When are you going to wise up, Collins?"

"Winstone was investigating Kantos, among others, and now here he is, shot dead execution style—just like Giessen and the rest. The two bodyguards were working for Winstone, and probably knew the assailants, since there was no sign of a struggle and their weapons are still holstered. I'm sure it's the same hit squad that took out the three German crime bosses, Winstone, Hilda. Now Kantos, his wife and son, and the bodyguards. There were no prints. The front door was locked. No shoot-out. They were just popped off as pretty as you please. No muss, no fuss. When are *you* going to wise up?"

Densmore studied Mason as he processed this.

"Go see for yourself," Mason said. "Have a good look at the wife and boy, then tell me there's not some kind of cold-blooded gang taking over."

Densmore stepped past Mason and headed for the stairs.

As Mason watched Densmore climb the stairs, he said to Abrams, "Now you see why I added Densmore's name to the list. Let's get out of here."

Outside, a gaggle of German reporters waited at the gate. They fired questions as Mason and Abrams wedged past them. Then, just outside the gate, Mason had the feeling once again that someone was watching him. He glanced around and spotted a car parked opposite their jeep. Mason froze in midstep. Sure enough, someone was staring at him through the driver's-side window. Laura sat in an elegant Mercedes 770, probably once belonging to some Nazi general, with her hands on the steering wheel and the engine idling.

She locked eyes with his and nodded toward the road, her expression conveying anger or fear. But just as Mason moved toward her, she revved the engine and drove off. Puzzled, he watched her race down the road. He recovered a moment later and got behind the wheel of the jeep. Abrams barely had time to jump in before Mason took off.

16

M ason had the accelerator pinned to the floorboard and shifted gears like a race car driver but, try as he might, the jeep was no match for the supercharged, two-hundred-horse-power Mercedes. Laura had a quarter-mile lead, and she was continuing to widen the gap, when she took a sharp turn and disappeared from view.

Abrams checked his pistol as if expecting trouble. "Who are we chasing? How many guys?"

"It's my ex-girlfriend," Mason said.

Abrams stopped what he was doing, looked at Mason, and holstered his pistol. "If you've got a beef with your ex, can you please settle it when you're off duty?"

Mason took the same sharp turn as Laura. The road straightened with a clear view ahead, but Laura was no longer in sight. Mason slowed the jeep and peered down each side street they passed.

"What the hell was she doing at the Kantos place?" Abrams asked.

"That's what I intend to ask once I catch up to her. She looked upset, whatever the reason."

"Admit it, you lost her. Now, if you'd have let me drive—"

Laura's car came out of nowhere and swerved in front of them, the tires squealing as it did so. Mason gripped the steering wheel and raced up on her tail, but Laura surged ahead. The two cars sped through the winding curves of Promenadestrasse, then Burgstrasse, heading north and toward the edge of town.

Mason shook his head. "If she wants me to follow her somewhere, she could have just said so."

"She can drive; I'll give her that. I haven't met her yet, and I already like her."

Laura made a hairpin turn onto a narrow street and took several more quick turns before pulling into the small parking lot of the Partenkirchen cemetery. She got out of the car, walked past the chapel, and headed for the cemetery park before Mason had a chance to come to a stop. There were no other cars in the lot, and the only other person in sight was an old woman trying to sweep away snow gathering under the chapel's portico.

Mason parked the jeep next to Laura's Mercedes, and they climbed out. As they walked across the parking lot, Abrams pulled his coat tight against the bitter wind that blew up the valley and scattered snow flurries that had started to fall. The two investigators entered a cemetery park divided into small squares and shallow rectangles and dotted with random clumps of trees.

Laura waited on a footpath to their right. She wore a tweed pantsuit under a beige wool overcoat.

"Secret Agent McKinnon," Mason said, "this is my partner, Gil Abrams."

Laura ignored the crack and held out her hand. Abrams shook it while sporting a grin big enough to dislocate his jaw.

"Okay, talk to me," Mason said to Laura.

"You like to get right to the point, don't you?" Laura said.

"Laura."

"Nothing to say about how I lost you then picked you up again?"

Abrams interjected, "I thought it was some pretty nifty driving, and I said so."

Mason silenced Abrams with a stern look, then turned back to Laura. "What were you doing at the Kantos house? How did you know about the murders?"

Laura suddenly looked past them to a man dressed in a black coat and hat who had just entered the cemetery. They all watched as the man headed down a footpath taking him to an area of bare-limbed trees. He stopped at a gravestone and bowed his head. Laura turned and walked in the opposite direction, prompting Mason and Abrams to follow her.

After a few steps, Laura said, "I was visiting some reporter friends of mine at the army press office when the call came in about the shooting at a residence on Hausbergstrasse."

"And you suspected it was Eddie Kantos's house."

Laura looked straight ahead as she nodded and chose another path at random.

"How do you know Kantos, and where he lived?" Mason asked.

"I told you I've spent months investigating the black market trade between Germany and Italy. That I disguised myself as an Italian and a Jewish refugee as a way of learning about the smuggling routes. Bolzano is one of the main points of distribution in Italy for smuggled goods and refugees. Most of the smugglers go through there at one time or another, and that's where I met Kantos through another contact."

"Met him, meaning what?"

"I'd heard that Kantos was a big operator in the black market, arranging and coordinating smuggling routes through the French and British zones of Austria to Italy, and I wanted to interview him. I also heard he was helping the Jewish Brigade smuggle Jewish refugees to Palestine."

"What's the Jewish Brigade?" Abrams asked.

Mason said, "They're Palestinian Jews who fought in the British Army, but a lot of them stayed on after the war to help smuggle Jewish refugees into Palestine."

Laura nodded. "That's right. So, to get to Kantos, I posed as a Palestinian Jewish journalist doing a story about non-Jews helping refugees reach Palestine. Kantos was a pretty fascinating guy." She turned wistful. "He was a rugged, handsome man, a real-life adventurer: ruthless, dangerous, but with a soft spot for the Jewish refugee plight."

Mason said to Abrams, "There's one thing you have to understand about Laura: She looks for ways to put her life on the line." He turned back to Laura and said, "So, do tell us more about the wild desperado with a heart of gold. He must have made your heart go pitter-patter."

Laura glanced at Mason and smiled, amused at his hint of jealousy. "Kantos was a major in the SOE, the British Army's Special Operations Executive. It was a clandestine espionage unit and conducted sabotage and raiding operations during the war. Kantos also participated in operations with French units of the SOE, and he was awarded medals by both countries. He used his hero status to gain special privileges from both the Brits and the French: travel passes, identity cards, even military escorts. And what he couldn't obtain through favors, he got through bribes or extortion."

"How did you know where he lived in Garmisch if you only met him once in Italy?"

Laura said nothing as they walked around the maintenance building situated in the center of the cemetery.

"Did you learn it from the same man who introduced you to Kantos?" Mason asked.

"What difference does it make? The reason I brought you here and I'm telling you this is to warn you. I'm scared for you, and I'm scared for me. If they got to the Giessen gang *and* Kantos, then no one is safe, including you."

"Then tell me who your source is. If he has a connection to any of these victims then he could have important information. We need to talk to him."

"I remember giving you my source in Munich, and he wound up dead."

"If your source is associated with Kantos, then he's already a target. And if they can get to Kantos, they sure as hell can get to your man."

Laura sighed and looked at the ground as they walked. "I should say no on principle, but the man is a creep. Willy Laufs. He runs a local small-time gang dealing in narcotics and prostitution."

Abrams appeared enthralled with Laura, his eyes widening with each revelation of her story. "And you were able to find this guy and talk to him?"

"He approached me. A sucker for a nice pair of legs." Laura stole a glance at Mason. "Don't worry, I was able to keep him at arm's length. He prefers adolescents, anyway. Of both sexes. He reportedly runs a brothel for high-end clients who share in his perverted tastes. I don't know where it is, but you shouldn't have any trouble finding it; some fancy villa on the west side of town."

"We'll find it," Abrams said.

Laura continued, "Willy's real value is his connections to the Sicilian mafia, mostly narcotics. He was a diplomat in the Nazis' Office of Foreign Affairs in Sicily, and that's where he made friends with the main crime families."

Mason said to Abrams, "Laufs must have been the one to bring up the Italian who put a gun to my head at the Steinadler."

Abrams whistled in amazement. "Then he works with Lucky Luciano's crew."

Laura stopped when the idea sank in. "Who put a gun to your head?" she asked Mason. "And how many times does that make it, now?"

"Don't worry about it," Mason said. "Keep going."

Laura shrugged and began walking again. "Willy's been a go-between for the crime families and Kantos and Giessen, not only for narcotics, but for every kind of black market commodity you can think of. He also facilitated the smuggling routes through Italy for Nazi war criminals."

"Damn, Laura," Mason said and shook his head. "You have a real death wish. Tell me those days are over."

Laura stopped and put her hands on her hips. "How incredibly patronizing of you. Yes, I'm finished with this particular investigation, but that doesn't mean I'm tying on an apron and running barefoot in the kitchen. I'm not going to swear off my career just for your peace of mind."

Mason and she had argued like this before, and he knew her better than she thought. "Bullshit. You're still not done putting your life at risk, despite telling me you're scared. You need the excitement. You're addicted to the thrills. That's why you just *happened* to decide on Garmisch to write up your articles."

Laura's expression softened as she looked at him for a moment. "Maybe." She smiled. "Here we are again. In the thick of it, you and I. You must know that's why I found you so attractive."

"Laura this isn't a game."

"You let me worry about that. I've taken some big risks in my time—"

"Yes, yes, I know. You've crossed glaciers and ridden in open bombers at twenty thousand feet."

"Let's talk about you for a second. Let's talk about how *you* love to put your life on the line. You charge in like an enraged bull, even if it means putting the people who love you in danger." Laura stepped around him and headed for the cemetery exit. Mason remained behind as he absorbed Laura's words.

Abrams caught up to her. "Do you have any idea who killed Kantos or Giessen?"

"No," Laura said. "Do you?"

"All we can figure is they knew each other, because the killers got the drop on the bodyguards and Kantos."

Mason charged forward and said to Abrams, "Radio in and have some MPs pick up Laufs. Tell them to sit on him until we get back to HQ."

Abrams quickened his pace and headed for the jeep. Mason stepped in front of Laura again to stop her. "For your sake, stop nosing around. Anyone even suspected of having the wrong information dies. Go home. Type up your articles and keep out of sight. I don't know who's next on the list."

Laura acted more excited than fearful at that prospect. "Mason, you've got to let me in on this. I promise I won't stick my neck out too far, but I'm going to stay involved with or without you. If it's with you, then we both have a better chance of getting what we want." She waited. "Well?"

Mason resisted parsing her words about getting what they both want. He looked in her eyes and saw reflected back the same feeling of excitement that drove him to the edge—the thrill of the chase. The very thing that had brought them together and pushed them apart. There was no way he could stop her. She would do exactly what she wanted. Finally he said, "So far, it's more questions than answers, conjecture, innuendos." He then told her about Winstone and Hilda, what he'd found out about them while probing into the circumstances of their murders, about Kessel,

Schaeffer, and the secretive Abbott. He told her about what Winstone had told him, how he'd claimed there were documents that could shake the army's very foundations. "I suspect the Casa Carioca is being used as a base of operations. I believe some ex-SS officers and a few of the Polish waitstaff are part of the hit squad with Kessel and Schaeffer at the head of it. It's all related: Winstone, Giessen, Kantos, their murders, and this group based out of the Casa Carioca."

Laura was writing down everything in her notepad and acted more excited with each new detail.

Mason said, "I want you to promise me you won't throw out accusations, headline your stories with question marks, without facts to back them up—"

"I don't do that kind of journalism. At least not if I know I can get the real scoop from a reliable source."

"Good, because if you put out this story before I can get all the facts, you could blow the investigation. They'll just cover their tracks and run for cover. That is, after they get their hands on *you.* You have to promise me you'll wait for me to bust whoever's involved before you publish anything."

She touched his arm in her excitement, and Mason almost recoiled from the electrical charge that it elicited. The sensation made Mason snap at her. "I'm not exaggerating about keeping out of sight. Where are you staying?"

She smiled as if realizing the effect her touch had on him. "A house in the Breitenau district. It's called the Alpenrose, in the foothills."

"Good. That's isolated enough. Stay home except to buy groceries. Tell no one what you're doing. I don't know Richard, so it's up to you whether you trust he can keep his mouth shut."

"You called him Richard."

"What?"

"I said you called him Richard. Did you have a change of heart about him?"

"Laura, I'm being serious. You want an incentive?" Mason asked and swept his hand toward the gravestones. "Just look around you."

"I get it. Don't worry."

"Oh, I'm going to worry, all right."

17

Mason and Abrams sat in a German DKW sedan parked in front of a line of warehouses situated two hundred yards from the train station. Several trucks and wagons were parked along the narrow street, but the investigators still had an unobstructed view of the activity around the warehouses. It was a little after four P.M., and the sun had already dropped behind the mountains. Though they were both attired in civilian overcoats, wool suits, and homburg hats, the temperature still felt like it had plunged twenty degrees.

Abrams wrapped his coat tightly around his chest. "How about we start up the car and get some heat in here?"

"Two guys sitting in a parked car attracts enough attention without letting the motor run."

"We've been here for an hour. It's going to get dark pretty soon," Abrams said, and he looked up at the leaden sky. "Looks like it's going to snow."

"You wanted to be a detective. You'd better get used to cold and boring stakeouts."

Mason and Abrams had spent the last two hours hitting all the known black market spots, circulating among the vendors, showing Yaakov's mug shot and asking about his whereabouts. The black market vendors, suspicious by necessity, considered the two healthy, clean-cut fellows flashing a mug shot doubly suspicious, and, despite offers of cigarettes in exchange for information, they returned only blank stares or adamant denials.

Finally one old man selling piglets hidden in a baby carriage gave them information for two packs of cigarettes. According to the man, a group of enterprising souls had set up a black market venue in two disused, interconnected warehouses, providing the vendors and customers a welcome chance to do business indoors and out of the cold. Yaakov, he had said, could be seen there frequently in the afternoons. The two investigators had already made a thorough search of the two warehouses, but no Yaakov. Despite zero assurances that Yaakov would show up, or that the purchased information was reliable, Mason had insisted they sit on the place. This was their last option on a very short list.

Abrams shivered. "Aren't you cold?"

"My feet are screaming, my side aches where I was shot, and my butt's sore, but then I think back to being a POW and nearly dying on a death march in the worst winter—"

"Oh, here we go again: old war-dog talk."

Mason chuckled at Abrams calling him an "old war-dog" less than a year after the war had ended. "Get out and walk around if you're that cold."

Abrams got out of the car and stomped his feet, but only a moment later he jerked open the door. "He just went into the second warehouse."

Mason got out of the car. "You take the first one to cut him off, and I'll go in the second."

Mason quickened his pace and entered the bustling warehouse. The place had the air of a flea market in chaos. People had set up their wares on whatever space was unoccupied: coatracks of fine clothes and furs, furniture, handcarts containing makeshift displays of jewelry, cameras, phonographs, even the entire contents of households, all competing for attention with vendors selling wood brought down from the mountains and farmers selling eggs, half-rotten apples, salt-cured pork, and handmade lye soap. Soldiers and citizens mingled together, bartering and haggling.

Mason scanned the area as he skirted the street-side wall. A few people eyed him warily, including several U.S. soldiers. He even recognized a couple of MPs from headquarters, but they were too busy flirting with one of the farm girls to notice him. Then, on the opposite side of the building, he spotted Yaakov talking to a woman selling something out of an open steamer trunk.

Mason moved for him, but for whatever reason, Yaakov chose that time to check his surroundings. His face widened in shock when he saw Mason. He yelped and bolted for the middle door connecting the two warehouses. Mason ran for the door to inter-cept Yaakov, pushing through the shoppers and dodging vendors' displays. The commotion attracted the attention of the two MPs, and they blocked Mason's path before Mason could catch Yaakov.

They pulled out their nightsticks, and one MP grabbed his arm. "What's the rush, buddy? You steal something?"

Mason pulled out his badge and yelled, "CID! Back off now, or I'll have you arrested for black market activities."

The MPs released him, but Yaakov had already crossed into the other warehouse. Mason hoped Abrams was on his toes, because at the pace Yaakov was running, they would lose him for sure. Mason burst through the connecting door. There were fewer people in this warehouse, and Mason could clearly see Yaakov hurtling for a back exit with Abrams in hot pursuit.

Despite Yaakov's speed, Abrams had a longer stride, and just as Yaakov breached the exit door, Abrams caught Yaakov by the coat collar. Abrams struggled to reel in a squirming Yaakov, and just as Mason arrived, Yaakov slipped out of his coat and took off again.

Abrams cursed and threw down the coat. Mason blew through the door and spotted Yaakov sprinting across an open field. Hunks of rusted metal and discarded railroad equipment lay like forgotten gravestones, and it was one of those relics buried under snow that became Yaakov's foil. With another yelp, Yaakov tumbled to the ground. This time, Mason got there first and seized Yaakov by both arms as he jumped to his feet.

Yaakov writhed and kicked. "I don't know anything! I didn't do anything. Leave me alone!"

"Calm down," Mason said and pinned Yaakov's arms behind his back. "We're not going to arrest you."

Abrams ran up and stood in front of Yaakov to cut off any further escape. Breathless, Yaakov gave up his struggle.

Between gulps of air, Mason said, "Jesus Christ, Yaakov, we're trying to save your scrawny hide."

"I'm the only one who can save me," Yaakov said as he tried to jerk free.

"Not this time," Mason said.

Abrams said, "They killed Eddie Kantos and his family."

Yaakov stopped his struggling and slowly looked up at Abrams. "His wife and child?"

Abrams nodded.

Yaakov became limp in Mason's hands. "I had nothing to do with that. I swear."

"That's not why we were looking for you," Mason said.

"Then what do you want?"

Mason loosened his grip and turned Yaakov to face him. "Yaakov, we know you were an informant for Agent Winstone."

Yaakov exploded out of Mason's grasp and took off running again.

"God damn it!" Mason yelled as the two investigators chased after him.

Yaakov made fifty yards before Abrams overtook him and tackled him. "He's as slippery as an eel," Abrams said as he held Yaakov to the ground.

Mason came up an instant later and kneeled next to Yaakov. "Sorry, but I have to do this." He handcuffed Yaakov's left hand to his right. He then lifted Yaakov off the ground and planted his feet firmly on the ground. "Are you done?" he asked as he tried in vain to brush away the wet snow and mud with his free hand.

Yaakov nodded.

"All we want to do is ask you a few questions," Mason said.

"Aha! Now you change from saying you want to save me to interrogating me."

"Because you ran away from us like a madman. And I noticed you didn't ask why we would want to save you. Pretty suspicious to me." He pulled Yaakov toward the street. "Come on, we're taking you into headquarters."

"Wait," Yaakov said and dug his heels in the ground. "Ask me what you want, but don't take me there. Please."

Mason stopped. "Winstone was killed because of what he discovered. And I'm positive some of that information came from you."

"Please, I beg you, don't ask me to get involved any further. If it gets back to them that I revealed information... I have more than myself to worry about. My family depends on me."

"Yaakov," Abrams said, "whoever killed all those people is probably after you. Give us their names, any information that can help us. That's the best way to assure your family's safety."

Mason said, "If you willingly withhold information, we'll be forced to take you in for impeding an investigation. You will be held and interrogated—"

"I survived three concentration camps," Yaakov said in anger.

"I was beaten, starved, forced into slave labor, while most of my family was either gassed or shot in mass graves. I endured everything the Nazis did to me. I can resist your interrogations."

"That's not what Mr. Collins meant," Abrams said. "If you're detained, you won't be able to protect your family. The killings will go on, and the murderers will remain free. We're sure you have vital information that could help bring them to justice. We want to help you and your family, but we need *your* help to do that."

"We can protect you," Mason said. "I suggested this before, but we can make sure you're safely transported to the Jewish DP camp at Feldafing. It's far enough away from here to be safe. You'll have shelter, food, and a dozen aid organizations to help you and your family."

"We could rot in a camp for years, waiting in line for a chance to emigrate, with no guarantees it will be Palestine. I do not want my child born on German soil. I will earn the money to bribe the British or pay smugglers to take us. Besides, the men who want me dead can find out which camp I am in and kill me there."

"Meaning American officers who are members of the gang?" Mason said.

"Yes. You see? You cannot protect me."

"Yaakov," Abrams said, "they're after you whether you help us or not. And if we can find you this easily, then how long do you think it's going to take them to do the same? You have a better chance working with us than going it alone. Trust us. Please."

Yaakov thought for a long moment as he trembled from the cold. He'd discarded his coat in the chase and his clothes were soaked from the snow and mud.

"Let's take you somewhere and get you warmed up," Mason said.

Yaakov looked from Mason to Abrams, as he considered the

offer. Finally he nodded and said, "My place. If we are to help and trust each other, it is important to me that you meet my family."

Mason and Abrams led him to their car. Mason took off the handcuffs and had him sit in the passenger's seat with the heat on full blast. Someone had already pilfered Yaakov's coat, but he refused Mason's and Abrams's offer to take one of theirs. On the way, they talked little except for Yaakov giving Mason directions. They drove parallel to the Partenach River then headed south. Finally Yaakov had Mason park the car on Klammstrasse, and then they walked to a small commercial district not far from the city park.

Yaakov led them into an alley. Fifty feet farther on, he opened a reinforced door, which turned out to be the rear entrance to a clothing store selling traditional Bavarian outfits, ironically run by a Jewish couple. Yaakov tipped his hat to the man minding the counter as they passed through the store and exited. They crossed a small street and entered a bookstore. Yaakov tipped his hat again, saying, "Shalom aleichem." They passed through a curtain and mounted a staircase.

Yaakov knocked four times at a door facing the stairs before unlocking it. They entered a small living room with an open kitchen. A pregnant woman in her late twenties sat at a small kitchen table and played with a boy of no more than a year old. Next to her, on another chair, a woman mended a girl's dress. A girl in her late teens read a book to three other children as they sat near the empty fireplace in the living room.

Yaakov introduced the two investigators, then gestured toward the pregnant woman. "This is Helena, my wife." Pointing to the others, he said, "Olga is my brother's new wife, and the boy with Helena is their son. The three young children near the fireplace are Olga's cousins, and the older girl is the daughter of a good friend of mine, who is no longer with us. My brother, Berko,

works as a ski-lift operator for pennies. He is a professor of literature, with a specialty in English literature. He lost his previous
wife in Sobibor. Our parents at Auschwitz. Also aunts, uncles,
cousins. We are all that is left. They all depend on me."

As they all said their hellos, Mason scanned their faces, especially the children. Four of them had already lost their parents, but
were fortunate to have found good people to take them in. But
Yaakov was one wrong step away from dead. And the killers had
displayed no remorse in killing Kantos's wife and child. He
pulled Abrams and Yaakov aside. "Yaakov, you can't stay here."

"I'm not going to a camp. You can't force me."

"Yes, I can. I can arrest you and have your family taken to a
camp."

Abrams looked at Mason as if he'd threatened to kill Yaakov
himself. "You can't."

Mason turned to Abrams. "They can't stay here, and they
can't stay with one of us. It's too cold to go to something like an
empty warehouse or cabin. Unless you have any bright ideas, I
can't think of a place they could go that someone in the army
wouldn't find out where they were. The only option is to give you
all new names with fake identity papers and get everyone to
Feldafing."

"I am not taking my family to this camp!" Yaakov said.

Abrams said to Mason, "Even if Yaakov was willing to go,
where are we going to come up with the fake documents?"

"I've got a good friend in the CIC in Munich. He could do it
in a couple of days."

Yaakov looked back at Helena, who appeared upset at the tone
of the conversation. He then gestured toward a battered dining
table. "We will discuss this later. Let us sit now, and I will tell you
what I can."

Yaakov asked Helena to make coffee, and they settled into
chairs around the table.

"How did you know Kantos?" Abrams asked.

Yaakov looked down and picked at a splinter of wood protruding from the tabletop.

"Yaakov…" Mason said.

"I lied to you gentlemen before. The day of the Steinadler raid. You were both kind to me, and I don't forget acts of kindness." Yaakov succeeded in removing the splinter then rotated it in his fingers. "I *did* work for Kantos… and Giessen."

"Doing what?" Mason asked.

"I was—how you say… an independent businessman, but most of my work was for them. I was a courier—running messages, documents, and correspondence. I made deals with diamond merchants and other black market wholesalers, and… well, some narcotics dealers." He leaned forward and raised his finger. "But I did those things for a good reason. Eddie Kantos said he would help me smuggle my family to Italy, then put me in contact with the Jewish Brigade. In exchange, I would do jobs for him—no questions asked—and earn money to pay him off."

Mason could have lectured Yaakov about making bargains with the devil, but it would serve no purpose. Then a thought came to him. "What if we can find and contact someone from the Jewish Brigade?" he said to Abrams.

"Don't look at me," Abrams said. "Just because I'm Jewish doesn't mean I have some kind of special Jew radar."

"Through Laura. She's been on the smuggling routes and she talked to Kantos about the Brigade. If I know Laura, she's met others like him, or she has contacts herself." He turned to Yaakov. "It might take a couple of days, but I think we can do this."

Yaakov beamed with excitement and grabbed Mason's hand, shaking it wildly. "That would be wonderful."

"But the only way this can work, and you and your family survive this, is if you stay put. You can't go out at all. Not even for food. If there's an emergency, have the bookstore owner go for a doctor. I assume you can trust him, since he's letting you stay here."

"His name is Isaac," Yaakov said, while still holding Mason's hand. "He's a good man." He pumped Mason's hand as he said, "Like you, my friends." He finally released Mason's hand and turned serious. "Now, how did you find out I was an informant for Agent Winstone?"

"When we searched his office, we saw your name written on his chalkboard."

"He promised to keep my name a secret. What was he thinking, writing my name on the chalkboard for all to see?"

Abrams said, "We don't know that Winstone was the one who did it. We feel certain that someone broke into his office, and there's a chance that whoever did that altered the information on the chalkboard to throw us off. It could be that they added your name as a dead end, to throw us off the path, or..." Abrams hesitated.

"Or what?" Yaakov demanded.

Mason answered for Abrams. "Or someone suspected you might be an informant, and hoped that we or the CIC would try to track you down. To see if you talked. Then all it would take is a crooked MP or CIC staff member to pass on that information, and you'd wind up like Kantos."

Yaakov groaned and let his head slump toward the table.

"Yaakov," Mason said, "you have to trust us. We won't divulge your name or even mention you exist."

When Yaakov nodded his agreement, Mason asked, "What did you report to Agent Winstone?"

"Mostly about Kantos's partnership with Herr Giessen and Bachmann."

"Winstone told me he had documents that could prove who is taking over the black markets, but we didn't find them in his home or his office. We suspect someone has taken them and probably destroyed them, but on the off chance they're still hidden, do you have any idea where they might be?"

"I know of no such documents. And I don't think he trusted me enough to tell me where they were hidden."

"Near your name on the chalkboard," Abrams said, "Winstone had written a Herr X and Herr Y. Do you know who they referred to?"

"No. Agent Winstone always spoke of them as X and Y. But..." Yaakov hesitated. "I think he put 'Herr' in front of the letters because he didn't want anyone to know."

"You mean they're Americans. Ones so highly ranked that Winstone didn't want to mention their names?"

Yaakov shrugged. "I believe so, yes."

"Winstone also had a Herr Z up there. Is that Sturmbannführer Volker?"

"I don't know."

"Did you ever meet Herr Z?"

"No. But he is as feared as Kantos. Someone who kills with pleasure, they say."

"And who is 'they'?" Abrams asked.

"Some of the low-ranking men who worked for Giessen."

Mason said, "I asked you about Volker before: He's tall, thin, with gray hair, a pronounced chin, and a pointed nose."

Yaakov shrugged again.

"Remember I said he also smoked Turkish cigarettes, with a gold foil tip."

When that didn't elicit a response, Mason said, "Cigarettes that smelled like burned flowers."

Yaakov's face lit up. "I remember that smell. I've seen a man like you described, but his hair is black. Once in a meeting with Giessen, and once at a house in the mountains. I was making a pickup, and I was taken to the mountain house blindfolded. Very secretive. There were maybe fifteen men. I recognized someone

I've done business with before, a third son of a baron of Silesia, and he was talking to a man like you described."

Mason checked to see if Abrams was writing this down, which he was.

Yaakov added, "There was an American officer there, too."

"You know his name?"

Yaakov shook his head. "I was only there a few minutes, and things felt very tense when I walked in. He was in uniform, which kind of surprised me. A major. Forty, maybe. Just a little taller than you. Not *big*, you know? But strong. Black hair, slicked back with enough grease to lubricate a tank, and big bushy eyebrows."

Mason looked at Abrams. "Schaeffer." He turned back to Yaakov. "Was Agent Winstone aware of Major Schaeffer's association with Herr Volker?"

"I have no idea."

Mason turned to Abrams. "Winstone had information on some untouchable American brass. Could be that Schaeffer's one of them."

"We should put a phone tap on the Casa," Abrams said.

Mason nodded and turned back to Yaakov. "Did you see any other Americans at that meeting in the mountains?"

"No one else was in uniform, and the few minutes I was there, I heard only German. There is one other person I haven't mentioned that Agent Winstone was very curious about." He leaned forward and lowered his voice as if that person had omnipotent powers. "A Lester Abbott. I never met him, but whenever his name came up people grew nervous. The rumors are that he used to be with the OSS."

"Not the CIC?" Abrams asked.

Yaakov thought a moment then shook his head. "I'm sure I heard OSS. Supposedly he turned bad when the OSS was dismantled. That's about all I know."

OSS stood for Office of Strategic Services, the wartime

American clandestine intelligence agency that had been disbanded in September of 1945. The files on the OSS missions and the people involved were sealed to all but those with the highest clearance levels, though stories were emerging of legendary exploits, and men and women of extraordinary bravery. But Mason had also heard his commanders in G-2 speak of the OSS in derogatory terms, considering it a rogue organization, with the higher ranks composed of Wall Street lawyers and bankers, and Ivy League academics, answerable only to the Joint Chiefs of Staff. A cabal of spooks, they said, who often exceeded their mandate and carried out unauthorized assassinations and sabotage and God knows what else beyond the eyes of army authorities. Mason had taken these rumors with a grain of salt, as the G2 was a direct rival of the OSS. And, it being a secret organization, Mason could confirm none of it, but he did know they were highly trained and, in the case of one gone bad, extremely dangerous.

Mason asked, "You have no idea what Abbott looks like, or where we might find him?"

Yaakov shook his head. "I've never seen him."

"How about the Casa Carioca?" Mason asked. "Do you know if it's being used as a black market base of operations?"

"All I know is that Agent Winstone was looking hard at the Casa Carioca, but security around that place is very tight. Hilda tried to get in deeper, but failed, or was killed before she could succeed."

Mason sat back, feeling overwhelmed, and yet he suspected that Yaakov's information was only the tip of the iceberg.

"How are we going to approach the American officers?" Abrams asked. "We have nothing on them except the word of an informant." He turned to Yaakov. "No offense."

"None taken."

"Our only leverage, right now, is going after the Germans,"

Mason said. "See if threats of prison can turn one of them." He turned back to Yaakov. "Anything else?"

Yaakov shook his head. "Every one of my sources is now dead."

"I want you to write down every German gang member you can think of: a description, an address, his function, any crimes. Even if you have no direct knowledge. If you just overheard something, innuendos, you didn't like his face. Write it all down."

"Are we going to try and bring them all in?" Abrams asked.

"As many as we can track down in the next few hours. We'll start with Willy Laufs."

Abrams whistled long and low. "We're going to have half the town wanting our hides."

"That's the idea."

18

Like pilot fish around a shark, four German lawyers followed Mason's every step. Whittman, a particularly tenacious lawyer, tried to cut Mason off. "Investigator Collins, you cannot hold my client—our clients—without specific charges."

The other three lawyers nodded in agreement. Mason ignored their protests and moved around Whittman to intercept a team of MPs that had picked up another German gangster.

One of the MPs said, "Hermann Auerbach, racketeering, suspected kidnapping, grand larceny."

"Put him in the room and get a statement," Mason said.

The MPs led Auerbach away, and Mason continued down the hallway in the main administrative building at the Sheridan barracks. The lawyers tried to keep pace, their scuffling footsteps and collective murmuring echoing off the hard surfaces of the corridor.

"Hermann Auerbach is also my client," Whittman said. "You can't do this."

"Military authority supersedes civil law in this case. He is to be detained for questioning, like all the others. If and when I am satisfied with his cooperation, he will be released into the hands of the German police. What they do with him and his pals after that is up to them."

Mason strode into a conference room that had been converted into a holding area, where MPs asked the arrestees preliminary questions before processing them and putting them into holding cells. He had recruited a dozen MPs to pick up the persons of dubious character on Yaakov's list, and another five to perform the preliminary interviews. Some of the arrestees yelled and stomped their feet in protest. In one corner Abrams had Willy Laufs, the person Laura had named in connection with Kantos. He looked surprisingly confident despite his recent ordeal and arrest. Mason would let Abrams handle Laufs for now. Abrams's softer approach could sometimes get results, plus he didn't want to get close to Laufs until he was sure he could keep his temper in check.

Willy Laufs's residential address hadn't appeared in any telephone directory, an official register, or even a police rap sheet, for that matter, but anyone in the know in the world of sleaze could point out Laufs's notorious compound, and generally without a moment's hesitation. It therefore required little effort on Mason and Abrams's part to discover its whereabouts. It was, in fact, not far from Winstone's villa, in the same neighborhood of walled estates on vast parcels of land. Of those who knew of its existence none would ever admit to entering the compound, let alone partaking of Laufs's repugnant offerings.

Willy had become a specialist in procuring teenaged and younger prostitutes of both sexes for wealthy clients who shared his appetites. He would pose as a priest and troll the ruins of German towns for desperate and starving orphans, recruiting them with a promise of food, shelter, and God's grace. These were the rumors, of course, as no one would admit to firsthand knowledge. Willy's brothels had been raided several times in the last nine months, and at various locations, but each time he'd been tipped off, and the raids uncovered nothing. Willy would then move on to another location, and the villa Mason's team had raided happened to be his latest and most opulent... at least according to the handful of locals in the flesh trade that Mason and Abrams had interviewed over the past couple of hours.

This sordid dossier had taken Mason and Abrams about two hours to glean from a handful of locals in the flesh trade. Mason had taken no chances of a tip-off this time, and they went into Willy's compound swift and furious with one M20 armored car to smash open the gates, and a squad of handpicked men to subdue the bodyguards. A dozen girls and boys from ten to sixteen had been liberated from forced prostitution. They had arrested three clients of high repute and deep pockets. And Willy himself had been caught in the act with a fourteen-year-old girl. It had taken three men, including a traumatized Abrams, to pull Mason off Willy before he could beat Willy to a pulp.

It had taken another three hours to round up the other thirty-odd men who were now in the conference room, all black marketers, gang members, and smugglers, and now it was close to ten P.M. Mason turned to look for the coffeepot and noticed he'd picked up a fifth lawyer. They burst into a renewed frenzy of protests. Mason held up his hands. "Gentlemen, please. You're not supposed to be in here. You're now interfering with an official investigation and subject to arrest. Any one of you could be a lucky guest of our fine facilities, with all the hospitality the American military can offer."

The lawyers fell silent, and Mason signaled two MPs to step forward. "These nice officers will escort you out. You can file your complaints with them."

The protests continued as the two MPs herded them toward the exit.

Abrams joined Mason. "Laufs isn't talking. Says he's no rat."

"He should have just said he doesn't know. Claiming he's no rat means he knows but isn't saying. We'll have a go at him after he spends a night in a cell with a few inmates who know he's a pedophile."

Abrams indicated the rest of the room. "I bet most of these guys won't give up a thing. They've all managed to beat raps before, and we've got nothing concrete to pin on them."

"One or two might sing if they see it's to their advantage. Besides, this little operation is to smoke out the bigger players. We'll see who blunders into our net." Mason then nodded toward the door. "And ladies and gentlemen, we have our first contestant."

They both watched Densmore enter and look around the room in astonishment. He zeroed in on Mason. "What the hell is going on?"

"Just taking a census of Garmisch's gangster community."

"Have you got anything on them?"

"No," Mason said. He wasn't about to tell Densmore about Yaakov's list.

"You're supposed to clear this kind of operation with me."

"I went to Gamin. All these men and women are involved in the Communist plot to steal army office supplies."

Densmore fell quiet as he studied Mason. He had never perfected the art of the poker face, and Mason could tell he was processing all this, trying to determine Mason's strategy. There was, however, something in his expression that Mason hadn't seen before—sincerity.

Densmore said, "I'd give you grief for going over my head on this, but you'd just ignore it."

"What do you want?"

Densmore seemed to have difficulty forming his words. "I've been thinking about what you've said: that we've got a turf war on our hands."

"And?"

"After looking at the murders in Kantos's house, the wife and son... That was a professional hit job."

"The real question is, do you now believe that Winstone and Hilda Schmidt were hit by the same group?"

Densmore glanced around at nothing while his hands fidgeted in his pockets. "Look, the methods are not the same, but if—I'm just saying if—you set aside the method of murder and consider the idea that these guys are pros, then, yeah, I can see the possibility."

"Then there's the three German gang leaders. Same execution-style murders, probably with silencers, a quick in and out, without anyone seeing. And think about this: They had to know of an imminent bust at the Steinadler, and know to wait out back and let Giessen, Bachmann, and Plöbsch come to them."

"Oh, come on. Now you're reaching."

"Then you're not going to like the next part. I believe that an ex-OSS agent and an American major managing the Casa Carioca are in league with some ex-SS officers in taking over the black market operations in this town—hell, this whole area. And my bet is there are more behind them. In fact, I was betting you were getting kickbacks to cover it all up."

Densmore's face twisted in anger. "I ought to break your neck."

"I wouldn't recommend trying."

"I don't know what you're playing at here, but I'm going to make a point to not give a damn."

Mason decided against saying any more. He'd let Densmore dangle a bit from the hook.

Densmore said, "Word of your antics has gotten to the provost marshal of Bavaria, Colonel Walton. He's making noise about getting you out of Germany."

"Yeah, Colonel Walton's threatened me before, back when I

worked under him in Munich. Said he was going to bust me down to private and transfer me to a border patrol in the mountains. He likes to blow a lot of hot air."

"Well, he blew it our way, because Colonel Udahl is ordering you to his office. I'm not expending energy to keep you here out of the goodness of my heart. I need an experienced investigator. You go, and all that's left of my CID detachment are kids still wet behind the ears. I'm asking you as a fellow cop, don't screw this up any more than you already have. Okay?"

Densmore walked away, and Abrams asked, "What do you think? Did we net one?"

"I don't know. First he's trying to throw a monkey wrench into this case, and the next minute he's just trying to save his skin. He's afraid of something, and he knows more than he's letting on."

"I don't see him having the ambition or imagination of a big player," Abrams said.

Mason nodded as he considered that. "Continue to supervise here. Try to put on some pressure. One of them might talk. I'll go see what the colonel has up his sleeve."

"You think *he's* slipped into our net?"

Mason shook his head. "He's one of the good guys." He started to go, then turned back to Abrams. "At least, I think he is."

COLONEL UDAHL'S office was on the top floor of the Rathaus. As a regional military governor, Udahl had been awarded the former mayor's office, though it was said that he rarely occupied said office. Instead, he was often absent, touring his domain, attending numerous ceremonies and political forums. A real hands-on kind of man, some said, while others claimed that "his highness" left the running of his kingdom to others while enjoying the royal perks of the job.

Colonel Udahl's sergeant secretary snapped to when Mason entered Udahl's outer office. "I'll let the general know you're here."

The colonel's outer office was meant to impress visitors. Framed photographs filled the walls, all of the colonel, of course: several with the colonel in African hunting gear kneeling before a dead lion or a rhinoceros with his high-powered rifle; the colonel reading a map with attentive staff; the colonel in uniform as the governor inspecting troops in Munich or speaking at a podium to a large group of German businessmen; the colonel shaking hands with the man himself—Ike. Curiously, none from the war. Then, in one corner, completely incongruous with the rest of the décor, hung an intricately carved Black Forest cuckoo clock. The clock reminded Mason of a similar one belonging to the depraved killer he'd hunted in Munich. The memory almost made him shudder.

The sergeant came out again and announced as if admitting someone to the king's court, "The colonel will see you now."

Mason entered a large office with wide windows overlooking the town and the inky black silhouette of the mountains. A sofa and chairs—austere considering the colonel's reputed champagne taste—sat at one end, with a boat-sized desk at the other. Colonel Udahl and, to Mason's surprise, General Pritchard, sat enjoying cigars in the high-backed chairs like two men at a gentlemen's club discussing the stock market or world domination.

Mason had expected a sharp reprimand for turning the town upside down in arresting the German suspects, the excessive use of valuable MP manpower, or bamboozling Major Gamin. Instead, Udahl offered him a cigar, which Mason declined. They invited him to sit. He declined that as well, thinking it bizarre to deliver a report about the five murders at the Kantos house, including a child, as if recounting an amusing story with a couple of the old boys. They insisted, so he sat in a chair facing Udahl, still refusing the cigar. Pritchard took the honorary spot on the sofa.

"You wanted to see me, sirs?" Mason asked once he'd settled into the plush sofa cushions.

Pritchard gave him a serious look. "General Clay has expressed great interest in your investigation."

"General Clay?" Mason said, stunned. As the deputy military governor of Germany's American zone of occupation, General Clay was the second most powerful American in the country.

Pritchard arched an accusatory eyebrow. "Someone sent him copies of your daily reports."

"My... I don't get it. Who would do that, and why?"

"We were wondering the same thing," Udahl said. "In fact, we suspected you, knowing your reputation for ignoring the chain of command."

Mason trolled through the handful of people familiar with the case, but he couldn't think of who would have done such a thing, unless... Gamin, the old, crafty buzzard, knew more about what was happening around him than he let on.

"You haven't answered us, Mr. Collins," Pritchard said.

"It wasn't me, and I have no idea who would."

Pritchard said, "Considering General Clay's acute interest, I thought it prudent to come down here myself and converse with Colonel Udahl about the situation. As you know, I've been interested in your case from the start, but now that General Clay is concerned, I am doubly so. In fact, I'm so interested that I halted the shipment of Agent Winstone's remains back to the States and ordered an immediate autopsy." He looked directly into Mason's eyes. "They found the missing parts of Hilda Schmidt's face." He paused. "They were in Agent Winstone's esophagus and stomach. Unchewed. In fact, by the lacerations and swelling in the back of his mouth and throat, it's clear that he was forced to swallow them."

A moment of silence passed. Mason tried to push away the images of those last horrible moments in Winstone's and Hilda's lives.

Udahl broke the silence. "Obviously Agent Winstone was murdered, and we want you to do everything in your power to find his killers. We're behind you all the way."

Pritchard said, "Because we have copies of you reports sent to General Clay, we're up to speed on your investigation."

"These recent arrests of Germans," Udahl said, "I assume you have something on these men to keep them in custody."

"Nothing specific, but they're all known offenders. Plus, all of them were identified by a reliable informant. And, please, sirs, don't ask me to tell you who—"

"Is it Adelle Holtz?" Udahl asked.

That stopped Mason cold.

"She was with you the evening of Winstone's death, was she not?"

"Yes…"

"What do you personally know about Fräulein Holtz?"

"I haven't seen her since that night," Mason said, lying instinctively, though unsure why.

"Well, if you had any plans to do so, you should know her background," Udahl said as he reached around the chair and plucked a file off a small table. He handed it to Pritchard, who opened the file and began to read:

"Adelle Katrina Holtz, a.k.a. Elizabeth Hertz, a.k.a. Katrina Hirsch. To her credit, she was kicked out of the girls' version of the Hitler Youth, but then she married an SS lieutenant. After his death she was sent to a labor camp. She got out of that by becoming the mistress of a particularly fervent Nazi thug, the deputy gauleiter of Salzburg, Josef Klee. That is, until she was caught with the man's personal valet. After the war, she was arrested in Munich for black marketeering and jailed for four months. She came to Garmisch in September of last year."

The idea that Adelle had been intimate with a high-placed Nazi shocked and disappointed Mason. It seemed in this town, lies and deceptions were everyone's game. "One of my main suspects is a Frieder Kessel. He's the assistant manager at the Casa Carioca. Do you have anything on him?"

Pritchard set down Adelle's file and looked to Udahl, who turned and pulled out another folder from his short stack. "Hauptsturmführer Frieder Kessel, the Ninth SS Panzer Division, awarded the gold German Cross and Knight's Cross. He was captured in Austria and held for six months. He's clean as far as war crimes go—unless you count him being a member of the SS. Nothing to indicate he's taken up a life of crime."

"Do you have any other suspects?" Pritchard asked.

"I don't have concrete evidence linking anyone, yet," Mason said, "but I'm looking at Kessel and a Major Schaeffer running criminal operations out of the Casa Carioca—"

"The Casa Carioca?" Udahl said. "Impossible. Do you realize how many of the army's top brass and MG officials go in and out of there? It's sponsored by, and for, the U.S. Army. It's like saying that because there are a few crooked congressmen, Congress is a criminal base of operations."

"I tend to agree with that idea, but that's another subject."

"Investigate whom you like, but don't involve the club."

"I'm sure Mr. Collins can be discreet," Pritchard said and turned back to Mason. "Investigate whom and where the case calls for. We'll not stand in your way." He turned to Udahl. "Why don't we show Mr. Collins what we have on Major Schaeffer?"

Udahl reached for Schaeffer's folder. "This file is classified. You will not share this information with anyone, refer to it in written reports, or use it as evidence without General Pritchard's or my permission. Is that understood?"

When Mason nodded, and Udahl continued, "Major Frederick Walter Schaeffer, born in Berlin in 1905. Emigrated to England in 1913, then to the U.S. in 1920. Joined the army in '26. In 1940 he trained with the British Special Operations Executive in Canada, and then joined the OSS two years later. He participated in several operations behind enemy lines in France, Germany, and Czechoslovakia, employing anti-Nazi Germans and escaped Polish and Russian POWs in demolition, sabotage, and targeted assassinations. Some of his methods are reported to have been excessive, even cruel. He was accused of theft and extortion, kidnapping and murder, but nothing was ever corroborated. However, he was such a successful operative that these allegations were dismissed, and he was awarded the Silver Star and Legion of Merit."

Udahl looked up from the file. "You'd better have more than hunches and innuendo to go after this man."

Mason said nothing, though he thought plenty: The man was an expert in espionage, sabotage, and assassinations, and he recruited ex-POW Poles. Skills he had carried out in the service of his country also made him formidable and dangerous in times of peace.

"As a matter of fact," Udahl continued, "General Clay is very concerned about you mentioning in your reports that you suspect high-ranking officers are involved in this crime spree. I want to emphasize again, if it looks like you're pushing against the army hierarchy, we want to be able to show them irrefutable evidence as to why. You run everything by me or General Pritchard. Everything. Is that clear?"

"Yes, sir," Mason said and pointed to the stack of files. "I don't suppose you have a file on an Sturmbannführer Ernst Volker, do you? An ex-Gestapo interrogator and a war criminal?"

Udahl shook his head. "I don't recognize that name."

"Is he one of your suspects?" Pritchard asked.

Mason told them about his suspicion that Volker had identified him at the Steinadler, and he recounted Volker's brutal interrogation techniques during the war. "He's associated somehow with this gang turf war. My informant puts Volker and Schaeffer together on one occasion." Before either of them could voice another warning about hunches, Mason asked, "What about a Lester Abbott? Possibly ex-OSS, as well?"

Pritchard looked at Udahl. Something passed between them. Udahl asked, "What do you have on him?"

"His name keeps coming up in my investigations. But no one can give me a description or tell me where I might find him."

"We'll check out his name and get back to you," Pritchard said.

"Another classified file?"

"I assume you have no evidence linking him, either," Udahl said.

"I find it interesting that both Schaeffer and Abbott were OSS."

"Because they were in the same organization does not make them guilty by association. The same could be said about you and Agent Winstone being in G2 together."

"Is there some question as to my involvement in Winstone's murder?"

Pritchard glanced at Udahl with a look of irritation. "I think we can move on. Have you made any progress in determining where Winstone might have hid his secret files?"

Mason shook his head. "A search of his office and safe didn't turn up anything."

"What about your informant? Could he yield more information?"

"I'm working on it," Mason said with a look that said he would say no more.

Udahl looked at Pritchard, who shook his head.

"All right, Mr. Collins," Udahl said. "That's all for now."

They stood and shook hands.

"Be sure to keep us informed," Pritchard said. "And if you need help plowing through the army's red tape, come to us. As we've said, General Clay has taken a keen interest in this case. Therefore, *we've* taken a keen interest, so don't disappoint us."

19

Mason lit a cigarette as he moved down the sidewalk on Hauptstrasse. It was after eleven P.M., but the later hour had done nothing to thin out the crowd of revelers. People still packed the bars and restaurants, or were spilled out onto the sidewalks, and had now spent hours consuming ample quantities of alcohol. Couples or groups of soldiers staggered along, laughing or yelling over each other in drunken competition.

Before Mason returned to the chaos at the Sheridan barracks, he needed time to think. Learning about Adelle's affair with a Nazi gauleiter weighed on him, but what occupied his mind more was that something puzzled him about the meeting with Pritchard and Udahl. It aggravated him like a buzzing around his ear. Usually he could pick it out right away, but not this time. Maybe he was slipping. Maybe it was because he had the unnerving feeling everyone had been being playing him for a sap—Winstone, Adelle, Densmore, Kessel... possibly even Gamin and Udahl—and being played had dulled his senses.

Mason came abruptly out of his thoughts when he had to dodge two army corporals and their German dates stumbling down the sidewalk and oblivious to their surroundings. One couple was so inebriated that they made a dash across the street in front of a moving car. The car screeched to a halt, the sound making Mason turn.

That was when he saw the car's backseat window roll down just far enough for someone to stick out the barrel of a Thompson submachine gun. Aimed directly at him.

Mason threw himself behind a parked car just as the machine gun fired. Bullets shattered the concrete wall where he'd been standing a split second earlier. The deadly spray followed his leap for cover. Bullets slammed into the car's metal body and blew out windows.

Mason lay flat against the car's rear wheel, curling his body for precious cover. Fragments of glass showered down. He could hear bullets, spent from piercing the car's body, ricochet around the vehicle's interior. What felt like minutes had lasted seven seconds. Then the engine roared, and the shooter's car sped down the street.

Mason leapt to his feet and pulled out his .45. He fired at the car's back window. The window exploded inward, but the car continued on and disappeared.

Just above the ringing in his ears, he heard a woman screaming, people yelling as they emerged from the various bars and nightclubs.

He leaned against the car and noticed his gun hand shaking.

THE SKATING SHOW was in full swing when Mason blew past the Casa Carioca's maitre d'. The man sputtered protests, but they were quickly drowned out by the band music. Mason wove through the standing-room-only crowd and between the tables. The waiters spotted him and stopped in their tracks. One of them put his tray down and tried to intercept him, but Mason held up his CID badge with such violence that the waiter hesitated.

Weissenegger, the boxer-turned-bodyguard, met him at the base of the stairs.

"Army business," Mason said. "I don't have a quarrel with you. Step out of the way, or I *will* arrest you."

Weissenegger glared at Mason as he stepped aside. Mason bounded up the stairs. When he reached the landing, he looked back. None of the waiters or muscle had followed him, and the patrons were all paying attention to their drinks, their dates, or the show. Mason turned and entered the hallway. Kessel and Boris, his bodyguard, came out of Kessel's office and stood in the middle of the hallway as if to block Mason from going any farther.

"You look upset, Mr. Collins," Kessel said.

Mason was about to respond when he saw two bodyguards flanking either side of a door at the end of the hallway. He looked back at Kessel and noticed the man looked uneasy and lacked his previous air of superiority. His boss was in the house.

Kessel shifted to block Mason's view and said, "Why don't we discuss things in my office?"

Mason pushed Kessel aside and charged down the hallway, but a moment later two baseball mitts for hands grabbed him from behind and pushed him against the wall. Boris ignored Kessel's orders to release Mason. Mason twirled, using his left arm to break the man's tenuous hold. But Boris was quick and grabbed Mason by the throat.

With the heel of his boot, Mason thrust his foot down on the tender bones of Boris's foot. The pain must have been excruciating, and usually it crippled a man, but Boris still took a swing at Mason. The swing lacked power and speed, and Mason deflected the blow. At the same instant, Mason jabbed Boris in the throat with rigid fingers, just above the hyoid bone. Boris's eyes popped wide. His hands grabbed his own paralyzed throat, and he staggered backward. His face turned red as he strained to take in air.

Mason knew the man would recover… eventually. He turned his back on Kessel and burst through the last door without knocking.

Schaeffer sat at his desk with his feet up and a drink in his hand. Mason's already explosive rage kicked up to full-blown fury when he saw the other man, sitting in a high-backed, red velvet chair like a king on a throne—Ernst Volker, ex-Gestapo major and torturer-in-chief.

Mason balled his fists. In addition to his fury, he felt an instinctual combination of repulsion and fear. He did everything he could to resist charging the man and crushing his neck. "You!" Mason said to Volker.

"We meet again, Herr Collins," Volker said.

"Shut up and stay where you are. I'll arrest you as soon as I'm done with Schaeffer."

"Relax, investigator," Schaeffer said. "I can vouch for him. Have a seat, and we'll talk."

Mason kicked the door closed, slamming it in the faces of Kessel's muscle. "Waving his falsified denazification papers at me won't work this time. I can testify that he tortured U.S. soldiers."

"You're addressing a superior officer," Schaeffer said calmly. "You will conduct yourself accordingly. You cannot burst into my office, acting like a crazed man, and threaten a civilian. Sit down and state your case, or I will have you arrested for insubordination."

"Your boys just shot at me. I don't like being shot at."

"Those weren't *my boys*, as you put—"

"Bullshit. You're the only operator with enough juice to order a hit on a CID investigator out in the open. And thanks to your hit squad, there aren't too many operators left."

"If I wanted you dead, I wouldn't have done it in such a clumsy fashion. Maybe whoever it was, simply wanted to warn you to back off of your investigation."

"You'd have to know the details of the shooting to think it was botched." Mason stepped forward. "I knew arresting every German racketeer in town would flush out the leaders. I know you and Kessel—and this scumbag"—Mason pointed to Volker—"are behind the murders of Agent John Winstone, Hilda Schmidt, Kantos and his family, and the German gang leaders."

"Those are very serious charges," Schaeffer said. "Do you have any proof?"

Mason leaned on Schaeffer's desk. "I'll get the proof and bring you down. Your warning didn't work. I won't stop. And if you do manage to stop me, then there are plenty of people informed of my investigation that'll be coming after you. You try to harm anyone to get to me, and *I'll* be coming for you." Mason straightened and removed his .45. He turned to Volker. "Get up."

Schaeffer stood up and picked up a document conveniently placed on his desk as if anticipating this confrontation. "This document states that Herr Volker was cleared by the XII Corps CIC detachment's commanding officer, Colonel Roberts. He has been officially sanctioned, and he's a valuable asset to the CIC. If you have a problem with Herr Volker, you'd better take that up with the colonel."

"I will," Mason said. "They might like to know what this man did in the service of the Third Reich." He waved his pistol for Volker to move for the door.

Volker obeyed. "Thank you, Herr Schaeffer, for your defense, but Herr Collins and I have some catching up to do. Haven't we? How you gave me vital troop positions and movements that aided us in capturing entire regiments in the Ardennes. I didn't torture him, as Herr Collins alleges. He gave it up willingly. I'm sure whoever interrogates me will be interested to hear what I have to say."

Volker's perfect English and soft baritone voice brought back those days of torture: the beatings, the electrocutions, the plunges into tubs of ice water, the sleep deprivation. Mason had never understood the idiom "seeing red with rage," because his experience of it was like gazing into a black tunnel. Everything around him disappeared except his tormentor's face.

It was only after Volker's head snapped back and he crumpled to the floor him, that Mason realized he'd given Volker a left cross to the jaw. Mason lunged, while vaguely aware of Schaeffer yelling for his guards. He had just enough time to bring his fist back to strike again when four strong hands pinned him and pulled him away. He struggled, but the men held him fast.

Schaeffer calmly walked up to Mason and leaned in. "You've got nothing," he said, elongating the last word to drive the point home. He slowly put his hand on Mason's gun. "Let me holster this for you before you shoot someone and get into more trouble than you already are."

Mason tried to free himself. No use. He knew he had to calm down and take the humiliation. He'd make up for it soon enough. He let Schaeffer take his gun. Schaeffer put on the safety and holstered it. He looked at Volker and tilted his head toward the door. Volker hurried out of the office.

Schaeffer turned back to Mason. "While you've been checking up on me, I've done the same on you. You have some reputation, investigator. I'm betting no one will mourn your loss. No one. Now, anything that happens next in here, it will be your word against a decorated officer's."

Without warning, Schaeffer gut-punched Mason, the fiery blast of agony forcing Mason to slump helplessly in the men's arms. He struggled to catch his breath.

Schaeffer grabbed Mason's hair and yanked upward. He put

his face in Mason's. "You come busting in here, gun drawn, and threatening me. You screwed up. I could have you put in the stockade for years. Now, unless you have concrete evidence, which I'm sure you never will, then I must insist you never step foot in this club again."

Mason summoned all the willpower he could muster to control his breathing and stare into Schaeffer's eyes. "Remember: You hurt anyone I know, and I'm coming after you."

The two men lifted Mason by the shoulders and dragged him out the door. Kessel stood at his office door and watched as the men pulled him along the hallway. Kessel held up his hand for the men to stop.

He said to Mason, "Are you able to walk out of here on your own? I don't want you upsetting the patrons."

Schaeffer was right: Mason knew he had nothing to pin on any of them—for the moment. Plus, he'd let his temper get the best of him and blown military and CID protocol. He had little choice but to make a tactical retreat. He nodded to Kessel. His diaphragm worked again, but he wasn't so sure about his legs. The men released Mason on Kessel's gesture. It took Mason a moment to steady himself. Standing upright made his whole torso ache, but he managed. He walked carefully down the stairs. One of the three bodyguards preceded him, partly to make sure he didn't cascade down the steps. As Mason crossed through the club, he caught sight of someone and nearly stumbled into the escort.

Laura sat at one of the tables with her boyfriend, Richard. Richard's attention was on the show, but Laura's eyes flicked wide when she saw Mason and she froze in mid-bite. Mason subtly shook his head as he passed her table. She understood the silent warning: She said nothing and remembered to chew.

20

Outside the club, the cold night air felt good on his face. It did nothing for the cramping in his gut—or his mind whirling with questions about Laura's sanity. His stomach heaved, but only a little bile and blood came up. He was sure he'd be peeing blood for a couple of days. He waited until he was deep in the Casa parking lot before spitting out the sour-metallic taste in his mouth. That was when he noticed Abrams leaning against a car.

Abrams threw down his cigarette and met Mason. "What happened in there?"

"I found Schaeffer. We had a little chat."

"Mason!"

Mason looked back and saw Laura taking quick steps across the lot. He looked beyond her, back to the club, but no one looked on. At least she had waited until deep in the parking lot to call out his name.

"Laura, what the hell?"

Laura caught up to them, her hard breathing creating puffs of condensation in the cold air. Mason took off his coat, though the movement made his stomach cramp. With some effort, he threw the coat over her shoulders.

"Are you hurt?" Laura asked.

"I knew I shouldn't have eaten the sauerkraut."

Laura let him know she didn't think that was funny. Another cramp made Mason lean forward.

"Lean on me," Abrams said. "We'll get you home."

Abrams put his shoulder under Mason's armpit and took some of his weight. Laura took his other arm. Mason let them help though he could have made the last few steps on his own.

"Must have been an interesting conversation," Abrams said.

"He showed his hand."

"Showed his hand, then buried it in your gut?"

Mason chuckled then recoiled from a spasm of pain. "That's about the size of it."

Laura helped him into the passenger's seat and slipped into the backseat. Abrams got behind the wheel, started up the car, and turned on the heat.

Mason turned in his seat to look at Laura. "I told you to stay out of sight, and you come to the worst place of all."

"I wanted to check out the club for myself. No one knows who I am."

"Does Ricky have any idea what you're up to?"

"What does that have to do with anything?"

"So, no. Poor sap doesn't know what he's in for: you chasing danger like a dog chasing cars."

"I came out here to see if you were okay, not to be insulted."

Mason turned to Abrams. "Tell her how ruthless these guys are."

"I'm not getting into the middle of a domestic dispute," Abrams said.

That quieted both of them.

"There's definitely something shady going on in there," Laura finally said. "Feels more like a Chicago mob hangout than an army nightclub. And, no, before you ask, I didn't talk to any of the employees. I simply observed. I see what you mean about the waitstaff. And the manager circulated through the crowd, shaking hands like a crooked politician. Then a group of colonels and generals went upstairs to the back offices."

"Kessel and Schaeffer's clubhouse of iniquity," Mason said.

Abrams said, "I've been trying to dig deeper about how the club operates, where the money comes from, where it goes, but I hit a brick wall every time."

"It's a neat little setup, that's for sure," Laura said. "And right under the army's nose."

"You should press charges," Abrams said to Mason. "An officer striking a CID investigator will land him in the stockade."

"He can produce enough witnesses to refute that claim."

Abrams shook his head. "I should have come along."

"I heard about the machine gun fire near the Rathaus," Laura said. "Was that you?"

"It was *for* me. This hit squad is picking off anyone with the slightest association with Winstone. At some point I'm sure Abrams here and I will be next on the list. That's why you need to get home and stay there."

"You've got to find those missing documents," Laura said. "If what Winstone told you is true, that should bust the whole thing wide open."

"We've searched Winstone's villa," Abrams said. "We've searched his office, his safe...."

"Well, search harder. You usually don't give up so easily."

Mason said, "Now, wait a minute...."

"I'd better get back," Laura said and pulled off Mason's coat. She opened the door then turned back. "And if either of you ever needs a safe place, you can always stay a few days with Richard and me."

Abrams thanked her. Mason said nothing, seeing no point in repeating why he considered that a really bad idea. They watched Laura until she made it safely back into the club. Mason felt another cramp coming on and slumped in the seat.

"Did you come by car?" Abrams asked.

"I wanted to rip Schaeffer's skull off, not wander around looking for a car."

"Why don't I drop you off?" Abrams said.

Mason nodded. Abrams pulled the car out of the parking lot, and they drove in silence for a while.

"I screwed up in there," Mason said as he stared out the side window. "I lost my temper. But I did confirm two things: Schaeffer's guilty as hell, and he's partnered up with none other than our mysterious Herr Z—ex-Gestapo major, Ernst Volker."

"The guy who tortured you during the war?"

Mason nodded. "I knew it when I smelled the Turkish tobacco at the Steinadler."

"Let's arrest him, then."

"First we have to find him, then convince the CIC it was a mistake to clear him of war crimes."

Mason filled Abrams in on what he'd learned from the meeting with Udahl and Pritchard: the autopsy confirming Winstone's murder, and Schaeffer's background. That not only was the mysterious Abbott ex-OSS, but Schaeffer was as well. He left out the part about Adelle's past. Then he briefed Abrams more fully on what had happened in Schaeffer's office. "Kantos was SOE, Schaeffer and Abbott OSS—could be some kind of connection. A brotherhood of trained saboteurs and assassins."

"Maybe we should follow up on the OSS lead. There could be other ex-OSS agents in league with Schaeffer's gang."

"Scary thought," Mason said, more to himself. "We'll see what we can dig up."

Abrams parked the car in front of Mason's house and started

to get out. Mason put his hand on Abrams's arm. "Thanks, but I can take it from here. And I was thinking... it might be best if you lay off the case. At least the fieldwork. They might decide to go gunning for you."

"I'm not going to sit this out. You can't ask me to do that. Besides, I'm already in too deep for them to ignore me."

"Back in Munich, I nearly lost my last partner. I don't want it to happen again."

"Partners don't leave their partner's ass hanging out in the wind."

Mason nodded, accepting the premise, but hoped he wouldn't regret it. He knew he'd blame himself if something happened to another partner, another friend. He exited the car and watched Abrams drive away.

After making a visual sweep of the area, he mounted the porch steps, unlocked the door and pushed it open until it was flat against the wall. The house was dark and silent. He pulled out his .45 and took one step into the living room. While watching for movement in the darkness, he flicked on a light switch, which illuminated a floor lamp.

If someone wanted to take a shot at me, they would have done it by now.... "Adelle?"

He waited. "Adelle, it's me. Mason."

He heard a rustling noise coming from the first bedroom off the hallway. Then a hand wrapped around the doorframe, followed by Adelle peering into the living room. She moaned in relief and ran to Mason, burying her face in his chest.

"I didn't hear from you for so long, I..." Adelle said.

Mason didn't return the hug. "You thought I'd been killed?"

Adelle nodded against his chest. "Or in the hospital."

Mason took her arms and broke the embrace. "All the reasons I could have been late, and you assumed I'd been gunned down?"

Adelle stepped back. "Why does that sound strange? Look at

how many people have already been killed." She backed away to get more distance from him. "You make it sound like I knew something was going to happen. When are you going to stop being a cop for more than thirty seconds? You suspect everyone is guilty."

"I do when I find out they've been lying. For instance, that sob story you told me about being arrested after your husband's death and put in a labor camp. But you left out that you were released because you were screwing a high-ranking Nazi gauleiter."

"I was twenty-two. I'd just lost my husband and father-in-law. I'd lost all hope and was facing death in a prison camp. I did what I had to do. I took a lover who saved me from prison. Go ahead, judge me. I'm a Nazi-loving tramp who doesn't deserve a chance."

Perhaps she was right, or perhaps Mason simply lacked the energy to continue. He'd expended every ounce of energy he had and felt an overwhelming need to sit. He shuffled over to the sofa and dropped onto the cushions. The onset of a raging headache reminded him that he hadn't eaten in twelve hours. He rubbed his forehead then noticed Adelle sitting in a chair opposite. She looked genuinely hurt, and he regretted pushing her so hard, but he wasn't ready to apologize. Too many people had lied to him, and, sadly, Adelle was at the top of the list.

Mason gave her a tired smile. "I forgot to bring more food," he said and resumed rubbing his forehead. "Is there anything left to eat?"

That was the best he could do in declaring his desire for her to stay.

Adelle seemed to accept this, and Mason admired her for it. She rose from the chair. "We have eggs and bread. Breakfast okay?"

Mason nodded and rested his head on the cushion back. He

stared up at the cracks in the ceiling as he thought. His headache flared when he thought about nearly having Volker in his grasp after all this time, only to lose him because of his temper. And there had to be a way to get to Schaeffer. Pritchard had warned him that he'd need hard evidence to go after a decorated major. The army protected their own, especially officers, and a war hero at that. Not to mention the probability that Schaeffer had a web of powerful yet secretive men behind him. Running a major black market operation required logistics, transportation, military passes, and travel orders, plus cooperation from the various security and law enforcement agencies. The army had branches serving all Schaeffer's needs, and with the unwieldy and chaotic occupation forces lacking top-to-bottom communication, each one operated autonomously and with ultimate authority. But which branches, and how many officers were involved?

A tangled web, indeed.

"Hey, are you awake?" Adelle demanded from the kitchen.

Mason raised his head and saw Adelle standing in the kitchen doorway. "Food's ready."

Mason hauled himself off the sofa, entered the kitchen, and sat at the small table. The scent of the cooking piqued his appetite, and he took in bites with barely a breath in between. After a few moments, he noticed Adelle staring at him.

"Did you love him?" he asked.

"Does it matter?"

"It does to me."

She took a few moments before answering. "He was kind and gentle to me, but I could never get past what he did. I never liked politicians *or* cops."

"And here you are…."

"I didn't think this was romance."

"You just do what you must to survive."

Adelle hesitated, looking into Mason's eyes. "Yes."

"Maybe in another time. Another place...."

"I suppose so," she said and rose from the table. She walked up to Mason, her body pressing into him. "I know that's the best you can do when talking of romance. I'm tainted, but so are you. Both of us came out of this war damaged."

She cupped his chin and leaned his head back. She leaned over and kissed him deeply. Mason responded and stood. They never broke their embrace as he led her to the bedroom.

A HOWLING wind stirred Mason from a troubled sleep. Adelle was awake and sitting up with her back against the headboard. She was naked with the bedcovers pulled up only to her waist.

"You're not cold?" Mason asked.

"I got used to it living at the labor camp. Besides, I like the cold."

"Not surprising coming from the Ice Queen."

"Speak for yourself."

Mason fluffed up his feather pillows to prop up his head. He lit a cigarette and stared at the ceiling.

Adelle took the cigarette from Mason's mouth and took a drag. "You were making quite a racket in your sleep, talking and moaning. Bad dreams?"

"No more than usual."

"The war?"

"That, and my time as a POW. What's your excuse? Why are you up?"

"Other than fearing for my life? I couldn't help thinking of how Hilda suffered. We seemed to fight constantly, but I still love her and miss her."

Mason took a long drag on the cigarette, trying to burn away the thoughts of Hilda's cut-up face and his friend forced to swallow the results. "Sometimes I dream about the victims in my murder cases. An occupational hazard. I got used to seeing dead soldiers during the war, but the civilians, the ones that were in the wrong place at the wrong time... like your sister. I never really get over those."

"Hilda knew what she was getting into. It wasn't exactly the wrong time and place for her."

"She's not as innocent as I made her out to be?"

Adelle became pensive as she helped herself to one of Mason's cigarettes. "What I mean is, she knew being with Winstone had consequences."

Mason turned to face her. "Was Winstone into something I don't know about?"

"That night, at Winstone's villa, I could tell what you were thinking, looking at all those things in his house."

Mason suspected the answer, but he asked it anyway: "That wasn't to make him appear as a black market kingpin for his cover?"

Adelle laughed. "He was covering his cover, then. With real gusto. His cook, Otto? He was Winstone's go-between with certain German royalty and industrialists, who are rolling in money. For astronomical prices, Winstone would certify them as denazified, or he helped place some in the new German local governments. He then used that seed money to finance some of Herr Giessen and Bachmann's schemes. Winstone was swimming in it. He and Hilda were planning to go to Switzerland just as soon as he cleared up some loose ends."

"What kind of loose ends?" Mason asked.

"I have no idea. I know that Giessen being murdered shook him. And I got the impression he knew who was responsible, but he refused to tell Hilda. All he would say was that as soon as they were safe in Switzerland, he was going to release some documents as revenge on the killers."

She stopped when she saw Mason's furrowed brow. "Look, I know he was a friend, and he *was* a good guy. I'm sure he was like all the rest; Garmisch has too many temptations for even a good man. I think releasing those documents was also his way of making amends. Even while he planned to sneak into Switzerland with a king's ransom. He was good for Hilda, though loving him and being involved with his schemes was her undoing."

"What exactly was her involvement?"

Adelle shrugged as she puffed on her cigarette. "She was Winstone's original contact with Eddie Kantos and Herr Giessen."

"Why are you telling me all this now?"

"Hilda made me swear to secrecy. She's dead now, isn't she?"

"Do you know where Winstone stashed all that money?"

Adelle smiled. "You want it for yourself, don't you?" She rolled toward him, pressing her bare breasts against his arm. "If you find it, then we can take it and go to Switzerland together."

If the documents still existed, Mason hoped that Winstone had stashed the money in the same place. And he saw an opportunity to buy Adelle's questionable loyalty, and her secrets, with a promise of a pot of gold.

Mason said, "Let's just say that if I find it, I'm not about to throw it in the river. Or hand it over to the U.S. government." And though this ploy was to persuade Adelle, he wasn't so sure what he would do with the money if he found it.

Mason got out of bed, fished through his pants pockets, and pulled out his CID badge. Inside the badge case, and tucked behind his photo ID, was the piece of paper he'd found in Hilda's suitcase. He brought it back to bed with him and showed it to Adelle. He knew he was taking a risk, but he didn't know anyone else who had been closer to Hilda. At least, the only one still alive.

"Does what's written on this paper mean anything to you?"

Adelle studied it for a moment. "No. Should it?"

"I found this concealed in Hilda's suitcase in her apartment. Very carefully concealed. Are you sure you don't know what this means?"

"I have no idea. Do you think it has to do with where the money is hidden?"

"Possibly. Or where Winstone hid his documents."

"Then why would Hilda have it?"

"It might not have anything to do with Winstone at all."

"I can tell you one thing about it: That's not her handwriting."

Mason looked at the figures neatly written on the paper.

Adelle continued, "She never wrote in block letters like that. And she was left handed, so everything sloped to the left."

"Then someone gave it to her for safekeeping."

"But if Winstone and she were going to Switzerland, then why would she have left this in her suitcase at her apartment?"

"Maybe he gave it to her in case he had to get out of town in a hurry or was arrested. Or she secretly kept a copy for the same reasons. Could be anything." He put the paper back in his CID badge case, making a show of it, letting Hilda see. When he got up to put the case back in his pants pocket, he deftly lifted the paper out of the case and palmed it. He went to the bathroom, ostensibly to pee, and rolled up the paper into a tight scroll and wedged it in a gap between a mounted shelf and the tiled wall.

Mason felt an attraction to Adelle, but he wasn't about to trust her. And sometimes he wondered if he felt a deeper bond with the murder victims than the living. So be it.

M ason rose early. He woke Adelle and offered to take her someplace safe, though he was unsure where he'd take her if she accepted. Instead, she opted to stay, so he left her with the same instructions: Keep the Walther pistol close, don't answer the door and stay away from the windows. His stomach still felt bruised, but that didn't stop him from downing a large breakfast at the officers' mess. He then used one of the mess hall phones to call Laura to arrange a meeting for later that afternoon.

From his billet to the officers' mess, then to headquarters, he had kept a constant lookout for gun barrels sticking out of car windows or figures lurking in shadows, but he made it to the Rathaus auxiliary building without ducking for cover. Not that he felt totally immune from an ambush even at the MP headquarters.... Finding Densmore waiting for him in his office, staring at the chalkboard and corkboard, made him all the more uneasy.

Without turning around, Densmore said, "Lots of names and lines on here, but are you any closer to figuring it all out?"

Densmore had every right to be in his office, but it still made Mason suspect he was there for more than a quick review of his progress. Oddly, Densmore seemed unfazed by his name being listed among the suspects.

Mason put his satchel on the desk and saw that the papers laid out on the surface were still in the same order as when he'd left. "Suspicions. A few leads to follow."

"I want you to gather what you have and write up a final report. I'm taking you off the Winstone case."

"You're what? You can't do that."

"As your supervising officer, I can."

"You had no interest in it beyond proving Winstone committed suicide, and now you're taking away a case you considered unwarranted?"

"When were you going to tell me about the autopsy?"

"If you'd been around, I would have told you last night."

"Well, now it's officially a double homicide, and since you're the only suspect, I can't very well let you conduct the investigation."

"Oh, come on, Patrick, you know I didn't do it. Until this moment, I'm the only one who's pushed for murder." Mason strode over to Densmore. "You wanted to file it as a suicide, despite my reservations. Tried to ship off Winstone's body without an autopsy. Release that Italian and anyone else that might have any connection to the killers. And now you're taking me off the case?"

"Those weren't my fingerprints in the victim's house. I wasn't there the evening of his death. I wasn't the last one to see him alive. And why are you so desperate to find his supposed missing documents? Is there something in there that might implicate you? You see? It goes both ways, buddy."

"Then you're doing all this because you're afraid. Afraid for you career or your life, I don't know."

Densmore said nothing, but the anger had dissipated from his face.

Mason saw an opportunity to persuade Densmore and brought his tone down a notch. "You saw the hits on the three German gang leaders. You saw the hits on Kantos and his family. His wife, his kid. I got back the ballistics report on the two shootings, and the bullets match one of the guns used in both. The killers have been careful up to now, but they did make this slipup. And Winstone was connected to both parties. He was bankrolling Giessen, and he had dealings with Kantos."

"How do you know this?"

"A couple of informants. The point is, I'm making real progress. I'm getting closer, and that's why someone tried to gun me down last night." He told Densmore about his experience at the Casa Carioca last night, that Schaeffer refuted nothing. About Volker, and how he'd been there chumming it up with Schaeffer. The mysterious Abbott, and how all three were most likely the ones doing the executions.

Densmore said, "After the shit you stirred up last night, I'm surprised you're still walking around."

"Is that why you're afraid to get involved?"

Densmore marched over and shut the door. "You're damn right, I'm afraid."

"The one thing going for me is that General Pritchard and Colonel Udahl are behind me. Someone has been sending my reports to General Clay, and he's instructed them to back me up. There are too many eyes on me right now for them to make a stupid move like that."

"I'm the one who sent Clay the reports."

"*You* did?"

Densmore nodded.

"Why? Did you suddenly get a conscience?"

"Fuck you, Mason. It's because you and I were city cops. Both of us screwed up when we were on the force, and we deserve a second chance. I didn't want to see you go down in flames."

"We both screwed up? What do you mean?"

"I know you ratted on fellow cops in Chicago."

"Yeah, for running a dope ring and killing my partner. What about you?"

Densmore avoided Mason's eyes. "Doesn't matter what I did. Either way, we both got burned, and we both deserve a second chance. After what I saw in the Kantos house—the wife and little boy..." He balled his fists as if struggling with an internal conflict. "I have to take you off Winstone. There's no way to justify letting you stay on when you're too personally involved. It goes against every procedure in the book."

"Then let me keep the German murders and the Kantos case. The crime rings. It's all the same case, really. I know if I can get to the bottom of those, it will lead me back to who killed Winstone."

Densmore thought a moment, then nodded. "I'm going to make you a deal. I'll take the case, but in name only. That way it looks like we're following procedure, and it'll buy you a few days before the provost marshal in Munich figures out what we're doing." He pointed his finger at Mason. "But as soon as any heat comes my way, you're out. You understand?"

Mason was surprised by Densmore's offer, but he maintained a neutral expression. Densmore never did anything for altruistic reasons. Either he was truly shaken by the brutal murders or this was a way for him to maintain control of the investigation. "Okay, we'll do it your way," Mason finally said. "Then first thing we should do is get a team of MPs to pick up Winstone's chef, Otto Kremmel. He was helping Winstone shake down wealthy Germans for denazification papers."

"That pompous kraut," Densmore said. "I'll take care of it, and then I'm going to personally nail him to a wall."

Mason took a pad of paper and a pencil from his desk and began writing. "Look, here's what I need, and I need it fast. Wiretaps on the Casa phones. A bulletin sent to all MPs to look out for Volker. MP surveillance on Frieder Kessel and Schaeffer around the clock. And if we can find him, the apprehension of one Lester Abbott."

"We don't have the resources for all that without help from the Munich detachment. If you want to keep this case, we can't attract any undue attention."

"Then make it our two junior investigators for surveillance: Wilson and Tandy."

Densmore nodded.

"The bulletins?"

Densmore nodded again. "If he's really a war criminal, then I don't care who signed him off. And I'll write up the orders for the Casa wiretap." Densmore started to leave as he said, "Remember, this only gives you a few days. You'd better get results soon."

After receiving Densmore's written orders for the wiretap, bulletins, and surveillance, Mason had a sketch artist draw up a likeness of Volker, then had Wilson and Tandy have the sketch printed and distributed to the various MP stations and post commanders in the area. Once the bulletins had been distributed, Wilson and Tandy began their vigil outside the Casa Carioca. Meanwhile, Mason coordinated with the surveillance techs to patch into the Casa Carioca telephones through the main switchboard.

By midafternoon, Mason felt satisfied that things were finally falling into place. That is, until Densmore and the two MPs returned to headquarters empty-handed. Otto had disappeared. Either his wealthy friends were hiding him, or he'd eventually end up on the growing list of corpses.

AT FOUR P.M., Mason made the twenty-minute drive down to the Eibsee Hotel. The sprawling three-hundred-room hotel sat on the shore of the impossibly beautiful Eibsee Lake at the foot of Germany's highest mountain, the Zugspitze. The American army had taken over the hotel and designated it a recreation center, so the herds of guests were a mix of American soldiers, their guests, and military government administrators. Mason crossed through the lobby and exited onto the broad terrace. There were couples or groups standing at the railing, admiring the lake and the surrounding snow-laden mountains, but only a few hardy souls braved the frigid temperatures to sit at the thirty-plus outside tables. Laura was among them.

A teapot, two cups, and a plate of bite-sized pastries sat in front of her. She had changed out of her reporter's outfit and now wore an ankle-length coat of navy blue velvet and matching hat. The blue ensemble, her red lipstick, black hair, and blue eyes—a kaleidoscope of sensuality that conspired to beguile Mason.

Mason came up to the table. "My butt's going to freeze to this chair."

"The places I've been, this is downright balmy."

Mason glanced around before he sat down.

"Relax," Laura said. "I come here every afternoon for teatime. There's always some GI who sits down and tries to pick me up."

"I was hoping we'd meet someplace more out of the way than this."

"I can't stay cooped up in that house twenty-four hours a day. This is my one time to get some fresh air and take in the gorgeous view." She crinkled her nose and sniffed the air in Mason's direction. "Nice perfume. Who's the girl?"

"What girl?" Mason asked and immediately felt foolish for the childish response.

"I hope she's good for you."

A waiter came over, and Mason ordered a coffee.

When he left, Laura looked at the lake and said, "This is one of my favorite places in Germany."

"Göring would agree with you; he took it over for the Luftwaffe during the war."

Laura ignored the remark. "What do you want?"

"I have an informant who's helped me out big-time on this investigation. He and his family are Jewish camp survivors, and they want to emigrate to Palestine. I want you to help them get in contact with someone in the Jewish Brigade."

She finally pulled her gaze from the scenery and looked at Mason. "You made a promise on the assumption that I could come through for you? Pretty brazen of you."

"Laura, can you do it or not?"

The waiter came back with Mason's coffee. Laura used the pause to pull out a cigarette from a gold case. She lit it and looked back at the lake.

"Romantic, isn't it?" she said. "You could almost forget the rest of the world. Just put everything on hold. Forget the tragedies, and the mistakes you've made." She turned back to him. "Did you know Richard Strauss came here to write some of his best music?"

"Feeling melancholy?" Mason asked. "Is domestic life with Ricky getting to you? Is he preventing you from putting your life on the line?"

"Meeting you here—anywhere—could put my life on the line. Like asking me to come out of hiding to track down some, let's say, disreputable people in order to contact someone I may or may not know in the Jewish Brigade. I can always count on you to put me in danger." She gave him a sad smile and touched his hand. "But I wouldn't have it any other way." She studied Mason for a moment. "What's this girl like?"

"You haven't answered my question."

"Answer mine first. Is she pretty?"

"Yes."

"What's her name?"

"Adelle, and she's—was—a skater at the Casa Carioca."

"Ah, now I see the connection. The damsel in distress. Your chivalry knows no bounds, Sir Knight," she said sarcastically. "Is she good for you?"

"Maybe. She can be intoxicating to be around, but she's likely to lead to one hell of a hangover. Does that satisfy you?"

"I should be jealous," Laura said and looked away as if taking in the view, but she acted more pensive than entranced. "It will take me a couple of days."

"You'll be saving a group of people who truly deserve it and helping make their dream come true."

After a long moment, Laura turned to Mason. "And when this is done, I think it's best we keep our distance." She opened her purse. "I mean it, Mason." She pulled out her billfold.

Mason held up his hand. "It's on me." He pulled out his wallet. "After all, this might be the last time I get to do this. And for more reasons than one."

As Mason counted out the correct change for the bill, he could feel Laura staring at him. She stood abruptly and came up to him. She kissed him quickly on the lips and walked away.

MASON ARRIVED at the Sheridan barracks in the early evening and proceeded to the conference room used to question the German suspects the night before. Abrams was talking to an American suspect, a sergeant, in a corner of the room.

When Abrams saw Mason, he turned the suspect over to the waiting MP and met Mason by the door. "That's Sergeant Whitney of the transportation branch. He was caught running stolen antibiotics and narcotics up to Munich."

"Did he give you anything?"

Abrams shook his head. "He never had contact with the distributor. He gets a note of where to go, which changes every time, and retrieves a key to a truck and its location. He then drives it up to Munich and leaves it at a designated spot that changes each time. He hops in an empty truck and drives it back to Garmisch. His pay is put in the glove box. There's always a different cargo as cover."

"He had to be in contact with someone for the initial setup."

"A Sergeant Hoffman, who was busted for sexual assault a few weeks ago and sent back to the States. Whitney says that even after Hoffman's bust the arrangements never skipped a beat. These guys are good. It's like a cloak-and-dagger outfit."

"That would fit Schaeffer's OSS background."

"Oh," Abrams said, remembering, "the servants from Winstone's villa are back in town."

Mason nodded. "We'll have a go at them when we're done here. Anything from the other detainees?"

"Most of them were processed and released."

"Did Willy survive the night?"

"The guards pulled him out of that cell before things got too far out of hand. He spent the morning in the clinic and is recuperating in a separate cell. I hear he's not going to be able to sit down for a while."

"Let's have a word with him."

They stepped up to Willy Laufs's cell. An MP guard let them in and closed the metal door behind them. Willy stood at the barred window with his back to the door and his head lying on his crossed arms. The guards had given him a one-piece uniform usually provided for army maintenance crews, as his clothes had been torn to shreds. He turned his head to see who had entered, then whirled around when he saw Mason. He had stitches above his left eye and several bruises on his moon-shaped face. He pleaded with them with eyes like green marbles pressed in soft dough. He deserved more of the same, as far as Mason was concerned, but Laufs had experienced enough to appease Mason's temper.

"You pick on a poor entrepreneur and let the big fish go free," Laufs said in German. "Even the Nazis left me alone as long as I cut them in. The bastards took more than their fair share, but at least I stayed out of jail."

"You got a taste of what's to come when you go to prison," Mason said. "On the other hand, for the right information, we'll consider leniency."

"I told your partner, I'm not a rat."

"Suit yourself," Mason said and called for the guard.

"Wait," Laufs said with panic in his eyes. "What are you doing?"

"We're putting you back in that other cell."

"Can't we negotiate?"

"No."

The guard came and unlocked the door.

Laufs panicked. "You can't do this! Do you know what they did to me?"

Mason answered in German, "Tell me who killed Herr Giessen, Bachmann, and Plöbsch, or it's the other cell. And this time, the guards won't pull you out."

"I don't know. Whoever killed them, I would like to shake their hands. Those two nearly put me out of business."

Mason motioned for the guard, who came in with his handcuffs at the ready. Laufs pleaded and begged, but the guard continued, then Mason helped the guard pull Laufs into the corridor. Laufs screamed at the top of his lungs.

Mason yelled over him. "Who killed Giessen and his partners?"

"I don't know. I swear to you."

"We know you were a go-between with the Italian crime families for Giessen and Kantos," Abrams said.

"We crossed paths, sure, but you could say that about anyone who uses the black market."

"Did you have anything to do with Giessen's or Kantos's murders?"

Laufs looked at Abrams as if dumbstruck by the question. "No."

"You have any idea who killed them?"

"No!"

Mason stopped the procession. "Why are you still walking around? They're bumping off anyone who had a connection to Kantos and Giessen."

"I am a small fish surrounded by sharks. I'm not a threat to them. I keep my head down and my mouth shut. They know this."

"So, you know who we're talking about."

Laufs sputtered, unable to speak through his panic. Finally he said, "I don't know who they are. Just that some incredibly powerful men are taking over. Please. I swear." And he kept repeating, "I swear," as if his mind might snap at any minute.

"Do you know a Herr Volker?" Abrams asked.

A tick of recognition passed across Laufs's face.

"You know him, don't you?" Mason said.

"Maybe he even threatened you," Abrams said, "telling you that anyone going against the new leaders would end up like Giessen and his pals."

"I don't know who you're talking about."

Mason turned to Abrams. "He's not going to give us anything." He and the guard began to push Laufs along.

"Wait, wait, wait," Laufs said in ever-increasing insistence. "Maybe I know Herr Volker a little."

Mason signaled for them to stop again.

Laufs caught his breath and said, "Volker was working for Giessen, but I heard he betrayed him. That's all I know."

"Where can we find Volker?" Abrams asked.

"I can't tell you where, because I don't know!"

"That's not good enough," Mason said and nodded to the guard for them to continue. Laufs dug in his heels and threw himself backward to stop their progress.

"Please, I will tell you all I know," Laufs said. "Just don't put me in there."

Mason gestured for them to take Laufs back to his cell. They pushed him in and pinned him against the wall. Mason removed the handcuffs and asked the MP to wait down the hall. Once the MP had closed the cell door and left, Mason faced Laufs. "Start talking."

Laufs rubbed his wrists and shuddered as he took a few deep breaths. "I swear I don't know who killed Herr Giessen or Herr Kantos, or the American agent for that matter. Yes, I did some deals with the Italians for Herr Giessen at the beginning, but once the contacts were made and business started rolling, they cut me out. But I heard rumors...." His voice trailed off as if unsure whether to continue.

Mason got in Willy's face. "You're about one heartbeat away from hell."

"Abbott," Laufs blurted out. "A man named Lester Abbott runs a very powerful gang. He's the boss. Nothing happens without his say."

"Describe him," Abrams said.

He looked at Abrams as if Abrams didn't understand. "No one I know has ever seen him."

"He's not a ghost. Someone must have seen him."

Laufs only shrugged in response.

"What about Schaeffer or Kessel working out of the Casa Carioca?" Mason asked.

"I've heard of them, but I never dealt with them."

"Come on, Willy. You want us to believe that with all your dealings with Giessen and Kantos, that you've never done any work for Schaeffer or Kessel?"

"Like I said, I was almost put out of business once I gave Giessen his contacts. I've just heard the same things you probably have, that a powerful gang has almost made a complete takeover of the area, and Abbott is the big boss. And not just Garmisch. Their connections run up to Munich and beyond. It's like an entire territory."

Mason and Abrams exchanged glances. That tidbit had only confirmed their suspicions: Colonels and generals had to be behind that kind of power.

"What about Agent Winstone?" Mason asked Laufs.

"What about him?"

Mason rubbed his forehead in frustration at Laufs's obfuscation. He was sure Laufs knew more and was saying only enough to keep him from being thrown into the other cell. At least Laufs was talking, though, and Mason knew they'd get nothing out of him if they actually did shove him in with inmates bent on beating a pedophile to death. He spoke slowly to keep his temper at bay. "Do you know who killed Agent Winstone and Hilda Schmidt?"

"I could think of about five people who would have wanted to murder him, but they're all dead. He apparently had a file on almost everybody that could have put them away for life." He added quickly, "Except for me." His eyes flitted between Mason and Abrams. "The man to ask is Otto Kremmel. Now, there's a grifter if there ever was one. He had Winstone snowed and half the Bavarian aristocracy eating out of his hand."

"We tried to pick him up this morning," Abrams said, "but he's disappeared. He's gone, Willy, along with your bargaining chip."

Laufs shook his head. "You just haven't been looking in the

right place. He wouldn't be too far away. He's hoping to find the money Winstone hid away, like everybody else. And the word on the street is that those documents are still out there. There's a big reward for anyone who can find them."

Abrams looked at Mason then asked Laufs, "Then tell us where we can find Otto."

"Try a filthy-rich widow who lives alone on an estate called the Stebenheim in Oberau. Otto's been romancing her for some months now. He's always trying to extract money from her, and get her to include him in her will."

Mason and Abrams exchanged glances again.

Laufs brightened. "I see by the looks on your faces, I gave you some interesting information, no?"

22

Mason and Abrams drove up the circular driveway and parked their sedan in front of what could pass for a small-scale French château. It sat on a low hill, overlooking the small town of Oberau, which lay six miles north of Garmisch. The stately Stebenheim mansion showed signs of recent neglect, with its windows shuttered and frozen weeds emerging from the snow left to accumulate on the estate grounds. The sun had set an hour before, leaving only a deep purple dome above the western mountains in an otherwise black sky.

The two investigators climbed the steps of the front, columned portico, with Mason noticing the absence of footprints in the snow as they did so. He knocked on the massive double doors. A crow cawed its displeasure for disturbing the silence.

"I'm surprised some army or MG officer hasn't claimed this as their palace," Mason said.

"I can see why," Abrams said as he looked around. "This place gives me the creeps."

Mason knocked harder this time. "Willy Laufs better not have sent us on a wild-goose chase."

"I'm still trying to get over the idea that you sent Densmore to search for Winstone's documents. I mean, after all, we're still not sure whose side he's on."

"I couldn't order the search without him knowing about it. And it was either having him go on the treasure hunt or coming with us. I want Otto alone for a while."

Before they'd departed for Oberau, they had gone by headquarters and told Densmore what Laufs had said about the reward for whoever found Winstone's documents. Densmore immediately put a squad together of MPs to do an all-out search of Winstone's villa. On Mason's advice, he also took along Winstone's servants, as they had been present during Winstone's renovations of the villa. The idea being that they could point out every filled crack and replaced floorboard, with the hope that, in one of them, they might find Winstone's documents.

"What if he finds them and turns them over to the bad guys?" Abrams asked.

"All I have to do is take one look at him, and I'll know he's trying to pull a fast one. The man's got the worst poker face of anyone I've ever met."

Mason decided not to wait any longer for someone to answer the door. He tried the latch. The door opened onto a darkened foyer. The two investigators silently readied their pistols and flashlights, then stepped inside. On their left and right were wide entrances to large rooms, and in front of them a long hallway. A grandfather clock sat silent in a corner of the foyer, and though the pendulum could have stopped swinging just a minute before they entered, Mason had the impression that the clock had ceased measuring time years ago.

Mason signaled for Abrams to take the right entrance and Mason moved toward the left. While listening for movement in the dead silence, he breached the door frame and stopped. With the beam of his flashlight, he swept the room. Elegant furnishings abounded. Religious-themed paintings that looked centuries old and priceless hung on the walls. Halfway across the room Mason's flashlight beam fell upon an old woman sitting on an intricately carved settee of embroidered silk upholstery. Her silver hair was done up in a bun, and she wore a gray wool pleated skirt and matching jacket.

"*Entschuldigung Sie, bitte?*" Mason said, asking her to excuse him for disturbing her.

The woman remained motionless as if she had become petrified at the same moment that the grandfather clock had stopped. To all appearances she had died in that position, but her forlorn eyes darted in their sockets as she stared at some unseen images of horror.

Mason holstered his pistol and moved to the woman's side. He heard Abrams step up to the door as he squatted to see into the woman's face. The woman finally turned to him. Tears formed in her eyes.

"What's happened, ma'am?" Mason asked in German. "Where's Otto Kremmel?"

The woman's eyes lost focus as she relived some horror, then slowly she turned and pointed to a closed door on the other side of the room. Mason stood and signaled for Abrams to follow. Abrams hurried across the room. Mason removed his pistol from his holster, then slowly turned the door knob. He looked at Abrams, who nodded that he was ready, and Mason pushed open the door. They took two steps into the parlor. The sight made them both freeze for a split second.

Otto hung by his neck from a heavy silk rope in the middle of the room. His hands hung at his sides, his body was still. Mason rushed up to take Otto's weight off the rope, while Abrams went to where the rope had been tied to a marble column of the fireplace. Mason could immediately tell that his efforts were useless. Otto was still warm but lifeless. Abrams untied the rope and helped Mason lower Otto's body to the floor. Mason checked

Otto's pulse, just in case. That was when he noticed the bloody message nailed to Otto's chest.

TOO LATE. WE HAVE YOUR LITTLE RAT FRIEND.

"Yaakov!" Mason yelled and ran out the door.

ABRAMS POUNDED the steering wheel and cursed as he raced toward town. "We should have hog-tied Yaakov to his bed. How are we going to find him in a town this size?"

"We're not going to find him. Right now we have to get to Yaakov's family before the killers do. Yaakov's probably being tortured as we speak. He could have given away their hiding place by this time. We may already be too late."

Abrams cursed again as he renewed his assault on the steering wheel. "If Yaakov is dead, I'll kill them all."

"You sure you're up for this?" Mason said firmly.

Abrams nodded and pressed on the accelerator. Mason gave him directions that took them in a circuitous route, all the time checking the mirrors and looking behind. Satisfied that they weren't being followed, Mason had Abrams park in the alley behind the bookshop.

After a visual sweep of the area, they went to the back door. It took several knocks to persuade the shop's owner, Isaac, to answer. He looked terrified at the sight of two men in uniform until Mason reminded him that they had been with Yaakov the day before. "Is the family still here?" he asked.

Abrams said something in Yiddish, which elicited another terrified look on Isaac's face. He said in German, "Follow me."

Mason and Abrams followed Isaac up the stairs. Isaac knocked on the door in a code.

The door opened a crack, then fully. A tall man with dark hair and thin beard stood at the doorway. The man was Yaakov's brother, Berko. He displayed the same terrified look as Isaac when he saw Mason and Abrams. Isaac introduced them, and said that they had been there to see Yaakov the previous day. Berko let them in. Yaakov's pregnant wife, Helena, let out a soft cry when she saw Mason and Abrams. Berko spoke softly to Helena in Yiddish. The entire family gathered in the small living room and looked expectantly at the two investigators.

"Yaakov has not come home for hours," Berko said in English. "We urged him not to go out, but he said he had to retrieve the bulk of the money he'd earned on the black markets." He threw his hands up in worry and frustration. "And he wouldn't tell any of us where that was. Why did he have to do that? We could have gotten along fine without it."

Mason lowered his voice so the others wouldn't overhear. "Berko, we have to get you and your family out of here quickly. This place is no longer safe."

"Where is Yaakov?" Helena demanded with rising panic in her voice. "We can't leave without Yaakov."

Berko spoke to Helena in a reassuring voice, though Mason could tell she sensed the worst had happened. "He can join us later," Berko said. "We'll make sure he knows where we are." He issued quiet commands in Yiddish.

The family immediately went to work, gathering clothes hung out to dry, the children's things, a bundle of food. The children looked bewildered but displayed no tears. They were obviously used to being pushed from one place to another, and a few of the children were old enough to remember the war, the fear, and the idea that you ran to stay alive.

Mason turned to Isaac. "Could you please go downstairs and watch the street? Warn us immediately if you see anyone or anything suspicious."

"How are we going to fit everyone in one car?" Abrams asked.

"We can manage," Berko said. "We take only what we need."

"When it's safer, we'll make sure you get the rest of your things," Mason said.

"Do you already have a place to go?" Abrams asked.

"Yaakov had a plan for this kind of emergency. A small maintenance shed in the mountains."

"Maintenance shed?" Mason said. "You can't live more than a few days isolated like that. It's snowing up there."

"It was a last resort," Berko admitted.

Mason shook his head. "I know a better place." He noticed Abrams's puzzled expression, and said to him, "She said if we needed a safe place…"

Abrams smiled and nodded. In ten minutes everyone had a bundle to carry. Helena tried to keep a brave face for the children, encouraging them and making it an adventure—flight took precedence over grief. Mason carried the smallest child and a bundle as he led the way down the stairs. Berko removed the mezuzah from the door frame and put it in his pocket.

Halfway down, Isaac ran up to them. "There are four men out front, and they have guns."

M ason ordered the family back upstairs, but Berko came down a moment later carrying an old shotgun. "I will help," he said.

"You know how to use that thing?"

Berko nodded as he panted with fear.

"Then stay on the bottom step and cover us," Mason said. "They could come from the front or back, so be ready."

They descended the stairs into the narrow hall that led to the front of the shop, an office, and the back door. Mason had Abrams watch the back door, using the office doorway for cover. Mason had Berko stand on the last step of the stairs and crouch behind the return wall. He then crept up to the curtain dividing the hallway from the front of the shop and peered through the gap. The bookshelves obscured a full view of the front shop window, but looking between the tops of the books and the bottom of the shelves, he could make out two men dressed in black moving toward the alley.

Mason looked at Abrams and signaled that one or two were heading toward the back. He then bent low, slipped through the curtain, and slid behind the first row of bookshelves. From there, he had a better view of what was going on outside.

Two men with black stocking caps pulled down over their faces stood by the front door and right-side window. Mason guessed they were waiting for the other two to get into position, with the plan to rush in at the same time. This portion of the street contained stores that had closed at seven P.M., so there was little traffic. The men could enter with little worry of witnesses.

Mason figured the two men going around back would notice the army sedan and take a few moments to check it out. He hoped the presence of the vehicle would be enough to discourage them, but in that same instant, the men in front pulled out submachine guns from their long coats and glanced around one last time.

Mason aimed his .45 at the one standing by the window. "Military police! Drop your weapons and put your hands up. My gun is trained on you."

The man jumped aside, using the doorframe as a block. Mason held his fire so as not to reveal his position. He aimed at the door. That was when the two opened fire, blindly spraying the room.

From the other side of the curtain, Mason heard someone kicking in the back door. Then two gunshots in rapid succession. He knew the sound well: a .45 Colt automatic—Abrams's gun. A man cried out in pain. The second man in the back opened fire with an automatic pistol.

That exchange prompted the two men in front to charge. But instead of going through the door, one leapt through the window. Mason fired and missed the first man, but when the second attempted the same thing, Mason was ready. He fired again, hitting the man's thigh. The man wailed in pain and jerked in midair, then landed hard on the sidewalk.

Mason raced to the opposite shelf, just as the first man fired at his previous position. Books exploded. The wooden shelf splintered. Book pages, ripped to shreds, floated in the air.

Mason stayed low and moved to the far end of the shelf. The first man stopped firing, and a moment of silence passed before another round of firing came from the back. A deafening boom followed—Berko's shotgun.

In front, the wounded man continued to wail in pain, and his companion yelled in English for him to shut up—American English.

Abrams came out noisily from the back.

"Get down!" Mason yelled.

A burst of machine gun fire erupted from the front. Wood, glass, and paper sprayed out like mini explosions. Mason went up on his knees to see if Abrams was hurt, but the movement gave his position away. Immediately, the shooter brought his machine gun fire to bear on Mason. Bullets buzzed narrowly over his head.

A moment later the firing ceased, followed by the sound of footsteps on broken glass. The men were making their escape. With one last spray from the machine gun, the men ran for their car.

Mason and Abrams rushed to the front as the assailants' car sped away. Mason checked Abrams and saw blood on his coat. "Were you hit?"

"That's the other guy's blood."

Mason sighed with relief. "We only have a few minutes before the MPs arrive. Let's go." He pulled a breathless Abrams toward the curtain.

"Aren't we going to wait for them?"

"I don't want anyone to see this family or have any idea where we're going."

Mason picked up his spent shells and instructed Abrams to do the same. When he entered the back hallway, he saw Abrams staring at the dead assailant.

"I shot him," Abrams said in a weak voice.

Mason gently urged Abrams toward the stairs. "Come on. You did the right thing. These men were coming to kill Yaakov's family."

Berko was already up in the apartment barking orders at the shocked and weeping women and children. Once again they gathered the bundles and hurried down the stairs. It took some urging to get them past the dead man. Mason made sure everyone, including Abrams, was settled in the car before returning to the hallway. Isaac sat on the stairs in shock. Mason turned the corpse on its back, pulled up the black ski mask, and shined his flashlight on the face. Just as Mason thought: one of the Poles from the Casa Carioca. "I'm sorry for all this," Mason said to Isaac. "The MPs will arrive in a few minutes. Say nothing about us or Yaakov's family being here. Just tell them to search the hospitals for a man with a gunshot wound in his thigh. You saw nothing else."

Isaac nodded.

"WHAT DO YOU WANT?" Richard was not happy. Not happy to answer the door after eleven P.M. Not happy to answer it in his bathrobe. And sure as hell not happy to see Mason there, let alone Abrams and eight apparent refugees.

"Sir—" Abrams was cut off when Laura spoke behind him.

"Richard, what is it?"

Richard stepped aside to let Laura have a look for herself. "What is all this?"

Mason shrugged as an apology. "I know you offered Gil and me safe shelter, but this family needs your help."

"Of course," Laura said. "Come in."

Richard grumbled, "Laura…"

Laura ignored Richard's protest and stepped aside. Mason ushered the family indoors, while Richard fixed his stare on Mason. In any other circumstances, Mason would have met the glare with equal contempt, but for the sake of the family, and Laura, he kept his eyes on the family as they gathered in the living room.

The men removed their hats and faced Laura. With one last sigh of exasperation, Richard disappeared down the hallway leading to the bedrooms. The baby started to cry, but the rest remained silent. In the car, Mason had told the family about Otto's body and the note indicting that the killers had probably abducted Yaakov. Helena could have thrown a tantrum, blaming Mason, blaming all Americans for putting Yaakov in harm's way, and though her eyes had conveyed that message, she had remained silent. Mason couldn't blame her; he had, perhaps, pushed Yaakov too hard, or underestimated the ruthlessness of the killers.

Laura smiled at the children and asked Mason, "Is this the family you asked me to help?"

Mason nodded and introduced them all, telling Berko and Helena that Laura was the person who would try to contact someone in the Jewish Brigade. They nodded their heads and softly expressed their gratitude. Mason then explained to Laura why he had brought them there. "I know this is going to be hard on you," Mason said, "but we had no other choice." Mason said to Berko, "I have no delicate way of saying this, but you will only be able to stay here a few days at most. If Laura is unable to make contact within that time, I think you should reconsider going to the Jewish DP camp in Feldafing."

"What has changed?" Berko asked. "Is it not as likely that they will find us there? I am determined to carry out Yaakov's dream for us all to go to Palestine. He has sacrificed everything for that. Thank you, but we will take our chances. I will find another place."

Berko turned to Laura. "We promise not to be a burden. And we can help around the house. Helena and Olga are excellent cooks. I can do repairs. Whatever you need."

"Don't worry about that now," Laura said. "I'm glad to help out. You all must be exhausted and in shock. Fortunately we have two extra bedrooms you can use. Let me show you."

Mason and Abrams waited in the living room while Laura helped the family settle in for the night. A few minutes later, Laura came back to join them.

"I know you told me we should keep our distance…." Mason shrugged. "Sorry about all this. I hope it's not going to cause a problem with Richard."

"He's slowly getting used to my form of insanity," Laura said and looked at Mason with a tender expression he hadn't seen since their affair in Munich. "You'll never cease to amaze me. Just like helping those orphans in Munich. You're whacking someone over the head one moment, and the next moment, this."

They held each other's gaze for a moment, until Abrams cleared his throat.

"I promise they'll only be here a few days," Mason said.

"They can stay as long as they need," Laura said.

"I told Yaakov's wife and brother that Yaakov has been taken by the killers, and that, chances are, he's not coming back. It's the same people, Laura. I told Yaakov to stay put, but he went out, and they found him, just like that. As hard as it might be, the family has to stay inside and out of sight. You, too."

She nodded. "Find them, Mason. Find them, and if there's no other way, put do them in a deep, dark hole."

24

M ason and Abrams left Laura's and descended the hill into town. Abrams had fallen silent. Mason knew why. "Have you shot anyone before?"

Abrams took a moment as if coming out of a deep thought. "Once. Maybe. Our squad of MPs entered a German village ahead of the regular troops. The town had surrendered without a fight, but there was a sniper in the church bell tower. We all fired at him, and someone got him, but no one really knew who."

"It's different when the man is right in front of you."

"I'm fine, okay? Let's leave it at that."

"You shot because you had to. Period. I don't want you brooding over this, because the next time you might hesitate, and you'll be the one on the ground."

"Did you ever shoot anyone up close?"

"A few times. Then there were a few times I should have and didn't. Right now, I regret those more." He said the last sentence with force, and he turned a hard left on the steering wheel.

"Where are we going?" Abrams asked. "The bookshop is the other way."

"No more regrets."

"What is that supposed to mean?"

"I should have shot Volker and Schaeffer last night in Schaeffer's office. Right there where they sat, right in the teeth of their smart-assed smiles."

"You're insane, you know that?"

"For some time now."

"Pull your shit together. You're not going to march in there and kill Schaeffer. All that's going to accomplish is putting your neck in a noose. Whatever guilt you feel about Yaakov is not going to be solved by gunning down that scumbag. There's still a slim chance that Yaakov got away, or we can track them down in time to save him. Turn the car around, and go back to the bookshop."

"You said it yourself: You want to kill whoever took Yaakov. Now here's your chance."

"Turn the damn car around!"

"Are you giving a superior officer an order?"

"Damn right I am. When you're acting like a crazed fool. We get the evidence, and we watch them hang."

Mason eased the accelerator, bringing the sedan back down to normal speed, but he stayed on course. He looked at Abrams: still green, still so young, not hammered by war and loss. It was like looking at a mirror that reflected Mason's own youth, a time before…. Maybe he could still hold on to some of those qualities. Maybe he could rein in some of the rage and remember his humanity. At that moment, he was glad Abrams sat across from him.

Mason turned the car around and headed back to the center of town.

They pulled up to Isaac's bookshop ten minutes later. Two jeeps, an ambulance, and an olive-drab sedan sat at odd angles in front of the shattered shop window. A bevy of MPs stood around in a circle and stared at something on the pavement. The headlights of the vehicles cut through the darkness and were aimed at same spot.

A few flashbulbs went off. The MPs talked excitedly, but no one appeared to be in a hurry to rush the victim off to the hospital. Whoever the ambulance had come for no longer needed emergency aid.

"A lot of activity for a dead gunman," Mason said.

"Oh, God," Abrams said and jumped out of the car.

Mason ran to catch up, and they stopped next to the group of MPs. "Who is it?" Mason asked, though he felt he knew the answer to that question.

The MP sergeant said, "There's not much left to identify. Looks like he was tortured before they killed him."

Mason and Abrams stepped through the MPs and stopped at the victim's naked feet. Mason almost recoiled from the sight. Abrams cried out and turned away. Through the bloody and swollen face, beneath the cuts and bruises, the man was barely recognizable, but Mason, like Abrams, could still tell who it was. Yaakov.

Mason felt his chest tighten from a wave of guilt and sorrow. He squatted near Yaakov's face and mouthed a silent apology.

"You two know this guy?" the MP asked.

Mason nodded and turned to Abrams, whose face was twisted with the same emotions that Mason had internalized. Abrams walked away. Mason watched him for a moment, then turned back to Yaakov. There were rope burns on his wrists. A wire was still embedded in his neck. He'd been strangled with it so forcefully that it had cut deep into his throat. He was shirtless, which showed he'd suffered severe blows and cigarette burns all over his torso. Yaakov must have held out for quite a while, as he also had burn marks on his earlobes, where electrodes had been attached. Torture by electrocution, on top of the severe beating.

One of the two medics asked if everyone was done, then they

put Yaakov's broken body onto a stretcher. Mason watched as the medics covered Yaakov with a blanket then lifted the stretcher. The jostling made Yaakov's bare arm fall out from beneath the blanket. It was the first time Mason had seen Yaakov's concentration camp tattoo. The tragedy of it all hit him like a blow, and he knew that image was now permanently burned into his mind.

"A tattoo on his arm,'" the MP sergeant said. "A Jewish DP, an ex-concentration camp inmate. Survived all that just to be killed in Garmisch."

Mason nodded and walked away. He scanned the area for Abrams and found him standing next to their sedan, with his face to the black sky.

"Come on," Mason said. "We've got work to do. There'll be time to grieve later."

Abrams nodded and fell in line next to Mason as they entered the bookstore. Isaac stood in the middle of the wreckage, the broken glass, books, and shattered shelves. He looked up at Mason with a sad expression.

"You're a good man, Isaac," Mason said. "You helped save an entire family. We'll help you as much as we can."

As they walked to the back, Abrams said, "How are we going to get enough cash to do that?"

"I'm going to persuade Schaeffer to pitch in... as soon as I wrench the cash from his dead hands."

Abrams slowed at the curtain, as if reluctant to gaze upon the man he had killed. Mason hesitated with him, then drew back the curtain. The back hallway was empty; the body had already been taken to the morgue.

Densmore came down the stairs and met them. "Where have you two been?"

"Working our case," Abrams said.

"Who's the victim outside?"

"A man named Yaakov Lubetkin."

"So where's the family?"

Apparently Isaac had broken down and told all. "Somewhere safe," Mason said. "What about your search of Winstone's villa? Did you find the documents?"

Densmore shook his head. "We had the servants point out every square inch of Winstone's renovations, and we spent hours tearing up every goddamned spot. Nothing." He rubbed his head. "I'm tired, Mason. I really am. So why don't you give me the rundown, and then we can all go home and get some sleep. Unless, of course, you have some other people you want to shoot tonight."

Mason motioned for Densmore and Abrams to follow him out the back door and away from the crime scene techs. "We didn't want to tell you, because we don't know who to trust."

"According to you, nobody."

"That's right, but I'm going to tell you anyway. Yaakov Lubetkin was an informant for Winstone, reporting on Giessen and Kantos, while he worked for them. Yaakov and his family are Jewish survivors, and we had worked out a deal to help smuggle him and his family to Palestine in exchange for information."

"That didn't work out so well, did it?" Densmore said.

"You want to hear the rest or not?" When Densmore answered with silence, Mason told him about what Yaakov had discovered, that Kantos and Giessen had a partnership running everything on the black market from apples to zinc, and salt to heroin, by the truckload. About Hilda's relationship with Giessen and Kantos, then her falling in love with Winstone. That Schaeffer and Volker, plus the unknown Abbott, were the ringleaders behind the violent takeover.

As Mason went on, Densmore became so tight with stress that his body seemed to shrink. Finally he held out his hands to stop Mason. "I don't want to hear any more—"

"Patrick, the body you pulled out of here was one of the waiters from the Casa Carioca."

"That doesn't prove anything. He could have been working as a hired gun on the side."

"I also wounded one of the assailants, and I heard his partner talking to him in American English."

Densmore shook his head as if warding off any more bad news. "I'm a cop, but I never claimed to be a hero. I advise you to let it all go. Put in for a transfer and take Abrams with you. Nothing good will come out of this."

"You think this will all go away if I leave? And who's going to step up and put these bastards down? You? Gamin? I've got a personal stake in this, and I'm already a target."

Densmore turned to Abrams. "I'm putting you in for a transfer. Whether you like it or not."

"That's what I advise," Mason said to Abrams.

"Sirs, I'm not backing out of this. I could never live with myself if I didn't help. Please don't do that to me."

Densmore gave Abrams a stern look but said nothing.

"I need for you to keep this quiet," Mason said to Densmore. "I still don't know who all is involved."

Densmore nodded. "I'll run interference for you, but don't ask me to get in any deeper than that."

"Whoever got to Yaakov got to Otto, too. We found him hung in a widow's villa with a note nailed to his chest."

Densmore grimaced, more from the weight of bad news than any sympathy for Otto. "Write it all up tomorrow. I don't want to hear any more. I'm getting out of here and see if I can get some sleep." He turned on his heels and strode off.

Mason said to Abrams, "I want you to check into a hotel tonight. Don't go back to your billet. Just go straight to a hotel, and make it one run by Germans."

"And what about you?"

"I'll do the same thing, but after I get Adelle out of there. I should have done that two nights ago."

"I'm going with you. I won't sleep unless I know you and she are safe."

"You going to make sure I brush my teeth and tuck me in, too?

"If that's what it takes."

~

ABRAMS STOPPED the car down the street from Mason's house, and as before, they surveyed the area. As it was past midnight, no lights shone in any of the houses, including Mason's.

"We go on foot from here," Mason said as he drew out his .45. "You enter by the back, and I'll take the front."

"This is getting to be an annoying habit. Have you always lived like this?"

Mason ignored the remark and exited the car. Abrams did the same, and they wordlessly moved down the street. Abrams hopped the low fence of a neighbor's yard to approach Mason's house by the backyard. Mason tried moving quietly, but his footsteps crunched through the frozen crust of snow. On the front porch, he unlocked the door and gently pushed it open.

The sound of a spring released under tension came first—a sound Mason knew too well, and one that made every nerve in his body fire at once. The next instant something heavy and solid hit the living room floor and rolled along the parquet.

"Gil! Grenade!" Mason yelled toward the back of the house. He jumped off the front porch and dived behind the porch's concrete riser.

At that same instant the grenade exploded, lighting up the snow in a hellish orange. The two front windows blew out. Glass sprayed onto the porch and rained down on Mason. He rushed onto the porch, kicked open the door, and entered the living room still full of acrid smoke.

"Gil!"

"Here!" Abrams yelled and stepped out from the back hallway.

Mason ran up to Abrams and checked for wounds. "Are you all right?"

"I can't hear too good," Abrams said, a little stunned. He tried to wave away the lingering smoke. "God damn, these people! This is fucked up!"

Mason rushed through the rest of the house looking for Adelle. She was gone, but so was the small bag of clothes she'd brought with her from her apartment. She must have figured out for herself that Mason's billet was no longer safe. Mason hoped she'd left town, far away from Garmisch, long before the would-be assassins had arrived.

Mason rejoined Abrams in the living room, and they both examined the area with their flashlights. The grenade had rolled to the center of the room and exploded, pushing the sofa toward the fireplace and turning two chairs to splinters. The grenade's shrapnel had ripped into the upholstery, shredded the area rug and disintegrated the floor lamp. Beyond the blast radius there were obvious signs that the intruders had torn the place apart: books pulled off the shelves, the contents of a cabinet emptied onto the floor, and the previous owner's record collection strewn across the floor.

Then Mason noticed a white piece of paper nailed to the inside of the front door. He walked up and aimed his flashlight on it. It was torn in places and blackened at the edges, but he could easily make out the message... BOOM!

Abrams came up to Mason and growled when he read the message. "We have *got* to put these people down!"

Mason felt proud of Abrams at that moment. The potent

warning had not scared him, but made him more resolute. After this latest stunt, Mason might have considered giving up and moving on, as Densmore had suggested. The force they were up against seemed too powerful and too clever, but Abrams's guileless remark had put it all in perspective.

Mason retrieved Hilda's note that he'd hidden behind the bathroom shelf, then quickly packed up a few clothes. Outside, a few neighbors had stepped out from their houses to see what had happened. An MP jeep and army ambulance pulled up a minute later. A medic cornered Abrams and insisted on examining him. Mason took the MP corporal inside and gave him a report of the incident. He kept the details vague, only heightening the corporal's suspicion that Mason was involved in something nefarious. Obviously, the corporal was not on Schaeffer's payroll, and Mason mentally added the man to his list of MPs he could trust.

An hour later Mason and Abrams checked into a German-run bed-and-breakfast. Doing so violated army regulations for both parties, but with some extra money, the proprietor happily looked the other way. With only a few hours left before sunrise, Mason doubted he would get much sleep. Schaeffer and his cronies were determined to tie up all their loose ends, including Abrams and him. As he lay on the bed in the darkness, images of Yaakov's torn body kept rolling around in his mind, the image of his tattoo was so clear, as if projected in the dark room. That was when it hit him: Yaakov's Birkenau tattoo on his forearm. The numbers.

Mason jumped out of bed and searched through his pockets. He pulled out the piece of paper from Hilda's suitcase. The numbers on the paper and Yaakov's tattoo were the same.

What possible connection could there be between Hilda's note and a concentration camp number? It being a coincidence was out of the question. Then why would Winstone use Yaakov's number? What did Yaakov have to do with any of it? If Yaakov knew where the documents were hidden, why hadn't he told Mason or Abrams?

The more likely scenario was that Winstone had simply used the tattoo without Yaakov knowing anything about it, as part of some code to finding their location. And since Laufs had said that a bounty was out for the location of the documents, it was remotely possible that Winstone had not divulged their location under torture. Perhaps he'd pointed to Yaakov instead, leading the killers to seek the information from Yaakov, and Yaakov had revealed their location under torture. "Perhaps," and "maybe": still more questions than answers.

One thing was obvious: Anyone connected with the location of the documents had been tortured and killed. The documents were in all likelihood in the killers' hands or lost for good. Now all Schaeffer had left to do was to clean up the loose ends. Present company included.

Dark thoughts on a very dark night....

25

Mason knew entering detachment headquarters came with a false sense of security. For all he knew, a good handful of the MPs and officers were on the Schaeffer gravy train. He and Abrams had eaten breakfast at the officers' mess, then Abrams had gone went to check that Wilson and Tandy were on the job watching the Casa, not sleeping.

He entered an auxiliary building in the complex and descended to the basement. The two technicians monitoring the phone taps of the Casa Carioca were in a room not much bigger than a broom closet. One technician, Archer, sat at the console, half-awake with a cup of coffee in one hand and a cigarette in the other. He sat up straight when Mason entered.

"Where's Lefebvre?" Mason asked.

"He's tracking down the addresses on some of the phone numbers like you ordered. There are about five that aren't officially listed. Could be numbers just lost in the system, but Lefebvre should be able to track them down."

"Anything come in?"

Archer gathered a handful of papers and handed them to Mason. "Pretty much mundane stuff. Those are the transcripts in

English and what we've been able to translate from German so far. Some of the phone calls were in Polish, so we should have those a little later now that we tracked down a translator."

"Why aren't you listening right now?"

"A light will blink if there's an incoming or outgoing call. But the circuits went dead around ten last night."

"What do you mean dead?"

"We started around noon yesterday, and the calls were sparse but regular. Then, boom, nothing. I thought something went wrong on our end, or with the Casa phones. But the main switchboard could no longer get a signal through. I had Lefebvre call the Casa reservations line on an office phone, and he got through. Somehow they've rerouted the phone lines through another relay center."

"I thought all local calls were routed through the main switchboard."

"No, sir. Most of them, but the outlying areas and the towns just north of here run through a series of others. The Casa used the main switchboard, but not anymore."

"Would there be a technical reason for them to change to another relay center?"

"Not one I can think of."

"Unless they found out their phones were being tapped." Mason thought a moment. "What about tapping directly into their phone lines at the club?"

"Well, sure, that's possible, but the club's got guys there around the clock, so we'd have to dig up the line somewhere in the network and tap in that way. We can do it, but it'll take some time... and probably another set of approval orders to give us permission to start digging around."

"I'll get you those."

Mason leafed through the pages. Archer was right. So far, the calls all appeared pretty mundane: supply orders for food, drinks, and linen; costumes for a new show; a maintenance problem with the retracting floor; a call for a piano tuner.

"Any one of these could be code for what they are really saying. Did you make up that list as I asked?"

Archer handed him a piece of paper. "Phone numbers in and out, especially the numbers that come up most often. They start with the most frequent calls at the top."

Lefebvre came in with a full pot of coffee in one hand and a sheet of paper in the other. He stopped in his tracks when he saw Mason and saluted.

Mason pointed to the piece of paper. "Is that the list of unregistered numbers?"

"Yes, sir," Lefebvre said and handed Mason the paper. "Traced down four of the five. Two are private residences. One is to a supply company, and the other a construction company. Both companies are in the German registry office, so they look legit. These numbers could have just gotten lost in the system."

Mason looked over the list. "Good work. Get those other calls translated and transcribed as soon as you can. I'll see about getting you orders to dig up the Casa lines."

Mason left the room and ran into Abrams coming from the other direction.

"I was just coming to see you," Abrams said.

"Come on," Mason said without stopping.

Abrams did a U-turn. "Where are we going?"

"Check out a few addresses the techs got from the phone taps."

They emerged from the basement and made a beeline for their car.

"I found Wilson and Tandy at the Casa," Abrams said.

"They have anything new?"

"Either they were spotted on one of their tails or someone tipped them off. Last night the driver took them on a joy ride all over the place, like he knew they were following him. Finally they ended up back at the Casa. Just to rub their faces in it, one of the Polish waiters came out with hot cocoa."

"Densmore's got to give us more manpower."

"Uh-huh."

Snow fell in big, wet flakes and had already covered the parked cars.

"A couple weeks 'til spring," Abrams said. "You wouldn't know it around here."

They got in their assigned sedan. Mason stomped his feet in a fruitless attempt to get warm blood to his frostbite scars. "It's going to get colder and snowier the way my dogs are barking."

Abrams started the engine and turned on the heat full blast. While they waited for the windshield to clear away the snow, Mason fished out his badge case and showed Abrams the piece of paper stashed behind his ID card.

"I found this hidden in Hilda's suitcase the day we searched her room."

"You're just showing this to me now? You sure have some problems with trusting people."

Mason shrugged by way of apology. "It may not have anything to do with this case."

"Then again, it might."

"I know that now." Mason pointed to the figures on the paper. "That letter and numbers are the same as Yaakov's concentration camp tattoo."

Abrams furrowed his brow. "Why...?"

"I wasn't sure why Hilda had hidden it so carefully, but it was something obviously important to her. But it's not her handwriting, according to Adelle."

"Winstone's?"

Mason nodded.

"But why Yaakov's tattoo?" Abrams asked.

"I don't know. That's why I'm showing it to you. Maybe between the two of us, we can figure it out."

"I'll summon all my analytical powers and get on that."

"Just drive, Sherlock."

ABRAMS EXITED the parking lot of the Alpspitz Supply Company and turned onto Alpspitzstrasse. Abrams struggled to see past the snow smeared across the windshield while Mason checked an unfolded city map.

"We're going to have to put chains on the tires if this keeps up," Abrams said.

Mason turned the map around several times to get their orientation. "Okay, turn left on St.-Martin-Strasse."

"How am I going to see the sign when I can't even see the street?"

"I had to walk in this kind of snow on that death march in the worst winter—"

"Give me a break, would you?" Abrams finally found the street and turned. "Tell me this place is last on the list."

"It is. It's also the farthest. South of town."

Abrams growled in frustration.

They had already visited the two addresses listed as private residences. One turned out to be a phone booth not far from the Olympic stadium, and the other, the apartment of Casa Carioca choreographer, Arnie Sobel. The Alpspitz Supply Company, the place they had just departed from, appeared to be doing legitimate business with the Casa Carioca, supplying everything from beverages to tablecloths and kitchen utensils. The supply company's books and a search of the warehouse had turned up nothing suspicious.

Ten minutes and another inch of snow later, Abrams drove

through a wide metal gate serving as the entrance to the final place on their list: the construction company, a two-story building of concrete surrounded by a high wall. They parked in the lot and approached several men in overalls who were off-loading an olive-drab truck with signs plastered on the door panels declaring Bachofen Bauunternehmen.

"Looks like a U.S. Army truck," Abrams said.

"Could be stolen. Though the army is already selling off some of its surplus."

The workers stopped what they were doing. Mason showed his CID badge to the one who looked like he was in charge, and said in German, "We'd like to speak to the owner or manager."

The man pointed to the building, then barked orders for the men to get back to work. The boxes were labeled in Italian, but Mason saw that several of the boxes had split open, exposing roofing tiles.

As they walked toward the building, Mason scanned the rest of the building materials stacked in the yard: bricks, concrete blocks, steel pipe, and slabs of marble. A man stepped out of the front door. Disturbingly, the man reminded Mason of a squatter Stalin: shorter, heavier, in his late fifties, and sporting a bushy head of black hair and matching mustache. He beamed a salesman's grin as if welcoming arriving customers. "What can I do for you, gentlemen?"

"Are you the owner?" Mason asked.

"Yes…" the man said tentatively. "Alfred Bachofen," he added and shook their hands.

"We're military police investigators, and we have a few questions."

"Please, come in out of the cold."

They entered a small lobby with a counter dividing the customer side from the office side, which held a couple of desks. A young woman sat one desk, while a lean man with slicked-back hair stood over her. They fell into silence and stared at the two investigators. Bachofen introduced them as his secretary and assistant manager.

"We'd like to interview your employees after speaking with you," Abrams said.

"Of course," Bachofen said as he raised the counter's divider. He led them past the desks and into a small, cluttered office. Bachofen retreated behind his desk, and they all sat. Mason studied him for signs of nervous tension, but he acted like he was ready to transact a sale with potential clients. Perhaps he had become accustomed to associating army types with big spenders. Even their serious faces and CID insignias hadn't thrown him off his game.

Mason said, "Your telephone number is 86271?"

"That is correct. One of them, anyway. We have two."

"Which one is 86271?"

"That would be mine. Why do you ask?"

"Do you have many dealings with the management at the Casa Carioca?"

Bachofen paused a beat. "Not so much in material anymore."

"Anymore?"

"Yes, during construction of the club, I procured certain materials and coordinated some of the labor."

"Any reason to be in frequent contact with them now?"

Bachofen's salesman smile vanished "I don't understand."

"We've been monitoring calls coming in and out of the Casa Carioca, and we've noticed quite a few calls to your telephone number."

"Well, I can explain. I do, from time to time, provide labor crews when required. Plus, during the construction of the club, I became friends with a few of the Americans supervising the construction."

"And who would that be?" Abrams asked.

253

"I don't understand why all the—"

"Just answer the question, please," Mason said.

"The original army engineer, Captain Brewster, for one. Then, subsequently, Major Schaeffer and his assistant, Herr Kessel."

"Major Schaeffer and Herr Kessel are under investigation for black marketeering and murder," Abrams said.

"Oh, my. I had no idea…."

"And all you talked to them about was the local elections, the weather, and the price of bread?"

"I presume that if you were listening in, you know the subjects of our conversations."

Mason noticed one lonely bead of perspiration on Bachofen's brow. "We would understand one or two calls in the course of a week, but three or four times in one day is rather odd, don't you think?" He pulled the pages of transcripts from his pocket and referred to them. "Two loaves of bread are six marks today. The weather is turning warmer, up a couple of degrees. The elections should be held tomorrow, if you want my opinion." He looked up from the pages.

Bachofen was speechless; breathless, in fact.

"Coded conversations, aren't they? The question is, what are they for? Shipments and receiving of contraband?"

Bachofen feigned shock and anger, opening his mouth several times, as if mute with outrage. "This is preposterous."

"Schaeffer recruited you and your business as a front for his black market trade."

Mason nodded to Abrams and they stood. "We'd like to take a look at your books and search the premises."

Bachofen balled his fists to hide his shaking hands. "You have no right… There has to be some regulation requiring you to produce a warrant to search my property."

"Come with us, please, Herr Bachofen," Mason said. "We'll start with what's being unloaded from the truck."

Bachofen sputtered as he wiped the growing perspiration from his brow. Mason led the way, with Bachofen in the middle. Abrams took up the rear in case the man decided to make a run for it—which was just what Bachofen's two-person staff had done. The outer office was empty. Mason quickened his pace. Abrams urged Bachofen to catch up, and they all rushed out of the building. The workmen had vanished as well.

"They must have beat it when we went inside," Abrams said.

Bachofen muttered, "Oh, dear."

Mason ran to the street and looked both ways. Footprints in the snow headed in both directions, but the office staff and workmen had disappeared.

26

M ason made Bachofen sit on a pile of boxes still inside the truck, while he and Abrams attacked the boxes unloaded onto the ground. Those boxes contained nothing but roofing tiles, as the labels had claimed, and he began to worry they'd jumped to conclusions. But ten minutes later, buried behind another two dozen boxes inside the truck, they hit pay dirt. Wedged between layers of tiles in one of the boxes, they uncovered a paper-covered bundle the shape and size of a brick.

Mason used his switchblade knife to slice open the package, revealing a compressed white powder. He said to Abrams, "What do you think? Heroin?"

"Can't think of another reason to be hiding it in boxes of tiles," Abrams said.

"Oh, dear." Bachofen nearly swooned and fell against the metal wall.

Mason and Abrams left him to his misery as they tackled other boxes, and each yielded the same hidden surprise.

Suddenly Bachofen leapt to his feet. "Please, I was only paid to look the other way. I have nothing to do with this. They call and tell me in code when a shipment will arrive and whether it will be put in one place or another. Never what's in the shipments."

Mason and Abrams ignored him, and Bachofen collapsed onto his stack of tiles.

"Go call this in," Mason said to Abrams.

Abrams jumped off the truck and disappeared. Mason turned to Bachofen. "Who else is receiving shipments?"

"I have no idea."

"Who calls you about the shipments?"

Bachofen looked up at Mason as if weighing the consequences of his response. "Kessel," he said weakly.

"Not Major Schaeffer?"

Bachofen shook his head with little conviction behind it.

"Never? It will go a lot easier for you if you tell me the whole truth."

"I'm doomed anyway. An expendable pawn, a fleck of dandruff on the shoulder of power."

"Have it your way," Mason said and jumped off the back of the truck. "Don't go anywhere." After shutting the truck's doors and throwing the latch, he walked up to the truck's cab and climbed in. He checked the glove box, but found only some badly folded maps of Italy and Austria, a pack of cigarettes, and a half-full bottle of schnapps. A search of the floorboards and under the seats yielded nothing, but when he reached behind the seats he pulled out a stack of neatly folded U.S. Army uniforms and several sheets of typewritten paper.

Abrams came up to the driver's door. "The cavalry will be here in a minute. How much you want to bet Densmore will be leading the charge?"

Mason showed him the stack of uniforms. "They had three sets of these stashed behind the seats." He then held up a sheet of official-looking stationery. "Schaeffer should have hired smarter guys. These bozos left behind written orders that got them across borders. Looks like they had another stop to make."

Two MP jeeps raced into the yard as if assaulting an enemy encampment.

"That was fast," Abrams said. "Densmore must have put out an APB."

Mason slipped the truckers' written orders into his breast pocket, and they met the MPs at their jeeps.

Mason approached an MP sergeant. "The company's owner is locked up inside the truck. Take him to his office and keep an eye on him. And rip out his phone before he has a chance to use it." He instructed the other MPs to remove and log all the bags of suspected heroin.

Ten minutes later, three more jeeps arrived on the scene, and, as Abrams had predicted, Densmore sat in the lead jeep.

Abrams gave Mason a subtle nudge. "Patton breaking through to Bastogne."

Mason smiled, then greeted Densmore and ran through the events leading up to finding the suspected drugs. An impressive pile of white bricks had already been stacked on the lip of the truck bed.

"Kessel and Schaeffer's contraband," Mason said.

"Can you prove it?"

"The company owner gets coded calls from the Casa Carioca about arrivals of shipments. He's inside. He already named Kessel as his key contact, but given some time and persuasion, I'm sure he'll give up Schaeffer."

A muffled pop came from the building. They all turned at the sound.

"A gunshot," Mason said.

Mason, Abrams, and Densmore rushed into the building. Inside Bachofen's office they found the MP assigned to guard Bachofen checking the man for a pulse—an unnecessary gesture, as Bachofen had a bullet hole in his temple and his eyes were frozen in death.

The MP looked up with a guilty expression. "I just stepped out for a moment. He was bawling his head off, and, well…"

Mason turned away before he said something he'd regret later.

Densmore said, "So much for your witness testifying against Kessel *or* Schaeffer."

Mason thought for a moment. "We've got the bait. Let's see what we can hook with it."

MASON SAT in the passenger's seat of the truck. Abrams drove. They both wore the outer jackets and caps found behind the seats. In back were four MPs behind a stack of cargo, which, according to the orders Mason had found, consisted of half the "roof tiles."

"Do you think they split the load to limit their loss?" Abrams asked.

"That, or the two halves go to different destinations. Sort of relay points for further distribution. No telling how many sites they have operating."

"This idea of yours may not work. What if one of Bachofen's drivers alerted them?"

"I'm betting they had no contact with the higher-ups in the operation. Bachofen was a pawn, but those guys were even lower than that. Of course, I could be wrong, and a bunch of trigger-happy yahoos with machine guns are waiting for us."

Abrams fell silent, but his knuckles had turned white.

"Don't pull off the steering wheel," Mason said. "We might need it."

They reached their destination, a U.S. Army supply depot in a remote area north of Garmisch. The depot was little used since the US 10th Armored Division had been shipped back to the States.

Now, it mostly housed mothballed tanks, heavy weapons, and armaments. MPs guarded the gates, but neither Mason nor Abrams recognized them.

One of the MPs examined the orders, then passed them on through.

"Didn't even want to look in the back," Abrams said.

"Either they're being paid to look the other way, or they're not real MPs."

They passed rows of tanks and howitzer cannons, all kept in top shape in case they had to be used again for a Russian invasion. At the far end of the sprawling depot stood several warehouses of corrugated tin. Most were shut and quiet, but the last in the row had a few men milling around.

Mason knocked on the back wall of the cab. "Almost there. Get ready."

Abrams took it slow, his back stiff and his breathing shallow.

"Take it easy," Mason said. "They don't look like they're ready to open fire."

"They're just waiting until we get in range."

After some additional encouragement from Mason, Abrams pulled up the truck in front of the warehouse. "What if they recognize us, or realize we're not the guys we're supposed to be?"

"We'll know soon enough. Remember, we're Germans in disguise."

Three men met the truck. One beefy corporal stormed up to Abrams's door. "Where the fuck have you guys been? You're three hours late."

Abrams said in German, "Crappy weather. We can't fly over the mountains. And the damned checkpoints—"

"I don't understand that kraut gibberish. Just get down and give us a hand."

Mason jumped down and moved quickly to the back. He

threw the latch and opened the doors. He said in heavily accented English, "Where *ist* Herr Schaeffer. Herr Kessel?"

"What the fuck do you care?" the corporal growled.

Abrams met them at the back, and Mason asked the corporal, "You sure this cargo is for you?"

"You think we stood out here in the freezing cold just to welcome you? Now shut up and start unloading."

Just then, to Mason's surprise, Sergeant Olsen emerged from the warehouse. They both froze for a split second before Olsen broke into a run.

Mason yelled to the MPs, "Now!"

Mason took off after Olsen. He heard shouts and commands behind him and hoped the MPs had surprised and overwhelmed the warehouse men, otherwise he just might get a bullet in his back. Olsen had long legs, but he was no sprinter. Mason got within twenty yards, pulled out his gun and yelled, "Olsen, stop!"

Olsen kept running. Mason pointed his gun in the air and fired once. "The next one's for you."

Olsen stopped this time. He kept his back to Mason and raised his hands. Mason maintained his gun aimed at Olsen's back as he walked up and patted the man down. Olsen had a nine-millimeter pistol in his belt and a Ka-Bar knife in his boot. "Nine-millimeter," Mason said. "Not your usual army-issue weapon." He patted Olsen down once more, just to be safe. "I expected to find your rotting corpse in the woods somewhere, Sergeant."

"If you don't send me to a stockade far away from here, that still might happen."

"You could have gotten out of Garmisch scot-free, but you just had to stay and team up with these cutthroats."

"You go where the money is."

"I never took you for a bright guy, but that's just plain stupid," Mason said as he handcuffed Olsen. He led Olsen back to the truck, where Abrams and the four MPs held Olsen's crew at gunpoint.

According to Mason's plan, Densmore and four MPs arrived in their jeeps five minutes later. Densmore did a double take when he saw Olsen. "Well, I'll be damned."

Mason pointed back toward the front gate. "The two MP guards are probably on Schaeffer's payroll."

"They aren't MPs. We picked them up. And just for the record, we don't know that Schaeffer's behind this."

"Why don't we ask Olsen?" Mason asked as they watched the MPs take away Olsen and his crew in handcuffs.

"Let's take a look at what's inside first," Densmore said.

Mason, Abrams, and Densmore entered the one-hundred-by-three-hundred-foot warehouse. Boxes, barrels, and crates labeled as powdered eggs, condensed milk, flour, sugar, and salt filled the space. A cursory search through the containers proved that most held what they advertised and were probably headed to the black markets all over occupied Germany. However, a number of them stacked in one corner claiming to contain powdered milk, actually held penicillin, amphetamines, medical-grade cocaine, and surgical supplies.

While Abrams and Densmore continued to bust open the containers like it was Christmas morning, Mason opened a wide double door leading to the rear of the building.

"You guys are going to want to see this," he said.

Abrams and Densmore followed Mason out the back, where two train tracks had been installed for transporting tanks and heavy cannon. Now the two tracks accommodated boxcars, hopper cars, and tankers. It took a few minutes to find a crowbar suitable for breaking the padlocks on the boxcars. That done, they went down the line, breaking the locks, pulling the doors open, and inspecting the contents.

They finally stood back and took in the scene.

Abrams whistled at the sight of it. The thirty cars were filled with petrol, coal, industrial chemicals, potatoes, steel, and aluminum.

Densmore said, "How could they have all this right under the army's nose?"

Mason looked at Densmore with a look that said, "You've got to be kidding."

"This is too big to move," Densmore said. "We'll have to post guards until we can sort it all out."

"Then we post guards on the guards," Abrams said.

27

U dahl was waiting at the entrance to the Sheridan barracks when Mason, Abrams, and Densmore arrived. As he approached the three investigators, a contingent of reporters followed. Mason caught himself looking for Laura among the gaggle.

Udahl directed the two photographers to step behind him. "No pictures of me. It's these men who deserve the credit." He shook the investigators' hands. "Congratulations, men. Job well done. General Pritchard sends his congratulations as well."

Udahl made a little speech to the reporters about cleaning up the town, and Mason being a big part of it. He declined to pose with the men, but insisted the photographers get group shots of the three investigators.

Mason finally had enough; he disliked the idea of advertising an ongoing investigation, and he never liked the idea of boasting to the press, especially when the ringleaders were still out there. The bust had taken a bite out of their profits, but there was plenty more where that came from.

"Sir, we'd better get back to work," Mason said.

"Yes, I understand," Udahl said. He turned halfway and spoke so the reporters could overhear, "No rest for the wicked, and even less for those who pursue them."

Inside the barracks, construction was under way to make it ready for the future expansion of the area's constabulary force. Mason, Abrams, and Densmore went straight to the cell wing, where the two fake MPs and the rest of Olsen's crew shared two cells. Olsen had been put in a cell at the end of the corridor and isolated from the rest. The MP guard unlocked the cell door and stood aside for the three investigators to enter. Once they were all inside, Mason noticed the MP guard hovering too close to the door. "We've got it from here. You can wait at the end of the hall."

The MP showed his displeasure, but complied, and when the MP was well out of earshot, Mason turned his attention to Olsen.

Olsen occupied the single bunk. He stared at the floor with his elbows on his knees and his head in his hands.

Densmore crossed his arms and exhibited a satisfied smile. "You're facing decades at Leavenworth. How does that feel?"

"I didn't do nothing that'd put me away for that long," Olsen said bitterly to the floor.

"I'm betting the court-martial judge and jury will see it differently."

"You know the drill," Mason said. "We've had this chat before. You give us information, and we'll do our best to see you get a reduced sentence."

Densmore turned to Mason. "You can't trust this guy. He set you up at the Steinadler."

"I didn't set him up," Olsen said, finally looking up. "He was made by that kraut."

"Volker?" Mason asked. Off Olsen's nod Mason said, "Now, there's a little piece of information you left out the last time we talked."

"I did what you asked. I risked my life to bring you in there."

"Strange that you got out alive, while three big-time gangsters and two bodyguards were executed in the alley behind the bar. How do you explain that?"

"Luck, I guess."

"Not so lucky now," Densmore said. "I don't think you understand how much trouble you're in, Sergeant. A previous bust for narcotics, aggravated assault, and now this…."

"I believe you left one out," Mason said. "Besides the ex-Gestapo goon, Olsen here was the only man to make it out of the back of the Steinadler alive. When I busted him, he was in possession of a nine-millimeter pistol, the same type of weapon used to kill Giessen and the rest. I'd say we can make a case for multiple homicides."

Olsen sat up straight. "What? I had nothing to do with that!"

"Five pros, all dead, and you without a scratch," Abrams said.

"Looks pretty damning to me," Densmore said. "A known thug and narcotics dealer, criminal gang member, and black marketer. Looks like we've got a winner, ladies and gentlemen."

"Yup," Abrams said. "Let's go tell Udahl."

"Wait! You can't pin that on me!"

"Oh, this looks very bad," Mason said.

"Bad for him," Abrams said, "but we'll look like heroes. Seems only fair he gets his neck stretched for killing those men in cold blood."

"You can't do this!"

"We may even be able to connect him to the other murders: Agent Winstone, Hilda Schmidt, Eddie Kantos, and his wife and child."

"I wanna see a lawyer."

Densmore threw up his hands in mock exasperation. "Now you've done it. Might as well pin a big sign on your chest, with 'guilty' in big letters."

Olsen's face turned red, and he pulled at his hair as if that might revive a few dormant brain cells.

"There's another way," Mason said. "You can make this all go away. Well, almost all of it. Save you from the gallows, anyway. Maybe shave off a few years at Leavenworth."

They all fell silent and waited. The only sound was Olsen's heavy breathing.

"Who's calling the shots, Olsen?" Mason demanded. "We want the big names. Not some low-level gunsels."

Olsen's face suddenly relaxed like a fifteen-watt light bulb of an idea had gone off in his head. "Kessel," he blurted out. "Frieder Kessel."

"That's all you got?" Mason said. "Not good enough. What about Schaeffer? He's the real boss, isn't he?"

"Schaeffer?" Olsen looked back down to the floor. "There's no way...."

"There's no way, what? No way you give him up, because you'll get shanked in the stockade?"

"There's no way, because.... He ain't involved."

"Bullshit," Abrams said. "We know he's the guy behind it all. Give him up, or we'll pin every one of those murders on you."

Olsen's face turned scarlet and he spat saliva as he shouted, "Then you're gonna have to hang me right now, because I only deal with Kessel!"

"What about Lester Abbott?"

Olsen calmed slightly at the subject change. "I've heard of him, but never seen him. Supposed to be some dangerous guy. That's all I know."

"How about Volker? You know where we can find him?"

"I've only seen him at the Casa. And that was only a couple of times."

"You're not good for very much, are you?" Densmore said.

"We got a deal or what?"

Mason turned to Abrams. "Ask the guard to bring us a pencil and paper."

Abrams talked to the guard, and a minute later Mason handed the pencil and paper to Olsen.

"Write down what you did, what Kessel told you, any other guys in charge, how the delivery system works. Everything."

"Then I won't get hanged?"

"That depends on what you give us."

"I don't spell too good."

"You're not applying for college. Just make sure we can read it."

Olsen went to work, and the three investigators stepped out of the cell.

"I'll supervise Einstein in there," Densmore said. "You and Abrams go ahead and pick up Kessel." He looked at his watch. "The club's just getting started, so please, don't go in guns a-blazin'. All right? And take a couple of MPs as backup."

Before Mason left, he said to Densmore, "Put him on suicide watch. I don't want to lose another witness. And no transfers. He stays here."

"Get the hell out of here, and go get Kessel."

THERE WERE a few early-bird diners at the Casa Carioca when Mason, Abrams, and two MPs entered the club. The maitre d' spotted them and nodded urgently to someone at the bar. He then took extreme interest in his seating chart as Mason and the others passed. Five musicians from the orchestra started playing a Dixieland jazz number. The waiters went through the same routine, stopping what they were doing and following them with hard stares.

When Mason and company reached the bottom of the stairs

they were greeted by the ex-boxer, Hans Weissenegger, and a companion only slightly smaller in bulk. They blocked Mason's way.

"Uh, boys," Mason said, "you do *not* want to do that. We've already put down one of your buddies at the bookstore."

"Major Schaeffer ain't here," Hans said.

"I'm not here for Schaeffer. Not this time, anyway. I want Kessel."

"He's busy."

"Look, Hans, I promised my boss I wouldn't create a scene."

"The only scene you're going to create is you flying out the front door."

"You saw what happened to Boris when he tried to stop me."

"Sorry. Orders."

"You know what? I'm kind of tired. This busting-criminals routine has got me drained." Mason drew out his pistol in a lightning move, pulled the hammer back, and poked it under Hans's chin. "No fight tonight, Hans. Okay?"

A few of the diners gasped, but the band kept the majority of the clients unaware of the altercation.

"Please, step aside," Mason said pleasantly. "I like you, Hans, so I don't want to make this an ugly mess."

Hans stepped aside, prompting his partner to do the same. Mason, Abrams and the two MPs passed the gatekeepers and mounted the stairs. Mason returned the Colt's hammer to the rest position but kept the gun drawn to dissuade anyone else from impeding his progress. He breached Kessel's office door first. Kessel sat at his desk and was on the phone. He hung up without a word.

"Placing orders for another shipment?" Mason asked.

"Yes, as a matter of fact. We're running low on champagne."

A quiet moment passed before Kessel rose from his desk, stepped around it, and offered his hands. As he did so, Hans and his partner appeared outside the door. The MPs tried to push them back but with little success.

"We tried to stop them, boss," Hans said.

"I know you did," Kessel said. "And I appreciate your restraint. We don't want to disturb the customers, do we?"

Kessel was calm, a vague smile even crossing his face as he looked at Mason. Mason moved forward with his handcuffs out. There was a serenity to Kessel's demeanor, and Mason answered in kind.

"Please, turn around and put your hands behind your back," Mason said. When Kessel did as instructed, Mason said, "You're not going to ask what the charges are?"

"I'm sure you'll get to that."

Mason took the hint: Kessel didn't want to talk in the presence of his men. Mason started to lead Kessel to the door, but stopped. He plucked Kessel's coat off the coatrack and laid it over his shoulders. "Wouldn't want you to catch cold."

Kessel nodded. "If we could exit the club as unobtrusively as possible, I would greatly appreciate it."

Mason held out his hand in a formal gesture for Kessel to proceed. When the group gathered in the hallway, Mason asked the MPs to go ahead and wait for them at the bottom of the stairs. "Holster your pistols, and pretend we're one big happy family out for a stroll."

The two MPs did as Mason had instructed. Hans and his partner started to follow them, but Kessel said, "You two stay here. No need for a parade."

"What do we do about managing the place?" Hans asked like a lost child.

"The show director will take charge. Do what Mr. Sobel thinks best."

Mason was about to escort Kessel down the stairs when he heard the door to Schaeffer's office open then close. He turned to the sound. His chest constricted at the sight of Adelle, who had just exited Schaeffer's office. She let out a little gasp when she saw him. They stared at each other for a moment. She then bit her lip and walked up to them, looking at Kessel, not at Mason.

"Frieder, where are they taking you?"

"Don't worry, darling. I'll be fine."

Kessel's words of affection made Mason's throat lock up. He stared at Adelle, but she avoided his gaze. *Now is not the time, Mason. Breathe and start walking.* He muttered to Kessel, "Come on," and forced himself to turn away.

If any of the club's patrons reacted to them escorting Kessel out of the club, Mason didn't notice. Fortunately, breathing, walking, and arresting bad guys came more or less automatically to him.

28

Kessel had all the confidence and composure of a businessman ready to negotiate a delicate transaction. He sat with his forearms on the long table and greeted Mason and Abrams with a "Gentlemen" when they entered a windowless room at the Sheridan barracks. The MP guard acknowledged their presence with a nod then exited.

The two investigators sat opposite of Kessel. Kessel's attitude puzzled Mason, but at least the "untouchable" confidence was gone and replaced by what Mason could best describe as relief, like someone ready to lay it all out on the table.

"Let's get started with the charges," Mason said.

Abrams opened a file folder. "Narcotics trafficking, black marketeering, grand theft, obstruction of justice, interfering with military police investigators in the course of an investigation, murder, conspiracy to commit murder—"

"Murder?" Kessel said in surprise. "I've not murdered anyone."

Abrams peered at him over the file folder. "You deny taking part in the murders of John Winstone, Hilda Schmidt, Yaakov Lubetkin, Edward Kantos—"

"I had nothing to do with any of those."

Though Kessel said it adamantly, Mason noticed him blink as if in a brief internal struggle. "Whether you actually pulled the trigger or not, you were part of the gang that did. That makes you at the least accessory to murder. Did you order the murders, Herr Kessel?"

"No, I did not."

"Do you know who murdered them, and did you willingly withhold that information from us?"

"Yes."

The directness took Mason by surprise. He took a beat to collect his thoughts. "Who are the murderers?"

"I have no direct proof—"

"That's hard for us to believe," Abrams cut in. "You worked closely with the gang responsible."

"I was, how you do you say... the front man. The fall guy. I was kept in the dark on all the inner workings of the organization."

Abrams pointed to an unseen spot in the open folder. "We have witnesses stating that it was you who called in the shipment orders, organized pickups and deliveries."

"I was given written instructions as to what to do when, whom to call, et cetera. The source of these instructions was never revealed to me."

"You had to get them from someone," Abrams said.

"They were left in a box in the back of the club. Each evening I was to check the box and carry out the instructions to the letter."

Mason slapped the table. "Come on, Frieder, you're Schaeffer's right-hand man. We're not buying any of this, so stop wasting our time."

"Difficult as it may be for you to believe, I'm telling you the truth."

"Who do you *suspect* are the murderers, then?"

"My guess is Major Schaeffer, Lester Abbott, and Ernst Volker. I also believe that some of the club's staff participated in some of the murders."

"Mr. Abrams shot one of the club's staff. One of your Polish tough guys."

Kessel inclined his head in agreement.

"We keep hearing about a Lester Abbott, but no one seems to have ever seen him."

"Neither have I."

"Then what makes you think he's one of the murderers?" Abrams asked.

"Overheard conversations, mostly. I believe he is one of the leaders of the organization."

"There's nothing you can give us to help locate him?" Mason asked.

"I'm afraid not."

"What about Ernst Volker?"

"Now, there's a despicable man." Kessel looked directly at Mason. "I understand you had some dealings with Volker when you were a POW."

"Maybe one day we'll get into my personal history, but right now, I want you to tell us where we can find him."

"Am I to get nothing out of my information?"

"That depends on what you have."

Kessel smiled. "That is like asking me to reveal my hand before you place your bet."

"We hold all the cards, Herr Kessel. Even if we can come to some sort of arrangement, there's still the German police. They'll want a piece of you."

"What I demand in return is not for myself. I want you to promise me that no harm or criminal charges will come to Adelle."

Mason felt his face turn hot with anger. Or was it embarrassment? He became aware of his own silence when Abrams stirred in his seat.

"I see you have feelings for her," Kessel said. "She does for you, as well. She said she saw the same qualities in you that she does in me."

At that moment, Mason was tempted to jump across the table and throttle Kessel.

Abrams spoke up. "We will do everything in our power to protect her."

"That's not good enough. I want to see that she is under your protection. She's frightened, and now that you have arrested me, I can no longer ensure her safety."

"Why was she so stupid as to go back to you in the first place?" Mason managed at last.

"She felt that I was the only person who could truly protect her. I told her she was foolish for thinking that way, but when people are afraid, they tend to do foolish things."

"Where is she now?" Abrams asked.

"You will find her at Hans Weissenegger's place. Hans is in love with her, though she's never done anything to encourage this."

Kessel wrote down Hans's address. "Hans is at the club, so she'll be alone. Knock three times, then twice. She'll know you've come for her. We arranged this when I heard you had raided the army depot."

Mason turned to Abrams. "Take a few MPs and bring her back here. I want to spend some quality time with Herr Kessel."

Abrams rose from his chair and leaned in to Mason. "Don't do anything crazy."

When Abrams left, Mason offered Kessel a cigarette, which Kessel accepted. They both lit up and stared at each other through a growing haze of smoke.

Mason finally said, "Why didn't you run when you heard of the army depot bust?"

"It was inevitable that you would come for me, and at the time it felt like the best way to end my involvement. I've had enough, and I had little desire to go on the run. I have yet to decide whether that decision was honorable or cowardly."

"How did you get into this racket if you didn't have the stomach for it?"

"Don't get me wrong; the commercial aspects of the group didn't bother me at all. We provided a service. The black market is really all the German people have to survive."

"Diluted penicillin and baby formula, narcotics. Did that really help the German people?"

"I'm a realist, Herr Collins. I was penniless and destitute when Volker approached me about coming to work for them. They offered me outrageous sums of money to be their front man."

"But then they started murdering people."

Kessel inclined his head. "Yes... Killing Herr Giessen and Bachmann, I didn't mind so much. They were horrible men. But then they killed Winstone and Hilda, and I knew it wouldn't stop there. I was very fond of Hilda. A sweet girl, despite her minor flaws of character. She's the one who introduced Adelle to me."

"How did you meet Volker?"

Kessel leaned back and regarded Mason for a moment. Mason could tell Kessel was calculating what to say.

Mason answered for him. "You were part of the group helping Nazi war criminals escape out of Germany."

"War criminals," Kessel said with bitterness. "Is it not your justice system that says innocent until proven guilty?"

"Oh, come on, Frieder. The evidence against most of them is overwhelming. Despite the horrible things they did, we didn't shoot them over open ditches like they did to the Jews. We've tried them in a court of law. And more than a few—too many, in my opinion—have been released due to weak cases or lack of evidence."

"All SS men are automatically arrested, considered war criminals, regardless of their actions. How is that just? If a few Americans in Patton's Third Army committed atrocities, would that justify condemning the entire group?"

"The SS guarded the concentration camps and gassed the inmates. They slaughtered millions of people. Tried to eliminate the entire Jewish population in Europe."

Kessel slapped the table. "But I did not. Nor anyone in my division. You cannot condemn us for what others did."

"You got off, didn't you? A tribunal determined you'd done nothing, and they let you go."

"I am not going to try to justify helping my comrades escape political trials. My loyalty is to my country and the men who fought and died at my side. You would do the same for the men you served with, if the circumstances were reversed."

Mason stubbed out his cigarette. "I don't see what qualities Adelle thinks we share."

They fell silent for a moment. Finally Kessel said, "I met Volker through the escape group. I despised the Gestapo, but I assumed since he was free, he had been judged innocent of any war crimes. I didn't know what Volker really was until after I'd accepted the job at the club. I accept my fate, Herr Collins. I no longer want to be a puppet for the organization."

"Very noble of you."

"I don't pretend nobility. Those men are wanton killers and will stop at nothing."

"So far, you've named Schaeffer, Abbott, and Volker as the leaders. Who else?"

"Only rumors, innuendos, speculation…"

"I'll help you along a little. For instance, I'm sure there are high-ranking officers involved. Generals even. This operation couldn't work without them. Come on, give it a shot. Give me some names, even if you just suspect them."

"I don't have any names. No facts. But, as you say, there's little doubt that there are American officers, in very high places in Frankfurt, Berlin, Munich, who, while they are not part of the operation, profit from its existence. In fact, I am surprised that you are still alive. If you get too close to the kings, you will have a fatal accident of some kind. Or a crazed person will gun you down. I urge you, for Adelle's sake, for your sake, stop this investigation now with my arrest."

"If you want to help Adelle, then help me stop them. That's the only way. And unless we do, all this—your confession and trying to protect Adelle—is all going to be pointless."

"And if I indicated to you where to stand on the tracks in front of an oncoming train, would you do it? Could you stop it? That's the power these people have."

"You don't have to stand in front of a speeding train to stop it. Just remove some of the rails and it will self-destruct."

Kessel reached for his pack of cigarettes and discovered it was empty.

Mason stood. "I'll get you another pack. Lucky Strikes, right?"

Kessel nodded.

Mason needed to clear his head anyway. He felt conflicted about Adelle, about Kessel. He stepped out into the cold evening and took in the fresh air. On rare occasions, during his years as a detective and investigator, Mason had experienced that antithetical bond that sometimes developed between cop and criminal, like priest and confessor. He was always fascinated by intelligent and compassionate men whose moral compass deviated to the polar opposite of his own. Mason had fervently wanted to bring

Kessel down, but now he'd accomplished that, he found himself resolving to do what he could for the man.

That brought him to Adelle. Battered and bruised, pushed and pulled by forces beyond her control, she had still maintained her dignity. She felt deeply, but, like Kessel, her morality had deviated off course. Yet Mason felt affection for her. The empathy he felt for both of them, actually, left him confused and made him wonder what that said about *him*. Perhaps some darker part of himself could emerge given the right circumstances.

Ten minutes later, Mason came back to the interview room with the pack of Lucky Strikes and two cups of coffee. They shared a few stories about the war, and, as Kessel recounted some of his experiences, Mason began to recognize at least one quality they had in common: a sense of duty and honor. And by the time Abrams returned with Adelle, the barrier between them as enemy combatants had eroded.

Mason and Kessel stood when Abrams led Adelle into the room. Adelle only glanced at Mason. She tried to smile, but it never made it. Rather than run into either man's arms, she stopped at the far end of the table between them. Abrams pulled out a chair for her and she sat.

"Herr Collins has agreed to our arrangement," Kessel said.

"There's a man I know in Munich," Mason said. "A German police inspector. He's a good man and a good cop."

"I'm not going to Munich," Adelle said.

"You want to be safe?" Mason said.

Kessel leaned toward her. "Adelle, you can't stay in Garmisch. At least not until this is all over."

"And when will that be?"

"Maybe not for a long time," Mason said. "You should get used to the idea that you can't stay here."

Adelle finally looked into Mason's eyes. "Again I am sent

away. For years men have sent me here or there, always ruling my life. Dictating who I see, what I think. I'm sick of it."

"We both want you safe," Kessel said. "And Munich is not so far away."

Adelle said nothing.

"It may take me a day or two to arrange," Mason said. "In the meantime, you can stay with a friend of mine here in Garmisch."

"You have no friends," Adelle said.

"She'd probably agree with you."

"She? A friend *and* a woman? That surprises me even more."

"She's a correspondent. She's smart, resourceful, and we no longer have any connection. They'll have a hard time tracing her back to me. Not in the few days it will take for me to get you to Munich."

"Your former lover?" Adelle asked.

Mason ignored the question and turned to Kessel. "Are you satisfied with this arrangement? It's the best we can do. I can't trust the hotels, or even our headquarters."

Adelle slumped in her chair and lit a cigarette. "You men talking about me like an item on the black market. So, Herr Kessel bargained a good price for me, I suppose."

Kessel nodded his agreement to their arrangement. "You should find Volker by following his mistress. She has an apartment on Höllentalstrasse, number thirty-six. Volker often boasts about their midnight rendezvous near Kurpark. But he's a cautious man, so their meeting place could have changed by now."

"I'm trying to get over the fact that Volker has a wife," Abrams said.

"She isn't the only woman to make a poor choice in men," Adelle said.

That seemed to take a bite out of Kessel, who gritted his teeth as he said, "Her name is Margareta Schupe—"

Adelle let out a chirp of surprise. "I know that guttersnipe. She's Schaeffer's part-time lover. She deserves both of them."

"How do you know her?" Mason asked.

"She's a skater—if you want to call her that—at the Casa Carioca."

Mason asked Kessel, "Since you're in the mood to give us information, what about Schaeffer? How about giving us something that could definitely connect him to the organization or the murders?"

"I'm afraid I can't," Kessel said.

Out of the corner of his eye, Mason noticed Adelle stiffen. She and Kessel knew something more. Maybe he could pull it out of Adelle or use her to persuade Kessel. "You help me get Schaeffer, and I can promise you a much lighter sentence."

Kessel just smiled, but Adelle fidgeted in her chair.

"All right," Mason said as he stood. "We'll make sure you have a comfortable cell, and I'll tell the MP guards to treat you well."

Kessel bowed his head. "I appreciate that."

"Let's go," Mason said to Adelle with a sharp edge.

Adelle rose from her chair and rushed over to Kessel. She wrapped her arms around his shoulders. He patted her arm, but said nothing. Adelle straightened and shot Mason a defiant glare then allowed Abrams to escort her out of the room.

Before Mason exited, Kessel said, "Treat her well."

Mason nodded and left.

T he usual ten-minute ride back to town took twenty due to the heavy accumulation of snow. When Mason pulled the sedan into the Rathaus parking lot, Abrams said, "I thought we were taking Adelle to Laura's house."

"You're not," Mason said as he paused in front of the headquarters' front entrance.

"Oh, come on. I wouldn't miss this little melodrama for anything."

"Sorry, no show tonight. You can get started on the report."

Abrams groaned as he got out of the car. "You want me to have a medic standing by when you return?"

Mason gave him a stern look and pointed at the entrance. Abrams sauntered off. Watching him made Mason smile.

"He's a good man," Adelle said.

"Boy, more like."

"The few times I've seen you smile was when you were with him. He's good for you."

"Unlike you," Mason said as he pulled out of the parking lot.

They were silent for a few minutes, then Adelle said, "I've known Frieder for a long time."

"You don't need to explain."

"He was my husband's best friend. When Aldrich died, Frieder helped me as best he could from wherever he was at the front."

"I don't need to hear this."

"I was the first person he came to see once he was let out of the POW camp. We were both lonely. We never loved deeply, but—"

"Adelle, that's enough."

"You're jealous. I'm glad."

"I'm mad. Every woman I know can't make up her damn mind. They come to me when they want a strong shoulder to lean on, then when they get what they need, they run off to play with the other boys."

"Ever think you drive them away?"

He looked at her, then back to the snowy road. "Yes."

"Was Laura your lover?"

"I'm not going to share my life story..." Mason stopped. "What possessed you to go back to the Casa, when that's the very place you escaped from?"

"Protection."

"Pro—" Mason hit the steering wheel.

"You couldn't offer it to me."

"Adelle, I'm a cop. What more protection do you want?"

"The kind you couldn't give me. You'll be long gone—dead or transferred, or you'll leave—and I'll be here to fend for myself. I can't live off principles. Or memories."

Mason had no answer for that.

"I fell in love with you," Adelle said, "but I couldn't see it was going anywhere. You're still in love with that other woman. I could see it in your eyes every time you looked at me. An American woman, and I'm the widow of your enemy, an SS lieutenant."

"That didn't matter to me. It's what you do now that matters."

Adelle scoffed. "No one thinks that way. Not even you. And you didn't deny that you still love that other woman."

"That's over. Okay?" Mason knew he had protested too much. He crossed the Loisach River and headed for the foothills of the mountains near Breitenau. "What were you doing in Schaeffer's office?"

"Are you worried I'm fucking him, too?"

"I don't want to know."

Adelle clicked her tongue in annoyance. "You don't hurt easy, but when you are, you're like a pouty child." She turned in her seat to face him. "I was looking for evidence. Frieder was sure there were records or a ledger, or something against him. Unfortunately I didn't find anything."

"And he sent you in there?"

"I went on my own. Frieder knew that one of these days Schaeffer would dispose of him, and he'd had enough of the killing."

"A saint, if there ever was one."

Adelle looked at him for a long moment. "You really had feelings for me."

Mason concentrated on the road. "The key word is 'had.'"

"Spite doesn't become you."

Once more, Mason had no response, and Adelle continued, "If you didn't have feelings for me, you wouldn't be acting this way."

"Like you said, I won't be around much longer, and you're going to Munich."

"I'll be staying with a friend of yours. Maybe you'll come visit."

"Maybe."

Adelle leaned toward Mason. "Who knows? With a little time…."

"I'm going to be dead soon, according to you."

"Yes, well, we can't have everything. But we can have a nice dance before the music stops. You see, I'm a romantic realist."

"I don't see us doing a waltz together." He paused. "But, now, the tango. That I can see."

Adelle chuckled and kissed him on the cheek. Mason started to say something, but the lights came out of nowhere, aimed at his side window, blinding him. His instincts took over. He jammed the steering wheel and his car spun on the icy road, but not quickly enough....

The speeding truck slammed into the car's rear fender panel. The violent impact felt like landing on pavement from a two-story window. The car whirled around. Through the shock, Mason heard Adelle screaming.

The centrifugal force pinned him against the door. He tried to protect Adelle even while struggling to gain control of the car. The world outside the windshield blurred past, the headlights flashing by a dark void, pavement, then trees.

Then he saw it. The tree seemed to be flying at them as if wielded by a giant, and it headed for Adelle's door. A split second later the car plowed into the towering tree. It ricocheted off the tree trunk, rising off the pavement and spinning 180 degrees before coming to a crashing halt. The two wheels on the driver's side hung off the edge of a twenty-foot-deep ravine.

Adelle lay limp against her door. Blood streamed from her head and face. Her body was oddly crooked from the waist up and her head leaned at an unnatural angle. Still, Mason kept calling her name as he tried to revive her.

Then he heard the crunch of gears as the truck backed up to align itself for another ram. Mason tugged at Adelle's body. He tried to pull her toward him, but the crumpled metal had trapped her leg.

The truck, now repositioned, moved forward, slowly at first as it slipped on the ice, but it quickly picked up speed and was now racing toward them. Mason tried once more to free Adelle. She felt like a rag doll as she slumped into his arms, but the metal would not release her.

In rage and desperation, Mason pulled out his .45 and fired through the broken passenger window. He fired five times at the charging truck. It was too dark, the headlights too blinding, for him to see what he might have hit.

The headlights and the truck's grille were on top of him. He flung himself backward, out the driver's door just as the truck collided with the sedan. He dived behind a tree a second before the truck impacted with the sedan. Like being shot from a cata- pult, the car became airborne. The rear fender hit the tree, flipping it around.

An instant later, the truck flew over the edge and swept past him in hell-bound pursuit, both vehicles tumbling and spinning before crashing into the bottom of the ravine.

Mason clambered down the slope, the snow and his shock making it difficult. He stumbled down the last four feet, then he jumped up and ran to the overturned car. Adelle dangled upside down, her leg still held firm by the crumpled door panel. There was no need to rush; she was dead.

He staggered over to the truck, which lay on the passenger's side. There were two men inside and both wore civilian clothes. The driver's body had tumbled onto the passenger, his head half gone from the impact of Mason's bullets. The passenger had fallen halfway out the door window, and the truck had landed on his chest. The man's eyes were frozen open to the black sky. Mason didn't recognize either of them. He had to bust through what remained of the windshield to search them, but they carried no IDs.

Returning to the sedan, Mason had the overwhelming need to free her from the steel and chrome coffin. Mason yanked at the door with all his strength. Over and over again he pulled at the door. Then, with one final tug, the door gave a few inches. That was enough. Adelle's body slumped onto the inside roof of the car. He pulled her from the wreck, despite pain that radiated from every muscle. He lifted her by her armpits and dragged her ten feet from the wreckage. He sat next to her and stared at nothing at all.

T he passing of time went unrecorded. Mason became aware of the ambulance and the MPs only when he noticed the red light sweeping across the snow and Adelle's bloody face. Flashlights and voices came to him, and he stood as MPs and two medics ran up to him. They asked him his name, and he responded. He summoned his strength and presence of mind, fished out his CID badge and identified Adelle. He started to explain what had happened, but the two medics took over and examined him.

"I'm okay," Mason said.

"No, sir, you're not," the sergeant medic said as he looked at Mason's head.

Mason touched his face and brought away blood. The medics took him by the arms and led him up the embankment to the waiting ambulance.

Mason jerked his arms free. "I don't need to go to the hospital."

"Let us determine that."

"You're not taking me to any goddamned hospital!" Mason yelled, which only made his head throb.

"All right," the sergeant medic said. "You're going to need a few stitches for your head."

"Patch me up, and let me go."

While the medics tended to Mason's head wound, another car pulled up. Abrams got out and ran up to the back of the ambulance. "I figured it was you when the call came in."

"Adelle's dead," Mason said, the words making his throat clench.

Abrams fell silent and put his hand on Mason's shoulder. Mason shot to his feet and pulled Abrams aside. "I need you to go to Laura's and warn her that Schaeffer might know where she lives. The only way the men in that truck knew where to intercept me was when I called Laura to make sure she was there. Most of the phones at the Sheridan barracks are on a common line, and whoever was listening heard me ask for an exchange in Breitenau. There's only one main road from Garmisch to there, so all they had to do was wait for me in a strategic spot. Eliminate two problems in one blow."

"I'll pull Wilson and Tandy off their surveillance and get them to go up there to stand guard."

Abrams started to leave, but Mason pulled him back. "Do that and come right back to HQ. I'm getting Volker tonight, and we say nothing about it. To anyone. Do you understand? I'm going to make him squeal no matter what it takes."

MASON SAT shirtless in a chair in a corner of the ground floor of MP headquarters. A doctor and medic examined him thoroughly, while Densmore stood nearby.

"You could have a concussion," the doctor said. "We need to get you x-rayed, and then observe you overnight."

"No," Mason said for what was probably the tenth time.

"You're as stubborn as an old mule."

"I don't want to waste time in a hospital."

"You've got bruised ribs and contusions on both thighs, not to mention the nasty laceration on that hard head of yours."

Abrams entered the lobby and walked up to the group. He gave Mason a subtle nod that all was taken care of.

An MP clerk came over to Densmore and handed him two sheets of paper. "The reports on the two in the truck."

Densmore's eyebrows rose as he read. He asked Mason, "You sure this wasn't an accident?"

"When a truck makes a three-point turn to slam into an already smashed car, it's not an accident."

"Well, the two assailants were MPs from the 508th in Munich. A Corporal Ivers and Private Frazier. They were reported AWOL two days ago."

"Munich?" Abrams said.

"You'd prefer they'd been from here?" Densmore asked Abrams.

"It means Schaeffer's got a long reach," Mason said. He expected Densmore to howl about accusing Schaeffer again, but he continued to look at the two reports.

Mason flinched with pain when the medic wrapped a bandage around his rib cage. The doctor tried to check his pupils again, but Mason tilted his head away. "I'm fine."

"Have it your way," the doctor said and put his instruments back in his bag.

Mason mumbled a "thanks" as the doctor walked away. His entire body was one big throb, but the pain of Adelle's senseless death hurt more.

The same clerk came up to them again. "Sirs, Colonel Udahl would like to see Mr. Collins and Mr. Abrams in his office."

"Now?" Densmore asked after looking at his watch.

"Right away, sir."

Densmore turned to Mason. "Good thing you're not in the hospital, or he would have insisted on wheeling you up there on a gurney."

"Calling for me, too," Abrams said. "This can't be good."

As Mason and Abrams climbed the stairs in the Rathaus' main building, Abrams filled Mason in. "Laura refused any help and wanted to send Wilson and Tandy away. She wants to stay put, and Berko said the same thing. I'm not sure her boyfriend was too happy about it."

"Damn stubborn..." Mason stopped himself.

"Don't worry, I only half listened to her. Wilson and Tandy are sitting in a car out front of her place, poor lads."

The two investigators were ushered straight into Colonel Udahl's office. The colonel waited for them on the sofa. He rose to shake their hands and said to Mason, "Glad to see you're okay. Sorry to hear about the German woman."

"A friend of yours?" said the booming voice behind Mason.

All turned to see Major Gamin striding into the room with a big grin as if making a grand entrance on a stage. Mason glanced at Udahl, who looked just as surprised as Abrams and he.

"You all look like you've seen a ghost," Gamin said. He stopped in front of them with his hands linked behind his back. He looked straight at Mason with one eyebrow pushed low. "Well?"

"She was the sister of the woman killed with Agent Winstone, and she was helping with—"

"Yes, I know all that. I've been catching up on your reports. Seems you stir up more trouble than you solve."

Udahl tried to change the subject by saying, "It's good to see you feeling better, Bob. It's been a while. Why don't we sit

291

down?" He made a gesture for all to sit, but Gamin ignored him.

"Sir," Abrams said, "those murders would have happened—"

"I don't remember giving you permission to speak," Gamin barked.

"This man has every right to speak," Mason said. "If you think you're gonna make up for lost time by being a hard-ass—"

"Mr. Collins, that will be enough," Udahl said.

Mason turned away from Gamin and asked Udahl, "Sir, you wanted to see us?"

Gamin took two steps toward Mason. "You have a black touch, Mr. Collins. People wind up dead when they're around you. And it will stop as of now."

"Major, please," Udahl said, but that was as far as he got.

"I'm transferring you out of here, Mr. Collins," Gamin said. "As far away as possible."

"Major," Udahl said, "this man stays until we can wrap up this case."

Gamin turned to Udahl. "He's under my command—"

"Don't make me pull rank and go over your head," Udahl said. He paused to gain his self-control, then looked at Mason. "I imagine your interview with Kessel yielded some useful information?"

"He says he was the front man," Mason said. "He received written instructions from concealed sources and wasn't able to provide further evidence." He noticed Abrams ogling at him out of the corner of his eye. Even if he could trust Udahl, he didn't trust Gamin, and he had no intention of mentioning the information about Volker.

"You don't feel you could get anymore out of him?" Udahl asked.

"He seemed sincere, like he was relieved to get things off his chest. I believe what he said is the truth."

Gamin fidgeted on his feet as if in a nervous frenzy. He said to Mason, "Colonel Udahl may want you to stay and finish this case, much to my objection"—he pointed to Abrams—"but day after tomorrow this man is on the first train for Frankfurt. He's to report to the 709th MP Battalion." He looked at Abrams. "That train leaves at ten-hundred hours. Be on it."

"Mr. Abrams has been invaluable to this investigation," Mason said.

"I don't care."

"If Colonel Udahl and General Pritchard, not to mention General Clay, are adamant about solving this case, then Mr. Abrams is vital—"

"Don't blow smoke up my ass. He's a rookie with about as much experience at detective work as I have at brain surgery."

"Then you must have quite a few satisfied patients—"

"Mr. Collins," Udahl said in a rising voice.

Mason turned to Udahl. "Sir, Mr. Abrams knows this case inside and out. He's performed as an investigator to the highest standards, and it would not only jeopardize the case, but it'd be unjust to punish him because of the setbacks."

"Mr. Abrams, what do you have to say for yourself?" Udahl asked.

Abrams cleared his throat. "Sir, I request that I be allowed to stay on. We're close. I know it. I will go where the army sends me, but I only ask that you delay my departure until we finish this."

"That may never happen," Gamin said.

"Give me a week, sir," Abrams said.

"Thirty-six hours," Gamin said. "And that goes for you, too, Mr. Collins. I don't know whose dick you're sucking, but it ends right now."

Mason wanted to slam his fist into Gamin's smug smile, though he wondered if this rabid-dog routine was another clever ruse to cover his involvement in the gang. First his stroke-addled charade, then this act. And now he was trying to torpedo the investigation by sending both of them away. It was time for Abrams and him to look closely at Gamin.

"Mr. Collins," Udahl said, "are you any closer to determining Major Schaeffer's role in this investigation?"

"Everything points to him, but he's been very careful about covering his tracks."

"Then find the proof you need ASAP. I'm depending on you to get it done. And Mr. Abrams, we appreciate all the work you've done so far for us, and I wish you all the best for your future in the army."

Mason and Abrams thanked them, saluted, and left. By this late hour, the corridor and stairway, in fact the entire building, had turned quiet. As they descended the stairs, Abrams said, "I'm not going to let them transfer me anywhere."

"Yes, you are."

"It doesn't make any sense. Why transfer me in the middle of an investigation when I've done nothing wrong? When we're so close?"

"That's exactly why you're being transferred. I think Gamin is doing this on purpose to cripple this investigation. For whatever reason, I think he's been putting on an act to cover up his guilt."

"You think Gamin is the lead guy?" Abrams shook his head. "I don't see it."

"He's in a perfect position to wield local power, but the lead guys are higher up on the food chain than him. We're talking colonels and generals, people with enough power to squash us both. And that's why I'm glad you're getting out of here before that happens."

"They're transferring you, too, you know," Abrams said.

"I don't think they plan for me to be alive long enough for that to happen. I know too much."

"I do, too."

They reached the ground floor, and Mason stopped to face Abrams. "Don't screw up your chances with the army. Keep your mouth shut and your head down, and you'll do fine."

"I don't want to stay in the army if it means I have to duck under a rock."

"I want to see you do well. Have a life and a career. In a couple of years this will all be history. They're giving you a gift. A way out, with excellent commendations and an exemplary record. All you have to do is keep quiet about all this. Do it. Now, let's go get Volker."

Mason noticed Abrams checking his watch again. "I bet the minute hand hasn't moved since the last time you checked."

"It's two past midnight," Abrams said. "Maybe we have the wrong spot. Maybe Kessel set us up."

"Maybe you want to be quiet just five minutes."

"I liked Adelle, too. You don't have to bite my head off."

"For once I'm pulling rank and ordering you to shut it."

Mason and Abrams had gone by Volker's mistress's apartment, but by the time they arrived, she had already stepped out. Waiting near Kurpark, Garmisch's city park, had become their only alternative. They sat in their car parked on the south side of the park, with a clear view of the main entrance and an isolated park bench. There were other park benches, but this one was under an umbrella of trees, making it the best for a clandestine rendezvous.

Apparently Mason had guessed correctly, as a woman, silhouetted in a lone street lamp, approached the bench. She wore an ankle-length ivory coat and a matching hat. The ensemble looked very expensive by the way the fabric shimmered in the light. She paused in front of the bench, looked both ways; her condensed breath swirled around her head as she did so. She finally sat, and the streetlamp illuminated one side of her face.

"That's her," Mason said.

"You sure?"

"Yep. Margareta Schupe. I interviewed her that night at the Casa Carioca about Hilda. I remember that face, and also how she moves—like she has well-lubed ball bearings in her hips."

"Didn't Adelle say that she was Schaeffer's squeeze?"

"Hence the out-of-the-way meeting place. She's stepping out on Schaeffer, and Volker's stepping out on his wife."

"Such naughty Nazis."

Mason chuckled despite himself.

Abrams pulled his gaze away from Margareta and looked at Mason as if trying to gauge Mason's intentions. "Even if you get Volker to admit to murder and name Schaeffer, kidnapping and torturing him—"

"Who said anything about torturing him?"

Abrams gave him a skeptical look. "Come on. Don't give me that. You do it, you'll never get him into a courtroom. This will more or less make him immune from prosecution. He could even try to get us in hot water with army prosecutors."

"The only courtroom I'd like to see him in is one for war crimes. My concern right now is to get him to talk. He talks, then we make sure his buddies find out about it. One way or another, this is Volker's last night of freedom."

"What are we going to do with the girl?" Abrams asked.

"We can't let her go. She'll run back to Schaeffer and tell all."

"Do what you want to Volker, but no harm comes to the girl."

"Apart from scaring her out of her wits, she'll be fine. Might make her think twice about the gangster-moll lifestyle." He noticed Abrams mooning over her. "Maybe she'll swoon into your arms."

A pair of car headlights appeared in the rearview mirror. The beams slashed across the asphalt. Margareta got to her feet and stepped to the curb.

"This is him," Mason said. They readied their pistols and watched as the car passed them. Mason recognized the 1938 Horch. "That's the car that was waiting outside Adelle's apartment when we went to get her."

Through the car windows, he saw a large-framed man driving, then Volker's distinct profile in the backseat.

"He's got his bodyguard driving him," Abrams said. "What do we do with that guy?"

"Time to wing it." Mason started the car and pulled ahead. When the Horch stopped next to Margareta, and she slid in, Mason hit the accelerator. The tires screeched as he raced up and stopped the car at an angle to block the Horch.

Mason and Abrams jumped out with guns up, aiming at the driver. It was Bolus, the muscle-bound bartender from the Casa Carioca.

"Hands up!" Mason shouted. "Don't make a move."

The driver did as he was told. Margareta screamed, jumped out of the car and started to run into the park. Abrams chased after her and tackled her to the ground. At the same moment, Mason rushed up to the driver's-side window. "Roll down the window. Slowly." When Bolus did so, Mason aimed his pistol at Bolus's head, reached in, and searched inside the man's overcoat. He pulled out a Lugar pistol and put it in his pocket. "Now take the key out of the ignition and put them in my hand." Bolus obeyed. Then Mason threw in his handcuffs. "Cuff yourself to the steering wheel."

The driver did what he was told while Abrams wrestled Margareta back into the car. Mason went to Volker's door and pulled it open. A glint of light reflected off metal. Mason ducked just as Volker fired a shot. The growl of the bullet zipped just past his ear.

Abrams put his pistol against Volker's temple. "Put it down on the floor. Easy does it."

Volker bent over to put the gun on the floorboard, but never made it all the way. Mason struck Volker across the temple with his gun butt, and Volker slumped in the seat.

Margareta screamed as she rolled herself into a ball. "Please don't kill me."

While Abrams tried to calm Margareta, Mason returned to Bolus and threw the handcuff key in his lap. "Take the handcuffs off and get out."

It took Bolus a moment to release himself and step out of the car. Noticing the man had a pronounced limp, Mason pinned him against the car. He pulled out his switchblade and cut open the man's pants leg. A fresh bandage was wrapped around his thigh.

"That's the exact spot I shot someone coming after Yaakov's family last night. What a coincidence."

Bolus's eyes popped wide with fear. Mason forced him to move around to the trunk. He fired two shots into the trunk lid.

"Wouldn't want you to suffocate." He gestured toward the trunk. "Get in."

"I'll freeze in there," Bolus said.

"I'm giving you a better chance than you gave that family at the bookstore." He aimed his pistol at Bolus's head, and Bolus climbed into the trunk.

Mason slammed the trunk lid shut and returned to Volker, who still lay dazed across the backseat. He cuffed Volker's hands behind his back. Volker moaned and started to come out of his stupor. His temple bled profusely. After applying a gag to Volker's mouth, Mason removed a canvas sack he'd stashed in his coat pocket and pulled it over the man's head. As quickly as they could, he and Abrams forced Volker and Margareta into their car.

Mason finished knotting the ropes that bound Volker's arms and legs to a heavy wooden chair. Volker sat quiet, stoic even, with the sack still pulled over his head. Only his heavy breathing betrayed his fear. Mason had prepared the villa's furnace room in advance of their abduction: the chair and the tableful of props to be used in the coming performance. Behind Mason sat the massive coal-burning furnace like a cast-iron medusa with its tangle of vent pipes stretching out to various parts of the house. After double-checking the ropes, he crossed the room and exited through a door of wood and banded iron, securing the latch behind him.

Abrams stood next to Margareta in the neighboring room. Her hands were bound behind her, but not to the chair. She still wore the gag that they'd been forced to use when she tried to scream for help. Abrams looked pained to see her that way, and Margareta pleaded for mercy with her doleful eyes. She struggled with her bindings when she saw Mason approach.

"Did you explain that we're not going to hurt her?" Mason asked.

"I tried, but I don't think she believes me."

Mason squatted next to Margareta. "What happens to you in the next hour or so is partly up to you. You're in the basement of an isolated house, so no one can hear you. But, for the sake of my ears, if you promise to keep quiet, we'll remove the gag. Okay?"

Margareta looked at Abrams then back to Mason. She nodded. Abrams stepped behind her and removed her gag. Margareta took in gulps of air, but she remained silent.

"Good," Mason said. "Now, if you also promise not to try and run away, then we'll untie your hands, too."

Margareta nodded again, and Abrams untied her hands.

Margareta rubbed her wrists and said, "What do you want from me?"

"We were only after Volker," Abrams said, "but we couldn't very well let you go."

"I won't tell anyone," Margareta said.

"Major Schaeffer is your lover, right?" Mason said more than asked.

Margareta looked at Mason as if she was unsure how to answer.

Mason continued, "Margareta, I'm afraid you have the worst taste in men I've seen since Eva Braun. Both Schaeffer and Volker have murdered about a dozen people. At least the ones we know about. Including Hilda Schmidt and Adelle Holtz."

"That's a lie!" Margareta said with little conviction in her eyes, like a child caught red-handed but denying it anyway. "I won't tell anybody. I swear. Let me go. Please."

As if on cue, she started to cry and covered her eyes with a trembling hand. Mason didn't buy it, but Abrams obviously did.

"Margareta," Abrams said, "we won't hold you any longer than we have to. Then you'll be free to go."

"I'm not sure about that, partner," Mason said. "I suspect Margareta here knew Schaeffer's and Volker's activities. That's aiding and abetting. She'll do some prison time."

Margareta suddenly recovered from weeping and gave Mason a fiery glare. "You've got nothing on me."

Mason looked at Abrams. "This lady would be a real good actress if she wasn't so obvious, changing her routines on a dime."

"I am…was an actress."

"There. You see, Mr. Abrams? She's an actress. I knew it."

Abrams looked puzzled by the direction Mason was heading.

"Not many jobs for German actresses these days, are there?" Mason said.

Margareta shook her head. "All I could find was that lousy skating job at the Casa."

"Not as much glamour or money, I bet." Margareta shook her head, and Mason said, "That's why you shacked up with Schaeffer and squeezed Volker on the side."

"A couple of cheap bastards," Margareta said.

Abrams looked shocked then disappointed that the potential flower of his eye had turned out to be bitter and jaded.

"I've got a proposition for you," Mason said.

Margareta barked a short, bitter laugh. "I hate cops. You couldn't pay me enough to open my legs for you two. That's what you really want, isn't it? You two will rape me and kill Ernst when you've got what you want."

"Miss," Abrams said, "that is not what's going to happen."

"You two make me want to vomit."

"But not your two scumbag boyfriends?" Mason said. "Now, before you let loose and ruin that obviously expensive dress of yours, listen to my proposition. You can make a wad of cash, plus you'll come out of this looking like an innocent victim. No jail time. No suspicion that you ratted on anyone."

Margareta couldn't hide her interest as Mason pulled out his wallet and fished out two hundred dollars—all the money he had until the end of the month. "How much have you got?" he asked Abrams.

Abrams still looked baffled, and not too happy to surrender money for a mysterious cause. He fished the money out of his wallet and counted it. "Fifty-two bucks."

Mason plucked the money from Abrams's clutches and said to Margareta, "That's two hundred fifty-two dollars. That's a lot of dough for a German."

Margareta looked him straight in the eye. "What do you want me to do?"

Mason entered the furnace room and left the heavy door open a crack. Volker lay facedown on the coal-stained floor. He'd obviously tried to free himself and had fallen forward with the chair now on top of him. He struggled with greater frenzy when Mason walked up to him.

"Now look what you did," Mason said. He jerked the chair violently into the upright position. He then yanked off the canvas hood. When Volker became used to the harsh light, his eyes popped wide for just a moment when he saw near the chair a wooden table displaying an array of blunt instruments. He recovered quickly and looked straight ahead with a dispassionate expression. Mason picked up a billy club and whacked the table with it. Volker jumped and blinked, then, with greater effort, he regained his composure.

Mason leaned in close to Volker's face. "I'm betting you're one of those sadistic bastards who can't take what he dishes out. I remember a similar basement and *your* instruments of torture. Now the world has turned. You know what comes next." Mason put the hood back over Volker's head. "I'm going to enjoy this."

Volker breathed heavily, and his body became rigid, which

triggered in Mason a primitive urge in him to do exactly what he promised, what he could have only dreamed of when Volker had tortured him so brutally. He could even smell the remnants of that sweet burned odor of the Turkish tobacco, the same musky cologne. That inner voice urged him to go ahead and return the favor. It took all of his will to keep from carrying out the punishment.

"You might be wondering why I'm keeping on the gag." He leaned in to Volker's ear. "There's nothing I want from you. There's nothing you could say that could make me stop."

A bloodcurdling scream came from the utility room, and Volker recoiled at the sound.

"My partner is going over your mistress. From her, we expect information, but she's trying to be brave and not talk. Braver than you, I think. That is, if we wanted any information from you."

In fact, Margareta was acting once again on an impromptu stage. She had agreed to take Mason's and Abrams's money for a one-night performance. "Ernst," she shrieked. "Please! Help me!"

Margareta screamed again, but if anything, it seemed to calm Volker. Apparently Volker was the kind of sadist who had little sympathy for the pain of others. Perhaps it even gratified him. It moved him only to the extent that it foretold what he would soon endure. Volker would react solely to his own suffering.

Mason picked up a thick rubber hose, very much like the one Volker had used on him. He laid it on Volker's shoulder and slowly pulled it across Volker's neck. Volker shuddered involuntarily.

Mason brought the hose up high then swung it across the sensitive part of Volker's shins. Volker jerked against his bonds, but only sputtered while trying to stifle cries of pain.

"Remember doing this to me?" Mason asked, and he did it again.

Volker couldn't control himself this time and screamed into the gag.

The creak of strained hinges caused Mason to turn. Abrams stood in the doorway. He looked with shock and anger at the rubber hose, then at Mason.

Margareta screamed again. "Oh, God. No. Please stop!" Even though Abrams—her designated torturer—was nowhere near her.

Mason walked over.

"What the hell are you doing?" Abrams hissed near his ear. "This is not what we agreed. That's why we're having Margareta do it. To scare Volker into talking."

With a lowered voice, Mason said, "He doesn't care about Margareta. Let me worry about how to handle him."

"No," Abrams said a little too loudly. "You're no better than him if you do this."

"This asshole deserves more. You know what he did to those people. He's the one who cut up Hilda. I'm sure of it."

"This is about what he did to you."

"To me, and countless others. My buddies. American soldiers."

"Don't do this, chief."

Mason pushed Abrams ahead of him into the other room. He shut the door and spun back to Abrams. "Don't question my methods."

"If I don't, who will? We're here to get information."

Margareta screamed, and Abrams said to her, "Hold off a second, would you?" Margareta shrugged, and Abrams turned back to Mason. "Give him a chance to talk."

"And if he doesn't?"

"Give it a try. Please."

Mason knew Abrams was right, though in his early days as a police detective he'd been taught, and practiced, the unspoken rule that if a man was truly guilty, then a few judicious blows were warranted. But somehow, this was different. The sheer terror of torture was too inhumane. Even for Volker.

"Let me try one more trick," Mason said. "It should push him over the edge. It won't hurt him… much." Off Abrams's skeptical look, Mason said, "You can supervise."

Abrams walked over to Margareta, and she did her best to seduce him with her eyes.

"You like my performance?" she asked.

Abrams pulled out his handcuffs. "Sorry, but I have to do this."

Margareta extended pouty lips. "You don't trust me?"

"Not even close," Abrams said. He handcuffed her to a water pipe and shushed her with his finger. He then followed Mason back into the furnace room and slammed the door shut.

"Your girlfriend has passed out, Volker," Mason said. "Looks like we can double-team you."

Volker panted beneath the hood. Mason retrieved the electrical cord he'd prepared earlier, with alligator clips attached to the two bare ends. He then yanked off Volker's hood. His ghostly pale face contrasted with the dried blood on his cheek and caked in his hair. He jerked his head back when Mason held out the electrical cord.

"This was your favorite torture method, as I recall. I still have the burn marks to prove it."

Volker tried to distance himself from the cord. He turned away and contrived a defiant expression.

"Let's try the earlobes first," Mason said, thinking of Yaakov's ruined corpse.

Volker swung his head wildly, but Abrams held him firm. Mason attached an alligator clips to each ear. He then stepped behind Volker, yanked his head back by his hair, and lifted the gag just high enough for the man to speak.

"Last chance," Mason yelled into Volker's ear. "Schaeffer's the one who ordered all the murders, isn't he?"

"I know the law. You can't do this. You'd better kill me, or run, because I'll see that you suffer until your last, agonizing breath."

"That's not going to happen, because you're going to be a drooling vegetable once I get done with you. You're not going to be able to remember your own name." He jerked Volker's head harder. "You and Schaeffer murdered Winstone and Hilda Schmidt. You carved up her face and stuffed the parts in Winstone's mouth. Didn't you?"

Volker tried to scream over Mason. "I don't know what you're talking about!"

Mason shoved the gag back in place and pulled down the hood. "We'll move on to other parts in a few minutes," Mason said. "Don't you worry about that." He noticed Abrams looking squeamish, so Mason winked at him.

"Let's get this over with," Abrams said.

Mason said to Volker, "My partner didn't get to experience what you put me through, so he's a little anxious to cut your throat and be done with it. I say, not quite yet."

Volker stiffened and huffed, trying to prepare for the worst. Mason walked the plug end of the cord over to a variable power supply with a large black dial that was plugged into an outlet. He plugged the cord into the power supply and threw the switch. It began a menacing hum. "Are you ready?"

Volker jerked against the ropes as if he already felt a searing jolt of electricity.

"Wait," Abrams said. He leaned in to Volker and talked in a low voice as if conspiring against Mason. "My partner is crazy over what you did to him. I can't stop him. He outranks me. You've got to give him something else to sink his teeth into. Something he needs more than torturing you."

Mason slowly turned the dial, the buzz of electricity getting louder. Volker sputtered and moaned at first, but it quickly turned to muffled screams. Then he went completely rigid. Mason kept the voltage low enough to make it excruciatingly painful, but not enough to do permanent damage.

Abrams screamed at Mason, "Stop!" But Mason waited another moment, then dialed it down to zero. Volker slumped forward against his bindings. He made a wheezing sound as he struggled to take in oxygen through his nostrils.

"That was at low voltage for only four seconds, Volker," Mason said. "Imagine thirty seconds turned all the way up. Imagine thirty seconds with the leads attached to your testicles. That's what you did to people."

"Chief, please," Abrams barked. He had tears in his eyes from witnessing such a horrible sight. He looked at Mason a moment longer, as if expressing that he finally understood what Mason had suffered under Volker. He turned back to Volker. "Quick, man. Give us something. If I put him on another track long enough, I can call this in to the MPs and get you out of here. But you have to help me."

Volker nodded his head violently, speaking unintelligible words through the gag.

Abrams said to Mason, "I'm removing the gag. He needs to breathe."

Mason smiled as he nodded. Abrams was doing a good job of playing along. Abrams untied Volker's gag, and Volker gasped for air as he muttered, "Please, please, please…" continually.

Abrams leaned in. "You better think fast, Ernst, or my partner will keep going."

Continuing the role of vengeful maniac, Mason said, "What are you two talking about over there?" He marched over to Abrams, simulating rage at his partner. "You said he needed to breathe. I don't want you coddling him and talking to him behind my back. I want to watch this man fry." He turned to Volker. "Hell with the ears. I'm going straight for the balls."

Mason started to pull on Volker's belt.

"No, please!" Volker screamed.

"Volker," Abrams said. "Say something."

Volker raised his head as if to scream it from the rooftops. "A deal's happening tomorrow. Schaeffer is personally supervising it."

"What kind of deal?" Abrams said, shouting now.

"A train is coming up from Austria."

"What's the train carrying?" Mason asked.

"Aluminum, chemicals, steel, and iron...."

"What else?"

Volker shook his head as he pleaded with his eyes. "That's all I know."

"Bullshit," Mason said and charged over to the power supply. As he reached for the dial, Volker screamed, "No!"

Mason went back to Volker and yelled close to Volker's face. "What else is the train carrying?"

Volker took a deep breath and closed his eyes as if the telling were painful. "There are two boxcars loaded with gold bars and currency from the Third Reich treasury. It was a shipment destined for Switzerland at the end of the war, but the SS men got only as far as Seefield, in Austria, before having to bury it. Some of those ex-SS men handed it over to the American authorities, and now it's being shipped to the American repository in Frankfurt."

"How's Schaeffer going to steal that kind of cargo off an American military train?"

"At least half the train is carrying German POWs released from Italy. They will have to make a stop just across the border to process the ex-prisoners and feed them."

"That's when they jump the train?" Mason said.

Volker nodded as he sucked in air. "Some of the MPs guarding the train are in league with Schaeffer, and Schaeffer has fake orders to turn over the boxcars of gold and currency to him."

Mason looked at Abrams. Even after everything he'd discovered about Schaeffer's organization, he found it hard to believe that so many people could be involved—MPs, senior officers issuing false orders—and that Schaeffer could manipulate the exact contents of an official train; especially that he could manage to attach such valuable cargo to a train hauling German ex-POWs. It struck Mason as unbelievable. It was ominous, even frightening.

"What time is the train supposed to arrive?" Mason finally asked.

"Around eight tomorrow evening. At the MP checkpoint way station south of Mittenwald."

Mason got in Volker's face. "You gave it up in about twenty minutes flat. You worked on me for a week, and I never gave it up. Isn't that right, Volker? You lied about that to Schaeffer."

Volker lowered his eyes and sputtered, "Yes."

Mason put the hood back on Volker's head, and Volker let out a yelp. "Please, no more," he said. "I did what you asked."

Mason signaled for Abrams to follow him, and they exited the room. Mason slammed the furnace room door shut, threw the latch and secured it with a padlock.

Margareta shook her hands, making the handcuffs rattle against the metal pipe. "Are you going to let me go?"

"Sure," Mason said. "Tomorrow night."

"Tomorrow? You can't do that. You promised."

"Now, don't you fret. We're *all* spending the night. Hell, you get to stay in this beautiful villa with two handsome men. What else could a girl ask for?"

33

A brams turned the car onto Kreuzackerstrasse, a small street in a working-class neighborhood. Though the houses were quite respectable by American middle-class standards, they seemed tiny after the sprawling villas in Winstone's part of town.

Abrams parked the car in front of a simple white stucco house with a sloping, red-tiled roof. Like many of the houses in this area, it had been divided into a triplex to house the bulging population.

"I still don't think this is a good idea," Abrams said. "In fact, I think it's crazy."

Abrams watched as Mason checked his pistol. "Aren't we here to ask this guy to help us?"

"You don't walk into a lion's cage without a chair and a whip."

They got out of the car and walked up a dirt path leading to the left side of the house. They stopped at a side door labeled 44C. Mason knocked and waited.

Abrams yawned. "Do you know how many times Margareta had to go to the bathroom last night? Uncuff and cuff. I think I got three hours of sleep, what with her yammering and trying to seduce me."

"At least you got the girl. I had to stare at Volker's ugly mug all night."

Mason knocked again, and Abrams said, "I half expected to see you'd beaten him some more during the night."

"Sure, I wanted to strangle him. Put him out of my misery. But I didn't."

"Oh, yes, the man showed incredible self-control," Abrams said sarcastically.

Mason glanced at Abrams, then punched the door. The whole door panel rattled in its frame. The door swung open.

Hans Weissenegger had to dip his head below the door frame. He wore flannel pajamas and looked like a giant-sized Papa Bear from the kid's nursery rhyme. "What the hell?" When he saw Mason, he snarled, "You!" and balled up his fists.

Mason held up his hands. "Hold on, Hans."

With one long step, Hans was out the door. He towered over both of them. "I ought to kill you right now for what you did."

"Kessel is fine," Mason said. "We're going to make sure he stays that way and does as little prison time as possible."

Abrams said, "It turns out, he was just a fall guy for Schaeffer and Volker—"

"Shut up, you," Hans said. "My beef is with this guy."

"Hans, we didn't come here for a fight, and I'm not going to apologize for arresting Kessel. We're cops. We arrest people who break the law. Kessel took the fall like a man. We respect that and will treat him right. He'll be out in no time. Now, I want you to calm down and listen to what we've got to say."

Hans thought a moment as he glared at both of them. "You'd better be damned about it. This is my sleep time."

"How about we go inside and talk? You've got to be freezing with just your jammies on."

Hans mumbled a curse and stepped inside, ducking first, and stood in the living room. After Mason and Abrams followed, Hans shut the door and crossed his arms.

Mason looked at Abrams with a here-we-go look. "Hans, we need you to do something for us."

Hans looked incredulous. "You want me to do something for you? How crazy are you guys?"

"Pretty crazy," Abrams said under his breath to Mason.

Mason glanced at Abrams before turning his attention back to Hans. "I'm trying to figure out how to say this without it being a blow to you...." He paused. "Hans, we have some bad news. Adelle was killed last night."

Hans's arms dropped to his sides, and his jaw went slack. "Who did that? I'll kill the son of a bitch!" The words had started out as a moan and ended as a roar.

"I killed the men who did it," Mason said.

"You were there?"

Mason nodded. "I was taking her to a safe place. They tried to kill both of us."

"And look at you. A couple of stitches."

Mason quickly told him what had happened the previous night with the truck slamming into the car. "Those guys were under orders. Some other people ordered the murder. And I've got one of them locked up in a villa."

"Why didn't you kill him?"

"We're cops. We don't kill people we arrest."

"Well, I'll do it. Who is it?"

"Ernst Volker."

Hans froze. Either he was too shocked to speak or afraid of the power behind the man.

"The other man is Schaeffer," Abrams said.

"Schaeffer..." Hans said in a weak voice. The concept of losing Adelle was finally sinking in. Tears formed in his eyes. He rubbed his head with one beefy hand then turned away. "They killed Adelle?"

"Hans, you have to listen to me. She knew too much. Anyone who knows too much winds up dead. Schaeffer won't stop. He'll kill anyone who even looks to be in his way. We've got to bring him down. And that's where you come in. Volker gave us a way to bust Schaeffer tonight. Up until now, we haven't found any witnesses still alive or any concrete evidence. If we catch Schaeffer red-handed, we've got him, and he won't do any more killings."

"You want me to go along as muscle? I'll get Schaeffer to talk —right before I break his neck."

"Actually, we want you to babysit Volker and his girlfriend."

"He's not in jail? Are you running a boardinghouse for murderers now?"

"We don't know which MPs are on Schaeffer's payroll. If we put him in jail, he could get word to Schaeffer."

Hans pondered this for a moment. "Alone with one of Adelle's killers?" He nodded. "Count me in."

WHEN ABRAMS DROVE up the driveway of Winstone's villa, Hans whistled. "Not bad. If you arrest me, do I get to stay here?"

Abrams parked and the three men entered the villa.

"The girlfriend's upstairs in the front bedroom," Mason said to Hans.

"And don't get any ideas," Abrams said.

"Who do you take me for, huh?"

"What I meant was, watch out for her. She'll make you feel like the sexiest man alive and promise you anything if you let her go."

"Who says I'm not?"

Mason led him down to the vast basement. They had to pass through several rooms to reach the furnace room. Mason unlocked the padlock, but before he opened the door, he said to Hans, "No beating on him. Scare him as much as you want. It's easy to do."

Mason and the others entered the room. Volker sat on a chair in a corner. He was handcuffed to a loop of chain that gave him a few feet of freedom. A bucket had been provided to relieve himself, and a table held a canteen of water and a loaf of bread.

Volker jumped out of his chair and huddled in the corner when he saw Mason, but when he laid eyes on Hans lumbering through the door, he looked like he would crawl into the bucket.

"You know each other," Mason said to Volker. "Hans is very upset about Adelle's killing."

"You keep him out of here!" Volker cried. "You have no right..." His voice seized as his body shook. He turned his face to the wall.

"See what I mean?" Mason said to Hans.

"Where's the challenge?"

"And remember what I said..." Mason then turned so Volker could hear. "Treat him just the way we talked about."

As he and Abrams left the room, Mason looked back at Hans and said, "Don't have too much fun."

34

Mason had the impression that every eye followed him and Abrams as they crossed the ground floor of MP headquarters.

Out of the corner of his mouth, Abrams said, "Have we got swastikas painted on our foreheads?"

"Half of them suspect we're up to no good, and the other half think we're about to cut off their extra income."

When they mounted the stairs the activity below returned to normal.

"Your assignment is to recruit MPs for tonight," Mason said. "Ones that aren't on the take and can keep their mouths shut."

"Do I look like the MP camp counselor? How am I supposed to know who's on the take and who's not? Most of these MPs are good guys, but my trustworthy detector doesn't seem to be working."

They entered Mason's office, and Mason shut the door. "MPs usually know about other MPs. The team keeping an eye on Schaeffer—Wilson and Tandy. They've just moved up from the MP ranks, and they've been good about keeping their mouths shut and doing their job. Have them help you find some more guys."

"We can't pull too many for this operation without raising suspicion."

"Ideally ten," Mason said as he laid his satchel on the desk and took off his coat.

Abrams let out a big sigh showing his discomfort with the assignment. As soon as he walked out the door, Densmore entered.

"I was just coming to see you," Mason said.

"Then you lost your way sometime between last night and eleven o'clock this morning."

"I had a few things to tend to."

"I believe it. You look like shit." Densmore closed the office door. "It wouldn't have anything to do with that incident at Kurpark, would it? People reported several gunshots and screaming. And an MP patrol checked out a vehicle parked there overnight. They found one of the Casa Carioca's employees frozen to death in the trunk. He had a bullet wound in his thigh that the ME figures was patched up about two days ago. About the time you shot a guy in the leg trying to kill your informant's family."

"Well, I'll be damned," was all Mason offered.

"Is that your handiwork? Blood on the backseat, tire tracks blocking the car, four sets of footprints....?"

Mason looked Densmore in the eye. "I still wonder how much I can trust you."

"I don't give a damn whether you do or not. Was that your doing last night?"

Mason could use another ally, but Densmore appeared to be neither friend nor foe. The man made most of his decisions based on saving his career and his skin. But Densmore already knew enough and had had plenty of opportunities to see Mason kicked out of the CID or put behind bars... or worse.

Finally Mason said, "That was Volker's car. The man in the

trunk was Volker's driver and a bartender at the Casa Carioca. The one I just happened to shoot in the thigh when he and the others came for Yaakov's family."

"What about Volker?"

"I've got him tucked away someplace safe."

"I'm not going to ask where."

"I wasn't planning to tell you. But there's one thing: Volker gave me a way to get at Schaeffer."

"*Gave* it to you, did he?" Densmore smiled slightly and shook his head. "All right, then. What's your plan?"

Mason gave a rundown of what Volker had told him about the train carrying valuable cargo and German ex-POWs from Italy. "Since the train runs through French-occupied Austria, part of the trip is supervised by French authorities. Just over the border they exchange supervision with Americans at a way station."

Mason walked Densmore over to a wall map of southern Bavaria. He pointed to a spot south of the town of Mittenwald and just north of the German-Austrian border. "The train will stop at this checkpoint to process and feed the ex-prisoners. From what Volker told me, about half the MPs guarding the train are under Schaeffer's control. They'll separate the train's load in half and have another locomotive waiting to hook onto the cargo cars. They have signed orders, official carnets, and paperwork to make the exchange."

"That's a major haul. We're talking millions of dollars."

"That's why Schaeffer's personally supervising. I imagine he doesn't want his crew getting any ideas."

"They'll be heavily armed. We should get half the battalion in on this."

"Get the battalion alerted, and I guarantee you, Schaeffer will be tipped off."

Densmore shook his head. "We can't risk losing that cargo. If Schaeffer gets tipped off, too bad. We'll get him on another bust."

"Abrams and I are being shipped out tomorrow. There won't be another bust. And Schaeffer will find another way of stealing it. We'll lose not only the cargo, but Schaeffer, too."

Mason could tell Densmore was weighing his options: Going in undermanned against a heavily armed and desperate gang was an enormous risk. And if they botched the operation, and command discovered they hadn't alerted the battalion, they would both go down hard.

Mason said, "If we catch Schaeffer red-handed and capture the orders authorizing the transfer, we might be able to trace their source. Bag the high-ranking officers behind them. You want to think of your career, just imagine what a bust like this could do. General Clay is watching this closely and putting pressure on Pritchard and Udahl—"

"Don't try dangling that in my face. I know you don't think much of me, but I didn't become a cop just to feather my bed. And don't think I don't know why you're doing this. I know about your deal with Pritchard, and how you'd benefit from this bust."

"That's at the bottom of my list of reasons why I want Schaeffer. He's either murdered or ordered the murders of a dozen people, including friends of mine and a mother and a child." Mason lowered his voice and took a step closer to Densmore. "It's now or never. Are you in? Or are you out?"

Densmore let out a big sigh. "I'm going to regret this."

IT WAS midafternoon when Mason drove over to the Sheridan barracks. Densmore and he had hammered out many of the details of the evening's raid, though Abrams was still out trying to form their squad of MPs.

Mason entered the barracks' cell wing and accompanied a jail guard to the end of the hall, to Kessel's cell. Kessel sat on the bunk with his back to the door and his head leaning against the wall. He remained motionless as the guard unlocked the cell and Mason took two steps inside. Mason asked the guard to step back down the hallway and not let anyone approach the cell.

When the guard's footsteps had faded down the hall, Kessel said, "You promised to take care of her."

"You heard what happened?"

Kessel shot to his feet and swung around to face Mason. "You promised!"

"Yes, I did," Mason said calmly. "It was an ambush. They knew exactly where to wait for us. They were trying to take us both out."

"I should have known better than to trust an American. She was German and meant nothing to you. Like all German girls, you Americans think of them as playthings."

"I felt more for her than you think."

Kessel dropped to his bunk. "At least you were honorable enough to come and face me."

"I underestimated Schaeffer's reach. We can't help Adelle, but we *can* bring the killers to justice."

"Justice. There's no justice possible when the cops are inept or corrupt."

"There's more than one way to carry out justice."

Kessel looked at Mason, his eyes showing he knew what Mason meant.

"For instance," Mason said, "thanks to you, I've got Volker. With a little persuasion, he gave me a way to get at Schaeffer. The one thing he refused to admit is any involvement in the murders of Adelle, her sister, Winstone, and all the rest. But I'm betting you know."

"I had nothing to do with that. I told you that already."

"But you know who did. And I don't want to hear any crap

about having no proof. You knew, and you let it go on. You did nothing to stop them, and now they've killed Adelle. That's why you're so upset. You had a hand in killing her just as much as Volker and Schaeffer. Now it's time for you to have some balls and tell me what you know."

Kessel jumped up and pointed toward the door. "I suppose now you'll promise to keep me safe, too. A promise you know you can't keep."

"If you insist on being a coward, and Adelle's killers stay free, then you're right: It's only a matter of time before they get to *you*."

"Get out! We're through talking."

Mason slowly went to the cell door and called for the guard. He then turned back to Kessel. "I'm going to have you transferred to another prison. I won't say which for obvious reasons."

"They'll have me killed for trying to escape."

"I'll get someone I can trust to drive you up there."

The guard unlocked the door, and Mason exited. He looked back at Kessel as he walked away. Kessel had resumed his position, with his back to the cell and his head against the wall.

35

M ason watched the road through his binoculars. "Here they come."

He and Abrams sat in the front seat of a borrowed army ambulance. Abrams used his own binoculars, and they watched as a jeep and two troop transport trucks proceeded down the two-lane highway. The small convoy was too distant to see the occupants clearly.

"How do you know it's them?" Abrams asked. "It could be just a convoy heading for Austria."

Mason checked his watch. It was 7:45. "The timing is right."

"What if Schaeffer isn't with them? Maybe he decided to sit this one out. Or someone tipped him off."

"Then we'll make the army very happy we saved their cargo, but we'll be screwed."

Mason and Abrams's ambulance was parked at the south edge of a wide, semicircular clearing in the narrow valley cut into the mountains by the Isar River. Less than a mile away from the Austrian border, a makeshift way station had been constructed as a border control point. Three train sidetracks branched off from the main line coming up from Austria and Italy, with each sidetrack divided by an open area of ten yards. A confiscated farm-house and two outbuildings sat in the middle of the clearing and served as offices and housing for two officers, six MPs, and a clerical staff of three. Next to the farmhouse, a large tent had been erected as a triage center for seriously ill, injured, or half-frozen ex-POWs and civilian refugees from the Sudetenland, who were often transported in open boxcars. Other tents housed teams preparing hot soup or served as the register station to process the incoming ex-POWs. The POW-cargo train was scheduled to arrive in fifteen minutes, and since the train carried close to three hundred ex-POWs and "prisoners of interest," army headquarters had sent down an MP captain and eighteen MPs from a POW facility near Stuttgart to take over control of the train.

Four MPs dressed as medics sat in the back of Mason's ambu-lance. Mason had already checked in with the chief surgeon in the triage tent and explained their presence by claiming that Third Army had sent them down as a combat-ready medical team to provide armed treatment for any of the "prisoners of interest" who might need it. On the north end of the clearing, Densmore, Wilson, and four more MPs hid just inside the tree line—half of them dressed as medical personnel and half dressed in Corps of Engineers' uniforms. The plan was that once the train arrived and the POWs disembarked, they would use the inevitable chaos of dealing with so many POWs as a way to blend in with the rest of the crowd.

After a few tense minutes of watching the convoy, Mason said, "Schaeffer's in the lead jeep."

A few moments later the convoy turned into the clearing and pulled in behind the farmhouse. Schaeffer leapt out of the jeep and strode like a four-star general up to the MP captain. The way station's lieutenant joined them, and the group shook hands, though the MP captain looked wary of Schaeffer's unexpected arrival.

"That answers one of our questions," Abrams said. "The captain's probably not on Schaeffer's payroll."

"Unless Schaeffer's buying his allegiance as we speak," Mason said.

Schaeffer showed the lieutenant and MP captain what Mason assumed were the orders and other official paperwork. The captain frowned and gesticulated wildly, then jabbed the paperwork with his index finger. He was obviously not happy about orders directing him to relinquish control of the valuable cargo, but while Schaeffer continued to argue, he made a hand signal for his men to exit the trucks.

As Mason watched Schaeffer's men climb down from their vehicles, he said to Abrams, "I count sixteen MPs and five railroad crew."

Densmore's voice came over the Handi-Talkie, "I recognize three of ours in that bunch."

Mason picked up the Handi-Talkie and said, "Yeah, and there's a couple of the MPs from Company A in Munich. And some of the MPs and railroad crew are Poles from the Casa Carioca."

Schaeffer's men milled around in groups of three and four. They avoided contact with the real MPs and slowly began to spread out, some heading to the north end and some the south. The Poles dressed as railroad crew headed in the general direction of Schaeffer's carless locomotive that waited with steam billowing on the sidetrack closest to the main line.

Densmore's voice came over the Handi-Talkie again. "Twenty-two to our twelve. This could get interesting."

"We concentrate on Schaeffer if this gets messy."

"There's train smoke coming up from the south. It'll be here in a couple of minutes."

"Remember, we let that train pull in and disembark the POWs.

We move only when Schaeffer's crew starts to separate out the cargo cars from the POW cars."

Mason watched as Schaeffer and the captain continued to have words. The way station lieutenant stood next to Schaeffer, butting in from time to time. Obviously the MP captain had no idea what was going down, but the lieutenant knew very well what Schaeffer had in mind.

Finally the low rumble and chug of a train came echoing up the valley floor. Then the train's whistle blew, announcing its arrival. Moments later the cargo train slowed to a crawl on the main line, while one of the German railroad workers threw the switch. The train rolled onto the sidetrack closest to the farmhouse. The train had fourteen boxcars, with a single passenger car separating the first five cars containing the valuable cargo from the final nine holding the ex-POWs.

When the final car cleared the main line the locomotive stopped. Immediately, a dozen French and American MP guards climbed down from the tops of the cars and took up positions around the train. They were joined by another six French MPs, and two French officers, and two American officers, who had exited the passenger car coupled in the middle. Then the captain's MPs and the way station MPs formed a second line. Everyone readied their weapons.

At the same time, Schaeffer's railroad workers set about preparing their locomotive and uncoupling the one that had brought in the cargo. The cargo train's engineer jumped down and started yelling at them until two of Schaeffer's "MPs" pulled him aside.

Except for Mason, little notice was taken of this altercation, as all eyes were fixed on the train and a French officer as he ordered his men to open the final nine boxcars. Three hundred haggard German ex-POWs, with worn and dirty uniforms, poured out onto the platform.

Mason said into the Handi-Talkie, "Okay. It's time." He then called to the men waiting inside the ambulance, "Let's go, guys. Nice and easy."

The four MPs dressed as medics hopped out and milled around the back of Mason's ambulance. As Mason had hoped, no one appeared to notice him and his team. Mason watched as Schaeffer intercepted two American officers who had exited the train's passenger car. The unhappy MP captain followed close behind.

Mason leaned in close to Abrams and said, "Volker said the two American train officers were in on it. The poor captain doesn't have a chance."

Schaeffer showed the two American officers his paperwork. They appeared content with the transfer, trading handshakes and nodding their heads—all a great theater for the MP captain's benefit. The MP captain was having none of it, and now found himself fighting against three higher-ranked officers.

Meanwhile, the official doctors and medics began circulating among the ex-POWs. A group of men came out from one of the tents and set up tables on the ground between sidetracks. Large pots of soup were laid upon the tables along with metal bowls. Once the ex-prisoners were checked, they lined up hungrily for the hot soup.

At the opposite end of the clearing, Densmore and his men casually emerged from the tree line. They meandered or talked among themselves, and again, with all the activity no one seemed to be aware of them.

Mason and his men would wait until Schaeffer made a definitive move to couple the cargo to his waiting locomotive, but Schaeffer and the MP captain continued a heated argument.

"Come on, captain," Mason said to himself, "let Schaeffer take his train." He said to Abrams, "The guy has to pick the one time to be smart and question orders and superior officers."

Schaeffer's train crew finished uncoupling the cargo train's locomotive, with Schaeffer's MPs forcing the cargo train's real crew to assist. The now-cowed engineer tooted one warning and pulled forward onto a maintenance track. Mason's and Densmore's teams merged with the outer fringes of the captain's MPs, the way station medics, and the soup detail.

Schaeffer's locomotive tooted its whistle, and, with a great rush of steam, it slowly backed onto the inside track. It finally struck the coupling of the lead cargo boxcar, making the whole train shudder.

At the same moment, another train's whistle sounded in the near distance. As if an air-raid siren warned of an imminent attack, everyone stopped and turned in the direction of the sound. A uniformed clerk suddenly rushed out of the farmhouse and went straight for the lieutenant. He spoke hurriedly, and, in turn, the lieutenant rushed over to Schaeffer.

Something was wrong.

Mason pulled his helmet down to his eyes, lowered his head, and intercepted the clerk returning to the office. "What's going on?" he asked as offhandedly as he could.

"It ain't good," the clerk said. "Another train carrying Russian ex-POWs is making an emergency stop. Trouble with the locomotive."

"Russian and German ex-POWs in the same station?"

The clerk nodded. "They're one of the last groups of Russian ex-POWs to be forcibly repatriated back to Russia, and they ain't happy about it. Not since they heard the stories of repatriated POWs being sent to Siberian gulags or executed for being exposed to the decadent West. The train's carrying guards, but the conductor radioed a warning that, somehow, a bunch of the Russians got hold of ten cases of schnapps. They're angry, drunk, and rowdy."

"Can't they hold the train off?" Mason asked.

"Nope. There's another train due to come through here in about thirty minutes."

Mason kept his head down and took a circular route back to Abrams. By then the railroad crew had separated the cargo boxcars and the passenger car from the rest of the train.

"What's happening?" Abrams asked.

"This could get really ugly."

Just then, the Russian ex-POW train eased into the way station and onto the middle track. When it came to a stop, the U.S. guards aboard it jumped down. The engineer climbed down from the locomotive cab and waved at Schaeffer's railroad crew to come check out the locomotive. Meanwhile, the Russians locked in the boxcars yelled and pounded on the doors. The lieutenant in charge of the second train ordered his men to form a line with guns ready. Then a sergeant moved down the line, opening each boxcar, yelling orders in Russian as he did so.

Seeing the line of MPs with their guns ready, the Russians calmly descended into the field dividing the two trains. They glared at the Germans, a few yelled insults, but they seemed intimidated enough by the armed guards.

Schaeffer's locomotive, now coupled to the cargo boxcars, slowly pulled forward. Schaeffer and his men moved toward it, which signaled his train crew to walk away from the Russian-POW-train engineer who had demanded their aid. The engineer yelled at them to come back, but the men ignored him.

Mason waved his hand, and his men moved in. He felt a rush of excitement. If they could surprise Schaeffer's men with guns drawn, then they had them. He hoped everyone knew their job, and that they could subdue and arrest all of Schaeffer's men without it turning into a shoot-out.

Mason zeroed in on Schaeffer, hand on his pistol but not drawn. Schaeffer sauntered toward his waiting train as if stealing a train was all in a day's work. Mason quickened his pace when

Schaeffer got within ten feet of his train, but at that moment a gunshot rang out. All heads turned.

A German POW dropped to the ground. A wild-eyed Russian held a pistol. He fired at the crowd of Germans again, and, as though it had been a starting pistol for a footrace, the Russians surged toward the Germans, blowing past the bewildered guards. Enraged, the Germans charged, and like a scene out of a battle on the Russian front, the two groups slammed into each other. The MP captain's men and the Russian-POW-train guards fired their weapons in the air in a vain attempt to quell the riot.

The ruckus had also caused Schaeffer to look back. That was when he saw Mason. Then he noticed the ring of men coming toward him. He yelled something Mason couldn't hear over the Russian and German melee. He and his men pulled their weapons and fired as they ran for the passenger car. Densmore's group was closer, and they opened fire. Mason's group charged for the train, but they had to shove or dodge their way through the fighting Russians and Germans.

One of Densmore's MPs went down, then one of Schaeffer's.

Mason lost sight of Schaeffer as he shoved or fought off enraged brawlers. Finally he broke through the crowd and saw several of Schaeffer's men had clambered onto the slowly moving train. They fired back at Mason and his men. Bullets whizzed past, and another man went down. Mason tried to get the MP captain's attention as he ran, but the captain looked confused as to what emergency to address first.

With a blast of smoke and steam, Schaeffer's train began to pick up speed. Only a few of its cars remained on the curved branch, and once all the cars had moved onto the main line, the train could accelerate.

Mason broke into a sprint with Abrams right behind him. He saw two of Densmore's MPs had broken off from the scuffle and were also running alongside the train, but they immediately disappeared into the steam and smoke.

Finally the MP captain realized that the precious cargo was being stolen right in front of him. He rallied some of his MPs to help Densmore's squad assault the men in Schaeffer's gang who had yet to make it to the train.

As Mason closed in on the passenger car, a man stepped out on the car's end platform and fired. Mason returned the fire. The man crumpled and fell to the tracks. With so many bullets flying around, he couldn't tell if it was his bullet that had brought the man down.

A moment later, Schaeffer's train cleared all the car onto the main line, and it picked up speed. Mason's lungs burned as he ran. He concentrated all his efforts on catching the train. He stared at the handrail and pushed himself to the limit. Finally he grabbed the railing of the passenger car and hauled himself up onto the first step of the rear platform.

"Mason!"

Mason looked back. Abrams reached for Mason's hand as he ran flat out. Mason caught his arm and pulled him onto the step.

The train was running under full power now, speeding through the narrow valley. Mason and Abrams held tight to the railing of the passenger car's platform as they tried to catch their breath. There was a single rear door with one small window, and as long as they kept their heads low, they were concealed. But from this position it was impossible to see how many of Schaeffer's men might be waiting inside.

As Mason reloaded his pistol, Abrams yelled over the noise, "How many?"

"At least five. Maybe more."

"Are we the only ones?"

"I think I saw two of Densmore's men, but I'm not sure they made it."

Mason looked back and saw a truck had pulled out onto the highway running parallel with the tracks. Even if it was Densmore with a squad of MPs coming to their aid, it would take too long for the truck to catch up. They had to do it alone.

Abrams's eyes were wide with fright. Being shot at had been bad enough, but now they had to charge blindly through the rear door of the passenger car of a fast-moving train. How many men? How many guns? Abrams looked at Mason.

Mason tried to calm Abrams with a confident smile. "Ready?"

Abrams nodded violently, making his helmet bob on his head. They both took deep breaths as they shifted in place just below the door's window. Mason grabbed the latch and counted to three.

He shoved the door open. Both ran in, yelling from fright and adrenaline, guns up and fingers on the triggers. They stopped fast. The two MPs from Densmore's squad that Mason had seen running alongside the train now had their Thompson submachine guns trained on six of Schaeffer's men. One of Schaeffer's men had a serious chest wound, while another had a superficial wound on his neck.

"How many more of Schaeffer's men?" Mason asked one of the MPs.

"We don't know."

Abrams leaned over and took deep breaths.

"He all right?" the other MP asked.

"Just winded," Mason said.

Abrams straightened, his face as pale as the snow outside.

"It's not over yet," Mason said.

Abrams nodded. Mason moved through the passenger car, with Abrams following close behind. As he passed Densmore's men he said, "We're going up front."

They stopped at the door, and Mason peered out the window. No one waited for them on the platform or the coupling area between the passenger car and first boxcar. They moved out onto the forward platform. The train rolled at close to full speed. The track, the ground, the snow-covered pine trees blurred by.

Mason yelled, "We have to go up and over."

"Are you serious?"

"It's the only way."

Abrams groaned, but he slid past Mason, climbed off the platform, and gingerly crossed the coupling. He grabbed on to the ladder leading up to the roof and took slow, careful steps upward. Mason followed. At the top of the ladder, Abrams peeked over the top and yelled, "Clear."

They both climbed up and stood on the roof, bent at the waist. The clack of the train wheels and the roar of the locomotive echoed loudly in the narrow canyon.

"Just concentrate on your feet," Mason yelled over the noise.

Abrams groaned and moved tentatively forward. Mason looked back. Densmore's truck was gaining, but still far behind. With careful steps on the rocking boxcar, they proceeded across the roof, then, three feet from the front edge of the roof, Mason signaled for them to crouch low. With guns up, they crept up to the edge and peered down. Two of Schaeffer's men clung to the boxcar rails and stood on the coupling.

Mason and Abrams took aim, and Mason yelled down, "Drop your weapons. Hands up!" When the two looked up in surprise, Mason said, "Do it now."

The two MPs slowly jettisoned their weapons and raised their hands.

"Hello, Richardson," Abrams said.

Richardson grimaced as if expecting something very painful in his immediate future, and he leapt off the train.

"Jesus," the other man said.

Mason climbed down and checked the man for weapons. He then called up to Abrams, "Take him back to the passenger car."

"What about you?"

Mason shrugged that there was nothing else they could do. After helping Abrams get their prisoner onto the roof, Mason began to cross the next set of boxcars. With each boxcar, he repeated the process, moving swiftly across, then checking each junction for more of Schaeffer's men. He had no idea what he would do if he encountered more men clinging to the cars, but fortunately the rest of the cars were clear.

On the lead boxcar, Mason crouched low at the gap between the car and the locomotive's tender. At that moment, the train's whistle blew long and loud. Mason rose high enough to see over the top of the locomotive. The train was barreling down on the town of Mittenwald at full speed. An unscheduled train hurtling through town could wreak havoc.

Mason jumped the gap and landed on the lower section of the tender. He crawled up to the higher lip of the coal storage section and looked down into the locomotive's cabin.

Schaeffer stood in the cabin with the engineer, fireman, and two MPs. One of the MPs had his pistol jammed into the engineer's neck. Mason aimed his pistol at the group.

"Nobody move!"

The MP holding the gun on the engineer whipped around and aimed at Mason. Mason fired once, and the MP went down. The rest of the group raised their hands.

"Stop this train. Now!" Mason yelled.

The engineer applied the brakes. The wheels screeched and steam billowed, engulfing the cabin and obscuring the men. Mason rolled quickly to the ladder, knowing Schaeffer would try something now.

The steam began to dissipate, but before Mason could reach the cabin platform, Schaeffer emerged, preparing to jump off the still-moving train. Mason was ready. He rushed across the cabin and grabbed Schaeffer by the collar. Rage gave him the strength to pull Schaeffer off his feet and propel him into a steel panel.

Schaeffer's head bounced back from the impact, and he slumped in Mason's grasp. He then spun, but the second MP and the fireman grabbed him to hurl him off the train.

"Let him go or you're both dead!" Densmore said. He and three of his MP squad had caught up to the train as it stopped. Their guns were trained on the men in the cabin.

The men released Mason and held up their hands. Breathless, Mason acknowledged Densmore with a nod, then shoved Schaeffer's head up against the steel panel again. He pulled Schaeffer's head back by the hair so he could speak into his ear. "I'm going to watch you hang."

B y the time Mason and the rest returned to the way station the riot had been reasonably subdued. The Germans and Russians had at least been separated. Those injured in the melee were sent to the hospital triage tent and medic station. Considering the amount of gunfire exchanged, there were only a handful of casualties from both Mason's and Schaeffer's crews.

Mason and Abrams saw that their men received priority treatment, then made sure they got into the first of the ambulances to arrive. The remnants of Schaeffer's crew were put into guarded trucks and sent back to Garmisch. Shortly after, two troop transport trucks of additional GIs arrived to ensure the Russians would, however reluctantly, get back on their train.

On the ride back to headquarters, Mason, Abrams, and Densmore celebrated by sharing a bottle from the Russians' supply of pilfered schnapps. But, like many moments in life, the elation rarely lasts, and theirs quickly evaporated when they were summoned to Major Gamin's office immediately upon their return.

Gamin and Udahl were waiting for them with glum faces.

Mason, Abrams, and Densmore stopped in the middle of the room, their medic uniforms covered in mud, soot, and blood.

Gamin marched up to them. "You jokers really did it this time."

"What would that be, sir?" Mason said. "Saving millions of dollars' worth of cargo?"

"Going behind my back. Risking men's lives. Taking on a dangerous gang with a dozen men—"

"Major Gamin, this is not productive," Udahl said.

"These jokers are still under my command."

"Bob, we just took into custody the ringleader of a vicious gang. They're not expecting marching bands and medals, but these men did their job."

Mason said to the room, "I think the major is most upset about losing out on a portion of the profit."

Gamin growled, "You son of a bitch—"

"Gentlemen, this is getting us nowhere!" Udahl said.

Gamin displayed a venomous smile. "It's all right. We've just about seen the last of Collins. You're both going back to Frankfurt for reassignment tomorrow morning, and in your case, Mr. Collins, I hope they send you to some mosquito-infested hellhole."

"That's enough from both of you," Udahl said and turned to Densmore. "You're the senior investigator. I'd like to hear a full report at this point."

Densmore ran through the events: what they observed prior to the German POW train arriving, Schaeffer's crew commandeering the valuable cargo, the unexpected stop of the Russian POW train, then the riot and ensuing shoot-out and chase.

"These two were on the train for fifteen minutes," Gamin said, indicating Mason and Abrams with a nod. "Did you check their pockets?"

"Major, please!" Udahl said.

A man cleared his throat just inside the office door. All turned to see Captain Hollister, the JAG senior trial counsel—the army equivalent of a senior prosecuting attorney—standing just inside the door. Mason had run across Hollister a few times with minor cases. With his craggy face, broad teeth, blazing red hair, and steel blue eyes, he gave off the air of a man close to madness. He could fire up the oratory of a Baptist preacher and wither a witness down to a shattered mess. When not performing in a courtroom, the man never cracked a smile, and at this moment he displayed an epic frown.

He marched into the room with his briefcase steady at his side. Without moving his head, he greeted everyone with curt nods and a soft "Gentlemen." Once he had his briefcase firmly planted on Gamin's desk, he turned to the room. "I've discussed the case with the deputy judge advocate general, the defense counsel assigned to Major Schaeffer, and the defendant. In my studied opinion, and from the advice of the deputy judge advocate general, the best prosecutable charges we have against the defendant are reckless endangerment, possession of unauthorized firearms, resisting arrest, possession of forged orders, and behavior unbecoming an officer—"

"What? Wait...." Mason said.

Hollister pivoted to face Mason. "Chief Warrant Officer Collins?"

"Mr. Collins is fine or we'll be here all day. What about murder, attempted murder, grand larceny, attempted larceny..."

"The defendant claims he fled in fear for his life. He says that in the confusion of the riot, he had no idea who was intent on killing whom. He observed you and your men advancing on him with weapons drawn after shots had been fired. You were not in uniforms identifying yourselves as military policemen, you did not call out who you were or your intentions—"

"Excuse me, sir," Densmore said, interrupting, "but they

opened fire on us, and I did declare who we were and our intentions."

"*Major* Schaeffer," Hollister said, putting the emphasis on a superior rank, "said that you did not, or, because of the noise of the riot, it was not sufficiently loud to be heard. He fled in fear for his life, and he had grave concerns about the precious cargo. He assumed you and your men were intent on stealing the cargo, and he felt it his duty to prevent you from doing so."

Mason said, "He tried to take those five boxcars using forged papers—"

"Major Schaeffer was under the impression they were genuine. The orders were for him to take charge of the cargo and ensure its authorized delivery—"

"He had men under his command wearing false uniforms. He had Polish nationals posing as train crewmen—"

Hollister continued, talking over Mason, "He was to use whatever means necessary to carry out those orders, as there was grave concern that a theft of the cargo by rogue army personnel might occur, and he claims to have recruited these men in good faith in carrying out those orders. One might condemn him for poor judgment or naïveté, but we have no proof he intended to commit robbery or that he was aware that the orders were forgeries."

"Don't you realize how ridiculous that all sounds? I have one of his partners in custody, and he's the one who informed me where Schaeffer would be, when, and for what purpose."

"Where is this witness?"

"I have him in a secluded location."

"The fact that you spirited him to a secret location without authorization, or neglected to take him to an authorized facility, is against regulations. Whatever testimony he may have provided will not hold up in any court of law."

"It was for his own safety."

"And could this witness claim he gave this information under duress?"

"Whose side are you on?" Mason growled.

"Mr. Collins..." Udahl warned for the second time.

Hollister's deadpan expression held steady as a marble statue. "I assume you are talking about Herr Ernst Volker. Frankly, I couldn't care less about this man's well-being. But if he takes the stand as witness for the prosecution, the defense counsel will tear the case apart. If what you say is true about Major Schaeffer, then I would be glad to bring the more severe charges against him, but until you can give me more credible witnesses or physical evidence, I can only bring the lesser charges to a court-martial hearing."

"What does that mean in jail time?"

"A stripping of rank, two to four years in Leavenworth. But considering his wartime record of valor behind enemy lines, it could go as low as a slap on the wrist and six months in confinement."

"Six months? He's either murdered or ordered the murders of a dozen people."

Hollister inclined his head solemnly. "Then give me what I need."

Gamin barked out a laugh. "Mr. Collins won't be around long enough to do that. He's on a train out of here tomorrow morning."

"That's a shame," Hollister said. "I tend to believe Mr. Collins, despite his ill-considered remark." He looked at Mason. "It seems you have twelve hours to come up with something that could help me bring more severe charges." With his head perfectly still, he rotated at the waist to scan everyone. "Any other questions?"

"Just see to it that Mr. Densmore picks Schaeffer's guards," Mason said. "Some of the MPs in this detachment are on Schaeffer's payroll."

Hollister nodded, but Gamin growled, "Couldn't resist another slanderous dig at my outfit, could you?"

Udahl said to Hollister, "Captain, you and I know that Major Schaeffer's story is extremely flimsy. He and his men fired on fellow soldiers."

"I agree," Hollister said. "However, there are no guarantees even those charges will stick. The judges may consider the major's take on the events as reasonable."

"Then it's up to you, isn't it? I've heard you're the best prosecutor we have. I'm depending on you to bring the most severe punishment possible."

Hollister bowed his head as a knight to a king's request. "If that will be all, I will return to my office."

When no one objected, Hollister turned on his heels to leave. He paused and looked at Mason. "If you do manage to discover anything further against the defendant, I'll be in my office most of the evening." With that, Captain Hollister left the room.

Mason felt like he'd been slugged in the stomach. He could endure any abuse Gamin cared to dish out, but hearing Hollister's concerns had taken the wind out of him.

A few minutes later the three investigators exited Gamin's office, and Densmore said, "I'm ready for an armload of drinks."

Abrams eagerly agreed, but Mason shook his head. "I have somewhere to go."

"Give it a rest," Densmore said. "You're not going to dig up what Hollister needs in the hours you've got left."

"I'll go with you," Abrams said.

"Not this time."

"Let him go," Densmore said to Abrams. "He's like a bulldog with his teeth clamped on a bull's ankle. He won't let go until he's trampled to death."

Mason refused to get into it with Densmore. The man had, after all, acted against his own self-interest when Mason had needed him most. "I appreciate what you did today," he told Densmore. To Abrams he said, "Get drunk for the both of us."

LANDSBERG PRISON, or, as the army had renamed it, War Crimes Prison Number 1, was famous for hosting Hitler after his failed rebellion and for being the place where he wrote *Mein Kampf.* More recently, the facility had become the U.S. Army's principal repository and place of execution for the worst Nazi war criminals. It looked to Mason like a modernized medieval castle, with two turrets sprouting green onion domes that flanked the main building. And with the lack of surrounding high walls, barbed wire, or guard towers, it hardly looked like a high-security prison at all.

An MP from the prison detachment led Mason across the prison grounds, where, behind the castle-like entrance, four main wings formed an X and were connected by a central guard tower. The MP pointed out a smaller two-story building attached to the main wings. "That's where Hitler was housed. The Nazis turned it into a shrine."

Mason said, "Can you imagine if a U.S. president had done time in prison that Americans would make a shrine out of it?"

"No accounting for taste, that's for sure."

The MP brought him to another small building branching off from the rest. A moment later Mason stood outside Kessel's wooden cell door.

The MP tapped on the door with his nightstick. "Herr Kessel, there's a CID investigator who wants to talk to you."

From inside came the creak of a bed frame. "Yes, come in."

The MP unlocked the door and stepped aside. Mason entered a dark room. He could see Kessel's silhouette in the moonlight. Kessel sat on the simple framed bed with his feet on the ground.

The MP went over to a small desk on the opposite wall and turned on a lamp. On the desk sat a few books and a half-finished letter.

The MP moved to the door. "I'll be just down the hall. Holler when you're done."

Kessel spoke only when the sound of the guard's footsteps had faded in the hall. "Sending me to this prison. Was that meant as an insult?"

"You're alive, aren't you?"

"The worst kind of Nazis are here. The ones who ran the concentration camps. You've shamed me by putting me in the same place as those mass murderers."

"Come on, Frieder. You're in a separate wing. All by yourself. Alive"

"There was a hanging this afternoon. I don't know who. I couldn't see. But I heard. The whole prison was silent. I could hear the trapdoor, and the rope strain as it snapped his neck."

Kessel fell into deep thought. Mason changed the subject to get him back on the problem at hand.

"We busted Schaeffer this evening, trying to steal the train Volker told us about."

Kessel looked up at Mason. "Then what do you want from me?"

"The problem is, the prosecuting attorney doesn't have enough to convict Schaeffer for the attempted train theft, and Schaeffer has friends in high places. He may just get off with less than six months in jail. Maybe not even that. You think that hanging was a bad way to die, wait until Schaeffer gets out and comes looking for you."

When Kessel didn't respond, Mason said, "I've got to pin those murders on him, and you're the only one who can help me. Now's the time, while he's still in jail."

"If Schaeffer has so many influential friends, then they'll just help him get away with it. It will be his word against that of an ex-SS man."

"If your testimony was the only thing we could hold against him, then you'd probably be right. But we've got him for suspicion of attempted train robbery. Holding false orders. Shooting at military policemen. He's the manager of the Casa Carioca, which has been tied to shipments of contraband. One of the Casa's Polish waiters was killed attempting an armed assault on a police informant's family. Two Casa skaters, Hilda and Adelle, both murdered. Believe me, with all that around Schaeffer's neck, there's no way the army can ignore your eyewitness testimony of murder. If you don't want to live the rest of your life looking over your shoulder, then help me stop Schaeffer. If you want to make up for just a little bit of Adelle's death and everything else you've done, then help me get Schaeffer. It's the only way."

Kessel sat in silence with his head hung low. Mason waited, letting him reflect on everything that had happened, and what would haunt him.

Finally Kessel said, "Volker and Schaeffer, along with three of their Polish staff from the Casa Carioca, murdered Giessen, Bachmann, and Plöbsch."

"And how do you know this?"

Kessel raised his head to look at Mason. "Because I was there."

"At the time of the murders? You helped kill them?"

Kessel nodded. "Schaeffer had wanted to hit Giessen's gang for weeks, but Giessen had gone underground when the turf battles erupted. The meeting at the Steinadler was their first since Schaeffer had decided to eliminate them."

"How did Schaeffer know where to do the hit? Was it Sergeant Olsen?"

Kessel shook his head. "Olsen had no idea about any of it."

"But I thought he worked for Schaeffer."

"He worked for Giessen. Only later, after the killings, did Olsen come to work for us. Volker also worked for Giessen, until he betrayed him to join up with Schaeffer. Being the inside man, Volker was to give up the meeting place, but even he didn't know where it would take place, only when. Like most of Giessen's gang, Volker had to be led to the meeting. Schaeffer had them tailed, then it was a matter of getting us all to the Steinadler and waiting out back for Volker to lead Giessen, Bachmann, and Plöbsch to us."

"And the German police? They were part of the plan?"

"Yes. Schaeffer had a select group of German police on his payroll who were to stage the mock raid. Once they got word of the location, they were to give us time to get in place before busting in, subduing Giessen's bodyguards and forcing Giessen and his partners to flee out back."

"But then my partner arrived early and screwed up that part of the plan."

Kessel nodded. "The two of you showing up was the one wrinkle in Schaeffer's plan. When your partner ran to the German police precinct for help, he insisted that the crooked captain bring the entire precinct force. Because of that, the captain could no longer control the outcome, and in the confusion two of the bodyguards got out with Giessen and the rest. In your case, when Schaeffer found out you had survived and started nosing around, he felt he had to move up his plans and eliminate anyone who might talk."

Mason shook his head in amazement at Schaeffer's ruthlessness. "That brings us to Agent Winstone and Hilda Schmidt."

Kessel closed his eyes. "Yes. I was there as well." He paused and looked pained to recall the event. "Schaeffer told me he only wanted to steal some of Agent Winstone's documents. I knew Adelle had a key to the villa, so I had a copy made. There were three of us: Schaeffer, Bolus, and me. Schaeffer and Bolus held them at gunpoint, and I was sent to search for the documents. Then, when I was searching in the library, I heard more men come into the house. I don't know how many, but I recognized Volker's voice, and heard one other man speaking English. Someone referred to him as Abbott." Kessel exhaled with a shudder. "I felt ashamed even then. I knew Volker was a sadist, and if he was there, Schaeffer intended to do more than steal Winstone's documents. And despite knowing that, I continued to search. I did nothing to interfere."

Kessel closed his eyes again. "When I was upstairs in the master bedroom, I heard the horrible screams. I froze as I listened. I'm not sure how long I stayed there, but I couldn't face going back downstairs. After some time there was a gunshot and everything went silent. I heard some of the men leave, then Schaeffer came up to find me." He opened his eyes and looked at Mason. "I only saw the aftermath, but Schaeffer's gloves were soaked in blood, and Volker still stood over Hilda's body admiring his handiwork."

Mason felt his anger rise, but he put it in check. He wanted Kessel to keep talking. "You never found the documents? Winstone never talked?"

"I heard him screaming about them being at his office. They could find them there. He gave them his office key and the combination to the safe."

"And they got the documents?"

"I believe so, yes."

"But according to Willy Laufs, there was still a reward out for their recovery."

"I heard that, too, but I don't know why. Maybe they didn't get what they wanted. Maybe Schaeffer suspected Winstone was holding back, but he said that sometime during Hilda's torture Winstone's mind snapped. They couldn't get any more out of him." He stopped and stared at some point in space. "That's why

Adelle ran into your arms. She was frightened and ashamed. And I swore never to participate in any other killings."

"You're a real saint."

Kessel looked at Mason. "Giessen and the others were cutthroats. I felt no guilt about what happened to them. But I had no part in the other killings."

"You just kept quiet about it."

Kessel had no answer for that.

"I need a description of Abbott," Mason said.

"They're very careful about concealing his identity. I've never seen him, and I didn't see him that night. He only came in after I'd gone looking for the documents. By the time I returned he was gone."

"Then how do you know it was Abbott?"

"I don't know for sure. I only know that I heard his name that night. Abbott is the real leader, and Schaeffer took orders from him the night we were at Winstone's."

Mason rubbed his face, trying to erase the horrible images from his mind. "Are you willing to testify? Tell them everything?"

Kessel nodded.

"I need you to write it down."

Kessel rose from the bunk with great effort, as if the weight of guilt pressed down on his shoulders. He sat at the desk and began to write.

"Put in there that you were present at those murders because you feared for your life if you didn't cooperate."

"You're asking me to lie on top of everything I've done?"

"Forget your damned honor for a moment and think about saving yourself from the same fate as that poor bastard today on the gallows. I'll put in my report that you were essential to helping solve this investigation and feel remorse for your actions."

"I am a condemned man. Nothing you will say can alter that."

"You're going to do some time in prison, but at least you won't have to keep looking over your shoulder for one of Schaeffer's men while you're there and, more importantly, after you get out. Schaeffer will hang for what he's done."

Kessel bent to the desk and resumed writing. "Don't make promises you can't keep, Mr. Collins." He stopped and looked up at Mason. "A dead man cannot make such assurances."

37

The U.S. Army had renamed a hotel on the south end of Garmisch the General Patton Hotel; an appropriate name considering General Patton's Third Army had ripped through the heart of Bavaria.

Mason knocked on the hotel room door again. This time with more force. A middle-aged man poked his head out of an adjacent room, pulled his beltless bathrobe tight around his round belly, and gave Mason a sneer.

Mason shrugged, then pounded on the door again. A moment later, Hollister opened it. He, too, had on his bathrobe, but was obviously still up, as his red hair was perfectly combed over his bald spot, and his blue eyes were still sharp enough to cut through steel.

"I wait until now to have a bowel movement," Hollister said through his permanent frown. "It's the one time of day I'm not disturbed. What is it that can't wait until morning?"

"Can I come in?"

"No."

"I'll just be a minute. It's important."

"So's my bowel movement."

Mason slipped in anyway and waited until Hollister closed the door.

"It's one o'clock in the morning," Hollister said.

"Justice never rests."

"What is it?"

"I have an ex-associate of Major Schaeffer who's agreed to testify that he personally partook in several murders with Major Schaeffer. He also will swear that he witnessed Schaeffer, along with another man, carry out the murders of Agent Winstone and Hilda Schmidt."

"How reliable is he?"

"Very."

"Not a hophead or crackpot?"

"He was a captain in the German army and cleared by the CIC. He has a clean army record and was a medal winner." Mason decided for now to leave out that Kessel was ex-SS.

Hollister fell silent for several moments, obviously considering the new development, though from outward appearances it looked as though he'd frozen in place. He finally nodded. "I'll pass it on to the new prosecutor in Frankfurt."

"What do you mean new prosecutor? I thought you were the prosecutor on this case."

"Not anymore. Orders came in this evening. Schaeffer's being transferred to Frankfurt tomorrow morning for a review of the charges and whether a court-martial is warranted."

Mason was speechless for a moment. "Warranted?" He stopped and turned away before he yelled something he'd regret later. "Who ordered the transfer?"

"The judge advocate general himself."

"Why? According to you, this was going to be a penny-ante court-martial."

"I'm afraid I forgot to grill the general about his motives."

Mason tried to think what this meant. "If a high-ranking

officer or MG official requested the transfer, would the judge advocate general change the venue and take it out of your hands?"

"You're serious, right? This is the army. They can do anything they want. My guess is the army brass view this case as a possible embarrassment."

"Someone wants to bury it."

"Probably. Now that the shooting's stopped, the army's fighting an image war for the politicians and people back home. Plus, there's an ideological war going on between democracy and communism. The Russians are portraying themselves as the ideal system for Germany, and the Germans haven't decided. They haven't had a real choice in a political system for fifteen years. The army doesn't want a scandal like this seeing the light of day. It would make us look incompetent, corrupt, and God knows what else."

"This move isn't political. This is about covering their asses and lining their pockets. Schaeffer's just the tip of the spear."

"And you want me to do what, exactly?"

"Show some backbone and fight to keep it here. If Schaeffer is facing murder charges, he might give up the ones protecting and profiting from him. If Schaeffer gets swept under the carpet, those same officers will just replace him with another, and the crimes and corruption will go on and on. Then imagine what will happen when the press learns the army tried to cover it up."

"If you're looking for a fellow crusader, you've knocked on the wrong door. I like the army. I like Garmisch-Partenkirchen. I like being senior trial counsel. Find someone else. Write a book. Whatever you decide, please do it elsewhere. Right now, I would like to get back to my bowel movement, and then bed." He opened the door. "Good night, Mr. Collins. And have a safe journey wherever the army sends you."

"I'll have my report about the witness on your desk by oh-eight-hundred tomorrow." Mason stopped at the door. "Do the right thing, and don't burn it or throw it in the trash. Send it with your file to Frankfurt."

Mason walked away without waiting for a response, and for the sake of the hotel's guests, he waited until he was outside to curse at the stars.

～

"You awake in there?" Mason stood outside Schaeffer's cell, in front of a steel door with a small barred window.

From the dark cell came Schaeffer's voice. "Fuck off."

Mason turned to one of the two MPs standing guard on either side of the door. Even Gamin was taking no chances that anyone could gain access to Schaeffer. He said to one of the MPs, "Is there any way he and I can talk in private?"

"Sorry, sir. Orders are to stay right here. We're not even supposed to let you near here, but this asshole shot a buddy of mine in that train bust."

Mason said into the cell, "You hear that, Schaeffer? You don't have too many friends right now."

Mason's eyes grew accustomed to the darkness, and he could see Schaeffer lying on his bunk with his arms behind his head, staring at the ceiling.

"I've got nothing to say to you," Schaeffer said.

"I didn't come here to chat. Just wanted to let you know that we now have a very reliable witness. This person will testify to being present when you killed Agent Winstone and Hilda Schmidt. You're going to hang."

"Whoever's claiming that is lying. Tell them they're dead."

"You go ahead and believe that. And now that we have your entire crew, one of them is bound to talk. I can guarantee that. The prosecutor will have enough evidence. If they don't hang you, you'll be put away for life."

A moment of silence followed, then Schaeffer said, "You've said your piece. Now get out of here."

"As much as I enjoy seeing you behind bars, I'm not here to gloat. Against my own interests, I'm here to offer you a deal."

Schaeffer swung his feet over the bunk and onto the floor. He suddenly lunged for the door, slamming into it with both fists. "Guards, get this man out of here!"

"Calm down, sir," the MP said. "We've already warned you earlier about making a racket."

"Give me the names, Schaeffer," Mason said. "Who's the real power behind your operation? Is it another OSS man? A commander, maybe?"

"I said fuck off."

"What about Lester Abbott? Where is he? Give me that at least."

"You don't know what you're talking about. Abbott was killed in the war."

"Not from what I've—"

Schaeffer banged the door and shoved his face against the window bars. "Volker told me how you squealed when he interrogated you during the war. You gave up troop positions. You named fellow intelligence agents. You admitted to spying." He yelled at the guards, "Do you hear that, boys? The coward standing next to you gave up information that got soldiers killed."

"I've got Volker," Mason said. "It took him about ten minutes to tell me all about your plan to rob the train. He even admitted to lying about me supposedly talking under torture. I went through a thousand times as much as he did, and I never said a word." He turned to the guard. "This is the guy who murdered that woman and child."

"The Kantos house?" the MP asked. "I was there. That was disgusting."

Schaeffer growled and turned away.

"Names, Schaeffer. And you can cut a deal. You might just get twenty years. That may seem like a long time, but it's a lot better than the hangman's noose."

With his back to the door, Schaeffer rolled his shoulders as if regaining self-control. He walked back to the bunk and lay down, resuming his previous position.

"It doesn't make sense you getting all the punishment, when the guys pulling your strings will go home with a pile of money and medals on their chests. They used you, abused you, and now they're going to let you hang or rot in prison. No, sir, doesn't make sense."

"They'll get they're just deserts. I'll see to that."

"From the end of a rope? I don't think so." Mason paused to see if Schaeffer would continue, but Schaeffer said nothing. "See you 'round."

Mason turned away and took two steps before hearing Schaeffer's voice echo off the cement walls, saying, "Mark my words, Collins: There'll be no rest for the wicked."

Mason stopped. That phrase... He rushed up to the cell door and out his hands on the bars. "What did you say?"

Silence.

Mason thought a moment. He then launched himself off the door and marched down the hall with urgency and purpose.

38

M ason exited his house—actually the army's house, his billet—with his duffel bag loaded to almost bursting. He locked the door for the last time and climbed into the waiting jeep.

"You know where they're sending you?" the MP driver asked.

"No, but I hope it doesn't include deep snow and subzero temperatures."

"Or live grenades."

"Amen, brother."

It was seven A.M. and still dark, though the rising sun cast a golden halo around the mountain ridges. He had three hours before he needed to be on the train—still time to stir up trouble. After a quick breakfast and coffee, he had the driver deposit him at headquarters. His case files and photos had been turned over to Densmore, but his typewriter was still there, and the uncomfortable chair —some things never change. It took him an hour and a half to type up three reports. One he left on Densmore's desk, along with Kessel's original written testimony. He then went by Hollister's office and left a report with Hollister's secretary, detailing Kessel's admission and involvement with Schaeffer's murder spree. He left out where Kessel and Volker had been stashed, only saying that Chief Warrant Officer Densmore would take custody of Volker that afternoon. He also included his visit to Schaeffer and his offer to exchange naming any high-ranking officers for consideration of a lighter sentence.

The last stop was Udahl's office. The colonel's secretary said he would be there in an hour, so Mason left his third and final report with the secretary. This version of the report repeated the same information as in Hollister's, but with one added piece of fiction: that Schaeffer would certainly talk, that he'd said he wouldn't go down alone.

Mason then retrieved his duffel bag from his office and descended the stairs. On the last few steps to the ground floor, his attention was drawn to the two MPs standing at the front entrance. They were dressed in the new uniforms for the fledgling U.S. Constabulary Force: the lightning bolt shoulder patch, yellow scarf, and yellow-and-blue-striped helmet. Though many months away from full force, these men, in their flashy uniforms, would take over much of the occupation zone's policing. Mason thought that if the army had similar uniforms in mind for the CID, then it was better he was planning to leave.

He saw Densmore near the watch commander's desk bending a few MPs' ears again with an exaggerated version of the train raid. *How many times will the poor MPs have to hear that one?* Mason wondered.

As he approached, Densmore dismissed his relieved audience and nodded at Mason's bag. "Did you put your bedroom furniture in there?"

"Once I stole everything out of your quarters, I didn't have room for anything else." Mason looked around then signaled Densmore to follow him to a quiet corner. "I left a final report for you, Hollister, and Udahl."

"I don't blame you for bypassing Gamin. Though I'm going to get an earful about that."

"You're mentioned heavily in Hollister's and Udahl's reports."

"I appreciate that."

"It's not exactly what I meant." Mason filled him in about where Volker was being held, and that he'd left Weissenegger guarding him. "I'm not sure what shape he'll be in when you find him. Weissenegger's an ex-boxer and was madly in love with Adelle."

Densmore laughed. "Just as long as he's still breathing."

"This is what I need you to take care of first. I've got Kessel tucked away at Landsberg prison."

"You're a wily son of a bitch."

"I need for you to ensure his safety. He's admitted to being present at the killings of Giessen, Bachmann, and Plöbsch. He also can testify to Schaeffer and Volker torturing and killing Winstone and Hilda."

"That's great news."

Mason told him he went to Hollister in the night with the information, and learned that Schaeffer was being transferred to Frankfurt that morning. "It could have already happened."

Densmore didn't appear that surprised.

"The thing is," Mason said, "as long as Schaeffer is still breathing, Kessel is in danger. He's been a stand-up guy, and I want to make sure he's treated right."

"And you're laying it at my doorstep?"

Mason got in Densmore's face. "If Abrams and I weren't being transferred, I would have taken care of it myself. Now's the time for you to step up to the plate and take a swing."

Densmore held up his hands. "All right. I'll do it."

"There's one other thing I need for you to do."

"Jesus, Mason. Do I look like an all-service police force?"

"I'm trusting you. Do not screw me on this one, or I will pay you an unpleasant visit."

Mason waited, but Densmore said nothing. "Abrams and I took Yaakov's family to a friend's place in Breitenau the night Schaeffer's men tried to kill them. I need for you to look in on them and help my friend get them to a safe place."

"Is that all? 'Cause I didn't have anything else to do but babysit your arrestees and a DP family."

"Frankfurt is just a train ride away."

Densmore let out a tired sigh. "All right. I'll do it." He held up a hand. "Unless you've got more, seeing as how I don't have much to do as the last real CID investigator in a gun-crazy town."

"That's it," Mason said and handed him a piece of paper with Laura's address. "I'll call her and tell her you're coming."

Densmore put the piece of paper in his pocket, accompanied by his usual tired sigh. "I'll drive you to the station," he said.

"I'd rather walk. It's only ten minutes."

Densmore cleared his throat. "Well, the thing about that... Gamin ordered that you're to be accompanied under guard." He pointed to the constabulary MPs. "Those two MPs are to escort you to the station. I was going to go along so you don't feel like you're under arrest or something."

"That lunatic must be really desperate to get me out of here."

"Looks that way," Densmore said and gestured toward the door. "Shall we?"

THE TRAIN PLATFORM'S departing passengers consisted mostly of GIs who had come on leave to ski or frolic with sweethearts or the local girls. A smaller group of WACs and nurses were assembled together near a couple of MPs, seeking shelter from the GIs who apparently still had plenty of frolic left in them. Mixed with this army contingent were the civilians, Germans, of course, and Americans brought over to help run the military government: lawyers, teachers, and CEOs who had volunteered to contribute their expertise.

Mason and Densmore found Abrams standing alone with his duffel bag and looking forlorn. He brightened when he saw Mason. He shook Mason's hand, then furrowed his brow when he realized the two MPs flanking Mason were there as an armed escort.

"Gamin isn't taking any chances," Mason explained.

Almost as an afterthought, Abrams shook Densmore's hand. "Are you part of the escort?"

"I'm here for moral support," Densmore said.

"Moral support? For us? Being shot at must have given you a whole new perspective on life."

"Be nice," Mason said. "Densmore's agreed to take care of Yaakov's family."

"I said I'd look in on them," Densmore countered.

Abrams stuck his finger at Densmore. "Nothing better happen to them, or I'll—"

Mason held up his hand. "I've already explained to him that Frankfurt isn't that far away."

The train pulled into the station. Since it originated from Mittenwald, only a few passengers exited. Then the crowd on the platform began to board. The two flashy MPs stepped in close to Mason and Abrams as a signal that it was their turn. The two investigators heaved their bags onto their shoulders.

Mason turned to Densmore. "Remember everything I told you."

"Don't worry."

"I'll probably be first to hear the outcome of Schaeffer's court-martial, since it's taking place in Frankfurt. With luck Schaeffer will break when he realizes he's looking at a possible hanging."

Densmore had a hard time looking at Mason. "About Schaeffer... I didn't want to tell you until now, because I was afraid of what you might do."

Mason waited. He knew he was going to hate whatever Densmore had to say next.

Densmore finally got up the courage to speak. "Schaeffer escaped this morning somewhere outside Garmisch. The sedan he was in had an accident with another car. In the confusion, Schaeffer got away."

"Son of a... I knew something like this would happen. It was fishy enough him being sent up to Frankfurt."

"Jesus, Mason, the MPs driving him had an accident."

"Bullshit!"

One of the constabulary MPs said, "Sir, it's time to go."

"Hold on a minute," Mason said to the MP, then turned back to Densmore. "Where exactly did it happen?"

"A couple of miles outside Garmisch, near Farchant."

"Who were the MPs doing the driving? Did anyone check to see if they were on Schaeffer's payroll?"

"Not everything's a Schaeffer conspiracy. Two of them were hurt. One seriously."

"What about the people in the other car?"

Densmore sighed before answering. "They left the scene."

"God damn it."

"Sir, you have to go now," the MP insisted.

"I'm not going anywhere."

"Our orders are to arrest you if you refuse. Major Gamin told me to tell you that he has a whole lineup of charges if we have to arrest you."

Mason changed to a conciliatory tone. "Okay, sure. I don't

want to be arrested." He started for the train car's steps when Densmore stepped forward and took Mason's arm.

"Don't do anything stupid," Densmore said.

"No. Of course not."

Densmore looked skeptical, but he released Mason's arm.

"See you around," Mason said and climbed onto the train. He joined Abrams, and they found two empty seats, which Mason had purposely selected to be away from Densmore's and the MPs' view. He reached into his bag and pulled out his .45 and a box of bullets, concealing both under his overcoat. He said to Abrams, "Look after my bag, will you?"

"I'm going with you."

"No, you're not. I'll beat you to a pulp if I catch you following me. Do you understand?"

Abrams glowered but said nothing. He looked more hurt than angry.

"I'll see you in Frankfurt," Mason said.

"The next time I see you it'll be in a casket."

"Then have a good life."

Mason checked the platform-side windows, then moved to the door at the front of the car. He slipped out and jumped onto the tracks. The train whistle blew and started to pull out of the station. He was sure the MPs and Densmore would stay on the platform to make sure Mason remained on the train, so he ran full out across several tracks and across an open field. By the time the last train car cleared the station, Mason had merged with the houses and disappeared.

IT HAD TAKEN Mason twenty minutes to find an unattended car in a quiet street. Another minute and a half later to hot-wire the ignition, and another fifteen minutes to drive over to Winstone's villa.

Mason found Weissenegger in the kitchen drinking coffee and eating an early lunch. He noticed the bruises on Weissenegger's knuckles.

"Is Volker still alive?"

"Can't breathe through his nose so good, but, yeah, he's alive."

"Once I'm finished with him, I want you to call the MP station and have them come and get him. Then lie low somewhere for a day or two."

"I ain't going anywhere but back home."

"Did you let Margareta go?"

"Last night at eight, like you told me."

"Did she say where she was going?"

Weissenegger smiled. "As a matter of fact, she did. She's at my place waiting for me."

"You big Romeo."

Weissenegger beamed with pride. "Thanks to you, I've had the time of my life. It don't make up for Adelle's death, but a little private time with Volker helped me get past my grief."

"Happy to be of service. Come on, let's have a little more fun at Volker's expense."

Mason and Weissenegger made their way down to the furnace room. Volker lay on a mattress on the floor. When he saw the two men enter the room, he crawled on his back toward a corner. Both his eyes were swollen. His nose sported a large bump in the middle and was still caked in blood. He curled up in a ball once he reached the wall.

Mason signaled for Weissenegger to stay where he was, then he walked up to Volker and crouched down next to him. "Considering what you did to all those people, Hans has been lenient with you."

"When are you going to let me go?"

"Let you go? Who said anything about that?"

Volker stopped breathing and tried to look at Mason through his swollen eyelids. "You promised you'd let me go. I've told you everything."

"No, you didn't. I know you're the one who cut up Hilda's face and jammed her body parts down Winstone's throat."

"He did what?" Weissenegger yelled and started to charge.

Volker covered his head with his arms. Mason held up his hand to stop Weissenegger, and, surprisingly, the man complied.

Mason said to Volker, "Why should I let you live when you did such horrible things to that poor girl?"

All Volker could summon was a pitiful moan. "Please...."

"I might show clemency, but you need to give me something in return."

Volker nodded violently, and Mason said, "There was a house or cabin in the mountains where you and Schaeffer would make transactions and strike deals. I want to know where it is."

Volker's face widened in surprise, at least as much as his swollen face would allow.

"Yes," Mason said, "I know about your little hideaway."

"I don't know where it is. I was always taken there blindfolded."

"I wouldn't advise lying again. Herr Weissenegger wants to tear you limb from limb for what you did to Adelle's sister. The only way to keep him from doing that is a word from me. Hans and I are pals now. Give me the location, and no more beatings."

Volker, in near hysterics, yelled, "You made me a promise before that you didn't keep. Why should I believe you now?"

Mason grabbed Volker's ankle and dragged him toward Weissenegger. Volker thrashed his legs and grabbed the mattress only to drag it along as Mason pulled him across the floor. "Wait! There's a fire road!"

Mason stopped but held on to his leg. "Go on."

"It's also a maintenance road for the ski lift. The road splits at the lift's second support tower. The left fork takes you to an old forester's lodge."

"How far up that road?"

"A kilometer."

"How will I recognize it?"

"A stone house with two chimneys. There's an iron horse's head mounted above the door."

Mason dropped Volker's foot. "You made a wise choice." He walked up to Weissenegger. "Go ahead and call the MP station. And keep him in one piece."

Weissenegger looked disappointed, but he nodded. When Mason moved for the door, Weissenegger asked, "Is Schaeffer the other one who killed Hilda and ordered Adelle's death?"

Mason turned to him and nodded.

"And that's who you're after next?" Weissenegger asked.

Mason took a moment, as he wasn't sure how to answer. "Yes…"

Weissenegger smiled and hiked up his pants as if ready to go into action.

39

"Forester's house" was a gross understatement for the elegant abode that stood before him. The sprawling two-story structure was more a manor than a functionary's lodge, with large, hewn-stone walls and a long front porch of varnished wood. It stood in a shallow, bowl-shaped field and surrounded by a pine forest, now laden with deep snow.

Mason stood just inside the tree line on a shallow rise. Fifty yards of open ground lay between him and the house. Smoke rose from one of the chimneys, signaling that someone was inside. If Mason had guessed correctly, Schaeffer was its current occupant, but it seemed odd that Schaeffer would come back here and not continue to run. Perhaps this was a rendezvous point for colleagues to spirit him away, or he'd come for a cache of money to buy his way to somewhere far away. Whatever the reason, it had been a bad calculation. One that Mason had counted on.

He heard the distinct click of a revolver's hammer being pulled back, then the touch of the cold barrel on the back of his neck.

"Let's show Schaeffer what I've found lurking in the woods," Weissenegger said.

Mason clamped his hands behind his head.

Weissenegger nudged Mason forward with the gun barrel. "It's now or never."

Mason stepped several yards into the clearing, and Weissenegger yelled out, "Schaeffer. I brought you a present."

Mason and Weissenegger slowly descended the incline toward the house.

"Don't slip, would you?" Mason said. "That thing might go off."

"I'm as sure-footed as a cat."

The front door opened, and Schaeffer came out onto the porch. He held a pistol at his side. "Well, I'll be damned." He stepped off the porch and waited at the bottom of the stairs. "Good work, Hans." He then held up his pistol. "Hold it there, though."

Mason and Weissenegger stopped.

"How did you get the drop on such a slippery fish?" Schaeffer asked.

"I followed him. He's got Volker at Winstone's villa."

"So Volker's who gave me up. I wondered where that rat had got off to."

Weissenegger said, "This guy wanted you so bad he forgot to look behind him."

Schaeffer waved his gun. "All right, come on," he said, though he kept his gun aimed in their direction.

Just as Mason took a step forward, two army light trucks came roaring down the driveway.

"This could be trouble," Weissenegger said.

"I wouldn't move a muscle if I were you," Mason said.

Schaeffer's face went wide with surprise. He whirled his gun around and fired two shots at the oncoming vehicles.

The four men in the lead vehicle returned fire as it skidded to a stop. Mason and Weissenegger remained where they were.

Running would just attract flying bullets. And just in case, Mason slowly crouched down. Hans must have seen the wisdom of this move and did the same thing. Schaeffer dashed across the field in the opposite direction, but the deep snow hindered his progress. The four men in the lead jeep jumped out, two of them aiming their guns at Mason and Weissenegger, while the other two took a few steps, aimed, and fired. A bullet clipped Schaeffer's arm, and he tumbled into the snow.

The second truck came to a more judicious stop. The covering on the truck kept the occupants in shadow, but the silhouette of the front passenger looked very familiar. When the front passenger stepped out Mason's stomach did a little flip, more from disappointment than shock—and not a small amount of trepidation.

"Mr. Collins," Udahl said with a satisfied smile.

"Colonel."

"Lower you weapon, Hans," Udahl said, "we've got it from here." He signaled for the two men to bring Mason forward. They seized Mason's arms and pulled him up to Udahl. Weissenegger followed them and stopped just behind Mason.

"I'm pleased to see you," Udahl said.

"I'm sure you are. You get to kill two birds with one stone."

"Looks like that inflated ego of yours got the better of you. Like coming here alone, for one, though that's typical of you, and something I was counting on. Trusting Hans, for another." Hans stepped over to join Schaeffer's men, and Udahl said, "Hans tipped me off that you were coming."

"If you can't count on your enemies, who can you count on? So tell me something. Should I address you as Franklin Udahl or Lester Abbott?"

A tic of surprise and irritation crossed Udahl's face. "I thought it fitting to use Abbott's name."

"It makes sense, since you were in the OSS, and part of the same team as Abbott and Schaeffer."

Udahl beamed like a proud teacher. "Yes, I was. Lester Abbott died when our OSS team was sent on a mission to Czechoslovakia. A debacle, really. A total fuckup on army intelligence's part. The Nazis knew we were coming. Schaeffer, here, managed to get away, but Abbott and I were captured and sent to the Gestapo. Abbott was a puddle of human flesh when they were done with him. He and I endured unbelievable torture—perhaps not so unbelievable to you—but my God, the damage they did to my body…" He paused and looked down to the snow as if remembering that time. He finally lifted his head and said to no one in particular, "Bring him over."

The two men dragged Schaeffer over and dropped him at Udahl's feet. Schaeffer cried out in pain as they forced him to his knees. Udahl squatted to face him. "I gave you an opportunity to run. You should have taken that opportunity." When Schaeffer said nothing, Udahl asked, "Where are those documents?"

Schaeffer looked up at Udahl with confusion in his eyes. "I don't have them."

Mason felt a flush of excitement. Winstone's documents still existed. No one had found them.

Udahl leaned forward to be in Schaeffer's face. "You didn't run because you wanted to save yourself by turning me in." Schaeffer started to protest but Udahl continued. "Don't bother denying it. Mr. Collins told me all about it in his letter."

"That's a lie!" Schaeffer yelled.

Udahl's voice hardened. "You came here to get the documents, the rat that you are. Now, where are they?"

"I'm telling you, I don't have them!"

Udahl stood and said to four of his men, "Search the house." He watched the men charge into the house, then turned back to Mason and frowned. "You look glum, Mr. Collins. Does it bother you so much, seeing an officer and war hero who's fallen from grace?"

"I see you more as a frustrated and bitter OSS agent who couldn't just walk away from the war."

"Did any of us, really? Over the course of our operations, in one form or another we in the OSS killed a battalion of men. We made victory possible, and at great cost. And when it was all over the OSS was deemed expendable, brushed aside and forced to swear a vow of silence. What we did and lost and sacrificed and suffered is all locked away in vaults. We became ghosts. Then a group of us finally made a decision. Why not put all our training to use for a personal cause? We made a pact to suck this rotten country dry. I know it won't last forever. Eventually we'll have to close up shop. But we'll disappear into the shadows with well-lined pockets."

"Is that what you think of yourselves? Noble outlaws? How about murderers? Sadists? Butchers of young women?"

"Now you're just boring me with your small-minded morality. It's simple. Life gives you two options: You die fighting or you die surrendering. I prefer the former. You, you've already surrendered to a system that uses you, that crushes you, and you wind up scrambling for the pennies thrown out into the hungry mob. I watched you grovel at Pritchard's feet just for a chance at being a police detective, and once they've chewed you up and spit you out, all you'll have left to look forward to at the end of your life is growing bitterness and fading memories. Pathetic."

Udahl nodded to one of his men, who came around behind Mason. He kicked Mason in the back of the knees, forcing him to kneel in the snow. Mason had been in this situation before, and it brought back haunting memories of another time. A Gestapo captain forcing him to do the same thing. Forcing him to his knees at gunpoint and demanding he choose between two equally doomed children. The very act, the memory, enraged him.

Yet, he would wait.

One of Udahl's men came out of the house with a look of worry. "We found about five grand but nothing else."

"The goddamned money's what I *came* for," Schaeffer yelled. "I don't have any documents. I wasn't going to rat on you. I needed the cash to get out of here."

In a swift move, Udahl grabbed Schaeffer's right hand, shoved a gun in it, and brought Schaeffer's hand up to his head. Then gun went off in a deafening explosion. Hot blood splattered Mason's face. Schaeffer slumped to the ground.

Suddenly, from the tree line, came the sound of a whistle blowing, and close to twenty men emerged from the surrounding forest. They were MPs with rifles and Thompson submachine guns. With them, to Mason's surprise, Abrams stood in the center of the line, alongside Densmore.

"Drop your weapons," Densmore said.

"I knew you'd come for Schaeffer," Mason said to Udahl. "But I needed evidence against you. You're under arrest for the murder of Major Schaeffer, Colonel."

One of Udahl's men opened fire and began to run. At the same moment, the rest of Udahl's men opened fire, using the vehicles as shields. Abrams, Densmore, and the MPs followed suit in a deafening fusillade.

The outburst of gunfire distracted Udahl for a split second. That was Mason's chance. He launched upward, grabbing Udahl's gun by the barrel and pushing it out of the line of fire. The gun went off, but because Mason had trapped the slide, the gun was now jammed. He then shoved his free hand into Udahl's wrist to disarm him, but the man was surprisingly strong and agile.

Udahl trapped Mason's free hand then elbowed him in the face. He twisted into Mason's body and flipped him. Mason hit the ground, but instead of continuing the attack, Udahl tried to chamber a round. Mason leapt up and tackled Udahl, while again trapping the man's gun arm. They traded blows as they rolled on the ground. Udahl fired the gun twice in desperation, the explosions rendering Mason deaf to any sound other than his heavy breathing.

One of the bullets ripped through Mason's overcoat and just grazed his shoulder. Mason jerked against the bullet's impact, and Udahl took advantage of Mason's break in concentration to get to his knees. Heedless of the bullets whizzing by his head, Udahl used his free hand to strike Mason once, twice, in the face. He tried to stand, using the power of his legs to wrench his gun hand free, but rather than pulling back in opposition, Mason rolled into Udahl and twisted the man's wrist. The man cried out, fell backward, and lost his grip on the gun.

Mason grabbed for the gun submerged in the snow. A mistake. It gave Udahl time to rise up and bring out a Ka-Bar knife. He lunged for Mason's chest. Mason used his leg to block. He had protected his chest, but the knife plunged deep into his thigh.

The searing pain paralyzed him. All he could do in the next instant was cover his chest and neck with his arms. Udahl rose up for another lunge with the knife.

But Udahl's thrust was cut short. Weissenegger grabbed him from behind. He lifted and pulled Udahl up and away. Udahl threw his elbows into Weissenegger's stomach, then slammed the back of his head into Weissenegger's face. Weissenegger grunted and staggered backward. Udahl whirled around with his knife and slashed Weissenegger across the chest.

Mason tried to get up, but his leg gave out. He crawled for the fallen pistol as Udahl sent another thrust of the knife at Weissenegger's chest. Weissenegger grunted and fell to his knees.

Udahl turned back to Mason and charged. Mason made a final lunge for the pistol, grabbed it, and flipped onto his back.

Through the blasts of gunfire, Mason heard Abrams yell in the distance, "Mason, no!"

Perhaps he could have warned Udahl to stop. Perhaps he could have shot him in the leg. But his rage blotted out his reason, and Udahl continued his deadly charge with his knife.

Mason fired twice, hitting Udahl both times in the chest. The .45 bullets had the force of a freight train, and they stopped Udahl's midair lunge. He crumpled and fell in front of Mason.

Udahl's death took the fight out of his men. They dropped their weapons and raised their hands. Two had managed to escape, but a handful of MPs went after them. Mason tried to see if Weissenegger was all right, but the pain forced him back to the ground.

He yelled to the sky, "Get a medic for Hans."

Abrams ran up to Mason and kneeled next to him. He pushed Mason's hands away from his wound and applied pressure.

"Hans needs more help than I do," Mason said.

"Densmore's taking care of it."

"You were supposed to be in Frankfurt by now," Mason said.

"Shut up and lie still."

"I'm going to kick your ass once they patch me up," Mason said just before he passed out.

M ason woke up with a hammering headache and a throbbing pain in his thigh. He'd come awake a number of times, like coming briefly to the surface in a warm ocean, only to descend again. But this time, he became fully aware of his surroundings. He lay in a bed cordoned off by a white curtain. An IV bottle hung above his head, with a tube attached to his arm.

Okay, I'm in a hospital... again.

He raised his head slightly, magnifying the headache. He smiled before dropping his head back onto the pillow.

Abrams sat slumped in a chair, with his head flopped backward, and snorted more than snored like he was searching for truffles in his sleep.

"How's a man supposed to get any sleep with that buzz saw going?" Mason said loudly.

Abrams stirred and rose up in his chair. "Hey, you're awake."

"I'm aware of that. Thanks. What are you doing here?"

"They let me hang around until you woke up so I could say good-bye."

"You weren't supposed to be anywhere near here. I promised you an ass kicking."

"Fortunately, not in your condition."

"How's Weissenegger?"

"Just came out of his second surgery. He's in bad shape, but they say he'll live."

"Good. I owe him."

"Margareta's with him. She actually seems to like the guy. Figure that one out."

Mason chuckled then shrugged as he thought back. "I can see it. He's a little slow but smarter than that I thought. It just takes him longer to get there. You know, he was the one who called Udahl. He pretended to betray me by telling him I was going to the forester's house to pick up Schaeffer. He almost had *me* convinced." Mason turned to get a better look at Abrams. "I didn't see you get off the train."

"The train was just about outside of Garmisch when I couldn't stand it anymore and jumped."

"I should have handcuffed you to the seat."

Abrams shrugged. "I knew what you were up to, but I didn't know where. So I went to warn Densmore. I got back to head-quarters right after you'd called him. Good thing I did, too. Densmore was only going to take a couple of guys with him." Abrams furrowed his brow. "How did you figure out Udahl was the guy calling the shots?"

"I didn't know for sure, but a bunch of little things kept tickling my brain: him knowing our informant was a 'he,' for one. That kind of started it. Then he knew about me seeing Adelle after that night at Winstone's, when no one but you and she knew about that. He kept throwing me bones, then telling me not to ruffle army-brass feathers. He warned me not to touch the Casa Carioca. Insisted that I report only to him and tell him everything. Then right after that witnesses would disappear, the wiretaps were blown. In one meeting, he already had files on exactly who I suspected, even though I hadn't mentioned them. Once General

Clay got involved, he threw Schaeffer at me to cover his ass. The fact that Abbott had been killed in the war. All this floated around in my head, but I never put it all together until Schaeffer used the same phrase Udahl liked to say, 'no rest for the wicked.' I played a hunch, leaving that letter for him, then having Hans call him."

"You gambled your life on a hunch."

"An educated guess."

"That was pretty stupid."

"Stupid's my middle name." When Abrams declined to argue that point, Mason said, "I appreciate you helping out."

"Don't mention it."

Mason noticed the MP standing guard outside the door. "If he's waiting to escort you to the train station, this time he'd better ride along."

Rather than laughing along with the joke, Abrams glanced at Mason's wrist. Mason started to raise his right arm to see what Abrams was looking at, but his arm lifted only a few inches before a pair of handcuffs stopped him. He shook his hand, making the handcuff rattle against the metal bed frame.

"What the hell is this?" Mason yelled.

A nurse rushed over and scowled. "Would you mind keeping it down? There are other patients in this ward besides your highness."

"Not handcuffed to their beds."

"Keep it down or I'll order a muzzle," the nurse said and stormed off.

"Gamin's gone over the edge," Abrams said. "He wants you kept in confinement until a court-martial hearing can determine whether you'll be charged with willful murder of a full-bird colonel. Not that rank should have anything to do with it, but in Gamin's mind, it's like killing the pope."

"Willful murder? Are they kidding?"

The nurse stomped over to the bed and called out to the MP

guarding the door, "Corporal, I need you to gag this man. He's disturbing the other patients."

The MP turned to the room, unsure what to do.

Mason held up his free hand as if surrendering. "That won't be necessary, ma'am. I'll be a good little prisoner-patient."

The nurse seemed satisfied that she'd gotten her point across and disappeared behind the curtain.

Keeping his voice to a roaring whisper, Mason said, "That son of a bitch. It was self-defense."

"I don't think it originally came from Gamin. The scuttlebutt is, it came from a higher source. Someone's trying to burn you."

Mason fell silent as he absorbed this. Whoever it was, they had to have major influence to push for murder charges when there were witnesses who saw Mason shoot Udahl in self-defense. "It's got to be someone in league with Udahl. Someone very high on the food chain. They're trying to cover their asses."

Abrams appeared to be debating whether to say more. Mason knew the look. It would be some brand of bad news.

"What is it?"

Finally Abrams said, "Volker's dead."

"What?" Mason started to yell it, but cut it off before the nurse carried through on her threat.

"Shot while trying to escape."

Mason hissed a curse. "What about Kessel? He needs to be protected. Get him some place safe. Anywhere."

"Don't ask me. I'm a lowly specialist three and about to be shipped out of here."

"If someone doesn't do it, he's a dead man. Maybe dead already." Mason fell back on his pillow. "They'll come after all of us: Yaakov's family, you, me." He pointed his finger at Abrams. "You watch your back out there."

"I intend to."

Mason jerked on the handcuff in frustration. "I've got to get out of here."

"And do what?"

"I'm working on it. I have to do it fast before someone sneaks in here and jams a pillow in my face. I need for you to tell Densmore what's going on and get him in here."

"I'll go by on my way out." Abrams stood. "They've got me on a supply convoy going north. No more jumping off trains for me."

Mason shook Abrams's hand with his free one. He held on longer than usual and looked into Abrams's eyes. "You take care of yourself. I was lucky having you as a partner."

"Who knows? Maybe we can again."

Mason smiled and nodded, trying to mask his doubt. "All right. Get out of here before Nurse Nazi throws you out."

Abrams paused as if he wanted to say more, but, instead, he waved a good-bye and walked away.

Now alone, Mason fell into deep thought. Udahl's crony bosses were still out there, plotting and killing off anyone who could be traced back to them. From what Udahl and Schaeffer had said the day before, the documents were still out there, somewhere. Udahl's men had searched the forester's house, Mason's billet, and Adelle's place, not to mention Winstone's villa the night of his murder. Plus, Mason and Abrams, then Densmore and a handful of MPs had all done several searches, turning Winstone's villa upside down. The documents weren't in Winstone's office or safe. If Winstone had planned to skip town, there was no way he'd leave them behind. He would have made sure they were quick and easy to access. That was why Hilda's note with Yaakov's concentration camp tattoo number made no sense. Having Yaakov hold the documents would have made it difficult to get to them quickly in case of urgent flight. And if Yaakov knew where they were hidden, he would have made sure they got into Mason's hands. It would have been his best chance of survival. They had to be in the villa. If he could just figure out where, he was certain that Hilda's note would make sense. And if he was going to determine where they were, he'd better do it fast. He thought back to every interview, every nuance, every detail....

Think, Mason!

"Already going stir-crazy in here?"

Mason looked up to see Densmore standing at the edge of the curtain partition.

Densmore walked up to the bed. "You should save your energy for the court-martial."

"You saw that was in self-defense."

"Yes, I believe it was. I put that in my report, and said so to Gamin and that JAG lawyer, Hollister. It fell on deaf ears. In most police departments that would have been a good shooting. But we're in the army, and, of all people, you shot and killed a colonel and military governor."

Mason had to agree: It didn't look good. "Abrams told me about Volker being killed while trying to escape," he said. "You've got to see that was a setup."

Densmore glanced at the door as if someone might be listening in. "Yeah, I can see that."

"Udahl's partners are still out there and active. They're going to make sure no one's left standing. That means you, buddy."

"You keep forgetting that if we're talking army brass, they— whoever 'they' are—don't have to kill you or Abrams or me. Just spread us to the winds. Make sure we're shipped off as far away as possible."

"Maybe for us, but not Kessel. You've got to protect him."

"And how am I supposed to do that?"

"Use your imagination. You're smarter and braver than you let on."

Densmore looked at Mason for a moment. "I'll do what I can,

but, speaking of spreading us to the winds, they're transferring me too. I'm being sent back to the States. They're going to put me behind a desk. Administrative duty. No more detective work. They might as well have killed me."

Mason got the message. Densmore didn't need to add that it was his fault.

"You think I blame you," Densmore said, as if reading his mind. "Well, not this time. We did some incredible work." He paused. "I know I've been more worried about saving my own skin and my career…" He moved closer to Mason's head. "That's why I'm doing this." He fished something out of his pocket, then looked back at the MP guard.

The guard had his face buried in a magazine. Mason felt the vibration of metal against metal, then the distinctive click of the handcuffs being unlocked. Mason kept still so the handcuffs wouldn't slip off his wrist.

"I left a paper sack on a bench in the hallway. There are some clothes inside. A set of civvies and a uniform, both out of your duffel bag. I couldn't get my hands on a coat, but I'm sure you can manage."

Mason glanced around the room as much as the loose handcuffs would allow.

"There's some windows to your left," Densmore said. "But I wouldn't try jumping. We're three floors up." He nodded toward the MP. "I'll let him take a bathroom break. He was at the forester's house and saw it all. He doesn't like you being prosecuted. He'll look the other way if I ask him to." He held out his hand. "Good luck. Don't take this the wrong way, but I hope I never see you again."

Mason shook his hand. "Take it easy, Patrick. And thanks."

"Get those bastards," Densmore said. He stepped into the hallway and spoke to the MP. The MP nodded and left without a glance Mason's way. Densmore hovered by the door for a few seconds as he watched the guard. He lifted his hat then resettled it on his head before slowly walking away in the opposite direction.

Mason slid off the handcuffs and pulled out the IV. His head spun when he stood up from the bed. Shooting pains in his thigh paralyzed him for a moment. He took a deep breath and forced the pain away. Miraculously, the grumpy nurse didn't see him limp out. He retrieved the sack that Densmore had left for him and slipped into the emergency exit staircase.

Mason had a tough time pulling on the pants and shoes, but he managed, and five minutes later he exited the hospital. Two hotels were just blocks away; plenty of parked cars to choose from. The biting cold relieved some of the pain in his head and thigh. His head spun from the loss of blood, but the adrenaline would keep him going... For a while.

That, and mule-headed resolve.

Mason leaned against a wall in the foyer of Winstone's villa. To his left, the living room, and to his right, the dining room, then the library. Ahead lay the staircase and the hall leading to the parlor, kitchen, and garage. The upper floor accommodated five bedrooms and three baths. Then the sprawling basement. A brutal, weeks-long search even in healthy conditions.

Where to start? Documents could be folded or rolled and inserted anywhere. Wherever Mason chose, he had to do it fast. The guard or the nurse had surely reported his absence by now, and it was only a matter of time before a squad of MPs came here to look for him.

He had retrieved the tools from the library where Densmore and his MP team had left them, and a flashlight from the kitchen. The effort of finding a car he could steal in the bitter cold, then driving with his wounded leg, had taken its toll. And now here he was, barely able to stand upright, let alone think clearly, running through all of Winstone's villa renovations again in his head. He reviewed the areas already searched, by himself and Abrams, then by Densmore and the team of MPs. The most logical and obvious places had been eliminated. That left the unlikely and the illogical, of which there were countless.

This is going to be impossible.

Blood had seeped from the freshly sutured wound. Both legs trembled. His whole body shivered. The cold was getting to him. It was cold enough in the villa to condense his breath. Cold and dark as a mausoleum...

The cold! Why hadn't he thought of it before? Winstone had relied on the fireplaces for heat. He'd refused to use the furnace. There wasn't even any coal in the storage bin.

Mason hobbled down to the basement and into the furnace room. Volker's mattress still lay on the floor, along with bloodstains from Weissenegger's beatings. Ironic to think that the documents could have been here, yards from Volker, this whole time.

He went up to the furnace and opened the feed door. The rusty hinges squealed in protest. He scanned the inside with the flashlight. Nothing but old ashes of burned coal heaped on the bottom. He shoved in his arm and searched the ashes, then felt up and around the furnace fire chamber.

Nothing. Reaching all the way in, his fingers brushed the far chamber wall. He cursed in frustration, making his headache rage. He felt weak from the effort, and the blood from his wound had soaked through his pants leg and created a stain as broad as his outstretched hand. He took a deep breath and stepped back, scanning the room for signs of fresh concrete or brick around the furnace. Every spot of wall and floor appeared untouched for years.

Out of having nothing else to inspect, he looked up to the ceiling. The dozen or more hot air ducts stretched in all directions and were tucked tight to the ceiling. Using the flashlight beam, he checked each one. The accumulated soot and dust appeared undisturbed. He traced each duct to its eventual destination, noting whether it was a specific room or area of the house. At the back of the furnace rose the main exhaust outlet, which climbed up through the ground-level flooring and vented into the library chimney.

The library, the room Winstone had renovated extensively, including the floor joists and supporting wall.

The major renovation work would have provided an ideal opportunity to create a well-concealed hiding place. That prompted him to step back and peer over the ventilation duct, where he caught sight of a short duct leading directly to the foundation wall. There was no reason to have a heating duct there. It served no purpose, as that level of the foundation wall was still below ground level.

After a frantic search, Mason found a ladder under the basement stairs. It took all his strength and willpower to bring the ladder to the furnace wall and climb the ladder's steps. His leg threatened to seize. His body felt both hot and icy cold. When he finally reached the duct, he felt a surge of excitement: Upon the top of the duct were faint handprints in the thin layer of dust. With a tenuous balance on the ladder, he used both hands to tug on the duct. The putty fixing the duct to the wall held firm. Mason took a deep breath and yanked several times. Finally the duct came loose and fell to the floor.

Victory and defeat. He'd found the hiding place, but inside was a small, brand-new safe embedded in the fresh concrete of the foundation wall.

He laid his head against the wall to recover his strength. His legs trembled. He found harder to think straight. He closed his eyes, but that brought on a wave of vertigo. He must have had a few brain cells still firing, because the image of Hilda's note, Yaakov's tattoo came to his mind: A47235.

He tried that as the combination, making the *A* into a 1: 14-72-35. The safe's lever refused to budge. He tried varying the combination, leaving off the *A*, or using a different number for it. Nothing worked.

He stopped. It didn't make sense. Why use Yaakov's tattoo number? Anyone who happened to make the connection would have assumed the same as Mason.

He quickly exchanged the letters in Yaakov's name for numbers: 25-1-1-11-15-22. Too many numbers. He tried putting the two 1s together as 11. Still nothing. His frustration grew and threatened to cloud what reasoning power he had left. He took deep breaths and tried to concentrate.

Perhaps it was a combination of the tattoo number and the numbers represented in Yaakov's name to get the three-number combination. But how many possible combinations could that yield? How long before his mind shut down completely? Assuming *A* equaled 1, he began to add sequentially the tattoo numbers, then Yaakov's name. Each successive attempt yielded nothing. He lost track of the ones he'd tried. He repeated himself. It became harder and harder to add simple numbers in his head.

He pounded the wall. "Come on!"

There had to be a methodical approach. With his mind closing down, the only way for him to perform this simple task was to speak out loud and use his fingers. In a final desperate attempt, he added all the tattoo numbers together plus the first letter of Yaakov's name— 46. Then the next three letters of his name—13. And finally the last two number/letters—37. He tried the combination, moving the dial slowly, making sure he counted the correct number of rotations for each: 46-13-37. He slammed down on the latch. The safe opened.

The absolute relief nearly caused him to tumble off the ladder. He laid his head against the wall to catch his breath, then he removed a series of folders bundled together and a cloth sack from the safe. He tucked everything under his arm and slowly descended the ladder. The relief had also brought on absolute exhaustion, which caused his sight to fade as if a heavy shadow enclosed him darkness....

You've got to get out of here, Mason.

Now that he had the prize, he didn't know if he could stand the utter frustration if, now he had the prize, the MPs came calling and clapped him in irons. No telling what would happen to the documents if they were taken back to headquarters. He had to put one foot in front of the other, climb the stairs, and go out into the cold—assuming he could even drive.

Someplace safe. Some place where he could have time to read the documents and recuperate some of his strength.

MASON SAT at the kitchen table. He had a blanket draped over his shoulders, and he nursed a second cup of coffee. One of the twelve file folders lay before him.

Laura came up to the table and slid a plate with a sandwich and potato chips in front of him. Mason started to open the folder, but Laura said, "Eat first. You need to get your strength up."

Mason let the folder cover drop closed and picked up the sandwich.

Two of the younger children in Yaakov's extended family ran into the kitchen, laughing and screaming as they played tag. Berko came out from the back of the house and scolded them and told them to go back to the bedroom. He smiled and nodded at Mason in a silent thank-you and another good-bye, then he left Mason and Laura.

It wasn't until Mason had reached Laura's house and recovered his senses that he'd finally looked into the cloth sack from Winstone's hidden safe. Inside was a bundled stack of bills amounting to fifty-five thousand dollars. A fortune by Mason's standards, but that amount was only a fraction of the profits from

Winstone's schemes. From a meticulous ledger Winstone had included with the files, Mason learned that Winstone had managed to smuggle over a million dollars of ill-gotten gains into a bank in Switzerland. The fifty-five grand was his and Hilda's traveling money, probably a majority of it meant for bribes.

Mason had decided to give Berko fifty thousand of it to allow him to pay—bribe—their way to Palestine. He'd offered the remaining portion to Laura for her troubles, but she'd declined, saying that Mason would most definitely need the five thousand for what he had planned.

Laura watched as he ate. "You're like a man born in the wrong century."

"How do you mean?"

"You should be wearing a suit of armor and declaring the Crusades an honorable cause. You'd have believed it was all about faith and divine grace, and not a land grab for power."

"I can't tell if that was an insult or a compliment."

"I think you know."

Mason looked at her while he bit into the sandwich. He didn't *know*, but figured it was a little bit of both. They sat in silence, him eating and her preparing her camera.

Laura finally said, "I've known you for a little over six months and, in that time, you've been to the hospital three times."

"I'm going to have to learn to be quicker on my feet."

"You use your head once in a while, and you might cut your trips to the hospital in half."

"Then I wouldn't have an excuse to see you."

Laura shook her head, even as she smiled. "What am I going to do with you?"

"Ditch Ricky and fall back in love with me."

"It's Richard."

"Where *is* Richard, by the way?"

"He's in Nuremberg for the Nazi trials. Göring is on the stand.

Richard has an interview with Göring; he's doing a whole piece on him, from his rise to power, up to the trial."

"Everyone wants to do stories about the Nazis."

"Evil gets bigger headlines."

"Why aren't you with him?"

"My work." Laura leaned on her elbows. "Maybe I should do a piece about your rise and fall."

"I'll rise and fall, and rise and fall again. But if some of the army brass get their way, I'll stand trial for something I didn't do."

Laura laid one of the files in front of her. "Then let's see what we can find to make sure that doesn't happen."

Mason pushed the empty plate aside. He opened a folder and began to read. Laura would finish reading a page, then photograph it and make notes.

Some of the files were divided by individuals: Herr Giessen, Bachmann, Plöbsch, Eddie Kantos, Volker as Herr Z, Schaeffer and Kessel, Udahl a.k.a. Abbott. Others were collections of wiretap transcripts, photographs, sighted meetings, or informant testimony—mainly Yaakov and Hilda Schmidt. Taken in chronological order, the files unfolded a lucid account of not only the growing power and complexity of Udahl and Schaeffer's organization, not only the rise and fall of Herr Giessen and Bachmann, but also Winstone's journey from determined yet naive investigator to an operative falling to seduction and corruption. Winstone's own rise and fall.

That revelation did not come in Winstone's own words, but Mason could read between the lines: Winstone had spent six months on the investigation, the progress slow at first, then the details poured in, with his best investigative work coming from his own involvement in intrigue.

Winstone began to profit from the very web of crime that he was investigating—until near the end. That was when he uncovered the bigger players. The ones with enormous power. By then, it had gotten out of hand, and he'd decided to flee with Hilda to Switzerland. But Mason doubted he would have found a truly safe haven. The men he'd uncovered had a very long reach.

Perhaps now that Mason knew more than Winstone, he, too, would no longer find sanctuary. He would always be looking over his shoulder, spending all his life on the run. There was a momentary sense of loneliness and sadness at that notion. Then he brushed those thoughts to the side.

Much of what the documents revealed Mason had discovered in the last number of days. Eddie Kantos appeared to be the pivot around which all revolved: his relationship with Giessen and Bachmann, his meeting Schaeffer and Udahl, using Willy Laufs as his go-between with the Italian crime families. He coordinated the smuggling routes using a contingent of Polish ex-POWs and Polish army brass and regulars, taking truckloads of luxury goods Germans had traded on the black market for food and medicine: gold watches, furs, diamonds, works of art, and the morphine and cocaine left by the collapsing German army. In exchange, petrol, heroin, household goods, and wine came up from Italy. Kantos had provided both groups' leaders rich contacts with German royalty and industrialists, and subsequently he'd provided, along with Otto, the same service to Winstone.

The documents told of Schaeffer and Udahl building their network through those alliances, and a loose partnership with Giessen and Bachmann. How they had helped Volker and ex-SS members slip Nazi war criminals out of Germany and into Italy and beyond, thereby accumulating favors from the German network, including informants and the locations of huge stashes of antibiotics, narcotics, hospital supplies, precious metals, SS coffers of diamonds and gold, and uranium left by the retreating German army. All the detritus of the crumbling Nazi war machine.

Winstone had written pages of reports about his investigation being stifled every step of the way. The same obstructions Mason had experienced: blown wiretaps, records missing or diverted, witnesses disappearing or reversing testimony. He recounted waking up one night and finding someone in his room and rifling through his desk. How he had hired Polish DPs as house guards, but that even they seemed to be working for Schaeffer.

Toward the end, possibly for his own survival, Winstone had stepped up the investigation and hired informants: Hilda, from inside the Casa Carioca, and Yaakov, who had black market contacts. Yaakov had done invaluable work, following and questioning people, gaining confidence—the perfect mole—and, at times, playing as a double agent. Yaakov would have made an incredible intelligence agent.

In the end, Winstone had obtained a damning set of documents. As he had said to Mason: "enough to shake the army to its core." Schaeffer and Udahl were only the tip of the iceberg, though, surprisingly, Gamin was only a pawn, his malady exploited by evil men.

As Mason stared at one last photograph, he had to sit back in his chair. Not from his weakened state, but from what the photograph revealed. It made absolute sense, but it was devastating all the same.

He looked up at Laura, who was furiously writing in her notebook. "Don't say I never gave you a valuable gift."

Laura stopped writing, picked up her camera, and snapped a picture of him. "Memories can be priceless. You gave me those."

They looked at each other for a moment, then Laura went back to photographing several pictures from Winstone's files.

"You publish whatever you want from all this," Mason said. "I only ask that you do it in a way that doesn't make the army out to be the bad guy. With sixty Russian divisions licking their chops at the rest of Europe, the army shouldn't be hit with a massive scandal."

"I told you before, I don't do that kind of journalism. That's like blaming the parents for their adult son's crime spree."

"I'm only willing to share these documents with you to shut down the guilty. I don't want the innocent caught in the line of fire. There are too many good men and women out there doing their best."

"Mason, I won't let this devolve into a raving diatribe. But what people read between the lines I can't control. You want to use me and the power of the press to bring the bad guys to justice, then let me do my job."

"I want to ask another favor. Don't put this out there for another twenty-four hours. I need that much time to slip out before it all blows up."

"Where will you go?"

Mason sat back in his chair. "That's an excellent question, Miss McKinnon."

"I don't know how you're going to get very far with that leg of yours."

"You patched me up pretty good. It should get me as far as I need. Where did you learn how to field dress a wound?"

"From spending time on the front lines in the Vosges Mountains."

"How about you come away with me?"

"So I can dress your many wounds?"

"Heal my broken heart."

Laura suddenly had a hard time holding Mason's gaze. "Why don't you spend the night and regain some of your strength?"

"Oh, no. That can't work. I may look tough, but I'm a squishy mass of sentiment on the inside. My heart couldn't take it."

"That's not what I meant."

Mason placed his hand on his heart as if suffering from pain. "You see? Even that could do me in."

"You can look over what I've written in the morning."

Mason smiled and looked into Laura's eyes. "I'll miss you, too. More than you can imagine."

They looked at each other for what to Mason felt like a long time.

Laura's eyes were moist but there were no tears. She said, "I'd ask you to write me from time to time, and let me know where you are, but wherever you go, headlines are sure to follow."

They fell into silence for a moment.

Mason finally said, "I should go. Did you have enough time for taking notes and pictures?"

Laura nodded. "Yes, and if I let you stay much longer, I might say or do something I'll regret later."

Mason stood. "I don't want to be responsible for that." He gathered up the files, then tossed a few of the more damning photographs next to Laura's notes. "Keep those. Just in case...."

Laura stood and walked over to Mason. She stopped inches from his face. "Forget what I said. Write me. Okay? I need to know you're all right."

They kissed for a long moment. Then Mason put on a coat from Ricky's closet, tucked the files under his arm, and left Laura watching him from the open front door.

The last of the troops passed in review in front of the dais on the parade ground, with Munich's sprawling McGraw Kaserne in the background. Presiding over the ceremonial inspection of Munich's armed forces were twenty-five officers wearing enough metal on their chest to forge a Sherman tank, while the army band played "The Washington Post" march. The officers finished their salutes of the passing troops and broke into informal groups.

Mason stood at semi-attention behind and to the left of the dais. One of the stipulations for allowing Mason onto the parade ground was that he had to wait until the ceremony had finished. He wore his CID uniform that Densmore had left for him at the hospital, another stipulation. He was fine with that, for it would probably be the last time he'd wear an army uniform, and he felt proud to do so.

The generals and colonels, military government officials, and U.S. congressmen began drifting down the stairs in twos and threes. Few paid much attention to him or seemed concerned that a CID criminal investigator stood at the base of the steps, while eyeing each of the dignitaries.

A few of the officers lingered on the platform. General Lucius Clay, the deputy military governor of the American occupation zone, was one of them. He talked with several other officers, while urging them to make their way to the steps. Finally the man Mason waited for began to climb down. He talked with a senator, unaware of or ignoring Mason's presence.

When General Pritchard stepped off the stairs, he finally looked at Mason. He stopped, turned, and displayed a big politician's smile. "Why, Mr. Collins. I'm gratified that you're still in one piece. Though probably unwise of you to show up here when you're a fugitive. The deputy provost marshal is still occupied on the dais, but I'm sure he'll be glad to take you into custody."

Mason held out a bundle of file folders. "I found Winstone's missing files."

Pritchard looked down at the files, then walked slowly up to Mason. The senator excused himself and walked on. The confrontation had drawn everyone's attention.

"Excellent work, Mason," Pritchard said and took the files.

"Some interesting items in there," Mason said. "You should have a look when you have a chance."

Pritchard put his hand on Mason's shoulder and tried to corral him away from prying eyes and ears. "Let's talk over here."

Mason refused to move. "General Clay found them very interesting, as well."

Pritchard turned white even while maintaining his smile.

"He found it especially interesting that you were the principal facilitator and beneficiary of the murders and thefts occurring in Garmisch-Partenkirchen."

"Whatever you think you read in there, or think you understand, is erroneous."

"Agent Winstone left little to the imagination. He discovered that you coordinated OSS operations through the Joint Chiefs of

Staff during the war and you worked closely with Colonel Udahl and Major Schaeffer. That you then directed and supported Major Schaeffer and Colonel Udahl in their criminal activities. Then it was just a matter of recruiting various other players in power to aid in your enterprise. Colonel Middleton of the quartermaster's office, General Davis of transportation, Captain Miller of the MG's public safety branch. Plus ten others. A neat little circle of friends."

Pritchard called out to four MPs guarding the entourage of brass. "You there. Arrest this man."

The MPs remained where they stood.

"You see," Mason said, "I worked out a deal with General Clay."

Pritchard glanced up to General Clay, who still stood on the dais.

Mason said, "He's so grateful for exposing your and Udahl's organization that he allowed me to personally hand you these documents and look into the eye of a murderer and traitor."

"You're still going to be arrested for shooting Colonel Udahl."

"No, I've agreed to leave the army, saving the army the embarrassment and dilemma of what to do with me. The press will release an in-depth story about you and your buddies, though it'll be delayed to give the army enough time to arrest the perpetrators and clean house before the story breaks."

"You didn't get everyone. And they will hunt you down—"

General Clay must have signaled for the MPs to take Pritchard away, for they suddenly had Pritchard by the shoulders.

"You're dead, Collins. Dead!" Pritchard yelled as the MPs led him away.

Mason looked up to General Clay, who appeared unhappy. He neither said nor signaled anything to Mason. Mason turned away, retrieved his can that he'd propped against the side of the dais, and limped across the field, while the band played "The Stars and Stripes Forever." He headed west, and he would keep going west until...

Well, that particular detail still eluded him.

Did you enjoy this book? You can make a big difference in my career!

Reviews are the most powerful tools in my arsenal when it comes to getting attention for my books. Like most readers, I'm sure you weigh reviews heavily once you've seen the book's cover and read the description. And without reviews, a reader might move on without giving a new author a try.

That's where you can come in: An honest review of this novel— or any of my other novels—just might be the thing that convinces them to read and discover new stories and authors. Like me!

If you enjoyed this book, I would be very grateful if you could take five minutes to leave an honest review on the book's Amazon page.

Leaving a review is easy:
1) Go to the book's page on Amazon
2) Scroll down to the reviews section and click the "Write a customer review" button just below the stars rating bars
3) Select a star rating
4) Write a few short words (or as long as you like)
5) Click the submit button

Thank you very much!

BOOKS BY JOHN A. CONNELL

THE MASON COLLINS SERIES

Madness in the Ruins

It is the winter of 1945, seven months after the Nazi defeat, and Munich is in ruins. A killer is stalking the devastated city—one who has knowledge of human anatomy, enacts mysterious rituals with his prey, and seems to pick victims at random. It falls upon U.S. Army investigator Mason Collins to hunt down the brutal killer. In a city where chaos reigns, Mason must rely on his wits and instincts, and he's driven to places he never could have imagined: from interrogation rooms with unrepentant Nazi war criminals to the bowels of the crumbling city.

Madness in the Ruins is the first in a series that will follow Mason Collins to some of the most dangerous and outrageous spots around the globe. **"...this is going to be a must-read series for me."** *~ Lee Child, #1 New York Times bestselling author of the Jack Reacher novels*

∽

Haven of Vipers

Mason Collins risks everything to hunt down a gang of ruthless murderers in a case that will take him from a Hollywood-style nightclub and a speeding train, to the icy slopes of the Bavarian Alps. As both witnesses and evidence begin disappearing, it becomes obvious that someone on high is pulling strings to stifle the investigation—and that Mason must feel his way in the darkness if he is going to find out who in town has the most to gain—and the most to lose...

Haven of Vipers is the second in the Mason Collins crime-thriller series that Steve Berry, bestselling author of *The Patriot Threat* and *The Templar Legacy*, said: **"Excitement melds with adventure as the tangled threads gradually unwind, revealing treachery coming from all directions. The whole thing is reminiscent of early-Robert Ludlum, and makes you clamor for more."**

～

Bones of the Innocent

Mason Collins grapples with a web of lies, secrets, and murder as he races against time to save the lives of abducted teenagers in a case as twisted as the streets of Tangier's medina. And as he digs deeper, he realizes everyone has a hidden agenda, including those who harbor a terrible secret. And just as Mason begins to unravel the mystery, the assassins have picked up his trail. Now, Mason must put his life on the line to find the girls and discover who's behind the heinous crimes before it's too late. If he lives that long…

Bones of the Innocent is the third in the Mason Collins series of historical crime thrillers that bestselling author Lee Child said, *"This is going to be a must-read series for me."*

～

To Kill A Devil

When a shadowy organization fails to assassinate Mason Collins, they go after his colleagues, his friends, and the love of his life. Mason knows the only way to stop the killings is to cut off the head of the snake. Armed with only the leader's code name, Valerius, Mason will trek across Franco's Spain to war-torn Vienna to kill the man responsible. But targeting the most powerful crime boss in Vienna promises to be an impossible task, and Valerius has something special in store for Mason.

~

A STANDALONE HISTORICAL THRILLER

Good Night, Sweet Daddy-O

1958 San Francisco

Struggling jazz musician, Frank Valentine, suffers a midnight beating, leaving his left hand paralyzed. Jobless, penniless, and desperate, Frank agrees to join his best friend, George, and three other buddies to distribute a gangster's heroin for quick money.

What he doesn't know is that George has more dangerous plans…

Inexperienced in the ways of crime, Frank quickly slips deeper and deeper into the dark vortex of San Francisco gangsters, junkies, and murderers for hire. To make things worse, Frank's newfound love, a mysterious, dark-haired beauty, is somehow connected to it all.

And when it becomes clear that a crime syndicate is bent on his destruction, Frank realizes that the easy road out of purgatory often leads to hell.

GET A FREE MASON COLLINS NOVELLA

Get a free copy of a Mason Collins introductory novella, *In Malicious Hands,* when you sign up to join my Reader's Group. This novella is not available anywhere else.

You'll receive occasional newsletters from me with details on new releases, special offers, and other news relating to the Mason Collins series.

To receive you free novella you can copy and paste this link in your browser:
https://johnaconnell.com/subscribe

ABOUT THE AUTHOR

John A. Connell is a 2016 Barry Award nominee and the author of the Mason Collins series. John has worked as a cameraman on films such as *Jurassic* Park and *Thelma and Louise* and on TV shows including *NYPD Blue* and *The Practice*. Atlanta-born, John spends his time between the U.S. and France.

You can visit John online at: http://johnaconnell.com

facebook.com/johnconnellauthor1

twitter.com/johnaconnell

bookbub.com/authors/john-a-connell

ACKNOWLEDGMENTS

I believe any work of historical crime fiction should be firmly grounded in reality, and though the principal plot and characters in HAVEN OF VIPERS are fictitious, many of the facts, circumstances, places and people are part of the historical record. I am deeply indebted to the scholars, historians, archivists and librarians for their work, passion and dedication to chronicling the postwar years. Because the story within these pages shares proximity in time, place, and context to *Madness in the Ruins,* I used many of the same sources in my research for this book.

And if you want to dive into the fascinating history of this time and place, I highly recommend the following books.

The list of sources is extensive, however, I would like to acknowledge those to which I turned time and again: Ian Sayer and Douglas Botting, *In The Ruins of the Reich* (1985) and *Nazi Gold* (1984); Atina Grossmann, *Jews, Germans, and Allies: Close Encounters In Occupied Germany* (2007); Wilford Byford-Jones, *Berlin Twilight* (1947); Edward N. Peterson, *The American Occupation of Germany: Retreat to Victory* (1977); Giles MacDonogh,

After the Reich: From the Libertaion of Vienna to the Berlin Airlift (1985).

∽

I would like to thank my incredible family and friends for all their love and support. To all the readers, booksellers, bloggers, and reviewers, I cannot thank you enough for your support of *Madness in the Ruins*, and your boundless love of books.

And finally, creating a book and building a writing career is a long and, sometimes, arduous journey, but my wife Janine, through her encouragement, guidance, strength of heart and mind, and supreme patience and love, has made the road rise up to meet me and commanded the wind to be always at my back. I am truly a lucky man.

Printed in Great Britain
by Amazon